The Torqued Man

The Torqued Man

The
Torqued Man

A Novel

Peter Mann

HARPER LARGE PRINT

An Imprint of HarperCollins*Publishers*

THE TORQUED MAN. Copyright © 2022 by Peter Mann. All rights reserved. Printed in the United States of America. No part of this book may be used or reproduced in any manner whatsoever without written permission except in the case of brief quotations embodied in critical articles and reviews. For information, address HarperCollins Publishers, 195 Broadway, New York, NY 10007.

HarperCollins books may be purchased for educational, business, or sales promotional use. For information, please e-mail the Special Markets Department at SPsales@harpercollins.com.

FIRST HARPER LARGE PRINT EDITION

ISBN: 978-0-06-321167-4

Library of Congress Cataloging-in-Publication Data is available upon request.

22 23 24 25 26 LSC 10 9 8 7 6 5 4 3 2 1

For Mom and Dad—my original readers

Our country has been depopulated, our people degraded, our industries destroyed. If Hell itself were to turn against English policy, as it is known to us, we might be pardoned for taking the side of Hell.

—EOIN MACNEILL, ARTICLE IN *FIANNA*

And the individual, powerless, has to exert the
Powers of will and choice
And choose between enormous evils, either
Of which depends on somebody else's voice.

—LOUIS MACNEICE, *AUTUMN JOURNAL*

Thou hast chosen an ill place to rest and slumber in, before the city of thine enemy.

—*THE HIGH DEEDS OF FINN MCCOOL*

The Torqued Man

The Torqued Man

S-E-C-R-E-T

Date: 05 September 1945
CPTN FLOYD WEEKS

BERLIN DISTRICT INTERROGATION CENTER
APO 755   US ARMY

TO:
CPTN CHARLES CARSON
OFFICE OF STRATEGIC SERVICES, BERLIN
APO 401 US ARMY

CHARLES:

Am sending the enclosed MS for your review in case it is of any value. It was found this morning in the remains of a bombed-out house in Schoeneberg following the arrest of former Abwehr agent Adrian DE GROOT. Little is yet known of DE

GROOT's activities during the war,
other than he was involved in
Spanish and Irish operations before
being imprisoned in 1944, then
later drafted into the people's
militia. At the time of his arrest,
he was living under the alias
Johann GROTIUS and employed by the
Real Estate and Labor Office at the
new Coca-Cola plant in Steglitz. He
is currently under interrogation
and seems eager to cooperate.

The Brits want next crack
at him, as it was SIS who tipped
us to his identity. I figure if
we can save them several hours of
reading, it would be the neighborly
thing to do. Anything in the MS
that can clarify the role of
Proinnsias "Frank" PIKE in his
affiliation with the Abwehr would
be of particular interest. PIKE, an
IRA fighter and socialist agitator
who escaped from a Spanish prison
in 1940, is thought to have gone

to Germany, where he disappeared during the war.

Please give this a look and send a report at your soonest convenience.

Yours,
Floyd

P.S. It appears there are actually two distinct MSS that have been collated either by their owner or the rubble women who found them. I leave it to you to puzzle out their relation.

1

JOURNAL

November 30, 1943

Frank Pike is dead.

The news is not surprising, and yet it still comes as a shock. Strange, given the perpetual state of shock life has become. I wonder if he ever knew how much he meant to me. I do feel partly to blame for the way things turned out.

Kriegsmann saw the body before the hospital was hit. Now it's a hole in the ground. I would have gone myself had I known he was there. But with this gash in my leg—damn that dog—and the mountains of smoldering rubble clogging the roads, it would have taken days just to get across the city. Imagine: Berlin burning all around him, and the man dies in bed from a fever. As though one needed other forms of dying these days.

Nonviolent death seems like one of God's little eccentricities.

According to Kriegsmann, he expired in the arms of a nun. Perhaps he had a chance to talk her out of her vow of chastity—one last thrust of the pike, as it were. Even in his beleaguered state, deaf as a post and limbs atremble, his skin cirrhotic and face caving in on itself, Frank Pike knew how to charm. It's a pity he never could find a proper use for his talents. For all his peccadilloes, questionable loyalties, and that ceaseless Irish garrulity—a verbal spigot for which there was no wrench, not even his handicapped German—he was, it must be said, a man of action. Or at least he could have been. It was our stymieing of his energies, those three years of forced indolence, that caused his undoing. Only in the Germany of today could a man of Pike's vitality become such a colossal waste. We may add it to the tally of murders foisted upon the world by our regime. Perhaps there are no nonviolent deaths after all.

I first met Pike in a Burgos prison in 1940. Despite the bleak setting, I felt almost giddy, as I'd just spent a week in the company of Himmler and would sooner have chosen to become an inmate there than suffer one more minute with that dullard.

I still shudder when I recall that trip. I had been assigned to be the Reichsführer's interpreter on his tour of Spain, a demotion that was part of the Security Office's attempt to flex its muscles over the Abwehr. I knew I was in for a miserable week as soon as Himmler boarded the train in San Sebastián. He immediately began complaining that the nitrate deficiencies of the Iberian soil had thrown off his digestion and were interfering with the rhythm of his bowel movements. As if that weren't enough, his wife had neglected to pack his bee pollen supplements, no doubt a malicious act, thereby dooming him to eight days of throat constriction and adenoidal hell.

To my horror, this harangue directed at everyone in his retinue—and to which we were obliged to listen attentively and fill the pauses with a *natürlich!* or *wie interessant!*—did not end when we pulled into Atocha but continued for days. Through the galleries of the Prado, where the Reichsführer insisted on seeing only the German and Dutch Old Masters and admired them without breaking stride, he lectured us on the wonders of the neti pot, the earliest Aryan form of medicine, a nasal-irrigation system for the warrior caste that led directly to the conquest of the decadent Hittites—it was all to be found in a proper study of the Sanskrit documents. Only when we came to Bosch's *Garden of Earthly Delights* did our group pause, as the Falangists and SS men all marveled at the ingenious tortures of the right panel, cooing like women ogling dresses in a window display.

The next day, the mayor of Madrid staged a bull-fight exclusively for the Reichsführer. A poor showing. The *corrida* hadn't yet recovered from the long siege during the war—the bulls were sluggish, the matadors timid. The regime had to bribe or coerce several hundred civilians to fill the stands and, to ingratiate themselves further with their Nazi guests, had chosen only the blondest, most Aryan representatives of Madrid. Serrano Suñer, who, as Franco's brother-in-law and lickspittle-in-chief, had been tasked with showing Himmler around the country, presented the Reichsführer with some fragments of a mixing bowl from an archaeological site in Segovia. "Hmm," said Himmler, examining the shards. "Could be a neti pot!"

"You see, Reichsführer," said Serrano Suñer, "we Spaniards are descended from the Visigoths. There is good Aryan blood running through our veins, like yours."

Himmler scoffed. No Aryan, he said, would make such a grotesque sport out of maiming innocent animals.

I hated seeing Spain papered over in swastikas. I state this with absolute sincerity, even while I admit my sympathies had once been with the nationals. I didn't want to see Spain go red—the churches torn down, the women renouncing dresses and dancing for overalls and agitprop, the vineyards collectivized and turned into Stalinist beet farms. In my naïveté, I had believed a conservative stand against the excesses of materialism would preserve the soul and, with it, art, which is always, in its authentic form, an expression of the soul. But those of us with a true preservationist impulse against the onslaught should have known we had no party to speak for us. I soon learned that Franco's regime, in its obsession with *limpieza social* and terror of foreign infection, was really only a rebirth of the Inquisition. Perhaps my idea of Spain, the one I saw threatened by the left, had never existed in the first place and was merely a postcard fantasy from my student days in Salamanca. But with Franco's victory, it had become clear to me that the caudillo and his Falangists were of the same stunted, loathsome issue as the thugs of our own regime.

By the time we reached Barcelona, I was about to tear my hair out. I had been buried in a deluge of utterances about poultry-rearing, Aryan pottery, and nasal hygiene. Stuck in my brain like a shard of glass was the phrase *Rudi, Deine Hände, bitte*. This was how Himmler beckoned his masseur, who traveled by his side at all times and was constantly realigning the Reichsführer's chakras.

On the eve of the pilgrimage to Montserrat, I seriously considered feigning illness. Himmler, through his study of bogus scholarship and his own lunatic theories, had concluded that the Holy Grail was hidden in the library of the mountaintop monastery and was dead set on finding it. I was lying in my bed at the Ritz, bracing for a day of temper tantrums and trying to will myself into contracting a fever, when a message came for me.

It was from the legend himself: Canaris. Only rarely did I receive a direct communiqué from the head of the Abwehr, and it was like receiving a lightning bolt straight from Zeus. Canaris was flexing his own muscles now—letting Himmler know he'd have to make do with another interpreter because his agent would be busy doing actual espionage. I was so happy, I ordered a bottle of cava and drank it in the bath.

I left the next morning for Burgos. My instructions were to recruit an Irishman currently serving a life sentence in San Pedro de Cardeña, but it felt like I was the one who had been freed from prison.

His name, Proinnsias Pike, was not new to me. It was my job to know the name of the man Franco once boasted of as his most important prisoner. Pike had come to Spain to fight fascists. He'd led the Irish Con-

nolly Column but was quickly promoted to staff officer of the International Brigades, where he spent the
following year organizing forces and directing propaganda. In the spring of '38, he was captured by an
Italian tank division at Gandesa and had been rotting
in prison ever since. When Ireland recognized Franco's government after the war, the caudillo commuted
Pike's death sentence to life in prison. In the meantime, Canaris had convinced Franco to let us have
him. That is, if he would have us.

San Pedro de Cardeña was a monastery the Falange
had converted into a prison camp and slaughterhouse.
Stuffed into its cells were nearly a thousand men from
the International Brigades and twice as many Basques.
At least, those were the numbers when I had visited
shortly after the end of the Civil War. Now, upon my
arrival a year later, the overcrowding problem appeared
to be improving. I had little doubt how. Of course,
there were still five or six men to each cell originally
intended for a single pious monk. And the place still
reeked of piss and blood and garlic, the latter owing
to the daily cooking of huge vats of soup, which along
with a moldy crust was the prisoners' only meal.

Spanish prison conditions had shocked even Himmler. At least back then. I'm certain the poultry
farmer has since orchestrated worse. But it is not an

exaggeration to say that in 1940 to have been a republican in Spain was as dire as being a Jew or communist in the Reich. Franco had enslaved the remnants of the Second Republic and was killing them through work and starvation. But Himmler, as he had remarked on our tour of a concentration camp outside Barcelona, saw no reason why purportedly European racial specimens—albeit second-rate ones—should be exterminated like this. After all, these were only ideological enemies, he contended, not racial ones. A few should be shot, certainly, and the gypsies and crypto-Jews naturally would have to go, but most could be reeducated. Serrano Suñer politely begged to differ. The caudillo's top advisers had conducted research definitively proving that Bolshevism was a congenital affliction similar to racial degeneracy. "That may well be," replied Himmler, annoyed. "But you people are mismanaging things all the same. With better sanitary conditions and a doubling of the prisoners' bread ration alone, their productivity could be increased tenfold."

A Carlist in a red beret saluted me and led me to the inner sanctum. The Cloister of the Martyrs, with its colorful twelfth-century Mudéjar arches, had been repurposed as an execution grounds by morning and a recreation area by day. A garrote stood in the center, beneath it a black stain on the earth, wet with the daily evacuations of strangled men. I was looking absently into this puddle of gore when the Carlist returned with a prisoner.

"You're Proinnsias Pike?" I asked uncertainly in English. He had the same shock of black hair on a pale, puckish face as the photo in my dossier. But prison had made him gaunt and hollow, hardly the strapping Irish street brawler I had been expecting.

"Unless you speak Irish, it's Frank. But most just call me Pike." In contrast to his appearance, his voice was an unblemished baritone with a cadence I found beguiling.

"Very well, Pike it is. My name is Johann Grotius. I'm liaison to the German Embassy in Madrid," I said, putting out my hand.

He gave me a quizzical look before taking it. I noticed his grip was shaky.

"Would you mind if we spoke for a few minutes?"

"Well, I've got to give a tennis lesson at two, and then it's lunch with the duchess, but I suppose I could squeeze you in."

"That reminds me," I said. I produced a length of fuet, a small wheel of Catalan cheese, and two rolls from my jacket. "Souvenirs from Barcelona." Pike's eyes ballooned in their sockets. "Please, this way," I said, leading him to a corner.

It was a warm August day, but Pike, in a soiled tunic and canvas trousers cinched with a rope, was shivering like he was out in winter. He eyed me warily. "You mind if we walk? Good for me to move my legs."

"Of course," I said, "but don't you want to eat?"

"We Irishmen have an astounding ability to move our mouths and feet at the same time."

We began to walk the cruciform path. Pike of course noticed my infirmity but didn't say anything. I have a mildly deformed leg—a clubfoot. My left leg is six centimeters shorter than my right, and my foot turns in on itself by about fifteen degrees. I wear an orthotic shoe, which allows me full mobility but not without a slight limp. Aside from the expected childhood pains of teasing and exclusion from sports, my defect did not mar my life until Goebbels mounted the rostrum. Then the comparisons came flooding in. That poisonous dwarf has made life for us clubfoots—at least those of us German clubfoots who are less than fanatical about National Socialism—a perpetual embarrassment. It seemed every Spaniard I had met in the last seven years had deemed it necessary to point out that I shared the same condition with *Señor Gebel*. One of them had gone so far as to nickname me *Gebelito*, which stung far more than any cry of "freak" or "goblin" had in the schoolyard. I was therefore grateful when, whether out of prudence or politeness, Pike declined to comment.

He pocketed the rolls and cheese and took small methodical bites from the fuet, chewing each piece to oblivion.

"It seems you've had a rough go of it here, Pike," I said.

He looked at me blankly, which made my idiotic statement appear all the more so. I didn't yet know his hearing was deteriorating.

"How are you getting on?" I asked.

"Oh, grand, just grand. You know what they say about Falange hospitality—always a fresh pot of tea, a warm bed, and a kick in the teeth. Tell me, is it true France fell in only six weeks?"

"Yes, along with the Low Countries. Denmark and Norway have capitulated as well."

"And England?"

"Still holding out, for the time being. But the Luft-waffe have many more bombs to drop."

"Will Franco join the fight?"

"It's unlikely," I said. Franco had of course pledged his allegiance to fight the international conspiracy of Jewish-Bolshevik democracy, but he demanded the Germans give him Gibraltar and half of North Africa, along with an endless supply of grain and gasoline.

The Führer had not taken kindly to this conditional offer of support, especially after he had just won the general his war.

"Look, Pike, I'd like to talk about your particular situation. I trust you've heard your death sentence has been commuted."

"I've been awarded a lifelong holiday here instead."

I handed him a cigarette. "So where does that leave you?"

"Trapped in a Trappist cell," he said melodiously.

"Yes, quite so, I'm afraid. That is, unless . . ."

"How come you don't sound like a German?" he asked.

"I'm sorry? Oh, you mean my English? Well, I suppose I have something of a knack for languages. I spent time in England as a student. And you?" I asked. "By the sound of it, Limerick with a New York twist. Tell me, do you still have contacts in America?"

"Surely you know I haven't been there since I was a pimply young cunt—or can't you tell 'by the sound of it?'"

I did know. His lawyer, who was one of our assets, had passed on copies of the correspondence Pike had on his person at the time of his capture. He had letters from a sister in New York, as well as friends in Ireland affiliated with the governing party Fianna Fáil, the

IRA, and the School of Celtic Languages at University College Dublin—all of which made him a particularly strategic asset from our point of view. Yet, unlike most prisoners, he appeared not to have written a single letter in the last two years.

"What is it you want from me?" he asked.

"Very well, since you favor the direct approach, let me ask you another question. What is it you want from life, Pike?"

"Well, I can tell you becoming a Nazi isn't high on the list. I'd say it's right below chewing off my own cobs."

"No one wants you to become a Nazi. I'm not a Nazi."

"You just work for them."

"I happen to be German. I work for Germany. I can't help that a gang of criminals and half-wits has taken power in my country and given us a war nobody wanted but one we are poised to win."

We in the Abwehr were encouraged to draw sharp distinctions between the Nazis and Germany as a way to disarm a potential recruit. I liked to think my frank contempt for the regime was particularly effective because, at least in my case, it was true.

"I have no choice but to work within these circumstances to bring about the best possible outcome."

"For yourself?" asked Pike.

"For the world, yourself and myself included. I'd like to help you, which will in turn allow you to help the people of Ireland."

"A charming notion," he said, laughing. "But I'm afraid not all us socialists have our dye washed out so easily."

"We want to send you back to Ireland. Helmut Kriegsmann said you would be amenable to the idea."

For once, he didn't have a clever reply. "Helmut the German sent you?"

I nodded. "He says you would know how to navigate the political situation there, how to heal the rift between De Valera's government and the IRA rebels and unite them in common cause against the British."

Pike laughed. "I haven't known anything for two years but hard Spanish stone."

"Well, you know enough to know this war is not like the last one. Germany is moving swiftly toward victory. Assuming the Russians stay out of the way, England will be defeated soon. Then the dream of a German Europe will be achieved. And with it, assuming we find the right allies, so will the dream of a united and independent Ireland."

"And what if Hitler's defeated?"

"It's possible, though it doesn't look like he will be.

Nor does it seem likely your fledgling republic will ever become whole unless it's backed by a military force that can actually defeat England. Wouldn't you like to help end partition?"

"To what end? So I can help turn Ireland into a German colony instead of an English one?"

"As far as I know, Germany has no designs on Irish sovereignty. It boils down to the simple equation that what's bad for England is good for both our countries. Germany can be a friend to Ireland, and Ireland can be a friend to Germany. But why trouble ourselves with geopolitical speculation? You must assess this situation realistically, Pike. This is about Ireland's fate, as well as your own. Nazis have nothing to do with it. The question you have to ask yourself is how, other than by working for us, do you plan to get beyond these walls?"

We circled the garroting post in silence. I stopped here and turned to him so that the execution site was in his line of vision over my shoulder. "Consider it this way. I'm offering you your freedom. And in return all I'm asking for is friendship."

2
Finn McCool in the Bowels of Teutonia: Concerning His Murderous Exploits in Berlin

The Bowels

**Here continue the high deeds of Finn McCool—
retainer to the Taoiseach of Erin and exiled captain
of the Fenians. Finn, who had hunted men through
the boglands of Erin and across the corpse-strewn
valley of the Ebro, was, at the moment we encounter
him, tracking his prey in the bowels of Teutonia.**

A horse cart brimming with viscera clattered down
the cobblestones of Horst-Wessel-Stadt. Its fumes
coiled up the saucer-sized nostrils of Finn McCool,

filling his wise brain with the fragrance of slaughter. The scent was unmistakable. Fouler than the spoiled rejectamenta sloshing in those sun-bleached barrels, fouler even than the fetid air of Friedrichshain, which reeked of dogshit and despair and industrial sewage gushing into the Spree. It was the scent of Morell. Dr. Theodor Morell. Homeopathic healer and physician to the stars. The keeper of needles. The Poisonous Mushroom. The personal doctor of Adolf Hitler.

Finn crawled along the quay, following the cargo of organ meat that had come from the far reaches of Slavdom. When the two guards became distracted by a girls' rowing team on the water, he slipped through the open loading dock and hid behind a metal staircase on the factory floor. Here was where they processed the offal into the life-giving serum that flowed through Hitler's veins. Finn had come to spike the punch. Though, from what he could see and smell from his clancular perch, there was hardly a need for skullduggery. The ingredients themselves were pure poison. Slimy sheep udders, putrefied bull pizzles, an ungodly stew of goat glands and equine vulvae that had traveled across the Ukrainian plains—these would surely kill any man, let alone a vegetarian like the Führer.

The truth was, Finn's heart did not warm to such a craven method of man-slaying as the slip of a Mickey. Not after the incident with the treacherous Fenian. No, he much preferred monomachy. To feel the hilt of his blade up against the guts, hear the deathgroans, taste the bloodspray. Of course, he stood no chance of getting in such close proximity to Hitler. Finn, as he crept from the staircase and up into the ventilation shaft, had a different plan.

It was rumored that the Führer had become dependent on his daily injections. He simply couldn't function without them. If the rumors were true, then one need not get to Hitler in order to knock him off his feet. All you had to do was eliminate the one man he relied upon to get through the day. Kill the doctor, and, with a bit of luck, it just might kill the patient too. To think that a feckless, rot-livered Fenian could, with the simple flick of his stag knife, bring this war to a halt—the thought made Finn laugh so hard he nearly gave up his hiding spot.

Fascists and doctors, Finn had come to understand, were kindred types, and the fascist doctor a lethal hybrid of the two. The fascist was known by his intolerance of ambiguity, overactive disgust reflex, and adoration of authority. The second type, the medical doctor, was of much older issue but exhibited many similar traits: the desire to impose order by excising foreign bodies, the infliction of pain, and the need to reduce reality to convenient contraries like healthy versus sick. The expression of these personality traits, given the right context, could be destructive on its own, but when spliced with the fascist, the result was without exception monstrous.

With Morell, Finn was circling his sixth kill. Seventh, if one counted that bit of bad business on the submarine, which he preferred not to do. The notches on his war club belonged to four Nazi doctors and one nurse, pedigreed party members all. Hitler's doctor, and with any luck Hitler himself, would be his crowning achievement.

The problem was that Morell, despite being morbidly obese and uniquely malodorous, was an elusive figure. Finn had sighted him but once, stood face-to-face with the man in his office, in fact. But no sooner had he laid eyes on him than the doctor was spirited away to a fortress in the eastern forests. Now his office was shuttered and his elite clientele of Reichskabinett members and film actresses was left out in the cold, clamoring for harder erections and softer stools. Like them, Finn faced the same intractable reality: that an appointment was simply out of the question. Doctors—they must be eliminated!

thought Finn in his wise brain. That was why he was here in the Hamma factory slithering through the ductwork and scraping his horn against hot metal. He needed a new path to Morell.

He wormed onward until he reached the vent above the factory office. Stilling his breath, he inched his face to the grate. A man was working at the desk below him with his back to the vent. Finn could make out his balding crown and sloped shoulders hunched over an account book. He should be going to lunch soon, at which point Finn could root around the files. Surely, one of those cabinets had a sheet with the doctor's home address on it. According to the rumors, the Führer had bought him a villa somewhere in the western suburbs in return for curing his eczema. But the problem was, there were several suburbs west of Berlin, many of them chockablock with villas. He'd asked his remaining friends among the *Wilden*, young misfits who roamed the lakeshores of the Grunewald, to keep on the lookout for the portly doctor, but so far the little Indians had turned up only a gold-collared hound and the body of a drowned infant.

Fifteen minutes passed, and the noon bell rang. Still, to Finn's surprise, the clerk remained at his desk. The Teutonians were usually so mechanized in their routine. Surely this man would not eat

at his *Arbeitsplatz*. The practice was considered
unhygienic here, belonging to the uncouth habits of
New York financiers and Hollywood film moguls—a
clear symptom of liberal-Jewish decadence. The
one o'clock return-to-work bell struck, yet the little
office mole showed no signs of abating. Finn could
hear him singing the sums to himself under his
breath as he tallied: *Einundvierzig, Fünfundsiebzig,
Zweihundertdreiundzwanzig . . .*

Finn's limbs [perfectly roped muscle] began to
cramp. The sweat gathered at the tip of his nose and
pattered onto the metal. He tried to adjust himself
but, in doing so, snagged his nipple on a raised
nailhead and let out a groan. The clerk paused in his
computations, lifted his head, and looked around for
something to confirm the report of his ears. Finn
remained frozen, exerting all the tendons in his neck
to hold his face away from the grate. Seeing nothing,
the man removed a cucumber, a jar of mustard, and a
heel of black bread from his desk drawer, gave Finn
his bald crown again, and returned to work.

Having decided he must wait the clerk out, Finn
withdrew his powers of sensual perception and retired
into the privacy of his mind, as he had done so often
during his years in the Spanish pit. He consulted
his repertoire of tales and, feeling fatigue for all

stories concerning his youth in Ireland, his criminal misadventures in New York, and his sobering political education in Spain, he decided to regale himself with the story of his ascension from the pit, chronicling his metamorphosis into the mighty hunter Finn. He would tell the tale of Finn McCool, secret death-dealing ambidexter, scourge of Nazi doctors, and redeemer of Europe—currently stuck in the bowels of Berlin.

3

JOURNAL

December 1, 1943

I picked him up in Hendaye late in the summer of 1940. The air battle for England was then under way (I might add that as I write, the RAF are certainly returning the favor in full).

Two civil guards drove him to the border in a black Hispano-Suiza, its silver stork piercing the veil of lit fog. Pike got out and walked across the bridge into France, where I waited. He was wearing a *Guardia Civil* uniform.

"Well, hello there, Mephistopheles," he said, taking my hand. "We never did shake to confirm the sale of my soul."

We drove through the night toward Paris. Pike said

little and looked out the open window, lapping up the air like a hound.

At dawn we stopped in Poitiers. It was his first breakfast in two years. It was also my first glimpse of his gregarious and libidinous personality.

"By God, did you see that?" he asked, after the bar girl brought our meal.

"What?"

"The girl, man. Your gorgeous lump of a waitress there. Did you see her arms? That's how I'd like to go—beaten to death by those fine, slender girl arms. I daresay women have gotten even prettier in the last two years."

I wouldn't have known.

"Say," asked Pike, "is it true Trotsky is dead?"

It was.

"Who killed him?"

"Well, he claims to be a jilted Belgian socialist, but he's almost certainly one of Stalin's NKVD men. Whoever he is, he was caught burying an ice ax in Trotsky's skull."

Pike shook his head. "And I thought that was just something the guards were saying to taunt us. Jesus, this coffee tastes like a dream."

It was nothing special, as I recall, but back then it

was still brewed mostly from real coffee beans, and not the chicory and dirt that currently fill our cups.

I noticed he had broken down his meal into little morsels and arranged them on the plate. He saw me observing him. "Prison habit. Made the bread last longer. We ate the pieces in order of least to most moldy."

"I would have thought it better to eat the moldiest first, knowing the meal will only get better."

"Well," he said with a mouthful of croissant, "you reveal your deep ignorance of strategy when it comes to consuming rotten organic matter. You see, the mold paints its flavor all over your tongue. It's sharp and it lingers. So, if you eat the moldiest bit first, the rest of your bread, even the untainted crumbs, tastes foul. But if you eat those few precious and miraculously unbesmirched pieces first, with a clean mouth and at the pinnacle of your hunger, well, then you've managed to experience pleasure in a place where there's only pain and privation. Like drawing yourself a cool heavenly pint from the brimstone of hell."

I told him that still it must have been awful to end every meal with a rancid taste in your mouth.

"Ah, but isn't that how life ends, Grotius—with a rancid taste?"

He had no illusions that it would end otherwise for

him. "I've eaten the best bits of life, and now that I've signed on with you lot, I'm onto the moldy parts. But at least I'm still eating. See, that's my problem. I'm still hungry for life, even after it's spoiled."

"*The maddest thing a man can do in this life is to let himself die,*" I said.

"What's that from?"

"The *Quixote*. Sancho to the Don on his deathbed."

"Well, God bless that peasant sage and font of squirely wit," he said, popping a bread ball into his mouth.

I knew then that I liked him.

Pike slept after we left Poitiers. I had taken two Pervitin with my breakfast and felt like I could drive all the way to China.

We were an hour outside Paris when he stirred. "Grotius! Of course! I've finally got it."

His shout startled me. "What? Got what?"

"Your name. It came to me in my sleep. Hugo Grotius. *De Jure Belli ac Pacis.* I can picture the spine on my father's bookshelf. Do you know it?"

"*The Rights of War and Peace.*"

"Is he a relation of yours?"

"Not that I'm aware of. Though I do have some Dutch stock in the family tree."

Of course, my last name was not really Grotius, but I was telling the truth. And I'm certain that the jurist Grotius had once been on our bookshelf too. That is, until my father sold off the family library. By the time I turned thirteen, all that remained of my grandfather Johannes de Groot's spectacular five-thousand-volume collection were two centuries of bound account ledgers, a Luther Bible, and an eighteenth-century treatise on rum manufacturing. "Nothing more a Flensburg merchant needs," I remember my father saying after the last cartload of books had been trundled away. Only later, after his death, did I discover that my father had kept a secret library of his own.

It seems fitting to note here, since the subject has come up and since this may well serve as the only meaningful record of my life, a word about my origins. My family was composed of the northern margins of Germany—Frisians and Dutch on my father's side, Danes on my mother's, with the odd Germanizing Saxon thrown into the stew. The De Groots had, amid the chaos of the Thirty Years' War and the decline of the Hanseatic League, shapeshifted from fishermen into merchants. A century later, Groot & Arnesen was the most prosperous firm in Flensburg. Sugar and rum from the Danish West Indies and whale oil from

Greenland passed through our docks and left behind their residue of capital in our coffers. At its height, the firm added its own rum distillery.

Our fortunes turned with Bismarck. When Flensburg was Prussianized in 1864, so began my family's long *Buddenbrooks*-like decline. "We were once the sweeteners of Europe," boasted my father, who was given to hyperbole, especially regarding the past. He was a fatalist and saw it as his duty as son and epigone to steer the family business on its predestined path to oblivion. Any attempt to change course or evolve with the times was seen as a betrayal. Although his entire identity was attached to an enterprise whose sole purpose had been profit, money itself was anathema to him, something to be spent or gambled away as quickly as possible. He regarded mercantilism as his birthright, requiring no more maintenance than a fresh coat of paint on the coat of arms.

By the time I was born, in 1902, into a patrician house beside the Marienkirche and the trappings of inherited wealth, all that remained of the family empire was the rum distillery. And it was bad rum at that, the kind you would see broken veterans drinking in the street. By 1921, the G&A Distillery had gone bankrupt and my father was consuming more alcohol than his firm was selling. Thankfully, I didn't witness this up close. I was in England at boarding school on money my family no longer had, part of a goodwill campaign to repair Anglo–German relations, and had just won a scholarship to study at university in Salamanca. By the end of that year, during my first year in Spain, my father's liver gave out.

I came back a month after the funeral to sell the house and tend to my mother and sister. One morning, while I was cleaning out his wardrobe, I noticed a small door hidden behind his staggering collection of suits. I pushed tentatively, and when I found myself on the other side, suddenly surrounded by a library of floor-to-ceiling perversions, I realized I had never known my father at all. Bodies contorted in horrible poses, pinioned by metal clamps and leather restraints. Wood and bone penetrating flesh. Pain and pleasure entwined. Images that continue to haunt me all these years later.

"Wonder what that musty old humanist would make of our little arrangement here," said Pike, still thinking of the jurist who shared my name. "We think—or rather, those of us who were fighting for a better world liked to think—we were making progress, little by little, century by century. But look what's happened in just a handful of years. Rule of law, international society of peaceful states, the universal dignity of man—all those four-hundred-year-old ideas of Grotius's out the bleeding window. To invoke those words today, well, you might as well be speaking Eskimo. And we have your boss Hitler—no, excuse me, I should say our boss Hitler—to thank for it."

I told him Hitler was neither my boss nor his.

"I wish I had your talent for self-obfuscation, Grotius. I hope that's something they'll teach me in spy school."

I said nothing.

"My father once told me Grotius had to flee the Spanish Netherlands by hiding in a trunk of books all the way to France," said Pike, stretching himself out in the cramped seat. "A longer, bumpier ride even than in this pile of metal. Speaking of which, what's a German like you doing behind the wheel of a Renault? Isn't it your duty to despise all things French?"

"On the contrary," I said. "As you'll soon see, the Germans love French *things*. It's only French people and their ideas they loathe."

Paris in the late summer of 1940 felt as though the whole SS had commandeered the city for a stag spree. Just the act of driving through at midday on a Saturday made me feel obscene. The Champs-Élysées reeked of champagne vomit and piss. Uniformed officers were outside drinking at cafés with their courtesans or walking their Great Danes in a victors' gait. I much preferred dour Madrid, even in its famished and war-weary state. It's not just that I resented Paris—which, like all foreign-born Hispanists, I do. We are distrustful of the city's easy charms and repulsed by its unchallenged claim to cultural supremacy. The Nazis wanted to conquer it, but in order to enjoy it. Even as conquerors, they were under its seductive spell. And this was what truly galled me. Seeing my countrymen, speakers of my language, the supposed descendants of Lessing and Goethe, lord their authority over a people all while playing out drunken tourist fantasies made me ashamed to be German. At least in Madrid the Francoist scoundrels I was working with had done this to their own people. I was merely an observer there and not part of an occupying force.

We dined at La Tour d'Argent. Canaris was of the school that assets should be overwhelmed by comfort—I suppose this was why I had been ordered to drive two hundred kilometers out of the way for lunch. But given Pike's recent circumstances, I think the effect was more jarring than anything. As we climbed the narrow staircase to the sixth floor, I noticed that the suit I had brought for Pike fit him like a bedsheet (I suppose he has always loomed larger in my mind). It was also still painfully obvious that he hadn't showered since leaving the Burgos dungeon. I watched him as he took in the elegance of the dining room, with its rich wood paneling, chandeliers, and huge windows overlooking Notre-Dame and the Seine. The man looked around the room as though lost in a forest.

"Don't worry, Pike. It's just like any other meal. You pick up food and put it in your mouth."

"Grateful you told me—saved me the embarrassment of gobbling it up with my arse."

"And no need to arrange the bites on your plate," I said. "None of the food is spoiled here. Though I'm afraid the same can't be said of the clientele."

We approached the table where Veesenmayer and Kriegsmann were waiting for us, and I summoned the bland professional tone I used when in the company of Hitlerites. I introduced Pike first to Dr. Edmund Veesenmayer, who at the time was serving as special adviser on Ireland with the Foreign Office. He was an SS man and ardent Nazi. And, as if that weren't revolting enough, a professor of political science. He wore his hair slant across his forehead in imitation of the Führer, and his veins bulged beneath his skin in such a way as to remind one of a turgid glans. He has since moved on to Zagreb, where he is no doubt busy with the slaughter of Serbs and Jews.

"And Helmut Kriegsmann I believe you already know."

"Helmut the German!" yelled Pike, embracing him and attracting the attention of other diners. I noticed that he spoke rather loudly, a bit too loudly for a spy.

Kriegsmann bothered me far less. In fact, I rather liked him. He was with the Brandenburgers, a commando unit dedicated to insurgency and sabotage, and he gave off the air of a swashbuckling adventurer—the kind of warrior specimen the Veesenmayers of the world secretly longed to be. Veesenmayer revered Kriegsmann for the very qualities he himself lacked but that he prized to the point of believing they were his own. Like a collector under the delusion that he, solely by virtue of possessing a beautiful painting, is somehow responsible for its creation.

Kriegsmann had been the mastermind behind Pike's release. He knew more about Ireland than almost anyone in Germany. Though that was an achievement rather easily come by, since nobody in Germany seemed to know anything about Ireland. Before the war, he'd been a doctoral student at Trinity, where he studied the migration habits of waterfowl, taught German, and fell in with the IRA. Pike was old friends with Kriegsmann's Irish wife, Val.

While the two friends caught up, I was left with

Veesenmayer. The man looked like he had been rubbed in oil.

"He reeks," he said, referring to Pike.

"As would anyone who's just emerged from San Pedro de Cardeña."

"I hear the Reichsführer was displeased by his trip to Spain."

"I'm not sure what you heard, but he seemed to enjoy himself," I said, recalling Himmler's daily temper tantrums.

"He said the Abwehr hasn't lifted a finger to track down German traitors who fought in Spain."

"Traitors? As I recall, the Reich was never officially at war with the republic."

"Communists, anarchists, traitors. It's all the same."

"Well, as Canaris sees it, it's not our job."

"So aloof, you lot. Nothing seems to be your job. That's why the Security Office has to do everything for you."

Himmler had made an agreement with Franco to let the Gestapo operate freely within Spain, in exchange for shipping back any rogue Spanish republicans found in the greater Reich. This arrangement was also an indirect assault on the Abwehr, as it meant Himmler's laboratory monster Heydrich would be watching over us, making sure Canaris didn't let things become too ideologically lax. Neither Hitler nor Himmler fully trusted Canaris. He was not a party member, and on top of that, he was an eccentric, a fox, a pirate captain sailing his ship of spies wherever he pleased.

"Mark my words, Grotius," said Veesenmayer. "Your lot's days are numbered."

Mercifully, the waiter arrived with our lunch. Though, after listening to these sinister admonishments come from Veesenmayer's lubricated face, I had lost my appetite. We were served *canard à la presse*, which was carved above our plates on a long fork. Pike's chin nearly fell onto the tablecloth. I was afraid he might be in shock. But he soon came to his senses and took up his utensils.

"Did you know that right here in this very restaurant is where Henry the Fourth first introduced the fork into French dining?" said Veesenmayer to the table in English, as though trying to prove his was as fluent as ours.

"What's this number?" asked Pike, gesturing at a little card that was presented next to his plate.

"It's the serial number of the duck," said Kriegsmann. "And it appears you've been served number 300,130."

"Is this a new German policy?" Pike asked.

Kriegsmann and I laughed. Veesenmayer looked annoyed.

"La Tour d'Argent has been serving the best duck in France for centuries. It is one of the oldest restaurants in Europe," he said testily.

We all began eating.

"Wait," said Veesenmayer, putting out his hand like a traffic guard. "We need new wine for the duck. This one's not right." He shouted for the waiter and demanded to see the wine list.

"Is this entirely necessary? This man," I said, gesturing at Pike, "hasn't tasted meat in years!"

"If you want to ruin your meal, you can be my guest," said Veesenmayer.

Pike continued eating. Kriegsmann and I looked at each other and recognized our mutual embarrassment at having heeded Veesenmayer's command in the first place. We, too, resumed eating.

"So I'm dining with barbarians," said Veesenmayer sulkily.

The waiter returned with what looked like a dictionary. Veesenmayer placed a pair of glasses on the tip of his nose, irritably flipped through the pages, and barked out a request for a 1921 Cheval Blanc.

When the waiter brought the wine, Veesenmayer, as punishment for our insolence, refused to let him pour for the rest of us. It was unclear if he was joking, but

Pike looked like he was going to smash the bottle over his head.

"You may think me a prig, Herr Pike, but I assure you there is nothing more serious than pleasure. And pleasure requires discipline."

"Gee, I'd sure hate to be your girlfriend," said Pike with a mouthful of duck, which he washed down after helping himself to a glass of Veesenmayer's forbidden Bordeaux.

The man had a contempt for authority and the tongue to match it. It was a miracle he'd survived a Falangist prison. I found it thrilling. And, it must be admitted, seductive.

Over brandy and cigarettes, Kriegsmann told us of his latest mission, which had been aborted due to weather. The North Sea seemed to be our most formidable enemy when it came to Irish operations. Operation Lobster was supposed to deposit him with a wireless on the shores of Dingle. But a storm caught them off the coast and nearly capsized the fishing boat. While Kriegsmann was undeterred, the Breton captain refused to bring her to shore in the storm and turned back. Pike, who was reeling from the wine, listened to his old friend Kriegsmann with eyes closed and a wan smile, like a child hearing a bedtime story.

After lunch, we drove to the château in the Loire Valley where Pike would undergo his training. I was to stay the weekend, make sure he was properly settled in, and then return to Madrid on the Monday train from Paris. I relished the idea of a quiet weekend in the countryside with minimal duties. I'd even brought a bootlegged copy of Zweig's *Erasmus von Rotterdam* and planned to spend the next day engrossed under a tree.

The château was an impressive Renaissance relic, with crenellated roof and Italian ornamentation that proved just how far the art of masonry had fallen in recent times. No doubt the house had been expropriated from those deemed racially or politically unworthy and somehow Canaris had finagled it into his possession.

Veesenmayer marched past us in a rage as we came through the front entrance. He was searching for the estate manager, Marcel, to berate him about some oversight with the driveway, and told us to go wait in the kitchen. Three other recruits were already there, smoking beside the stone fireplace. An American, an Alsatian, and a Bohemian German. All of them were abnormally tall, their heads nearly brushing the copper pots that hung from the arch.

We appraised one another in silence until a cherubic

man descended the staircase and clapped his hands together. *"Moin, moin!"* he shouted, with a mischievous smile and a cheek full of cut tobacco.

He introduced himself as Captain Arne Töller and welcomed everyone to his "House of Deception." He was clad in green riding pants, a loose white tunic, and a Greek fisherman's cap, his Mediterranean flair contrasting comically with his Plattdeutsch, which reminded me of my northern upbringing. Captain Töller then proceeded to explain that for the next few weeks these promising recruits would learn some "handy little tricks"—namely, encryption, wireless communication, invisible inking, and explosives—that would transform them into "masters of deception."

What strange characters the intelligence community employs, I remember thinking when Pike nudged me. "I haven't a clue what this fella's on about."

Embarrassed that I had never broached the subject before, I asked Pike if he knew any German.

"Sauerkraut, Danke schön, Flugzeug—what more could I need?"

I sighed, and for the second time that month, I took up the role of interpreter. At least it wasn't for Himmler.

Pike was given a room in the château and I was put up in the carriage house, in somewhat shabbier quarters than I had hoped for. The room was damp and smelled of mold, the bed canopy sagged with dust and cobwebs, and the mattress felt like it had been packed with bones. But at least there was a tap and a stove for boiling water. I had just drawn a bath for myself when I heard a knock at the door.

Exhausted from so much driving and a heavy meal, I pretended not to hear. I turned the faucet back on, hoping my visitor would take the hint. But the knocking persisted. I wrapped myself in a towel monogrammed with the initials of the previous owner and went to the door.

It was Pike. "Grotius—my interpreter, my liberator—I've another favor to ask."

"Certainly, Pike, but can't it wait until I've had a bath?" I said more testily than I had wished. I suddenly felt conscious of being undressed in front of him. I had a slim upper body that I took pride in keeping in a groomed and toned state, in hopes it offset the condition of my leg. I noticed Pike survey me in my nakedness down to the hem of my towel.

"I'm afraid it can't, Grotius. It's been two years and counting. . . ."

I looked at him blankly.

"Don't you see, man, I've been thinking about that girl from the café, and those women on the streets in

Paris, and even that plump old countess at the table beside us at lunch. I won't be able to learn a lick of spy work 'til I've let my Jap's eye have a proper wink and pumped all this jip from my brain."

"Well, what do you want me to do about it?" I said. "There are no women here."

I didn't know whether he saw the hanging implications of that statement. I hadn't either until I uttered it and then feared he'd think I was offering an alternative. Unless, of course, it was he propositioning me.

"What's the closest town?"

"Tours, but it's been all but destroyed."

"Is there a town that's not been destroyed?"

"Well, Orléans, I suppose. Though it's probably an hour's drive."

"Then you've got to take me to Orléans. If only for an hour."

I told him he was mad. I said I was sure a trip could be arranged eventually, but tonight was out of the question. "You don't even have papers, Pike. What if the authorities detain you? You do realize part of the job of being a spy is to evade detection." I reminded him that, according to Franco's government, he had escaped, which meant the French authorities and the Gestapo would send him back to Spain.

"But that's why I need you to come with me, Grotius. Flash those Abwehr credentials at whoever gives us trouble."

I laughed. "The Gestapo in Orléans won't set great store by the fact that I'm a diplomatic liaison in Madrid."

"Are you sure there's no way I can convince you?" said Pike, slowly this time, as his gaze wandered down to my towel.

Before I knew it, he pushed me backward onto the bed, dropped to his knees, and, pulling loose my towel, took me in his mouth. The suddenness and excitement of it all was too much. I felt the wetness of his tongue, his hardness against my bare leg, and before I could truly appreciate the first intimate touch I had experienced in years, I came.

Pike stood and wiped his mouth on his shirtsleeve. "Shall we go, then?"

4

Finn McCool in
the Bowels of Teutonia

The Pit

The smell of the morning's executions still hung in the air when the screw took Finn from his cell. Was this it? he wondered. His name had not been called. But, then, that hardly mattered.

Every morning for two hundred days, the priest would intone the roster of damned souls. And every morning they would call his name. At the O's his body would begin to shake. Oppenheimer, Ordoñez, Orozco, Orsen, Ortega, Peña, Perec, Pérez, Pike—each time the sound of it stabbed him. Even now, whenever he heard the Spanish pronunciation of his old name, *Pi-que,* the name he had known before he became Finn, he felt a sting inside his brain. Every morning the screw Clemente rattled the cell door open and led him out to the cloister garden, behind the other condemned names. In the early days, when the list was long, the prisoners were pushed against the stone wall and shot. After the numbers thinned, the garroting post was erected. Every morning for two hundred days Finn was made to stand and watch the executions, waiting for his own, until he alone remained in the garden and was then taken back to his cell.

Four hundred days had passed since his name had last been called. But here was the screw Clemente, wearing his same weary expression, nudging Finn down the ambulatory with his baton. In the garth, the garroting post shimmered in the midday sun. Three crows hopped around the pool of vomit at its base, pecking at half-digested bread, while guards hauled the last corpse away. Neither paid Finn any mind.

As he assured himself he would not die today, a voice behind him spoke.

"I told you I would come."

Finn turned to see the dark, kitelike face of the lawyer Baroucin. He had seen the man only once, at his trial. If it could be called that, though nothing was tried. It had lasted twenty minutes and the presiding military judge had sentenced him to death, as he had the other dozen prisoners from the International Brigades that morning. The Baron Baroucin, who spoke Spanish with a French inflection and looked every bit the reactionary aristocrat, had politely asked the judge to consider reducing the sentence to life imprisonment. The judge denied this request, and that was the last he had seen of his lawyer.

"I have some news," he said.

Finn, who was not keen to guess the contents of his lawyer's mind, stared at him.

"Franco has commuted your death sentence."

Finn considered these words, taking them apart and putting them back together again. It seemed he had already died many times in this courtyard.

"So I'm to live out my days here, then?"

Baroucin edged closer to Finn and whispered in his ear. "Not exactly."

The baron took Finn by the shoulder and escorted him to the far end of the courtyard, away from the guards. "I can't say much, but Lieutenant McGrath is a friend."

Gerry McGrath had been a fellow officer in the International Brigades. Finn had not heard of him since he was taken at Gandesa and feared that, like most of the IB men there, he had been captured or killed.

"Just keep silent while I talk, and listen very carefully. British intelligence has learned that the Germans are planning an Irish operation to coincide with an invasion of England and that they aim to recruit you as an agent. The details of the plan are unknown, but we have intercepted messages sent between the Abwehr office in Madrid and the Foreign Office in Paris. An Abwehr agent, likely a man named Johann Grotius, will be coming to make you an offer of collaboration in exchange for your freedom. McGrath says you should accept this offer. Don't act too eager, but accept. Once you are out of Spain, they will likely take you to a training facility in the Loire before bringing you to Germany. We have a contact in Orléans at a brothel called La Pucelle. Find a way to get there, ask for Mamie, and ask her for an Alouette."

"An Alouette?"

"It's a kind of verse. She will tell you more. Now, shake my hand if you understand this and agree to it."

"Does De Valera know about this?" asked Finn.

Baroucin handed Finn a crumpled five-pound banknote. "Read it."

On the back, written in the runic hand of his Taoiseach, Éamon the Valorous, with whom he had once passed notes through the bars of a cell, was a message:

Éire must remain officially neutral, but I'm trusting you to be our Finn McCool in the lands of the Gilla Dacar.—E.

So, thought Finn, there's still some fight in the old dog after all.

"Now eat it," said the lawyer.

Finn wadded up the five-pound note and swallowed it. "That's the best meal I've had in years."

"The most expensive one too, I imagine," said Baroucin. "Now shake my hand and, for godssakes, good luck."

And these were the memories Finn brought to sustain himself on his voyage to Teutonia:

—A grilled rabbit, caught and eaten on the purple wastelands of Aragon.

—The face of Arturo at the garroting post, tendons burst from his neck, eyeballs sprung from their sockets.

—The gamey smell of the vellum in the Manuscripts Room of University College Dublin.

—The black nose hairs of Dr. Vallejo-Nágera, visible just above his clipboard, as he expounded on his theory of congenital Marxism.

—The wind on his face while he and Seán Hogan clung to the running board of a commandeered postal lorry.

—The pursed lips of the Chekists in the lobby of the Hotel Florida as they tallied the ideological sins of the clientele and drafted kill lists in their heads.

—A warm loaf of pumpernickel from Liebermann's, fruit of his first theft.

—The sweaty thighs of Lucy O'Donnell during the premiere of *Modern Times* at the Savoy, the night before he left for Spain.

—The prim face of Seán Russell after he had expelled Finn and his fellow socialists from the IRA.

—The pint of porter gracefully drawn at JJ Bowles pub.

—The three Asturian boys, no older than fourteen, lined up and shot in the back of the neck, while their fathers were made to watch and the priest looked on.

—The house thief in Mountjoy who called him China and gave him a friendly tug in the library when the screws weren't looking.

—The jug-eared potato head of that fascist cunt Eoin O'Duffy as he led his Fine Gael goons through the streets of Cork, screaming about godlessness and civilization.

—The sour breath of Herr Doktor Wagner as he leaned to fit the electrode harness over Finn's face.

5

JOURNAL

December 4, 1943

The bombings have finally stopped—at least for now. The cellar held out fine. Remarkably, the house suffered only some roof damage and a few broken windows. The only injury I sustained throughout the ordeal was at the very start, when Frau Obolensky's terrier, driven mad by the planes and sirens, took a chunk out of my calf. But there's been no sign of her or her little beast ever since.

I count myself fortunate, as several of my neighbors are completely bombed out. The apartment block on the corner had its entire façade blown off. Now the private lives of others are visible to all. Yesterday I saw an old man on the toilet of his second-floor flat. There he sat, pants at ankles, reading his *Völkischer Beobachter* and smoking his pipe, apparently unperturbed by the winter air and onlookers. I felt like I was seeing a diorama in an anthropological museum: the twentieth-century Berliner at his morning ritual. I even heard him give a little grunt of satisfaction but couldn't tell whether it was in response to his freshly moved bowels or the Reich's air raid on Bari.

This past week has felt like a strange and terrible holiday. Existence on hiatus. I was surprised to find I had not been as frightened as I'd expected to be. At least not most of the time. The duration is too long for that kind of fear. Instead, it's a steady hum of anxiety, more tedium than terror, at once stifling and with a vague sense of freedom given the suspension of every-day duties. I remember feeling the same way when I had measles as a child. Except of course for the threat of being crushed into rubble.

Yet when one hears of all the madness happening outside, it seems safest to take one's chances in the cellar. As though fires and falling buildings weren't enough, there are rumors several man-eating animals escaped from the zoo when it was hit. I overheard a woman at the butcher this morning say she saw a tiger ambling down Uhlandstraße, and the block warden Herr Eich is convinced there are now crocodiles in

Hindenburg Park. Perhaps one of them made a meal of poor old Frau Obolensky and her dog.

All in all, I was quite well off down here. I had an ample supply of bread and cheese, a crate of apples, several gallons of water, two bottles of Hungarian brandy, a straw mattress, a bucket full of wood shavings, and a battery-powered radio. I could have lasted another week without much discomfort.

A far cry better than being packed cheek by jowl with strangers. I've suffered the indignity on two occasions— once in my apartment block's common cellar and once in the public shelter of the Zoo flak tower—and vowed never again. Picture a crowded bus depot with shrunken ceilings: hard wooden benches teeming with sour-shirted workers, mothers overladen with suitcases and sniveling children, and sanctimonious party members making sure no foreigners fill the seats or anyone cracks a now stale but still subversive joke about Göring, who promised us Berlin would never be attacked by air. Then the shaking starts and the Hindenburg lights flicker; meanwhile, the air is dank with the smell of fear and poor dental hygiene. No, I'm not one of those people who find comfort in shared suffering or in whom crisis bolsters a sense of fellowship.

What has really sustained me this past week is this notebook. Perverse as it sounds, I've even returned to the cellar to continue writing. Something about life aboveground always sapped my will to write. And yet down here, hunched over the dim glow of the kerosene lamp, the words seem to come naturally, as if of their own volition.

The problem is now I am not sure what it is I'm writing. Initially, upon hearing the news of Pike's death, I felt a sudden impulse to set down a record of his passing and the terms of our acquaintance. I thought this would require no more than a few lines—a brief eulogy in the vein of "This man lived upon the earth and I knew him," and nothing more. Yet my pen took a major detour almost from the start and seems to have embarked on a journey of greater scope and peril than I anticipated. I see now, having read over these pages in the light of day, that I have put down things any one of which will earn me a one-way ticket to the *Lager*.

Very well. My silence has been broken. I will continue writing down here.

And then I will burn every page.

I have only scattershot images from the remainder of my time at the château. Waiting in the car outside a brothel in Orléans in a state of nervous agitation. Spymaster Töller drilling the recruits on dashes and dots while decanting an ancient Sauternes. Kriegsmann carrying a stack of gelignite from the garden shed like a bundle of kindling. Pike collapsing with exhaustion after his first mandatory training run; the others playing croquet in the afternoon sun. Veesenmayer dressing down the cook for leaving the tops on the radishes. Me, under a pear tree, staring at the pages of *Erasmus von Rotterdam*, unable to read a word.

Then of course there was the debacle with the wireless. Perhaps I should have seen it as a foreshadowing of the perpetual misadventure that life with Pike would come to entail.

It was my last afternoon there. Pike, under the guise of practicing with the wireless, sent a message to the Madrid station, which went as follows:

Julius Caesar left a breezer
On the coast of France.
The King of Spain tried the same,
But he left it in his pants.

Rather than see this for the childish prank that it was, a nervous secretary in Madrid, likely Frau Linden, interpreted Pike's message as pregnant with urgent meaning. Was Franco moving against Gibraltar, hoping to force Churchill into another Dunkirk? Were the British attempting another landing? Or was Mussolini up to something in the western Mediterranean? This doggerel inspired a frenzied morning of questioning and reprimands between Madrid and Berlin. Veesenmayer, who had already shouted himself hoarse at the domestic help, nearly had an apoplexy.

"Sorry, Herr Veesenmayer," said Pike. "The mind's a bit clotted from all that bad prison air, but I'll get the hang of it quick enough."

Veesenmayer looked at me with murder in his eyes. "Your Irishman better shape up, or I'll be sending him back to Franco."

I returned to Madrid in a state of confusion. Pike had been as nonchalant about our encounter as I was wrought. Of course, I did my best to present a composed façade during the rest of my time at the château, and perhaps I carried it off. While it is possible Pike was as internally racked by the same heady cocktail of desire and embarrassment as I was, I doubt it. He seemed to have regarded the act as about as meaningful as pouring someone a beer.

I had no expectations to see him again. He would stay on at Töller's spy school for a few more weeks and then would likely be put up somewhere in Germany or Belgium before his mission to Ireland. My domain was Spain. Now that Pike was soundly out of the country and into his new role, there was no reason our paths would cross again.

I vowed to bury myself in work. Our staff had been growing by the week since the war began, and now our offices in the embassy were loud with bureaucratic hum. An arsenal of radios, telephones, mimeograph machines, and typewriters pumped information in and out of our walls from our satellites in Badejoz, Barcelona, Bilbao, Burgos, Cádiz, Santander, Seville, Valencia, Valladolid, Vigo, and Zaragoza. Radio surveillance from Africa, ship movements from Gibraltar, internal gossip from Franco's government, arrests, executions, food shortages, car manufacturing, armaments, tide charts, film distributions—it all came into our ears in Madrid. And though much of this information was sent on to HQ in Berlin, a substantial portion never left our KO. For Madrid was the real heart of Canaris's fiefdom, and he liked to know things no one else knew. Occasionally, the old fox himself would make an appearance in the office but never to talk about work or the war. Instead, he would wax lyrical about a Jerez he had just tasted or the impeccable grace of Manolete when slaying a bull. Once, upon learning I was a translator, he asked my opinion on the work of the writer Leopoldo Lugones. Sadly, I had little to offer other than I knew he was Argentine.

"*Hombre,*" he said, grabbing my shoulder like we were intimate acquaintances, "*hay que leerlo.*"

Under the pretense that the Iberian Peninsula was critical to the war effort, Canaris actually spent more time in Spain than in Germany. Though the real reason, rumor had it, was that he couldn't bear to be within driving distance of Berlin for fear he'd have to accept Hitler's dinner invitations.

The Madrid KO was run by Canaris's old friend Wilhelm Leissner. A former publisher in Nicaragua, Leissner was an adventurer and bibliophile who collected information like he did first editions. Ever since our operations had expanded from a half dozen people run out of the back office of an import-export business to the towering bureaucracy it was now, I rarely saw *Lieber Gustav*, as everyone called him. But he was a warm if somewhat mysterious figure whose worldly and avuncular mien had made me forget, at least in the early days during the civil war, that I was working for the military.

After Madrid fell and our own war began, Leissner moved us into our well-appointed offices in the embassy. My principal task was to collect information on foreign nationals in Spain, which I then presented to the various department heads in tidy, thorough reports. Those who I suspected were enemy spies I passed on to the counterespionage agents in Branch III, who sometimes shared this information with Franco's people. Those foreigners who I thought could be used for our own interests in espionage and sabotage I earmarked for Branches I and II, respectively. Needless to say, this was a big undertaking, as Spain was teeming with spies of every denomination. And initially, when each of us did three or four jobs, I did a bit of everything—from compiling dossiers to actual recruitment, even some basic forgery, which I had learned on the job.

But now the KO had grown so big, we were outnumbered three to one by clerical workers. I spent half my day in meetings, coordinating with my counterparts.

Despite my vow to redouble my labors when I returned from France, I found it all but impossible to do so in this environment. I was irritable. Whereas before I had hardly noticed the noise of the office, now the incessant ticking and clacking of the teletype drove me to distraction. To make matters worse, Himmler, true to Veesenmayer's prediction, had his Security Office minions breathing down our necks, demanding copies of documents. They had even come to the office unannounced to strike thuggish poses and spew threats.

I began slipping out every few hours for a walk in the Retiro just to clear my head. The ennui I had felt during Himmler's visit had grown into an acute melancholy. Spain had lost its charm. At least during the civil war, there had been a sense of dynamism and possibility. But it had now become clear that Franco was using his new powers not to restore civility to a fractured nation but to exact revenge on the one half that had been against him. A grim paranoia had corroded the traditional ebullience of the Spanish character. Too little food and too many executions. And, to be honest, too many Germans.

I had kept a tight grip on my impulses in Madrid. Pike had been my first encounter since a passing incident with a legionnaire more than three years earlier. I had been in a tavern in Burgos, drunk on vermouth, when I caught the eye of a truly perfect specimen: a Mediterranean godling in tight green breeches, golden skin bursting from his open-necked shirt, and a red tassel dangling over his brow. But we just avoided being caught by the man's commanding officer, a notorious sadist. I then found out a few weeks later that the soldier had been discovered while engaged in another tryst, in the same tavern toilet, this time with a fellow legionnaire. The two men had been flogged nearly to death and were languishing in a military hospital when the news reached me. This near miss with one of the bridegrooms of death, as the Spanish Legion called themselves, was enough to frighten me into celibacy for the next three years, such that I had almost succeeded in becoming a stranger to my own desires.

Now, on my wanderings through the battered Retiro, I felt the longing creep back into my blood and found myself furtively eyeing young men again. Not that I was prowling the park for illicit liaisons or anything like that. Rather, my encounter with Pike had perturbed me. And the erotic element was only one part of a general perturbation of the soul that he had induced.

I had been in the habit of trading cigarettes for books with a black-market bookseller on the Cuesta de Moyano. Beneath his table of *siglo de oro* volumes and nationalist works by the likes of Pemán and Maeztu, my procurer, Alfonso, had a vast catalog of authors who were banned in Spain or Germany or, as was often the case, both. Names like Proust, Clarín, Mann, Gide, Woolf, Lorca, and Wilde found their way into my bag in exchange for the Balkan Gold cigarettes that filled an entire closet in the Abwehr office and were there for general consumption, bribery, and barter. I would walk to a shady corner of the park, tucked away from the view of passersby, where a half-ruined Romanesque church lay in hiding. It was far older than anything else in the park, though something about its placement seemed staged, like it had been relocated by a Romantic landscapist of the last century hoping to add a splash of medieval nostalgia. There on a cool stone bench inside the roofless hermitage, I would sit and read my contraband.

But as I reclined in the apse, trying to lose myself in *The Immoralist*, I found my thoughts inevitably turning to Pike. Not just about our encounter, but also his situation and its bearing on my own. His had dramatically and unquestionably improved. He was no longer rotting to death in a cell. And even if he wasn't entirely free, he was certainly freer than he had been in Burgos. My offer had given him a choice that was so clearly better than his previous lack of choices that it hardly constituted a decision, let alone a difficult one. After all, he was now working in some tangible albeit tangled way toward Irish independence. Yet his glib remarks about making a deal with the devil chafed something within me I couldn't quite identify. I was certainly no stranger to duplicity and deceit. Striking fraught bargains with desperate people was a staple of my job. Even if no one else had outright called me Mephistopheles before, the analogy was self-evident. So what was it that bothered me?

Feckless ruminations such as these filled my days in Madrid for two weeks, then came to an abrupt halt when I received a telegram from my sister. The cancer had spread from her cervix and eaten its way through her bladder. The doctors had given her three months at the most. To further complicate matters, she had a six-year-old daughter, my niece, Gretchen, who was an invalid. The poor child had cerebral palsy and required around-the-clock care. My sister's husband had been killed in Norway in May, courtesy of a sniper's bullet in the throat, which meant once Maike was gone, something would have to be done about Gretchen. She asked nothing of me in the telegram, but I knew what was required. Our parents were dead. Klaus's were alcoholic wrecks. I was her only family left. Of course, I couldn't become the child's nursemaid myself, but I could arrange for her care and serve as her legal guardian.

I applied for immediate transfer to Berlin, assuming there would be some use for me in the hive of Abwehr HQ, even if it meant a demotion to clerical work. Imagine, then, my surprise when my transfer was granted but with an assignment to Branch II, where I was to be the case officer of our sabotage agents awaiting deployment. Among them: one Proinnsias Pike. He would be assuming the name Frank Finn when he arrived in Berlin the following week. It was then I realized—or, rather, finally admitted to myself—that ever since I left France, he had been haunting me.

December 8, 1943

My sister, Maike, lived in a small cottage by the Wannsee. Her husband, Klaus, had been a gardener at Sanssouci before he was called up. They met at a gymnastics holiday on Rügen and, after marrying, settled on the western outskirts of the city so that he could go on tending the Hohenzollern shrubberies. Misfortune had followed my sister from a young age—accidents, illnesses, my father's neglect, the demands of my senile mother—and finally caught her in its trap there on the idyllic lakeshore. Klaus, almost too stupid to be despicable, was a brownshirt and active party member. After Gretchen was born and it became clear that the child was enfeebled, Klaus threw himself into politics and drink. Though my sister never admitted as much, I could tell that he beat her. And Gretchen too.

I was of course far removed from all this, busy with my work in Spain. After earning my doctorate in philology at Marburg, I'd realized I would never become a full professor and, furthermore, that the thought of teaching both terrified and depressed me. So I moved to Berlin to become a translator. I would never be rich or acclaimed, but I harbored no ambition to be either. I wanted only to be part of the symbolic world. To live among books and through them. A quiet life of internal passion was the ideal I set for myself, and with my facility with languages and a boom in small publishing houses and periodicals in the late twenties, I fell into it quite easily.

After the crash, however, work became increasingly scarce. By 1933, I decided enough was enough and left Berlin for Madrid, where the new republican government and its campaign to bolster culture offered the prospect of work. But the machine-gun street politics I left behind in Germany followed me to Spain, as though it had stowed away in my luggage and erupted upon arrival. It looked as though the republic was going to be overthrown by the communists at any moment. Largo Caballero—the Spanish Lenin, as he was fond of calling himself—seemed positively gleeful in his threats, shouting on the floor of parliament about the bloody revolution right around the corner. Anarchists vowed they would beat him to it and, as a show of faith, started burning churches. At the same time, José Antonio gathered his altar-boy sadists and law-school thugs into the Falange, and the long preamble of assassinations, arsons, and uprisings began.

I was scraping by, translating essays from German

and English for Ortega y Gasset's *Revista de Occidente*, when one afternoon at a café on the Calle de la Montera an elegant man in a pince-nez approached me. He asked if I had translated the essay by Max Scheler in the most recent issue of the *Revista*, and by the time our conversation ended, Lieber Gustav had given me my first assignment for the Abwehr.

It was harmless enough, translating radio broadcasts and parliamentary proceedings. Not exactly literary, but it paid five times what I got for wrestling with phenomenology and vitalist metaphysics. I never envisioned myself working for the state, let alone the Nazi state, but it never seemed that way to me. I was working for Lieber Gustav, and he was working for Canaris. And Canaris, while technically working for Hitler, seemed always to be operating outside the traditional boundaries. For example, at least two of our officers in Madrid were *Mischlinge*, for whom Canaris had managed to procure certificates of Aryan blood.

Plus, I was in Spain. As far as I was concerned, I had fled Hitler. But with the changing political situation, my responsibilities gradually evolved until, by the time civil war broke out in the summer of '36, I, Sonderführer Adrian de Groot, had gone from being a marginal member of the intelligentsia to an intelligence officer recruiting from among my former kind.

In the intervening years, I had seen my sister and her family only a few times: at my mother's funeral, at Gretchen's christening, and once at their cottage for Christmas. Klaus and I loathed each other. He was the quintessence of the uneducated petty bourgeois, with seething resentments against all foreigners, against anyone who might know better than him, against anyone or anything that might puncture his delusion that he was a member of the highest race and the greatest nation on the face of the earth. This little beer-swilling, wife-beating clod of humanity whose sole occupation in life was to trim weeds had adopted for himself all the noble entitlements, privileges, and petulance of royalty, though with none of the refinement or enlightenment that is the preserve of true nobility. Here was the gardener who, when he looked in the mirror, saw Frederick the Great. Such a specimen would be laughable if he weren't so vicious.

Gretchen was a sweet child. At three, she was just beginning to show signs of her affliction. A stiffness that would erupt in spasms, difficulty chewing and swallowing, occasional seizures. She hadn't yet learned to walk or speak real words either. All of this alarmed Maike and angered Klaus. But, in spite of her troubles, she was a jovial and attentive little creature, and she smiled and laughed at least as much as she cried and coughed.

As far as I recall, I have threatened another human being with violence only once in my life. It was the morning after Christmas, 1937. Klaus had drunk himself blind the night before and was still in a stupor. Maike was trying to feed a bit of potato to Gretchen, but she kept coughing it back up. Pained by the ordeal, the child began to cry. I tried to focus her attention on a pair of painted wooden foxes I had given her for Christmas, while Maike worried the potato between her fingers into ever tinier morsels. When Gretchen choked for a third time, Klaus got up from his chair by the door, stomped across the room, and grabbed his daughter by the jaw. He wrenched her mouth open and, like he was fattening a goose, crammed potato down the helpless child's throat.

"You little imbecile," he shouted. "Too stupid to chew your own food!"

Maike hung on his arm, sobbing, and screamed at him to stop. I sat there in total silence, shocked by what I had just seen. But after the ordeal was over, and Maike had taken little Gretchen to the toilet, and Klaus had returned to his chair by the door, I rose from my seat and calmly approached him. I said that if I ever learned he'd so much as raised his voice to that child, I would abuse every power at my disposal to brand him an enemy of the state and have him detained, tortured, and executed in as gruesome a manner as the Gestapo saw fit.

He must have thought these were absurd words coming from a diplomatic translator, for that was my official public title. But my threat had not been empty. I took measures to ensure that, should Klaus make one false step, a tip to the police regarding what lay beneath the floorboards of his cottage would land him in a concentration camp for sexual deviants. As it happened, the Norwegians put a bullet in him first.

I arrived in Berlin in mid-September, not two weeks after receiving my sister's telegram. It had been three years since my last visit. The city was screaming with the growing pains of Hitler's building campaign, as though to prepare residents for the screech of metal and taste of crushed stone to come. Posters assured us that these yawning pits of earth would soon be a monumental testament to the strength of the German *Volk*.

The gash of the new East–West Axis offered a glimpse of the glorious future in store for us, one in which the human dimension was so dwarfed as to be annihilated. To walk west on Unter den Linden into the Tiergarten was to enter into an uncanny landscape of illusion, like a carnival funhouse *en plein air*. To hide Hitler's new boulevard from enemy air assaults, the pavement had been turned forest green, while overhead a canopy of wire netting recalled the autumnal colors of the erstwhile trees, bulldozed to make room for the planting of hundreds of steel flagpoles whose evergreen foliage flapped synthetic red and black.

Though not nearly as haggard as Madrid (but, oh, how similar it feels now, as the bombed-out modern style sweeps across Europe!), Berlin, when compared to the effervescent city of my memory, felt ersatz and flat.

That was not my only shock. I had expected my sister to be weak but was not prepared to find her as I did. A nurse greeted me at the door and showed me into Maike's room. I barely recognized the creature occupying her bed. Her body looked like it had been sucked by a powerful vacuum. A pile of bony angles and cavities was propped against the soured yellow of the bedsheets.

"I thought you said three months" were the first words that fell stupidly from my mouth.

Maike shrugged with her eyebrows. Her breathing was labored. It was clear she was in agony.

"Where is Gretchen?" I asked.

I leaned in close so I could hear her. She said she'd been taken to the hospital a few days ago, after Maike took a sudden turn for the worse. I told her at least it was a relief knowing Gretchen was in expert hands and being looked after there, until I could make more-permanent arrangements.

Meanwhile, a look of terror had crept into my sister's face. I assumed it was in response to the pain eating away at her. But then her eyes fixed on me with great intensity.

"They will kill her, Adrian."

Maike pointed me to the bedside table. I noticed that the portrait of Hitler that once stood atop it was gone. Inside the drawer was a stack of forms from the Reich Committee for the Scientific Registering of Serious Hereditary and Congenital Illnesses and a medical treatise. She then spent the rest of her strength whispering their meaning to me.

Before Klaus went to war, he and Maike had argued constantly about Gretchen. On their last visit to her pediatrician, they had been given a tract. "Permission for the Destruction of Life Unworthy of Life." Klaus had read it and thereafter hammered away at Maike about their ethical duty to contribute to the health of the *Volk*. Yes, of course he loved Gretchen, but was it morally justifiable that they should burden society and the Aryan race with the energy and cost it required to keep a useless, unhealthy organism alive? Maike, naturally, was horrified to hear their daughter spoken of in such terms and was relieved when Klaus marched off with the Wehrmacht. But, soon after, she began getting letters in the mail from the Reich Committee for the Scientific Registering of Serious Hereditary and Congenital Illnesses informing them that her daughter, who was suffering from "severe idiocy, incapable of work," had been approved for treatment at a nearby asylum in Brandenburg.

Maike had never registered with this institution and could only assume it had been the work of Klaus, perhaps in collusion with the pediatrician. She ignored the letters. But she had also begun to hear rumors from the woman at the bakery who was the mother of a quadriplegic boy. With or without the parents' consent, she told her, the doctors were killing crippled children.

I wouldn't have put anything past this regime, but I didn't believe Maike when she told me. It sounded more like a myth that expressed the fears of German mothers during wartime than a piece of credible information. I assured her Gretchen would be fine and that I would fetch her from the clinic first thing.

My sister died during the night. And just like that she was gone. We had not been close, but she had been a permanent part of the landscape of my life—one that was warmer and gentler than most other features of that harsh terrain. We had come into this world through the same portal. And now, by one entirely her own, she had exited it. In place of tears came snatches of Novalis: *Afar lies the world—sunk in a deep grave—waste and lonely is its place. . . . Vain hopes of a whole long life, arise in gray garments, like an evening vapor after the sunset.*

I spent the next day making arrangements for the burial. After that, I told myself, I would find a nursemaid and then I would retrieve my niece. I certainly couldn't have done so any sooner, as my hands were full. Not to mention, I had no idea how to tend to the child's needs on my own.

Then Pike arrived. I vowed to fetch Gretchen as soon as I got him settled in.

6

Finn McCool in the Bowels of Teutonia

Valley of the Nymphs

And this was the manner by which Finn traveled from the Spanish pit to the bowels of Teutonia:

By the conveyance of a slender man, with manicured hands, milk-white skin, and the eyes of a candlelight reader. A lonely man. A torqued man—pulled one way by inclination, and another by propriety—which was reflected in his warped left leg and involuted foot. With merchant's blood but literature in his heart, he had become a reluctant middleman for book-burners.

The Torqued Man pulled Finn out of the Spanish pit and charioted him to the land of the Franks. For this kindness, Finn blew the Torqued Man's horn. It was a gleaming instrument, small but well made, and Finn blew a clear melody into the horn, which for a short spell made the Torqued Man loosen his contorted frame.

"Now that I have repaid my debt," he said to the Torqued Man, "I wish to visit the valley of the Frankish nymphs, whose charms are sung as far as Erin."

It had been many seasons since Finn had embraced a nymph. He found their limbs even longer and plusher than he had remembered as they sat astride him and rode away his years of loneliness. He was rinsing himself in the sink, whistling a Frankish tune, when a rotund old whore walked in.

"*Putain,* that pitcher is for drinking, not washing your cock! Do I look like I want to walk down to the well after every *fils de pute* squirts his load?"

Finn apologized and put his pants back on. "Are you Mamie?" he asked in uncertain French.

"Who's asking?"

"An admirer of verse. I've come to hear a rhyme."

"A rhyme? What kind of rhyme?"

"I've been told to ask for an Alouette," he said.

Her expression softened. "Well, in that case I must warn you, monsieur," she said, switching to English, "my rhymes are quite filthy, and the only place that's fit to hear them is the toilet. Come."

Mamie led Finn down the hallway to the lavatory. It was in use. She pounded on the door. "*Putain,* you were in there when I walked by five minutes ago. Get that ass up and go stuff it with a prick!"

A pretty blonde came out and stuck her tongue out at Mamie. "You want in, it's all yours."

Mamie gathered up her skirts, pushed Finn inside, and closed the door behind her. The smell of a fresh, beefy shit hung thick in the air. Finn was astonished such a basso profundo of stink could have come out of such a tight young ass.

"*Mon Dieu,* that *putain* doesn't mess around," said Mamie, turning on the water line behind the base of the toilet. "Smells like she painted the walls with it."

She sat Finn down on the commode, lit a match, and blew it out above his head.

"Now we can talk," she said in a low voice he could just make out from beyond the enormous laced bosom that shaded him and obscured her face. "So, what did the lawyer tell you?"

"Nothing, except that I should find you."

"*Putain,*" she said, fanning herself with her hand. "I did not expect you so soon. The *Boches* want to send you to Ireland? Do you know when?"

Finn told her he just arrived and knew virtually nothing.

"Knowing nothing is not an option in this business. You know more than you think." Mamie proceeded to wring him for information. He told her about his lunch in Paris, about the château run by the spymaster.

"Is this Kriegsmann at the château with you?" she asked.

Finn nodded.

"How long will you be there?"

"I'm not sure. A couple of weeks is what one of them said."

"*Putain!* I cannot get a wireless set for you in less than that."

She frowned into the abyss of her own cleavage and began muttering to herself.

"What is it?" Finn asked.

"*Mais, putain!* Can't you see I'm composing? Let me think!"

A minute later, her brow unfurrowed.

"*Alors,* here is what you will do. Repeat this rhyme after me: *Julius Caesar left a breezer / On the coast of France. / The King of Spain tried the same, / But he left it in his pants.*"

Finn did as instructed.

"Good. Now, if this Kriegsmann leaves for a mission without you, you send that rhyme to the Madrid KO. You and Kriegsmann together, you must send the following verse: *Julius Caesar fucked a geezer / On the coast of Greece. / The King of Spain tried the same, / But only fucked as far as Nice.*"

She made Finn repeat it back to her.

"If Kriegsmann goes, the farting rhyme. You and Kriegsmann together, the fucking rhyme. No one goes, no rhyme. *C'est compris?*"

"Yes," replied Finn. "But won't this make the Germans suspicious?"

"Of course. But you will say it was only a stupid joke. You were bored. You wanted a laugh."

Mamie told him that from this point on he must play the role of the incorrigible Irishman—all Teague Land jests and bog witticisms and thinly concealed melancholy. Try their patience. Booze and whore and lark about. Yank at your leash. Take the piss and tell tales and prove to them at every turn that they may have your allegiance, but they don't own you. That is the best cover for a double agent, said Mamie, for it was the quiet, obedient ones who were most suspect.

She told Finn to return in two weeks, this time alone and on a bicycle mounted with a wine crate, and she would have a wireless set for him. If anything happened before that time, he was to use the rhymes.

"Any questions?"

Finn had a hundred questions, but he didn't yet know what they were. He shook his head.

"*Alors, fous le camp,*" said Mamie. "I have to shit."

7

JOURNAL

December 9, 1943

He had put on several kilos, I noticed, as we greeted each other at the train station.

"Well, look who it is—Mephistopheles! I should have figured you lived here."

"Only since this week," I said. "Welcome, Mr. *Finn.*"

"Oh, right," said Pike, falling to a conspiratorial whisper. "And what am I to call you now, Grotius?"

"Fluss. Emil Fluss."

"Emil Fluss? Jesus. Sounds like something you pour down a clogged drain."

His cheeks were ruddy and, while he still didn't look exactly healthy, it was clear his strength had returned.

I sensed not a shred of awkwardness from him about our previous encounter. On the one hand, this was a relief, as it would not be an obstacle to our work together. On the other hand, I was vexed I did not feel the same as Pike. Or rather that I did feel something, whereas he felt nothing. For him, masculine encounters seemed to be a way to pass the time when women weren't about.

I later learned from Pike that in prison he'd taken to men both as an expedient and an act of defiance of the pieties of their Carlist guards. An example of what he referred to as his "congenital smart-arsedness," and which I came to know all too well. He had renounced the Church at a young age, along with all of its prohibitions and "levers," as he called them. And when I expressed amazement at how he, an Irishman no less, could free himself from centuries of institutionalized guilt, he told me, "It's simple, Grotius. I just removed all the levers." Though how he did so I never learned.

I set Pike up in a stately operations house in Schöneberg, right next to Hindenburg Park. At the time, it was occupied by three Breton nationalists, our Russian housemaid Frau Obolensky, and a den of rats. The Bretons—Armel, Alan, and Jannik—had been recruited to hasten along the fall of France, which had come too quickly for them to help. Now they were on ice and peevish that the Reich authorities of the Occupied Zone appeared to be reneging on their promise of an independent Brittany.

But this sulky trio, who spent most of their time playing cards, drinking cider, and urinating out the second-floor window, brightened when Pike moved in.

"An Irishman is good luck!" said Alan. "We try do in Brittany what you do in Ireland."

"What's that?" said Pike. "Free some but not all the country, then fight a calamitous war against your own people?"

The Bretons, who barely spoke English, looked at one another uncertainly.

"I'm only taking the piss," said Pike. This did not clarify matters, but at least they saw that Pike was laughing. He then said something in a Celtic tongue that made them all laugh and applaud.

"You speak Breton?" I asked.

"Studied Old Welsh at university. Recall it was fierce similar to the way you lot talk."

I asked what he said.

"He say, 'I drink dirt wine,'" said Jannik, clapping Pike on the back.

"Well, it was supposed to be 'I drink red wine,'" said Pike. "But I suppose both are true."

The charwoman Frau Obolensky came out and

began yelling in her whiny Russian about the piss on the windowsill, as she stomped around emptying ashtrays with one hand, holding a freshly killed rat in the other. Then she noticed Pike. She dropped the rat, brushed imaginary crumbs off her bosom, and bowed.

Frau Obolensky was the widowed aristocrat of an infamous White Russian general. They had fled the Bolsheviks and, like so many Russians, burrowed so thoroughly into the exile enclave of Charlottengrad as to convince themselves they never left Saint Petersburg. They went to their Russian shops, read their Russian papers, drank their Russian tea, and never, unless it was absolutely necessary, interacted with Germans. For that would puncture the illusion and remind them of the bleakness of their dispossessed state. They were like those Trojans of the *Aeneid* who had taken refuge on the island of Buthrotum, where they built a replica of Troy before the fall and consecrated themselves to a life of morbid nostalgia.

But when the general died and every last kopeck was squeezed from their belongings—even the family samovar—Frau Obolensky had been forced to find work beyond the sanctum of the Russian enclave. Now in her late fifties, this woman, whose uncle had been the governor-general of Finland, was trapping rats and mopping piss off the windowsill.

My sister had wanted me to have her cottage in Wannsee, but I wouldn't think of it. It smelled of musty quilts, Sam Browne belts, and death. And though I was given the use of a car, it still felt too far from the city. Instead, I moved into a furnished flat next to the Schöneberg Rathaus and a short walk from Pike's residence on Nymphenburger. I had myself officially added as an occupant at his house too, so I could come and go as I pleased without raising the suspicions of the block warden.

As for the cottage, I intended to donate Maike's belongings to the Reich Charity League and sell it. That is, as soon as I had Gretchen installed somewhere.

December 11, 1943

My commanding officer at Abwehr HQ was Edelbert von Lauhusen, an Austrian aristocrat and morphine addict. He disdained Nazis as much as his old friend Canaris, or for that matter I, did. But according to aristocratic modes, his disdain was expressed as total indifference. For him, Hitler, along with the rest of the vulgarities of the twentieth century, didn't really exist, because they had no right to. To oppose them would require endowing them with a reality as substantial as his own, which was unthinkable. Instead, National Socialism was like a fly buzzing around the dining room—a nuisance, to be sure, but he wasn't going to allow it to ruin his *Tafelspitz*. Maintaining such an attitude while occupying the position of a high-ranking intelligence officer during wartime required not only centuries of good breeding but massive quantities of barbiturates. The only times I ever saw Lauhusen animated were when discussing his two passions: Italian cabinetry and Persian cats.

As you might expect, Lauhusen ran Abwehr II in a blasé fashion, granting his agents wide latitude and troubling himself as little as possible with day-to-day affairs. He knew literally nothing about Ireland. While this hands-off approach suited me fine, it unfortunately allowed for the meddling of others. Canaris and Ribbentrop had agreed to make the Irish cell a joint venture between the Abwehr and the Foreign Office, which meant Veesenmayer laid claim to half the reins. And with Lauhusen's drug-induced inner exile, the fanatical scholar and SS man had no trouble imagining only he was in charge.

Three days after Pike arrived, Lauhusen summoned us to his plush office on the Tirpitzufer. Veesenmayer was there too, with his usual Macassar sheen. He'd just flown in from Paris, and it was clear he'd upped his Pervitin dosage. He paced around the room, circling

Lauhusen at his desk, who, heavy-lidded and serene, looked like a lizard sunning himself on a rock.

"Exciting news, gentlemen," said Veesenmayer. "Word's come from Ribbentrop: Operation Dove has been approved."

"Already?" I asked. I had just settled Pike into his new home and had looked forward to accustoming him to life here in Berlin.

"What did I say?" snapped Veesenmayer. "Let's dispense with the idiotic questions, shall we?"

The plan was simple. Simplistic, in fact. Deposit an Irish agent via U-boat in Ireland, where he would mobilize the fighters of the outlaw IRA, unite them with the state security forces, and, when the time came, help launch a joint invasion of Britain with the Wehrmacht. Our embassy in Dublin would place a red flowerpot in the window to signal that the German landing was under way.

But now Veesenmayer said there would be two agents.

"Two agents?" asked Pike. "Is Helmut joining us, then?"

With a tinge of jealousy, I noticed the excited tone in Pike's voice when he asked about Kriegsmann.

Veesenmayer reached across Lauhusen's desk and pressed the intercom. "Send him in."

In walked a balding man with an upturned nose and the sanctimonious air of a priest. Pike jolted when he saw who it was.

"Proinnsias Pike, as I live and breathe," said the man.

"Seán Russell, the holy-water clerk of the Fenians. So you've come for a Nazi holiday as well?"

The two men made no move to shake hands. They just stood staring at each other.

"Veesenmayer tells me you two fought together in Ireland," said Lauhusen in English, with an accent thick as Viennese cream. I could see from his eyes that he had no clue on which side or in which war.

"Oh, Herr Russell and I did a bit of everything together, sir. That is, except blow up women and children. That's strictly your interest, isn't that right, Seán?"

Russell gave only a stare in reply.

"Well, come tomorrow you boys can add riding in a submarine to your list of shared experiences," said Lauhusen, like a condescending aunt.

"Now, Herr Lauhusen, sir, are you quite sure they let weasels on naval vessels?" said Pike. "Because Seán Russell is the most authentic specimen of mustelid ever to emerge on Irish soil."

"You shut that gob of yours, Frank, or I'll surely be shutting it for you."

"Gentlemen, please!" I interrupted. I sent for the secretary and had her usher the two of them to the hallway, where, I hoped, they would be too embarrassed to hurl insults in front of a woman.

"What is going on here?" I asked.

"What do you mean?" asked Veesenmayer defensively.

"You do see that those two aren't exactly friends, don't you?"

"Nonsense. That's just how the Irish are."

"Yes," said Lauhusen, "a bit of jousting, as it were."

"Where did Russell even come from?" I asked. "And why wasn't I informed?"

"The Foreign Office does not have an obligation to keep the Abwehr apprised of its every endeavor. We smuggled him out of America, and he arrived in Genoa only two days ago. Consider yourself informed."

"So he's had no training?"

"He's a well-trained soldier, and he knows explosives. More important, while Pike ran off to Spain to fight with the reds, Russell took control of the IRA. He was their chief propagandist and, unlike Pike—who, as far as I'm concerned, is a question mark—Russell's unflinching in his support of a German–Irish alliance. In fact, as acting head of the IRA, he formally declared war on England."

"Yes," I said, "and I can formally declare myself Holy Roman Emperor. A fat lot of good it will do."

"Pike had every reason to accept our offer, not necessarily out of loyalty to our cause, whereas Russell is fully committed. The two of them go together. Along with you."

"Me?"

"I thought we agreed to dispense with the idiotic questions, Sonderführer," snapped Veesenmayer. "The U-boat crew doesn't speak English. The Irishmen have no German. You shall accompany them until they reach Galway. You'll be driven to Wilhelmshaven at dawn, and that is all."

Once again, my linguistic talents had become a curse.

I had never been in a submarine before. While the idea of puttering along the seafloor in a pressurized tin can never sounded appealing in the first place, doing so in the company of two warring Celts who refused to yield the last word was, I can now say, an experience to be avoided at all costs.

The sun was hardly up before the two of them began bickering. I had thought the one consolation of my being press-ganged would be to spend a few more days with Pike, but instead I found myself in the role of captive audience and occasional moderator to his feud with Russell. They were like enemy siblings, dredging up decades' worth of grievances. By the time we reached Bremen, I could recite the litany of transgressions myself. Pike had sold out Ireland for international socialism by forming the republican Congress and, in doing so, had gone soft on the English. For this mortal sin, Russell had him excommunicated from the IRA. Alternatively, Russell had disgraced the IRA and the entire cause of Irish independence with the civilian bombing campaign in England the previous year. If Irish independence was to be won by spilling working-class blood and placing the nation above all else, Pike argued, then the kind of freedom they wanted was enslavement. The two loathed each other, yet even this seemed to be an expression of an underlying camaraderie, of the bond between men who had faced death and taken life together. And they both, despite their enmity, appeared glad to be going home.

The captain and crew of U-65 were enjoying their last smokes when we arrived. A wet and chilling wind, to which the sailors seemed impervious, was blowing in from the sea, such that it was a relief to descend into the ship's airless bowels. At least, at first. But as my mind gradually registered that it was encased by several tons of combustible diesel coursing through thousands of steel pipes, regulated by evil-looking valves and gauges that looked far too susceptible to malfunction, and I realized I would spend the next two weeks in this belly of a mechanical whale in the company of twenty other men without a ray of sunlight or fresh air, my knees buckled and my stomach dropped.

It was clear Russell was experiencing similar effects. He looked pallid even before we submerged, declining the poppy-seed roll and kudzu coffee Frau Obolensky had packed him for breakfast.

"Oh, dear, the boat ride bothers our man's tummy," said Pike. "Quick, Grotius, fetch the antacids!"

"I'll have you know I have an ulcer, you little prick. It's a serious fucking condition."

"Perhaps it's your conscience, Seán. Murderin' women doesn't sit well in the stomach."

"Neither does the sound of your cock-arsed mouth," he said, as he retreated through the portal to his bunk.

Shortly thereafter, the captain—who looked like a Baltic seafarer from the last century, with thick side whiskers, a nose like a Bartlett pear, and an unlit pipe lodged in the crook of his teeth—called the three of us into the map room, where he briefed us on how to behave beneath the sea.

We were to use only toilet 1. Toilet 2 was filled with fresh food and would be serving as a temporary larder until we ate through it. Water was strictly for drinking, and only a liter per day at that. Deodorant was to be worn at all times. No running, shouting, or smoking. No entering the nerve center, no touching the valves, no touching the torpedoes, no taking food out of the mess, no shaving, bathing, or buggering, and no touching the steam pipes unless you wanted to turn your hand into a seared pork chop.

Captain von Stockhausen barked this at us, then turned on his heels.

My seasickness improved and by dinner I was even hungry. The table was impressively set that first night, with wheels of semisoft cheese, boiled cod and potatoes, hard-boiled eggs, coils of garlic sausage, loaves of rye bread, and heaping bowls of apples and oranges. Yet knowing this bounty had come from the toilet—one surely scoured with naval diligence yet nonetheless befouled by many anuses—did much to dampen my appetite.

In the officers' mess where we dined, Russell was still suffering stomach pains. He gnawed tentatively on a corner of bread and groaned.

"Something wrong with him?" the captain asked me in German.

"Seasickness, I suppose."

"The lack of oxygen can affect a man too. Makes

one tired and irritable most often. But it can throw off the system altogether if you're not used to it."

I translated for Pike and Russell.

"Oh, I wouldn't worry about that, Captain," said Pike. "Russell here's had his head up his arse his entire life. I'm quite certain he's used to the lack of oxygen."

"Always the wit, Pike. You'd have made a better vaudeville performer than soldier. Maybe an extra Marx Brother—Micko. I'm sure they'd have welcomed you as a fellow Jew."

The captain waited for me to translate what Russell said, but I demurred. "Just a silly inside joke, I'm afraid, sir."

"That's another rule here I forgot to mention," he said, irritated. "No inside jokes at the table. In fact, it's best if there are no jokes at all. After all, a submarine is a serious place."

"Yes, Captain, of course." I relayed this new prohibition to the Irishmen.

"I've never cracked a joke in my life, Captain," said Pike solemnly, "and I don't plan on starting now."

Captain von Stockhausen gave a curt nod and then went back to cutting his food. Slowly, a high-pitched sound began to escape from his mouth, until he couldn't contain himself any longer, and he exploded in giggles.

We all looked at the man, uncomprehending.

"No jokes! Ha ha, gentlemen, really! The look on your face," he said, pointing at me, and then burst into tears of laughter. "I was just joking, you see! I love jokes! Inside jokes too, so long as I'm on the inside, of course."

He let out another giggle and then brought himself under control with a long sigh. "Now, if I'm not mistaken," he said, pointing his fork at Russell, "you mentioned something about Jews? I simply adore a good Jewish joke. Go on, then, let's have it."

Matters went from bad to worse. The fresh food from the lavatory soon ran out, replaced with unconscionable canned slop that looked like it, too, had come from the toilet. Every time we surfaced or submerged, I felt like my organs were shifting within me. Meanwhile, the captain's flare for Jewish jokes reached an intolerable crescendo, and Russell was soon too sick to come to table. He now had a fever and was vomiting into a bucket beside his bunk. Our quarters would have smelled ripe enough as it was, what with the lack of bathing and the flatulence-inducing fare of our diet. But Russell, even on an empty stomach, was farting to outpace the rest of us. And the scent of his sick bucket, mingled with the already noxious air, made every breath in that room a punishment.

The only blessing in all of this was that he was too sick to trade insults with Pike, who had finally left the sick man alone, save for a few savage words about the smells he was emitting.

Then Russell began vomiting blood. Copious amounts of it. Black and the consistency of coffee grounds. The ship medic who examined him couldn't make any conclusive diagnosis, but he surmised it was a perforated ulcer.

"Will he live?" I asked.

"If it's what I think, his gastric juices are leaking into his abdominal cavity. His only hope is surgery."

"What did he say?" Russell moaned.

"Your ulcer has likely burst your stomach," I told him.

"How long does he have?" I asked the medic.

He shrugged. "Two, three days at most."

Pike and I conferred with the captain in the map room. We were in the middle of the North Sea. Our closest landfall was Orkney, which was out of the question. The Bay of Galway, our intended destination, was still several days out. But we might make it to Killybegs, maybe Sligo, in four. Or we could return, three and a half days back the way we came, to Germany.

I turned to Pike. "If the medic's right, Russell won't make it to Ireland."

Pike remained hunched over the map table in silence.

"Even if he does, it's unlikely you'll be able to get him to hospital."

He paced the room for a minute, then punched the steel wall. "The bastard. Just when I smell the peat smoke, he goes and punctures his bleedin' stomach."

Russell died two days later, on our way back to Germany. The captain said a few words, then ordered his body wrapped in a swastika and launched into the sea. We radioed Berlin the news.

Pike approached me at breakfast our last day on the ship. Since the decision to abort the mission, he had not said much, keeping mostly to his bunk to read and covertly smoke.

"There will be another mission, right, Grotius? I'll have another chance to go back?"

"You're no use to us stuck in Berlin," I said. Of course, I was secretly elated he was returning with me.

"Good," he said, as though convincing himself that turning back had been the right decision. "But I have to say, this plan was total shite. Look for the red flowerpot in the window? Unite the clans into one big happy army? Jesus, are we schoolboys? You'd think an intelligence organization could come up with something a bit more, what's the word . . . intelligent?"

We went back to our quarters after breakfast. The other sailors were on duty, and with Russell and his evacuations finally gone, the room smelled only faintly abominable. I watched Pike peel off his clothes and climb into his bunk, so nonchalant in his nudity. He turned back at me and saw me looking at him.

"Say, Grotius, you ever sucked a man's cock at the bottom of the ocean?"

8

Finn McCool in the Bowels of Teutonia

The Boat

In the weeks following his poetry tutorial in the Frankish brothel, the Teutonians schooled Finn in the arts of wireless song and invisible runes. They also taught him to make great bursts of fire with which he could blow down doors and set the woods ablaze. Once he had mastered these arts, they brought Finn to their demon city in the black heart of Teutonia.

He arrived at night to a bustling metropolis in total darkness. Not a light in any window or on the streets. Just shadowed motion and sound. Cars motored by in silhouette. People scuttled along the pavement, the less fortunate of them hurrying to make it home before their curfew. The infernal buzz of Anhalter Bahnhof was concealed from enemy planes and the eyes of God by a giant shroud.

The Torqued Man was waiting for him there. "Welcome to Berlin," he said, as he looked at Finn with awoken longing. "Here I am called Fluss, for I am, like the flowing river, a creature without fixed form."

He led Finn to his guest dwellings in the Nymphenburg. A group of Bretonese hunters, who had been huddled around a fire in the main hall, stood and raised their horns to him in welcome. Then a plump Ruslandish hausfrau named Obelinka sat him down to meat. When he had eaten and drunk his fill, Obelinka led him up the steps to his room, her seasoned haunches bouncing cordially through her shift.

After a spell of rest, during which Finn bedded down in Obelinka's furs and clashed horns with the Bretonese, the Torqued Man returned to his door.

"You set sail for Erin tomorrow."

Not only was Finn going home, the Torqued Man told him, he was to have a companion. And who should it be but a balding imp from the ancient days before the Spanish pit: the treacherous Fenian Seán Russell.

Finn's mind teemed at this sudden apparition from the past.

Russell and he had once fought side by side against

the lackeys of Angleland. But much evil had passed between them since. While Finn and his exiled hunters went to Spain to fight the fascist cunts in manful combat and free the good Spanish folk from their overlords, Russell poisoned the remaining Fenians against the cause of brotherly socialism. Then, while Finn was stuck in the Spanish pit, Russell led them further astray. He had the Fenians set cruel traps for unsuspecting Anglelanders, catching folk in alehouses and depots and tearing them limb from limb.

Finn could not forgive Russell this treachery against not only himself but all the freedom-loving folk of Erin. And he knew his Taoiseach, Éamon the Valorous, would, could he speak to him, demand justice.

It was a warm summer evening, the night before they were to set out for the Northern Sea. Finn and the traitor Russell sat in the living room of Finn's dwellings in the Nymphenburg, looking out the open windows into the blackness. Obelinka had just brought them a bottle of *Apfelschorle* on a tray with two small, metal-handled tea glasses and a bowl of ice.

"Would you look at us, Seán?" said Finn, donning the cloak of amiability while he fingered a saltshaker filled with rat poison pinched from Obelinka's pantry.

"A coupla dumb paddies reunited in the arms of the Huns."

"Who'd've thought? Bleedin' heart Frank Pike gone off to make Spain red, and now he's living under the swastika? I hope the colors didn't confuse you."

"They call me Finn now, Seán."

"Finn? Larger than life now, are you—the great Fionn MacCumhaill?"

"Precisely. Finn McCool in the bowels of Teutonia."

"Bowels of Teutonia. Ah, that's a good laugh, that. Speakin' of, I've got an appointment."

Russell stood and went to the hallway toilet.

He came back some minutes later.

"What do you make of the German shelf toilet, Seán?" asked Finn, the emptied saltshaker safely back in his pocket.

"Foul business. I've streaked it something dreadful."

"Can't be avoided. It's designed to keep the memory of the past alive."

"They're a queer lot, these Germans."

"What can you say? They're fixated on their own history."

Finn reached for the tray of drinks. "Come, Seán, try the cider. *Apfelschorle*, they call it."

"Better not. Damn ulcer's put the bag clean out of order. He won't stand for even a nip."

"Well, then, this *Apfel*'s 'shorely' your man—nary a drop of spirit in it."

"You don't say. . . . Well, alright, then. . . . My, that does have a refreshing tingle to it."

"They add a touch of ginger to it, I'm told. A salutary burn."

"I'll say. Well, I'm told ginger's good for the bag."

"Yes, Seán, and so it is."

"Say, Pike—er, rather, Finn—I do hope there are no hard feelings about that whole bit of bad business in '34. We were fraying at the seams, and I was just trying to hold things together."

"Don't think of it, Seán. Different times those were. What matters now is the future."

"That's the spirit. Things are quite changed since you were last there. De Valera's worse than the English now. Any decent republican soldier is either dead or in lockup. Why, you and I are practically the only ones still angling for a fight. Us and O'Duffy, that is."

"Eoin O'Duffy is a fascist cunt," said Finn.

"I won't deny the veracity of it, but at least he knows Ireland's best bet is with Germany. And he's changed his tune toward the IRA. You two have more in common than you might think—barring, of course, your hatred of God and Church. Once we're back home, you ought to chance your arm at a rapprochement."

"That's sound advice, Seán. I'll have a think on it. Now finish your cider. We'd better shove off to bed. Fluss'll be coming for us at five."

"Say, what do you make of that fella?"

"Who, Fluss? Oh, I dunno. Not bad for a chat once you loosen him up. I rather like him, as much as you can like a man without respecting him. A well-meaning coward, I suppose." Not, thought Finn, a vile, bomb-blasting coward like yourself.

"Lord knows the world's rife with those. Well, g'night, then."

"G'night," said Finn.

By morning, Russell's guts had begun to corrode.

"How'd you sleep, Seán?"

"Shite. Ulcer's acting up something ferocious."

"You want to take a cider for the road? I think Obelinka has more in the icebox."

"Nah, I don't think it was any use. I need milk, calcium tablets. Feels like it's burning clean through my spine."

Russell groaned the length of the ride to Wilhelmshaven. He wouldn't even look at the breakfast Obelinka had packed. The Torqued Man seemed annoyed but didn't say anything. Finn, by contrast, was solicitous of the man in his care. After all, in some perverse way, that's how he regarded Russell—as his patient. He had learned from Dr. Vallejo, his tormenter in the Spanish pit, that showing concern and administering mild relief to a patient whom one is simultaneously torturing can itself be a form of violence.

That first night on the submarine, the vomiting began. Russell excused himself early from dinner and took to his berth. He never left it again, except to fill the bucket with the steaming evil that came pouring out of him. The seamen's disdain for their three guests was clear from the looks they gave Finn in the corridors. Short three beds, they were forced to share bunks and sleep in shifts. And if that weren't enough, they now had to put up with an unholy stench.

Only Finn could stand the foul air, and that was because he could smell justice in it. He attended to the dying man, wiping his forehead down with a damp cloth and emptying his bucket into the one toilet that wasn't filled with perishable food. But after two nights of agony, he began to regret the method he'd employed. Not the murder itself, mind you, but its means. The killing was too underhanded and the dying too protracted. He had quickly exhausted the pleasure he got in seeing Russell retch out his innards. Now he was just watching an animal suffer in its trap, and this brought no joy to a noble hunter like Finn. Only doctors could watch over a dying man and remain unperturbed.

As Russell's agonies continued, Finn's ministrations became sincere, if only to ease the man's anguish and hasten his death. But no amount of damp cloths, even ones laden with genuine pity, could make the ordeal any less horrible.

The Torqued Man came to Finn in the sleeping quarters. All the other seamen were gone and at their stations. Finn was leaning over Russell, wiping the bile from his chin.

"The medic says that if we return to Wilhelmshaven, Russell may yet live."

Finn looked down at the treacherous Fenian. The poison would run its course soon enough. Or, if not, he would find a way to speed things along.

He had dreamed of Erin every night in the Spanish pit. But it was his childhood he dreamed of, and the shores of that land were forever unreachable. The real island, that stifling, arseways place he'd left for Spain, was a neutral country in a world at war, and there was no room for neutrality in Finn's heart. To go home now would be to sideline himself from the fight. Instead, he would return to the bowels of Teutonia, where he could gut fascism from within. The Anglelanders would surely find better use for him there. As his Taoiseach had written him, the proper place for Finn was in the land of that evil giant, the Gilla Dacar.

"Let us turn back," said Finn with appropriate solemnity, while deep within he felt a new horizon of possibility explode into being.

The Torqued Man nodded and left to inform the captain.

Finn returned to Russell's bedside. He leaned down close, so as to face him eye to eye. "I just want you to know, Seán," whispered Finn, "it's not your ulcer that's killing you."

Too weak to speak, the dying man looked at Finn and gurgled his final testament.

The treacherous Fenian shat and vomited blood for two more days. His tongue turned black, and he choked on his own entrails. Finally, when they were but thirty leagues from the Reich naval hospital, he died and was flushed into the sea.

9

JOURNAL

December 17, 1943

A horrible night spent courting death. The bombings have returned with a vengeance. This time I felt the end bearing down as the walls shook and dust rained from the ceiling. But I had no great epiphanies. Just a vague sense of disappointment that this is what my lonely forty years on earth have amounted to.

A freshly painted hellscape awaits me outside, but I'm in no rush to go out and meet it. Right now, this cellar and this pen—my refuge, my distraction, my ordering principle—are all I wish to acknowledge.

Veesenmayer met us at the port. As expected, he was irate.

"If there's anything you wish to confess now," he said to me, "I assure you it will be better than confessing it later."

He bit angrily into one of the Vitamult bars he was always munching in the vain hope it would bring him closer to his *sportlich* ideal.

"Confess what?" I asked. "The man was clearly ill. He said he had stomach problems from the moment he arrived in Berlin."

"Well, an autopsy would have easily borne that out, but you conveniently jettisoned his body into the sea!"

"Those were the captain's orders. Neither Pike nor I had any say in the matter," I protested.

"Was there any sign of enmity between Pike and Russell?"

"Only what was already apparent from the start. No one was under the illusion they were fond of each other, though that's hardly a motive for murder."

"The driver who took you to Wilhelmshaven said the two of them quarreled the whole way there."

"I believe it was you who assured me the Irish often show affection through teasing."

"What do you know of their history together?"

"No more than you."

"Pike didn't talk to you about Russell?"

I shrugged. "Just jokes. Captain von Stockhausen insisted that we keep things light."

I had no desire to fuel Veesenmayer's paranoia with the complex history of grievances I had heard in the car. This would only make life more difficult for everyone. But I had no doubt that Pike was innocent. "Look," I said. "It was Pike who volunteered to return to Germany, all on the slim hope that Russell might survive. He could have been in Ireland and entirely out of our control, had he so desired. Now, if he killed Russell, what motive could he possibly have had to come back?"

"Plenty, if he's a spy."

Veesenmayer narrowed his eyes at me like a bad actor playing a villain and said he would be taking statements from the captain and crew once they returned from their next mission. "Something reeks here, and I promise you I will find the source."

And to think I was the one who had just spent a week breathing vomit and flatulence.

On the ride home, I reflected that I had once made a living translating Evelyn Waugh and nearly burst into tears.

December 18, 1943

After the U-boat debacle, I finally went to the hospital in Brandenburg to see my niece. But when I arrived, the head doctor, a man named Heinze, told me Gretchen was sleeping and should not be disturbed.

"But I only wish to see her. I won't bother her."

"I'm afraid she is ill at the moment. It's better for her to rest."

"Ill? With what? Is it serious?"

"Just a touch of pneumonia. Should be nothing to worry about. But that's why it's imperative she not have visitors now. Perhaps you can see her in a few days, when her strength has returned."

I'd like to think I protested more, but I didn't. The doctors surely knew what was best. And this man Heinze seemed competent. If they wanted to destroy her, as Maike had feared, why were they being so careful about her pneumonia? There was no talk of killing children here. Besides, I had my hands full with work. I decided I would come back at the end of the week to check on her.

As it turned out, caring for my invalid niece would have been a far cry easier than keeping alive an Irishman who was hard of hearing, unable to speak German, and prone to willful perversion. I felt like a nagging mother. "Did you do your shopping? Did you use all your ration cards already? Do you have your passport? Have you been practicing your German? What happened to your coat?" Fortunately, Pike was a neutral noncombatant and had only a loose cover to maintain in Berlin. If he had actually been working as an agent in enemy territory, he would have been arrested within a day.

There were only a handful of rules:

—Don't draw attention to yourself.
—Obey all laws and air-raid sirens.
—Refrain from associating with other foreigners, criminal elements, and Jews.
—Maintain your cover at all times.

Pike broke them all. He'd sooner sell his coat for black-market sausages than wait in the butcher's queue or try to outrun a gendarme than pay for a fare before boarding the U-Bahn. He traded his ration cards for the attention of prostitutes. He would play cards with the Bretons and then, dead drunk, wander halfway across the city to the underground brothels in the east. Miraculously, he was never arrested. Perhaps the Irish really were lucky.

I decided what Pike needed more than anything

was a routine. Keeping him out of trouble would be for his protection as well as my own. Now that the idea he might be a Soviet spy had infected Veesenmayer's mind, I had to make sure nothing fed his suspicions or extended their reach to me. This job required vigilance. Though, it must be admitted, I also simply craved the sound of his voice, the nearness of his body. Of course, I couldn't be by his side at all hours, as I still had other assets to mind—like the Bretons, who were becoming something of a nuisance. But I made Pike my chief concern.

Rarely a day went by from the fall of 1940 to the following spring—save for a brief interlude at Christmas—apart from him. We soon developed a little ritual that made those months rather bearable, even with my unmet longing and hidden grief.

I would call on him at four for tea. The flat was at its warmest then, having soaked in all the southern light during the day, and the Bretons, who kept nocturnal hours, had usually retreated to their rooms for a nap. Frau Obolensky, despite her culinary ineptitude, could make a decent pot of tea, and occasionally she could scrounge together the eggs to make a cake, which, if washed down with sufficient tea, was edible. Around six, we made our way through Hindenburg Park and repaired to the Ratskeller beneath Schöneberg town hall, where we would trade our ration cards for a liter of beer and whatever was the modest special on offer.

Throughout this, there would be words. So many words. It was more conversation than I had ever had with another person, and rather than finding it exhausting, as I would with most people, I found it exhilarating. Though not a natural conversationalist like Pike, I rose to the occasion in his company. Yet the dynamics of our relationship ensured that he was always the subject and I the interviewer.

He meandered through stories from his youth in Limerick—about his father, who was a Parnellite and schoolteacher, about his mother, who was run over by a train when he was still young, about his older sisters, who helped raise him until, at the age of twelve, he was sent with one to America, to the tenements of the Bronx. There he learned to defend himself in daily brawls among the gangs of other immigrant children, so that when he returned to Ireland with his brother-in-law in 1919, the Irish War of Independence just begun, he was ready to fight. And, having been laid low by the first wave of Spanish flu the previous winter and survived, he now felt truly invincible. He joined Hogan's flying column, and, as part of a squad of men who couldn't yet grow a beard among them, was soon racing all over the country, gunning down British soldiers and seducing the peasantry. Pike had a way of studding his discourse with so many astounding details, all mentioned nonchalantly in passing, that I was always asking him to back up and elaborate on something. This would of course take him into another bewildering thicket of memories. I came out of our conversations feeling like a man emerging from a dense wood, with the burrs of his colorful past stuck all over me.

One day he mentioned his mother's Jewish ancestry. "Your grandmother was a Jew?" I asked in a hushed tone, leaning across the park bench.

"She was. Or at least part of her was. As was my grandfather. And, as these things often go, so was my mother—that is, until the train got her."

He said his grandmother was a descendant of Portuguese Jews who drifted to Ireland during the Inquisition, while his grandfather was a Yiddish-speaking Vilnius Jew of more recent vintage. "That's how I come to have a preternatural grasp of the German tongue."

"That means you are part Jewish, then," I said.

"Well, I can't read the Torah and I haven't been trimmed."

That much I knew, I thought, summoning the taste of him.

"And as far as the Holy Ghost fathers who taught me

theology are concerned, I'm an incorrigible reprobate who imperils the sacrament of infant baptism. The only time I've felt like a genuine member of the tribe was when a gang of little fuckers on Colooney Street lobbed a stone in my eye and called me a dirty Yid."

This news concerned me. At the time, the Abwehr had in its employ a handful of Jews, even here in Berlin, but Veesenmayer was a model anti-Semite.

"That's why they packed me off to America. Pugnacious as I was, and what with the whiff of a pogrom in Limerick, they worried I'd get my head kicked in. But when I got to New York, nobody thought me anything other than Irish. Suppose there's only so many things a person can be in the eyes of another. Felt far more Irish in America than I ever did in Ireland. And when I came back, I felt just plain queer. Truth be told, I always felt a bit askew on the island. All the same, don't go telling Obelinka. If she knew I was part Yid, she'd probably spit in my tea."

Frau Obolensky was not the only one from whom this information should be withheld. "Veesenmayer already suspects you're taking orders from the Kremlin."

"Oh, but I am. And I'm here to put an ice pick right in Hitler's heart."

"For godssakes, Pike, lower your voice!" I whispered, forgetting to call him by his alias. "There are ears everywhere, and they all hear better than yours do."

We were both children of the new century. Pike was born a year after me, in 1903. And though I am not one to set any store by generations, as is all the rage, I do think we, the first European crop of the twentieth century, were stamped by our era. Too young to fight in the first war but wide awake for it. The prewar world would always feel like our childhood home, whereas for the current generation, our lost world existed only in fiction and the tired recollections of old men. The effect was that, well before the age of forty, we felt adrift in our own age, sensing that the world in which we lived was not the one from which we had come. The current war has only exaggerated our sense of being dislocated in time. Even for those whose hearts still beat after the last bomb has fallen, there can be no talk of genuine survivors. Something of ourselves—essential and irreplaceable—will have been left behind.

We were also men of letters. This provided us with a common refuge and outlook. We saw the world refracted through books. And despite the obvious differences in our personalities, our tastes overlapped considerably. We both loved Poe, Baudelaire, Chesterton, Conrad, Cervantes, Dumas, Baroja, Simenon, Maupassant, Hoffmann, Huxley, Lawrence, London, Lermontov, Turgenev, and Gogol. Neither of us, unlike what seemed to be the rest of the reading public, could find any use for Hemingway or Anatole France. And whereas I could not muster the cerebral humor to appreciate Swift or Sterne, both of whom he adored, he could not abide Mann or Zweig, who were favorites of mine. Though, perhaps as a conciliatory gesture, he said he thought their English translations had been poor. Out of fear he might have been unwittingly referring to one of my early labors, I never asked him which specific works he had read.

Pike had once dabbled in Celtic scholarship and even written a novel. It had been published by a small Dublin press in 1933. *The Blue Veil* imagined a future Ireland, taken over by a Catholic syndicalist organization much like the fascist blueshirts and ruled by a priggish general modeled on their leader O'Duffy. I still hear Pike's refrain—"Eoin O'Duffy is a fascist cunt"— which issued from him reflexively whenever the latter's name was mentioned. *The Blue Veil* belongs to what the Americans are now fond of calling "science fiction." The plot, as I recall him telling me, revolved around the discovery of a band of ancient Celtic warriors preserved in a state of hibernation beneath the peat bogs of the Blasket Islands. These slumbering time travelers are awoken by the last survivors of a decimated underground resistance who had been banished to the isles and who, together with the resurrected Celts, free Ireland from fascist tyranny.

I told him I would like to read his novel, but he laughed off the idea. "I wouldn't presume to waste your time, Grotius. Besides, that little pile of drivel is long out of print. The publisher had the remaining copies pulped before I left for Spain."

"Do you still write?" I asked him.

"It was a youthful itch. Took me a decade to finally get around to scratching it, but now I seem to be cured."

"I would have thought the enforced solitude of prison would drive a writer to take up the pen again."

"As you should well know from your visits to San Pedro, there was no room for solitude in my cell. And when the pace of executions finally slowed and I had a bit of space for myself, I was denied pen and paper."

"Why?" I asked, recalling my surprise that Pike's file contained no letters.

"Doctor's orders. They were running tests on us International Brigaders. I suppose they didn't want us divulging all their experiments."

"What kinds of experiments?" I was well aware

that San Pedro was a brutal place, yet I hadn't really thought of Pike as a victim until now.

"Oh, nothing worth boring you about. Measurements, blood samples, and the like. We used to laugh about it. Though they didn't help my hearing out much. Poured some grotty fluid in my ear one too many times."

"I suppose it could have been worse."

"That it could."

We talked often of Spain, the one beyond his prison cell. The Spain that was the most beautiful country in Europe, filled with the proudest people in the world. We had both gone there to escape and to experience its vitality firsthand. And we both, from opposing sides, saw it destroyed.

There was so much we could agree on about Spain. El Café Negresco on Calle de Alcalá. The simple perfection of *pulpo a la gallega* and a chilled albariño. The intoxicating geometry of Moorish architecture. The genius of Velázquez. The bibliomania of Unamuno. The grand Cervantine tragicomedy of living in ideals while mired in matter. And the light. Magnificent, singular rays of light that have never once pierced the slate skies above northern Germany or the British Isles.

Only when we veered toward women or politics

did our feelings misalign. He was truly puzzled that I didn't find Spanish women to be the most dizzyingly erotic creatures on the planet. I reminded him that I didn't really think of women that way at all.

"But surely you can appreciate their beauty, even if you don't want to fiddle with their parts. Though I can't say I really know what that's like, since I have a bodily attraction to all beautiful bodies. Now, I know that makes me an abnormal, as they say, but I've always thought that made the most sense. If you find a body beautiful, why wouldn't you want to do beautiful things with it?"

I blushed. I wanted to ask him why, since presumably he had found my body beautiful enough on two previous occasions, he no longer seemed interested in doing beautiful things with it. But I could never initiate such a conversation or be so bold as to make an advance. It is simply not how I am constituted. I told myself we had settled into a comfortable relationship as friends and colleagues. I didn't want to upset that, even though part of me desperately wanted to do just that. The cost of such a decision was that whenever I was near him, I felt a throb of suppressed longing that only over time, I suppose, matured into something else. But does that first flare of passion ever really go out? Or is it just buried?

"Well, all I can tell you is I find Spanish women imperious and demanding," I said. "And if they're not the new beer-swilling, pants-wearing republican type, they're haughty and fussy and remind me of death."

Similarly, Pike could not understand how I, while finding Franco repugnant and his treatment of the losing side criminal, had given my support to the corrupt forces of the Catholic Church and Spanish aristocracy.

"We are talking about priests who wield guns and pray for their bullets to find their victims' hearts. I've seen them face-to-face, Grotius. I've been whipped by a holy man's pistol."

I told him I had no doubt there were dastardly types on the nationals' side, just as there were on the left. And that my support had not been for the Church or aristocrats but rather against Russian Bolshevism.

"How many times must one say it?" he groaned. "The republic was not Bolshevist!"

"But you yourself admit the Russians were running the show."

"Only after no one else in the world was willing to help. Stalin was the last hope the republic had, and he wasn't so keen on saving it as much as controlling it. He revealed just how committed to liberation he was when he cozied up to your Hitler."

"Stop saying 'my Hitler.' I didn't vote for him. And he's as much yours as he is mine, now that you've signed on to fight with us."

Pike laughed. "Whenever we fight for something, we always fight against something, whether we want to or not. Conversely, whenever we fight against something, we're also unconsciously fighting for something. But there's no way of telling if those hidden 'fors' or 'againsts' are going to be any better than the 'fors' or 'againsts' we think we're battling."

"What on earth are you talking about?" I asked.

"I'm talking about damned if you do, damned if you don't. That's the damnedness of choice. But that doesn't mean it's all the same. It just means there are a lot of ways to be damned, and that's what makes up the burden of having to choose. Choosing precisely in which manner you wish to be damned.

"And in Spain, it was the free-thinking, dissident left—who, for all their flaws, are the only source of humanity left in the world—that I chose to defend, damned though we were. If, for example, you, Grotius, had been of the mind that a lettuce picker should be allowed to learn to read, and a librarian should be allowed to fill his shelves with the freely chosen words of his fellow man, and a woman should be allowed to become more than a mere aperture for semen and screaming infants, well, then, you would have chosen to fight for the Second Republic. But by choosing that, you would also have tacitly chosen to place your life and labor and moral judgments in the hands of Stalin. Those of us who made that choice, well, we were damned by our choices. But, even in hindsight, I'll choose that particular damnation time and again over the other way."

"You mean the way I am damned?"

He nodded. "You'd have been far better off in the republic, even one under the shadow of Stalin, than under Franco."

"Me? A bookish homosexual who has no patience for door-slamming, sloganeering, or other acts of mob idiocy. You really think I would have fared any better in Stalinist Spain?"

I had startled myself with my own frankness, with that word that never passed my lips but was always whispering in my thoughts. There was a brief silence between us. He knew I was right.

"The way I see it," I said, regaining my composure but with the fight now gone out of me, "you and I are extinct breeds whose instincts told us to run in opposite directions, but both ways led us off the same cliff."

"Now you've got it, Grotius. That's precisely what I mean by the damnedness of choice. And that's the reason I'm here."

I realized that there was some part of me that was disappointed with Pike for having chosen to come over to our side. Maybe he'd done it for Ireland. Or maybe he was without principle and simply wanted to live. But how could I or anyone else short of Socrates reproach him? After all, I had chosen the same without ever having had my back against the wall.

But there was a dimension to Pike that seemed untainted and untamed, and this was the part that drew me to him. This was also the part that seemed most threatened by his affiliation with us. I dreamed that if I could somehow protect him, his singular, rebellious spirit would rub off on me, and I would be changed.

And in a small way, I suppose this dream came true.

10
Finn McCool in
the Bowels of Teutonia

Cloudwatcher

Once back in Berlin, Finn unpacked the transmitter Mamie had given him and informed the Anglelanders of the aborted mission. He told them of Russell's death, which surely must have elated them, though he declined to spell out his role in it. He let them know he was at their disposal in Teutonia and game for sabotage, assassination, perhaps an uprising. Whatever they thought best.

But the response from Angleland was . . . weather reports. That's what they wanted. The shape of the bleeding sky.

He passed that first fall and the long winter that followed reporting on cloud cover and waiting for a mission. The city offered plenty of diversions, especially compared to his prior residence in the pit. At night, he would descend into the warren of alleys between Alexanderplatz and Hackescher Markt, where trussed *Mädchen* and feral-looking rent boys sold themselves beneath darkened storefronts. The stores themselves did brisk after-hours business, selling sausage and butter to shoppers looking to reach beyond their rations. The blackout had been good for the black market, turning it quite literally into a commerce in darkness.

As the streets here were too narrow for motor cars, only people's pocket torches and the green glow of their lapel pins kept them from colliding. Everyone spoke in hushed tones, not out of need for secrecy but simply because the dark prevailed upon them. And yet never, not even in the streets of Dublin, had Finn witnessed so much public drunkenness. He could smell it on the passing breath of strangers as he jostled against their silhouettes. The entire city was drinking itself numb.

Back in those early days of the war, he could trade his clothing ration cards for a kilo of liverwurst, a jug of *Kräuterlikör*, or a tin of tea, which he brought home to Obelinka. His money, which the Teutonians so kindly supplied him, went to the companionship of warm bodies. A *Wandervogel* who'd had his wings clipped, a Mitzi with a heavy bottom—whoever was willing to cozy up to him for a few minutes of human touch.

He would stay out late and sleep until the sun had warmed the flat. In the afternoons, over cider, he schooled his Bretonese housemates in the cautionary tale of Fenian history. Like all histories of colonial peoples, it was a story of boiling rage and despair, seasoned with just a dash of hope.

The Bretonese well understood the early conquests of the Normans. And they saw the sixteenth-century incursions of the Tudor monarchs of a piece with the centralizing schemes of their Frankish kings. As for the brutal settlement of Erin that followed, over three centuries of Anglelandish usurpation, the enserfment of the native Catholic peasantry, and the transformation of the island into a plantation colony? Well, this the Bretonese rather feebly equated to the sporadic terror campaigns and encroachments on regional sovereignty during the French Revolution.

But what they couldn't yet possibly know was that liberation, that long-sought golden dawn, when it finally came, would be so obscured by rainclouds of grievances and the foul weather of factionalism that hardly a ray of light poked through. Finn told them how the war to drive out the Anglelanders had given way to a civil war, splitting the Fenians in two. But that was only the first major split of an endless series of splits, reversals, and tentative reconciliations. Such that Éamon the Valorous, the man who once rejected the Anglelander peace and the stooge government of the Free State, eventually became the leader of it. And the Fenian comrades he outlawed, who had once, like Finn, leaned toward the internationalist horizon of socialism, were lately so enamored of Catholic nationalism that they were now bunking up with their old enemies, namely that blueshirt-turned-greenshirt cunt of a fascist Eoin O'Duffy. This, he told his fellow Celts-in-arms as they guzzled their cider and let fly abundant streams out the window, was the future that awaited them.

When the Bretonese went to sleep off their afternoon drunk, the Torqued Man would come for tea. And in the evenings the two of them would repair to his Ratskeller, where Finn performed his stage Irishry, with its melodious yatter and wit. The horn-blowing he'd given up, for he sensed an unbalanced longing in the other. A possessive love that Finn McCool, unbound and uncageable, could not abide. Frankly, it withered his horn.

The Torqued Man saw in him someone to whom he could justify himself. He and Finn were kindred spirits, he said, their predicaments virtually the same. They were both exiled humanists, shipwrecked by history, stuck in the employ of fascists, living in a state of inner dissidence but making the best of it.

Finn, not one to violate the code of hospitality, humored his host. He spouted his cheery cynicism, which flowed from his mouth as easily as ale flowed into it, and let the Torqued Man believe that he was now nothing more than a lazy idle schemer, waiting to be sent home. But really Finn was waiting for something else—waiting for his destiny to find him here in the bowels.

11

JOURNAL

December 21, 1943

That fall, while Pike and I developed our convivial routine—though after the U-boat our relationship became entirely and inexplicably chaste—plans were being made for Operation Dove II.

This time Pike would team up with a half dozen SS commandos and his old friend Helmut Kriegsmann. The latter had been trying to smuggle agents into Scotland via Belgium and had nearly drowned on his last mission, thanks to a failed bilge pump. The new plan was for Pike, Kriegsmann, and the commandos to parachute into the Aran Islands and pose as archaeologists. Kriegsmann and his archaeological team would hide out there, while Pike proceeded via ferry to Galway and then on to Dublin. There he would make covert contact with De Valera and arrange a meeting between the leaders of the army and the outlaw republicans. Once an alliance had been forged, Pike would contact Kriegsmann, who would then cross into Northern Ireland with his archaeologists and launch a sabotage operation in advance of the marine invasion of England.

I reported this to Pike at his flat one afternoon, having just come from a meeting with Lauhusen and Veesenmayer.

"Is Kriegsmann in town, then?" he asked, brightening.

I told him he was still recovering in Belgium.

"'Cause he'd know this plan is an absolute disaster. I mean, Jesus, do you really think a whole team of German archaeologists won't draw attention on the Aran Islands?" he asked, pacing the living room. "It's not the most cosmopolitan of locales, you know."

He said we had grossly overestimated the IRA's capabilities. Russell's last great incendiary act before he died, according to Pike, was "to have blown a giant load of smoke up Veesenmayer's arse." The Standartenführer's hope that Russell, Pike, or anyone else, including Jesus Christ himself, could unite the factions of the Irish Republican Army and then unite those with De Valera's government were so patently barmy that they could be the premise of a fairy tale.

"I'd sooner believe the SS has a magic cauldron that brings dead soldiers back to life," he said.

I told Pike he'd more or less read Himmler's mind and mentioned that he'd saved me from the Reichsführer's Grail quest to the top of Montserrat.

Pike laughed. "I made it up there once, during the war. Wasn't a monk about the place then. The anarchists had run the little arseworms out."

Frau Obolensky had just come out with the afternoon tea and made a sour face. Like many of the White Russian exiles, she knew both English and German but refused to speak them unless forced.

"Oh, sorry, dear," said Pike, giving her a gentle pat on the back as she lowered the tray onto the table. "She doesn't like when I say 'arse' or 'cock' or 'cunt' or 'fuck,' isn't that right, old girl? And I suppose 'arse-fucking,' 'cock-arsed,' and 'cunt-fucked' are off-limits too?"

She wagged her finger at him, muttering in Russian but smiling nonetheless. I had never seen Frau Obolensky smile before, and the sight of her gums and recontoured face startled me.

I brought this up later that evening, on our walk to

the Ratskeller. "How did you manage to charm that dour woman?" I asked. She detested the Bretons, and she seemed to have no positive feelings toward me. The only time she ever addressed me of her own volition was to accuse me of stealing the saltshaker.

"Oh, little Obelinka, she's a right lump of sugar."

"More like a lump of arsenic," I said.

"Do you really want to know the trick?" Pike asked. He had picked up a slender stick in the park and was swinging it like a fencing foil. "It's all a matter of finding a person's most vulnerable point, the part they hide from others because they're too scared to show it. Then you let them know you see it and that you like it."

Pike's strategy took me aback, not so much because of the technique but because I now realized—recalling how he looked at me in my towel—that he'd manipulated me in precisely that way.

"So what's Frau Obolensky's most vulnerable point?"

"Hers was easy, as is often the case with older women."

"And what's that?" I asked.

"Her samovar, naturally," he said, placing his hands in a uterine form over his crotch.

"Oh, you can't be serious!" I yelled.

"As a Jesuit, man. She's a proper nymphomaniac."

Had the man really bedded the widowed house-maid? She was nearing her senescence, and most of her curves were now in her jowls.

"That is truly repellent," I said, somewhat more huffily than I should have, then furious at myself for feeling like a jilted suitor.

"Well, you know what they say: One man's amorous act is another man's criminal degeneracy."

My hypocrisy was obvious, but it only made me sulkier.

After we had walked a block or two in silence, Pike began laughing. "Jesus, Grotius, can't you Germans take a joke? Frau Obolensky's samovar hasn't had a drop in it since the day she fled Russia. The way to that poor woman's heart is simply to praise her cooking, which, I might add, is wojus. That, and refrain from micturating in the living room."

"Well, it's hard to tell with you," I said testily. "God knows you've been cavorting with nearly every warm body you come across."

The most recent was Frau Winter, a secretary at Abwehr HQ whom I'd brought in to give Pike German lessons. After a month of thrice-weekly lessons, Pike was still unable to string a sentence together, which was suspect given that he was, like me, a student of languages. He spoke Old Welsh, for godssakes. I knew something was amiss.

One day I made a point of visiting him when I knew he would be having his daily lesson. Frau Obolensky let me in and told me Pike was in his room.

"Is Frau Winter here?" I asked.

Frau Obolensky gestured upstairs with her head.

"*Ja, Deutschstunden!*" said Jannik, who then burst into laughter with the other Bretons huddled around the coffee table.

As I approached the door, I heard noises that were neither German nor English but nonetheless perfectly intelligible.

These liaisons would have been none of my business—after all, I was not the man's chaperone; well, not exactly—except that his teacher was the wife of a colonel in Abwehr III. I should have pounded on the door and shouted that he and Frau Winter would be wise to confine their study methods to those that would not impregnate the colonel's wife, but instead I had just listened, disturbed by the commingling of my envy and arousal.

We descended the steps to the Ratskeller. The long, notoriously reverberant staircase was protected from the elements. As a result, Winter Relief collectors, most of whom were Security Service informants, made a habit of loitering there and accosting patrons for donations. These funds were supposedly intended for the unemployed and destitute, but it was common knowledge that, since the work-shy and vagrant had been corralled into concentration camps, the money, like everything, went to the war. In the face of these collectors, with their incessant bell-ringing and long, admonishing stares, it was imperative to be engaged in conversation. For they preyed upon silence and, once engaged, would hound you until you had coughed up a wad of marks. In exchange for this extortion, you received an idiotic pin of Bismarck, Hindenburg, or, if you were oh-so-lucky, Hitler, which only marked you as an easy target for the next barrage of collectors.

The trick was to appear engrossed in a banal topic, and Pike and I devised a sort of game around this, usually on the topic of films.

"I just saw *Wunschkonzert*," I said, fixing my eyes on Pike when a collector leered into view. "What a beautiful love story! What true German sentiment! A masterpiece!"

As we had rehearsed it, Pike would respond to whatever I said with an enthusiastic sigh of approval. This was an amendment of our original, too-ambitious plan, which had required him to utter a verbal response. On top of his then-limited German, he had no ear for accents, and even those languages he spoke fluently, like Spanish, were sung with the same Hibernian melodies and harp-strummed R's.

Once inside the Ratskeller, the informers had a much harder time. The basement acoustics made the ambient noise deafening, yet the booths, separated by high-backed walnut benches that looked like rows of stowed toboggans, created little pockets of privacy. This was one of the reasons I chose the Ratskeller. It was an oasis for those of us who had the luxury to pretend that the Germany before Hitler still existed. The decor was vaguely nostalgic and safely subversive, with framed "Max und Moritz" cartoons and *Simplicissimus* covers that conjured the respectably sybaritic prewar era. Nothing too irreverent or democratic, plenty of nationalism but of the pleasant, bourgeois-living-room sort. Like those old cartoon maps of Europe, where the nations are personified according to type and all squished together along the amusing confines of their borders. To top it off, they served Flensburger Pils, one of the few things from home I genuinely missed. Though, in the face of rationing, the beer's consistency had become more watery than I remembered.

We made it through the collectors' gauntlet and grabbed the last remaining booth as I called to the waiter for two beers. He brought them immediately and opened the swing tops with a satisfying pop. Pike took a long draw of his straight from the bottle while I poured mine into a glass and surveyed the room. I thought I caught a glimpse of a familiar face at the bar as we came in, but his back was now turned to me.

Having just moved here, I knew hardly anyone. I did not socialize with my colleagues and had a mild dread of encountering them outside work. The only Abwehr officer who was something of an intimate was James von Moltke. He was working under General Oster, our deputy head, on legal matters I knew little about. We had been close for a short spell in our youth, until things fell apart. But enough time had passed that we were once again practically strangers.

We met at Balliol College, Oxford, where we were both studying for the Michaelmas term—he in law and I in literature. The two of us were just enough alike to be completely different. He was a Junker of pedigreed Prussian warriors, and I was the penniless scion of Baltic merchants. Twin products of our nation's Greek-obsessed *Bildungsplan,* we represented the forking branches of a humanistic education: justice and beauty. He was studying international law and human rights following the Hague Convention, while I was working on my dissertation: a study of the picaresque tradition in Cervantes, Grimmelshausen, and Fielding. As a result, I thought him a bit of a moral crusader and he thought me a decadent aesthete. Nevertheless, our fellow students at Balliol regarded us together as "the Germans," even though on account of his South African mother he was only half. We soon accepted the pairing and fell in with each other. Our relationship grew intense. He shared my inclinations, but his sense of piety—his family were Christian Scientists, and he'd become a devout Evangelical—made everything an impossible torment. By the time we left at Christmas, we were no longer speaking. Now, nearly fifteen years later, the two of us were working out of the same government building, supplying military intelligence with our humane expertise—he in international law and I in my work, which I suppose has something to do with words. I had seen him only once in the halls at HQ, just enough time to exchange awkward pleasantries.

As for acquaintances from my previous life in Berlin, I had lost all contact with them. I'd heard about the fate of some. The bookseller Lehmann had been killed while defending his shop. The son of the family in the neighboring flat had been taken for questioning by the Gestapo and subsequently hanged himself. Bruno, a jazz singer with whom I had spent many an evening entwined and even once gone to Köln, had been interned. As had so many. A few of the luckier ones had fled. But there were far more ghosts of that doomed world still haunting this city. These I dreaded seeing and, so far, had managed to avoid.

Pike asked for a translation of our staircase banter, as was his custom. I told him about *Wunschkonzert*, a saccharine film based on a popular call-in radio hour, where people could request songs and dedicate them to their sweethearts away on duty. Carl Raddatz plays a fighter pilot in the Condor Legion who has to leave his gal to go drop bombs on Spain.

At mention of Spain, Pike pricked up and pressed me for more details. "Was it any use?" he would ask, which I soon learned was his way of determining if the film had been good. He had a peculiar habit of using me as a filter for films. I would see them on my own and then summarize them for him. If he was sufficiently interested by my account, he would then go see the film himself.

When I once suggested that he and I could just go to the cinema together, Pike demurred. "Watching films is like shitting, Grotius—it's best done alone."

I was still recounting the synopsis when Pike interrupted. "Sorry to cut you off midstream, Herr Fluss, but I've got a piss in me the bards will be singing about for centuries to come."

Soon after Pike left for the toilet, I sensed a presence hovering over my shoulder.

"I thought that was you, Adrian."

I looked up, startled at the sound of my real name. It was the figure from the bar. He looked terribly familiar, but I still couldn't place him. "I'm sorry . . ." I said.

"Egon. Egon Schulz," he said. "Don't you remember me?"

I was stunned. Egon Schulz had been the editor of the small press that published my translations of Valle-Inclán and Azorín. I knew him as a fiercely intelligent and dashing young intellectual. But this person in front of me was a human ruin. He was younger than me, but he looked every bit of fifty. His eyes were buried beneath folds of red skin, and his beard was so patchy you could see the tendons in his jaw.

"Of course, Egon," I said. "Forgive me, it's been so long. How are you?" I asked stupidly.

"Things have been better," he said. The press had gone bankrupt in '35, and for the last three years he had not been allowed to work.

"And you?" he asked. "You went to Spain to translate, right?" I could see the skepticism on his face.

I nodded. "Yes, yes. I've only just moved back."

"What were you working on there?" he asked.

"Oh, a bit of this and that," I said. "Chesterton, Eliot, some Benn. Nothing terribly important."

"And what are you doing here in Berlin?"

"I'm a cultural liaison to the Spanish Embassy." This was my official title, even though I had never set foot past the vestibule of the embassy. "Purely clerical stuff, mind you. Not much *Dichtung* or *Wahrheit*, I'm afraid."

"All the same, it must be nice to work," he said.

I nodded.

"Well, I won't intrude on your conversation anymore," he said, looking over at Pike, who had just returned to the table. I didn't introduce them, which was the prudent course, though my sense of etiquette still registered the shame.

"Good luck to you, Egon," I said, which, as soon as it escaped my lips, struck me as so banal as to be cruel. I wanted to tell him to find a way to emigrate at all costs, to get as far from Germany as possible, to tell him I was on his side even though it looked like I wasn't, to tell him everything sickened me, including my own complicity. But instead I said, "Good luck."

12

Finn McCool in the Bowels of Teutonia

Birdsong

And this was the mission the Anglelanders finally gave Finn:

H e was to infiltrate an Irish radio broadcast out of Berlin. The Irland-Redaktion was run by a German Gaelic scholar named Hartmann and had just begun sending out anti-British propaganda over the airwaves. The Anglelanders were certain Hartmann would be delighted to have Finn's help. He was to report to them on the group and, if he secured a spot on air, he could use his broadcasts to send secret messages over the airwaves.

This was certainly a step up from weather reports,

though it fell far short of the assassination-and-mayhem campaign he was pining for. Rather than his destiny, it was another desk job. Had the universe misheard him?

He had fallen into the same trap in Spain. Mustered his own brigade of fighters from the streets of Dublin and Cork, rousted them from their lives of criminal indolence, hack writing, and soap selling, and dragged them across the sea on the promise he would lead them in battle. But, as soon as they arrived in Albacete, the Comintern leader André Marty made him a major in the International Brigades and assigned him to political work. And so, while his Connolly boys were off at the front, he was at a desk in Madrid, brewing instant myths and sloganeering. The work consisted mainly of twisting the military defeats of the republic into epic tales of heroism and distilling the swamp of moral ambiguity into a Manichean showdown. It came natural enough to him. It's what he'd been doing ever since the Fenians interned in the Curragh saw he knew his way round pen and paper. But it was the same old story. Finn the Hunter was always "promoted" to Finn the Bird Caller. Everyone wanted what was in that wise skull of his, when he would have been much happier using it to knock out some fascist cunt's teeth.

At first, he'd actually believed the Popular Front slogans he was obliged to spout. "The fight for freedom has to be won everywhere before socialism can be established." But after a year, tired of speaking a predigested language and having realized the Comintern was more interested in sustaining the image of a heroic stand against fascism than the actual lives of republican soldiers, he said to hell with his pen and reenlisted as a private. Through the intercession of his friend Gerry McGrath, a Liverpudlian Irish who'd just become commander of the British Battalion, he was able to keep his major's rank. Within a week, he was at the front at Gandesa, just in time to be outflanked by a tank division of Italians. He was taken prisoner before firing off a single round. The only violence he'd been party to was at a bar fight in Madrid, when he smashed a *caña* over an American writer's head. The man had been too drunk to even notice.

Finn had known the hunter's life, once, when he was younger. The flying-column days—a glorious blur of freedom, adrenaline, and combat. He hardly ate or slept. Just replenished himself on whiskey and the warm thighs of Munster farm girls, who giggled whenever he talked for them in his toughest Bronx accent. It was a golden age, but it was over before he could savor it. At the time, he never had even a twitch of awareness that this boundless, life-drunk feeling might one day dim. Yet already by his late twenties a corrosive nostalgia had taken root. The street fights in Dublin began to feel like reenactments of lost youth. Like he was chasing a phantom, the thing in itself always just out of reach.

But the wanting had never left him. During his years in the pit, his lust for action had become a life-sustaining delusion. The fantasy of Finn the Hunter took shape in the corner of his brain like an easy chair he could sink into for hours at a time. He could spend an entire torture session in the forests of Erin. While Proinnsias Pike was having his tongue burned and his genitals skewered in the name of racial hygiene, Finn the Hunter was laughing with his merry Fenians round the fire, the scent of freshly slaughtered fascists wafting off their spit. Now that he had actually escaped the pit and regained his liberty, it was his duty to carry Finn off the page, so to speak, and onto the streets.

In the meantime, he would do as the Anglelanders wished.

He tracked the Gaelicist Hartmann to his lair in the Funkhaus. Rather than simply present himself as an aspiring radio personality—this struck Finn as artless, if not suspect—he decided to orchestrate a chance encounter with one of the Redaktion's employees. One day he saw Hartmann exit the broadcasting house accompanied by a small dapper man in a cream suit. There was a certain fastidiousness about the way he carried himself that made Finn suspect he would easily succumb to his charms.

Finn took to following the wee dapper man around the city. He seemed to be a scholar of sorts, as he spent his mornings at the university. But he often concluded his days at a dismal pub in Kreuzberg, where he passed the better part of the evening. It was there that Finn engineered his introduction to Archibald Crean.

The Pickled Herring, as the shebeen on Dresdener Straße was called, with its warped doorframe and choking air of unventilated coal smoke, was inviting only to those truly dedicated to the art of self-poisoning. The bar was run by a husband and wife who ignored the customers and spoke to each other in insult. It felt like family. Everyone huddled around the stove with the kaput dampener, sitting on three-legged chairs, their spokes long ago plucked to feed the flames. Those who could not get stove space were crammed together at the back half of the bar, farthest from the windows, which, even in May, leaked in chill.

The clientele was refreshingly international. Foreign workers from the recently conquered nations of Europe kept the bar full of custom all evening. Housed in dormitories resembling an open prison in the north of Kreuzberg, they used the Pickled Herring as their living room. There were even a few Orientals and lapsed Mussulmans among them. The *Herrenvolk* were greatly outnumbered here. They had likely fled after Hitler's war for racial purity brought a tidal wave of foreigners into the heart of the Reich and right into their *Lokal*. The few who remained, Finn speculated, were chastened communists, original patrons from the bar's former days as a Spartacist pub, who had learned to shut their mouths and swap their revolutionary ideals for five brain-softening liters of *Helles*.

Finn was on his third pint when the Irish radioman walked in, carrying a portfolio bag. He scanned the room, took in Finn's presence nonchalantly, and sat two stools over. The bartendress finished picking her nails before pouring a beer and sloshing it on the bar in front of the man. Finn had received the same unwelcoming service. He was beginning to sense it was part of the place's charm.

"*Danke, Effi,*" said the man.

Effi went back to her nails, this time the left hand.

"Any mail?" asked the man in polished German.

"*Na, ja . . .*" said Effi, not looking up from her fingers. Then, at the top of her lungs, "Hey, any mail for *den Dreckmann?*"

"*Kunsthändler,*" the man gently corrected her.

Effi shrugged. Her husband's shouted reply came from the back room. "Get it yourself, you lazy sow. It's under the register."

"One day I'm going to cut off his dick. Mark my words," she said to no one in particular. She handed the mail to the Irishman.

"*Danke, mein Schatz,*" he said, with the same unflappable politeness.

Finn watched as the man went through his correspondence. When he opened his satchel to deposit the letters, Finn noticed the pale-green spine of a familiar book. He ordered another beer, drank half of it, then, when the moment was right, knocked over his glass.

"Aw, for the love of Jaysus," he muttered in an exaggerated version of his own inflection, as he stood and shook the beer from his coat sleeves. "Ya feckin' eejit."

The ploy appeared to work. "Sorry, couldn't help

but overhear," the man down the bar said, "but might you be Irish?"

"Congenitally so. And by the sound of it, so are you. A man of the North, I take it?"

"Archibald Crean of Belfast," said the man. "The Danzig of Ireland. But I'm afraid you're a bit harder to place."

"Frank Finn. Limerick by way of New York and Dublin."

"*Ach so,*" he said, as the Teutonians did whenever a matter had been settled. "Refreshing to find another *paisan* here in the Reich."

"It is, that. I've been so smothered in incomprehensible German, I can barely recall how to speak."

"Do you not know German, then?"

"Oh, I can get by well enough, but there's no joy in it like speaking the native tongue, now, is there?"

"So it is," said Crean.

"Did I hear you say you were an art dealer— *Kunsthändler, oder?*"

Crean paused. "Yes, of a sort. At least that's how they know me here. I'm actually a scholar by day."

"Is that right? In German?"

"No, no. English and Irish literature, though I do

dabble in the old Germanic epics. I'm here giving courses at the university."

"Is that so? On what topics?"

"At the moment, shapeshifting and necromancy."

"Fascinating stuff, that. You're doing the Ulster cycle, I take it?"

"Naturally."

"Then indulge me in a question I've long harbored about your man Cú Chulainn."

"With pleasure," said Crean, delighted to have stumbled upon a fellow Celticist.

"When Cú Chulainn undergoes his torquing, with all his flesh twisting itself into knots and his organs going arse over elbow inside him, is it a fit that seizes him? Or is it self-induced?"

"Yes, well," said Crean with a laugh, "you've gotten to the heart of the paradox of the Torqued Man and really the central question of my course. You see, I'm interested in how we modern individuals, as well as whole nations and races, might harness the chthonic forces that are so well documented in ancient literature."

"Is that so?" said Finn.

"So it is. Now, as to your particular question about Cú Chulainn, it is whether he transforms himself by will or passively undergoes a fit?"

"Precisely."

"Well, as I tell my students," said the scholar, drawing the green book from his satchel, "we must always keep our speculations grounded firmly in the text."

"How do you like that?" said Finn. "Is that the Royal Irish Academy text I see before me, the one taken from the *Book of Leinster*?"

"It is indeed!" said Crean, impressed. "I've been playing about with a translation, triangulating from the *Leinster* manuscript and Windisch's German edition of 1905, which includes material from the *Yellow Book of Lecan*. Would you like to hear?"

"By all means!" said Finn.

Crean cleared his throat and, intoning in a deep murmur that he imagined was the mist-shrouded voice of the bard, recited the celebrated *riastradh*, the torquing of the *Táin's* Ultonian hero:

The first Torque seized Cú Chulainn and turned him into a contorted thing, unrecognizably horrible and grotesque. The bunched sinews of his calves jumped to the front of his shins, bulging with knots the size of a warrior's clenched fist. The ropes of his neck rippled from ear to nape in

monstrous, incalculable knobs, each as big as the
head of a month-old child.

Crean inhaled in preparation to go on, but Finn
beat him to it and, just to be sure the man was totally
in his thrall, declaimed in the original Irish.

*He sucked one of his eyes so deep into his head
that a wild crane would find it difficult to plumb
the depths of his skull. His cheek peeled back
from his jaws so you could see lungs and liver
flapping in his throat; lower and upper palate
clashed like a pair of mighty tongs, and a stream of
white-hot flecks broad as a ram's fleece poured
from his mouth.*

"Fair play to you!" said Crean, astonished.
"So, would you say it's something of a self-induced
seizure?"
"What's that?"
"What happens to your good man Cú Chulainn."
"Ah yes, of course," said Crean. "You see, the
grammar contains the paradoxical answer to your
question. The first convulsion *seizes* him; it makes his
sinews *jump* and muscles *ripple*—all involuntary. But

then the second phase of the transformation consists of voluntary action—he *sucks* his eye deep into his head.

"So, if we pay attention to the sequence as it is given here, and I believe we should, then it's rather the opposite of self-induced seizure. The Torqued Man is transformed for battle first through an unconscious physiological reaction that he then harnesses and develops through conscious changes. He is acted upon in such a way that it causes him to act. The process, in short, is dialectical."

"Yes, I see," said Finn. "Just like drinking."

"Drinking? How do you figure?"

"It's simple, really. The beer is poured: thesis. The beer is drunk: antithesis. But the beer has not really been negated. Instead, it has become, as they say, *aufgehoben* inside me. And this first synthesis will become the thesis of the next spagyrical turn within my guts."

"The dialectics of drinking," said Crean, now attuned to the game. "Gives a particular Hegelian stamp to the term 'spirit.'"

Both men laughed at their shared inanity.

"The Torqued Man's transformation is rather the opposite of the shapeshifters in the Icelandic Sagas," said Crean. "Do you know them?"

"Oh yes, though it's been ages. I devoured them all

THE TORQUED MAN · 157

one summer on a sea voyage from the States back to
Erin—just me and Snorri Sturluson packed in a cozy
hammock in steerage. Now, what was the one about
your man the poet with the temper? Elvin? Egon?"

"You mean *Egil's Saga*."

"The very one! Now, take your man Egil—a poet
who can just as well kill a man with an ax as split him
in two with a line of insulting verse. That's what's
thrown the time out of joint, I tell you. The cleavage
of word and deed. The world would be a great deal
more honest if all artists fought and every soldier
sang."

"Hear, hear," said Crean, thumping the bar with
his fist. "Though the one I was thinking of is *The
Saga of Hrolf Kraki*."

"Is that the one with all those shield-biting
berserkers?"

"Precisely. One of the great shapeshifting moments
in all of literature. You see, there the Vikings very
consciously bring about their alteration. A self-induced
seizure, as you say. Some speculate that the mead they
ingested before battle was laced with a mind-altering
fungus."

"What I wouldn't give for a good mind-altering
fungus," said Finn with a sigh.

Crean turned back to the bartendress, who was

rolling a cigarette with the dregs of butts she'd swept from the floor. *"Effi, haben Sie irgendeinen Pilz mit bewusstseinsverändernden Kräften?"*

"Up your ass."

Crean cackled. "It's great sport trying to get her goat. But she's a phlegmatic old bird. *Eine echte Berlinerin.*"

The first silence between them fell.

"Where are my manners?" said the Belfastman. "We dove headlong into literature and I didn't even ask about your vocation. Surely you are a scholar too. . . ."

Finn waved him off. "Me? No, no, nothing of the sort. Just an enthusiast of the native works." Finn repeated what the Torqued Man had told him to say: that he coached football at a gymnasium in Charlottenburg and taught the lads a bit of English.

"Well, you speak a fine Irish from the sound of it."

"Can't take much pride in that," replied Finn. "Just something my father taught me before I was too old for it to be a chore."

"I'm afraid mine is all hard won, and I still can't really speak it, though I can blunder my way through reading." Crean finished his pint. "Say, this might strike you as a queer sort of question, but would you have any interest in being on the radio?"

"Radio?"

"You see, I do a bit of graft for an Irish broadcast here. Nothing terribly political, mind you, just some cultural matters. Let the folks back in Ireland know who their friends are in these confusing times, what with all the poison England spews over the airwaves. But what we really need is a broadcaster in Irish, someone to reach the folks in the *Gaeltacht* is the thinking. Now, I can't promise you the job, but I could put you in touch with the man who runs the service. German fella, positively mad for all things Irish. That is, if you'd be interested."

13

JOURNAL

January 1, 1944

A new year, but what is there to celebrate? Can it possibly get worse? Will it ever get better? The air attacks have continued more or less unabated for six weeks. If it keeps up, there won't be any city left to bomb. The smoke is so thick most days, I can't see more than half a block ahead. But that is still enough to see things that beggar description. Yesterday I saw two women butchering a dead horse on the street. Its mangled carcass lay half-sunken in a crater containing the remains of whatever cart and driver had been attached. To think, a few years ago those same women would have fainted at such a grisly sight. Now they're licking their lips.

My own image is no less frightful. I've taken to

wearing a pair of alpine goggles and a damp neckerchief over my face whenever I venture out. Recently,
I happened to catch a glimpse of myself in a shattered
windowpane and nearly jumped out of my skin. I look
like a highwayman from some horrific future.

Plans for Dove II continued through October, though
none of the SS commandos Kriegsmann found passed
muster. Half of them couldn't speak English, and the
rest, when told Pike would be in charge, refused to
take orders from a foreigner. "*Nicht arisch,*" said one
with hyperthyroidal eyes, after looking at Pike's features and deciding he lacked the racial qualifications
to command. Kriegsmann said he could sort them out,
but Pike made clear he thought it a terrible idea to
have these murderous adolescents scuttling about the
islands in thin disguise.

Finally, thanks to Kriegsmann's intercession, it was
agreed: Dove II would involve only Pike and Kriegsmann, who would now be deposited on Lough Key
via seaplane. Pike was satisfied with this arrangement
and seemed to relish having his old friend in town. Of
course, I couldn't help but wonder if they were, or had
ever been, more than friends.

Lauhusen, who had been either absent or comatose at
our prior meetings, one day suddenly insisted that the

operation name be changed from Dove to Sea Eagle. "A magnificent creature," he said, beholding one in his mind's eye.

But the date kept getting pushed back. November came and went. By December, the RAF dominated the skies over the English Channel, and Operation Sea Eagle, along with the entire plan to invade Britain, was shelved.

With all British Isle operations on hold until spring, Kriegsmann relocated to Copenhagen, joined by his wife, Val, from Dublin. They invited Pike to spend Christmas with them. And when I drove him to the station, he seemed as giddy as a schoolboy bound for holiday. I recall being annoyed, but then as soon as he was gone, I became depressed.

I had tried again to see Gretchen in the hospital but was once more put off by the head doctor. Her lungs had healed well enough, he assured me, but she was currently receiving a battery of tests. Perhaps I could come back later during visiting hours, I was told. But I had to tend to a petulant Indian nationalist whom Lauhusen had saddled me with for the week.

Somehow the better part of a month had passed since my last visit to the hospital. But I was finally making permanent arrangements for Gretchen's care. I had even found a woman in Potsdam who could reside at the cottage. I spent the weekend cleaning it, stocking it with provisions, and disposing of a few unwanted items.

Chief among them was the trunk full of my father's harrowing bequeathal. I had planted it in a crawl space three years earlier as part of my threat to Klaus. But I could not bear to be in the cottage knowing it was still there.

I set out with the trunk in Klaus's dinghy. The lake was already starting to freeze along the banks. I rowed out far from shore to the middle, where the lake was still liquid and receptive to secrets, and heaved it in. But rather than sinking, the trunk surfaced upright and bobbed placidly along the current. Not what I had hoped for, but it would do. I watched the wind carry my obscene patrimony up toward the Grunewald, where it would soon be someone else's problem.

When I returned home to my flat, there was a package waiting for me. In my fatigued state, I half thought my gift to the lake had been returned to me in shrunken form. But the sender's address was the Brandenburg State Welfare Institute, where Gretchen was being kept. I felt a surge of guilt. I promised myself I would fetch her tomorrow morning, doctor's orders be damned.

I poured myself a brandy, brought a penknife over to the kitchen table, and cut open the parcel. I peered inside and there, packed in wood shavings, was a brass urn and an envelope.

The slip of paper, stamped with the seal of the hospital and signed by the head doctor, stated the following information, as matter-of-fact as a weather report:

NAME: Gretchen Ehlers
AGE: 6
TIME OF DEATH: December 13, 1940, 15:10
CAUSE OF DEATH: pneumonia

Above Dr. Heinze's signature was the phrase: *Our heartfelt condolences.*

I lifted the lid of the urn to see with my own eyes what I refused to believe. But in my agitation, I jostled its contents so that a plume of ashes billowed up and rained onto the table. There, scattered in my kitchen, floating in my drink, were the powdered remains of my niece.

January 3, 1944

I wish I could report that Gretchen's death was the injustice that pushed me finally to take a stand against this gang of criminals. That this unforgivable death, this murder of an innocent child under the guise of social hygiene, transformed me then and there into an agent of furious vengeance.

But that is not how life works. Revenge is an outdated concept. In the face of the modern state, individual action is so ineffectual as to be nil. Yes, I could have killed the doctor who killed my niece. I certainly wanted to. I would have loved to slit his throat as well as that of the nurse who gave the lethal injection. Once I even found myself, having apparently driven to Brandenburg in a fugue state, standing outside the hospital, shaking. But what was I doing there? Could I be certain that Gretchen had not actually died of pneumonia as the death certificate said? Was I really prepared to kill? Even so, what would my lone act have done to abate the murderousness that has infected our entire society, even its healers? What other options of resistance were open to me? I could have stood in the street denouncing this regime of killers, only to find myself clapped in prison and executed within the week. Whom would that help? Certainly not my niece. Nor my sister. Nor me.

Instead, Gretchen's death, like my sister's, felt like something another version of me was experiencing on a distant planet. If I am honest—though it was impossible to admit to myself at the time—while I was racked with grief and guilt, I was also relieved. Relieved that

Gretchen was no longer my responsibility. No sister, no niece, no ties to Flensburg, no future obligations arising from the contingencies of kinship. No doctors, nurses, or medicines, no tedious afternoons of caring for the sick. But the fact that this felt liberating meant I was not so different from my despicable brother-in-law. And that was an ugly truth I was unwilling to face.

The first week without Pike and our routine to anchor the day I felt listless. I walked the frozen paths of the Tiergarten. I read Hans Fallada, one of the few still-published authors, along with Jünger, I could stomach. I even rode out to Spandau and strolled through the rebranded Winter Solstice market, where I felt like a ghost among the living. Even in its paltry, redacted state, with corn-flour gingerbread cakes and marzipan SS soldiers, it was enough to make me feel the aching absence of a family, or a friend—someone with whom to huddle away winter's loneliness.

I kept imagining the cozy scene at the Kriegsmann flat in Copenhagen, with its mélange of Celtic and Nordic customs. The Danes excelled in intimate festivities. A candlelit evening with a dozen friends, thick in their woolen sweaters, their cheeks red with *gløgg*, dancing around the tree and singing like drunken wood sprites. No doubt the Irish brought their own time-honored rites of merriment to the table too. Pike had said Val Kriegsmann was a warm and hospitable woman, though, knowing Pike, I took that to mean something else entirely.

Wandering the empty streets and recalling memories of my former life here, I realized what a charmed and precarious existence I had back then. I took everything for granted. My youth. My freedom. Everything. I was translating Spanish and English novels for a small publishing house. The pay was a pittance and I lived in a lightless tenement in Prenzlauer Berg with faulty plumbing. My family's money had long run out, as had its credit. But I didn't feel poor. On the contrary, I felt I had been promoted to the highest echelon of society: the world of arts and letters. I was scratching out a living through my words. In obedience to the words of others, of course, but it felt like enough.

During my first few years in Berlin, the Nazis were a laughingstock. I would have taken them as a serious threat only had I run into a drunken SA gang on the street, smashing bottles and singing their battle hymns. But on the political stage they were a sideshow of miscreants and softbrains. How could we take them seriously? By the time we realized we had to, it was too late. In 1932, my sister married Klaus and moved to Berlin. Shortly after, I decided I could not live in the same city as my family, especially with an ascendant brownshirt clod as its newest member, and left for Spain.

But those six short years here had been so effervescent, it was hard to believe they belonged to the same life. It was in Berlin I came to accept my inclinations and, for the first time, began regularly to indulge them. The clubs by Nollendorfplatz promoted the homoerotic in a way that, as tasteless as much of it was, I found freeing. Of course, I was hardly a habitué of the demimonde. I had then, as I still have, a rather tightly wound constitution. And barroom orgies, cum cocktails, and spanking dungeons are as foreign to my character as Hitlerism is. However, the occasional dalliance with a bathroom-stall line boy or a night in a hotel with a curious English tourist was entirely to my taste.

It did me a great deal of good, these fleeting intimacies. I could feel the accumulated pressure of the years pour out of me. I gradually became bolder and, in the company of a friend, attended a few parties at Zauberflöte. I would skip the first- and second-floor dance pits, which were too noisy and grossly American, and emerge on the third floor at the Oriental Casino. With its Byzantine opulence, it was like coming to life in a Gustave Moreau painting. Stuffed snakes and ivory tusks patterned upon the wall, satin and leather divans draped with sable furs, plush Turkish rugs that tickled the soles of your feet, honeyed brandy served in hammered-silver goblets, the dim red light of Moorish lanterns that cut geometric shapes through the air thick with myrrh and opium smoke. Upon entry, all guests were equipped with a Venetian mask, a red silk smoking jacket, and a boiled-leather ring for maintaining one's enthusiasm.

On weekends in the summer, when I couldn't bring myself to suffer the day away in front of a dictionary, I ventured out to the Motzener See, to the nudist territory of New Sun Land. Unlike most of the *Nacktkultur* organizations, which were run like a military camp, with a strict regimen of group showering, group gymnastics, racial-hygiene lectures, javelin-tossing contests, and a close monitoring of erections, New Sun Land was apolitical and let guests spend their time and show their arousal as they saw fit. You could play volleyball or sing songs if you liked, but most people, including myself, were content to bathe in the sun, admire the magnificent human forms on display, and, if one was lucky, engage in a mutual caress.

All of these amusements had of course long since disappeared. Even the right-wing, pseudo-Nietzschean homosexuals of Adolf Brand and the greased Aryan sun wrestlers of Hans Surén had been absorbed into the SA, then purged. Only nude burlesques remained, since even the Führer could appreciate the gratuitous use of pure German skin to excite a crowd. That's not to say the confounding spectrum of human desire narrowed because Hitler showed up. But it had gone to ground. When it dared show itself at all, it was now housed in illicit basement dens or in the wild corners of the city's forests, places I was not desperate or intrepid enough to seek out.

What I missed most about the old Berlin were the books. Lehmann's, in which I spent more hours than I did my own bed, had been burned to the ground. Virtually all the best bookshops had been run by Jews, and now their Aryan expropriators filled their windows with an artful blend of drivel and German classics. As a result, the latter are losing their meaning. Granted, Schiller and Hölderlin still sing. In fact, their voices cry out with even more beauty and urgency than they did in peace. But to know they are no longer allowed to share shelf space with the likes of Heine and Mann is dispiriting. One hears a dissonant note in the distance, ruining the harmonies. And the stamping of poor Nietzsche with the Nazi seal of approval seems a fate worse than oblivion.

Even having lived through it, it's impossible to understand how all that chaotic energy of those years after the war—with passions reaching out into every direction, into every corner of belief, into every possible arrangement of bodies and ideas—was so thoroughly channeled into a single, unitary project of death. When each day brings unprecedented assaults on civility, each one enough to make you gasp with rage and disbelief, you gradually grow accustomed to this new form of breathing, until you hardly notice you are hyperventilating.

Feeling abandoned, I spent Christmas at the cinema. I even saw *Jud Süß*, a grotesque affair, and an absolute rape of Feuchtwanger's novel, though admittedly well made. Then, as though Goebbels and his film studio had designed a private hell just for me, I saw *Ich Klage An*. A stilted drama about the heroic compassion of doctor-led euthanasia. *Gnadentod*, as the regime is fond of calling it. Why, it almost sounds like a Christmas miracle—the gift of "mercy death."

I saw *Ich Klage An* another three times that month, and then several more the following year. I was compelled to it by occult inner forces, like a murderer who keeps returning to the scene of a crime. I was convinced that something would be revealed to me, that some clarity would be gained about Gretchen's death, the state's culpability, and my role in it all. But each time, I left the theater feeling more furious and powerless than before.

14

Finn McCool in
the Bowels of Teutonia

First Hunt

**And this was how what had once looked like a
string of follies owing to poor choices and rotten
luck showed itself to be Finn's destiny weaving its
curvilinear arc—like the bronze cords of a Fenian
torque.**

As both Crean and the Anglelanders had predicted,
the Gaelicist Hartmann was eager to bring him
into the broadcasting booth. Come summer, he was
piping messages of Teuto-Hibernian brotherhood.

His labor consisted of singing the high deeds of
Fenian heroes from Brian Boru to Patrick Pearse
while decrying Anglelandish rapine across the

centuries. No secret messages had been requested from him as of yet, but he had sent along notes on the personnel.

In addition to Hartmann and Crean, the Redaktion employed a cross-eyed Welshman named Bevan, an American Irish named Joyce, and a disturbingly attractive redhead by the name of Rosaleen Lynch. Disturbing because her fine-boned body housed a disgusting soul. Several times now he'd heard the end of her broadcast, in which "Emerald Rosie" worked herself into a frenzy of hatred for the Jews, whom she referred to alternatingly as "the rapists of Europe," "defilers of the white race," and "the perverts of mankind." Her hour always concluded with the jarring terset:

Remember your enemy, my sweet Irish children.
You must destroy him before he destroys you.
May God punish England and death to the Jew.

The graft was easy enough, but it struck Finn as a screwy form of warcraft. The Teutonians had enlisted him to be a layabout in Berlin, while the Anglelanders were having him chirp anti-British pap in Gaelic in the company of unhinged anti-Semites. He doubted the sheep farmers and turf cutters of Connacht even had radios, let alone the ability to influence foreign policy. It seemed this war was being waged by morons on both sides.

Speaking of morons, he'd run into P. G. Wodehouse during his first visit to the station. Sporting a checked yellow cravat and spats well over a decade out of style, the man looked as if he'd stepped out of the pages of his own inane novels. He'd just given a broadcast, making cheeky observations about his hard luck in a German internment camp—rereading Shakespeare on his lumpy cot, forced to smoke tea leaves when the tobacco ran out, and other atrocities. He and the missus were living rather better now in the Hotel Adlon, selling off diamonds for beefsteak and writing supplies.

Finn asked if the Teutonians had put the screws on him to do the radio.

"Oh no, nothing of the sort. I simply saw a chance to play to some laughs. Awfully quiet in the hotel suite, isn't it? Ethel hasn't laughed at a joke of mine in years, and these Jerries can't understand a bloody word I say."

Either old Wodehouse had gone daft, or he, too, was a double agent. Either way, nice a fella as could be, that Plummie. He'd even invited him to play tennis.

Finn was beginning to have serious doubts of his own efficacy, when one evening the thickets that had obscured his path for so long suddenly cleared and the way of the hunter lay open before him.

Crean had stuck around the studio to congratulate Finn after his first seven o'clock broadcast. After demonstrating a gift for oratory, he had been moved to an earlier time slot, bumping the surly Welshman Bevan to a later hour. At this, Crean was jubilant. He insisted on buying Finn dinner. "Come, you must be famished after all that bellowing and exhortation."

Finn, not one to put up a fight against a free meal, agreed. "Truth be told, I could eat a nun's cunt through a convent gate."

"That's the spirit," said Crean, clapping him on the back.

They ate black-market *Eisbein* at a restaurant a few steps off the Molkenmarkt. The proprietor addressed Crean obsequiously as "mein Herr" and brought a bottle of champagne, which he insisted was on the house.

"This is quite an organization you've got here," said Finn. "The university must pay its visiting lecturers well."

Crean laughed. "No, no, these perks—which I'm quite happy to share with you, Finn—come from my auxiliary vocation."

He couldn't mean the radio broadcasts. "The art dealing, you mean?"

"Precisely."

"Not that it's any business of mine," said Finn, "but isn't the Pickled Herring a rather queer spot for selling art?"

"I have different locales to cater to my different clients. You see, I deal in an art that has a niche appeal. And while not suitable to everyone's tastes, it cuts across class and rank."

"Intriguing," said Finn, between mouthfuls of smoked pork, pureed peas, and sauerkraut.

"I'm glad you think so. In fact, this very table is yet another of my impromptu galleries. Only here I service a more elevated clientele."

The proprietor removed their plates and returned with a small humidor and two snifters, into which he poured an exquisite Armagnac pilfered from the cellars of the Occupied Zone.

"I'd be happy to show you a wee sample of my collection," said Crean. "Though I must warn you, the art I deal in concerns matters of an erotic nature."

"I see," said Finn.

"Often of an unconventional sort. And some of these pictures are, well, shall we say, not met with favor by the authorities."

"Ach so," said Finn, imitating Crean. "Might these

pictures be the reason that guileless barmaid at the Pickled Herring refers to you as *der Dreckmann?*"

Crean made an annoyed face. "Yes, though she only reveals her ignorance. While I grant that this art is controversial and decidedly erotic, it is not smut."

He reached into his portfolio and pulled out a large envelope. He placed it on the table before Finn.

"Go on. Have a look."

Finn unsheathed three photographs and fanned them across the table.

It was, in fact, smut. Though not like any he had ever seen. While prudery was an alien concept to him, Finn felt an instinctual revulsion well up at the sight of these photos. He swallowed it back down and proceeded to inspect them with a disinterested curiosity. They depicted:

A skinny youth, bound and gagged, buggered by two men in white coats.

A stern-looking male nurse collecting ejaculate on a spoon, presumably to feed to the patient whose mouth was held open by a mechanical device.

A hooded man hanging upside down, suspended from a gibbet by his feet, with his foreskin being stretched in a metal clamp by a fully clothed attendant.

"What do you think?" asked Crean.

"Well, the compositions are certainly thoughtful. Tightly framed scenes, dynamic angles, that sort of thing. And while I'm no expert, they seem to be well made. I've always gone in for that high-contrast style."

"And as regards the subject matter?" asked Crean.

"A bit too clinical for my tastes, I'm afraid."

"Well, that's just one of several genres I deal in. There are also schoolmaster scenes and a forest-dungeon tableau. But," asked Crean, "the homoerotic nature doesn't bother you?"

"Oh, God no. A man's ass is as good a place for a prick as any other. But these photos remind me of going to the doctor. Which is about the least erotic thing I can think of." Finn shuddered, remembering the battery of tests that had punctuated life in the pit.

"Funny you should mention doctors," said Crean. "Many of my clients are doctors. In fact, I have a very important one coming here tonight to make an acquisition."

"Is that so?"

Crean leaned toward Finn and lowered his voice. "I always make sure to know a bit more about them than they tell me. A sort of insurance policy in this line of work."

"Prudent," said Finn.

"And this one tonight, Dr. Wagner? Well, he's the head of the Reichsärztekammer."

Finn jolted as though kicked. "I'm sorry, did you say Wagner?"

"That's right. A real muckety-muck, as they say."

"Dr. Gerhard Wagner?" asked Finn, floating out of his body and up to the corner of the room.

"The very one," said Crean. "Why, do you know him?"

"No, no. Just saw his name in print a while back, something about new breakthroughs in medical research." His own voice sounded strange and distant.

"Of course. These Germans have a keen grasp of health as a total concept. And from what I hear, Wagner's one of the pioneers of the new medicine. God knows we could use something like that back in Ireland. Can you imagine all the miserable souls who've been leeching the lifeblood out of the Celtic race? Ah, but you'll never get a proper eugenics program going there with the Church in the way."

"Isn't that the truth?" said Finn, nodding his head to the mournful lack of state-sponsored death back in his homeland. But while Finn's fleshly vessel carried on in the company of Crean, his mind went back—to

the Spanish pit, where he first met Dr. Gerhard
Wagner.

The screw had pulled him from his cell for the dawn
executions. Only that day, instead of being taken to the
garroting post, he was led to a cold and empty room.
The white paint on the walls smelled fresh, though he
could still make out palimpsests of spattered blood. In
the corner on a long table was a mounted camera. Its
eye would soon record every inch of his body. An hour
later, two men in white coats entered. While the screw
hovered nearby, the white coats unpacked their heavy
black valises and arranged their instruments on the
table. A stopwatch, a thermometer, a pad of gridded
paper, three ballpoint pens, a set of calipers, syringes,
a pack of needles, a jar of cotton wool, vials of different
hues, two scalpels, tongue clamps, arm restraints, a
leather head harness, a small flashlight, a ball-peen
hammer, metal rods of various circumferences, and
two sets of black rubber gloves.

One of the white coats snapped on the gloves, while
the other introduced himself. "I am Dr. Antonio
Vallejo-Nágera," said the man in Spanish, "and this is
my colleague, Dr. Gerhard Wagner."

"Take down your trousers," said Dr. Wagner in
accented English.

And so, with that first urethral probe, began a twelve-week battery of tests designed to measure the bio-psyche of Marxist fanaticism.

Vallejo-Nágera's theory, as he expounded it to Wagner across the unclothed body of their Irish specimen, was that Marxism was a congenital affliction. Just as Mongoloids possessed a series of physical traits that directly correlated with their inferior intelligence, adherents of communism and all other variants of antisocial, left-wing revolutionism were characterized by aberrant psychologies and submental brain function. He would be the first to document the full biological portrait of those suffering from the red sickness. Which would be of tremendous value to the health of all nations. Through the use of preventative social policies based on sound medical evidence, Marxism could be eradicated from Europe.

Of course, many thousands were already irredeemably afflicted. These would have to be weeded out and eliminated. Vallejo-Nágera's study would save authorities immeasurable time in identifying and sequestering these diseased minds, who up to now had hidden in plain sight. But with any luck the doctor would soon have a system of facial, cranial, and genital recognition that would lay bare the contours of born Marxists, making them as plainly visible as a Jew.

Though the Spanish doctor was technically in charge of the study, it was the German who performed all the examinations. While Vallejo recorded the results on the legal pad, Wagner groped and prodded the prisoner's body until it yielded knowledge. Finn could tell he liked to work with his hands. To feel naked flesh through his gloves and against the starched fabric of his coat. He always leaned in close, his face almost grazing the patient's skin, the better to smell his fear and humiliation. Finn was haunted by the man's breath, a revolting synthesis of coffee, chorizo, and quince jam, which was as appalling as the painful experiments they conducted on him.

But the worst of the ordeal was Wagner's smile. During the more invasive of the examinations, there were moments when his face, which otherwise bore the stern look of a Prussian professional, would undergo a hideous transformation. Whenever Finn flinched, whenever his body betrayed him, whenever his nervous system overrode his spirit and the scent of helplessness filled the room, Wagner's thin lips would crack, and in the growing chasm of teeth and tongue bathed in a sheen of rancid saliva, a smile would emerge. It was the sign of a private pleasure born of coerced intimacy. These were the moments, Wagner's smile told Finn, that made the practice of medicine so rewarding.

After another brandy to steady his nerves, Finn thanked Crean for dinner and left. But instead of going back to his dwellings, he found himself circling the Molkenmarkt and eventually planted himself in the shadows of the government building opposite the restaurant.

He fingered the small folding knife in his pocket. Not exactly the man-killing ax a hunter of his stature merited, but Finn McCool could gut his enemies with a hangnail if circumstances required it. He had taken his revenge on Wagner so many times in his mind, always with a battle-ax and always with the doctor in his white coat, that Finn didn't recognize the portly man in hat and gabardine jacket who walked by him and entered the restaurant. But when he came out twenty minutes later and the light in the doorway caught his face, Finn looked upon the bland profile of his tormenter.

If the Reichsärzteführer saw Finn, he gave no sign of it. Nothing about him betrayed that he was in fact a sadist carrying a kilo of illicit pornography in his briefcase. Instead, he looked like the self-satisfied and preeminent citizen he was—a respected leader of the

Doctors' League, director of the euthanasia program, and all-around exemplary National Socialist.

Finn's grip tightened and loosened around his knife in rhythm with the doctor's footsteps. The streets were still crowded here in Mitte. He would only follow him for now, he told himself. He would track him to his home, and then, after knowing where he lived, he could take his time setting the perfect trap.

But what if he was sent back to Erin before he could follow through? Though talk of another Irish mission had grown increasingly abstract over the last few months, there was still a chance he would be shipped off in another submarine at a moment's notice.

Wagner had just turned at Spittelmarkt and was now walking along the narrow canal of the Kupfergraben. It was quiet here and even darker than the rest of the city. Finn saw his moment and decided to seize it.

His jerkin burst at the seams as his abdominal muscles popped into high relief [like muffins rising in the oven]. His great lumps of thigh meat [white as un-befouled snow] began firing like two fulling hammers, carrying his shapely feet in silent, deer-quick patter over the pavement. Leaping at the Teutonian, he clasped a catcher's mitt of a hand over his rank mouth and pinned him against the rail of the canal.

He flashed his hunting blade and lodged its tip just beneath the man's eye.

"*Guten Abend,* Herr Doktor."

The doctor screamed a muffled reply.

"Do you remember me?"

Wagner shook his head.

"There were so many of us, yet there was only one of you. You and Dr. Vallejo, that is. In a little white room in San Pedro de Cardeña?"

A flash of recognition shone on the doctor's face.

"So you do remember. I was one of your Irish Marxists. I believe 'social imbecile with strong psychopathic tendencies' was your professional assessment."

Finn leaned in and whispered in Wagner's ear. "You'll be glad to know, Doctor, that I'm doing this for the health of the *Volk.*"

And with that, Finn plunged the knife deep into the man's belly, just below the navel, and jerked it upward until the hilt caught at the sternum.

A dreadful stench hissed from Wagner's innards, which had become, for lack of a better word, outards. And from his mouth came a torrent of blood.

Satisfied that his work was done, Finn pulled the knife from his chest and, grabbing the good doctor between the legs, heaved him over the rail.

15

JOURNAL

January 6, 1944

I spent the winter not thinking about my niece. In an idle moment, I would often catch myself not thinking about her. I learned then that to remember you are forgetting is itself a form of mourning.

It was Pike who was on my mind. I used both his company and my fixation with him to stanch the wound of Gretchen's death. With Operation Sea Eagle on hold through the winter, we kept to our routine, sexless but at least together.

He had returned from Copenhagen heavier, filled with stories and a bundle of books. Kriegsmann's wife had brought a whole duffel bag from Dublin to catch him up on the last five years of Irish literary life. He couldn't stop talking about one of them, a comic novel by a writer named O'Brien. "Utterly deranged and brilliant," pronounced Pike. He said he'd laughed so hard his organs hurt. But when I asked if he might lend it to me, he put me off, saying he was making a thorough study of it.

Val Kriegsmann, a name I soon tired of hearing, had also passed on clippings from the Dublin press wondering what had become of the illustrious republican Proinnsias Pike, who had gone off to fight Franco and never come back. Apart from those that judged him dead, various theories had surfaced as to his whereabouts. He was living incognito in Buffalo, New York, driving an ice truck. He was teaching English at a university in Guanajuato, Mexico, raising funds for an anti-fascist insurgency in Spain. He had been arrested by the NKVD in Zaragoza and was now in exile in Siberia, covered head to toe in tattoos. None of them dared guess that the radical republican and socialist was collecting checks from the Abwehr and wheezing his way through winter in Berlin.

In March the Bretons were given the ax, and I was tasked with moving them out. I was not unsympathetic to their plight, but at the time I was able to cloak myself in a protective glibness. I see it now for what it was: a state of denial expressed as cynicism. Of course it was

188 · PETER MANN

an unpleasant business, I told myself, but I was simply driving a car from one place to another. Besides, I thought, at least the living room would no longer smell like a latrine.

It was around then that Veesenmayer called me into his office. Unlike Lauhusen's, which occupied a roomy corner overlooking the Landwehr Canal and looked like a gentleman's study, Veesenmayer's office was about as cozy as an engine room. On the walls hung a portrait of Hitler and maps of Europe and the Balkans. His desk was stacked neatly with internal reports and a large jar of Pervitin, which he chewed like dinner mints.

He was a specialist on the South Slavs, having written his doctoral thesis on German settler communities in the southern Hapsburg lands during the Balkan Wars. It was amazing how often he found occasion to bring it up in the course of conversation. "The living *Völkerkundemuseum* of Europe"—that was his vision for the Balkans under future German administration. An outdoor zoo of nearly extinct peoples, where industrious Aryans could go on weekend trips to indulge their curiosity, taste a *ćevapčići*, wash it down with a *raki*, watch Serbs in traditional dress dance a *kolo*, then shoo them back to their mountain dugouts until the next tour bus arrived.

But Veesenmayer was in no mood to discuss the Balkans that morning.

"Sit down," he said, pretending to look at one of his reports. I noticed it was littered with the telltale orange crumbs of a freshly devoured Vitamult.

I sat.

"As promised, I've taken statements from the captain and crew of the U-boat regarding Russell's death."

"Yes?"

"And Captain von Stockhausen said something very interesting." He looked up at me with bloodshot eyes. I noticed he was grinding his teeth.

"Oh?" I said, pretending to suppress a manufactured yawn.

"He distinctly recalled an episode at dinner on the first night where Russell and Pike were arguing—"

"That's hardly distinct! They bickered every minute they were together."

"Don't interrupt. As I was saying, during this particular episode, the captain clearly remembers that Russell called Pike a Jew."

This caught me off guard. Then I recalled Russell's gibe about the Marx Brothers, which had triggered the captain's deluge of Jewish jokes. It had seemed meaningless then, but that was before Pike revealed to me his mother's ancestry.

"That's absurd," I said. "Captain von Stockhausen barely speaks a word of English."

"It doesn't take much English to understand when someone is called a Jew."

"We were talking about the Marx Brothers! Russell called the Marx Brothers Jews, not Pike."

"Marx certainly was a Jew, as I'm sure his brothers were too. But you have no business discussing him or his Jewish-Bolshevist rot!"

"Not Karl Marx, Herr Standartenführer. The Marx Brothers. They are an American comedy act. They make films."

"This is all beside the point! What matters is that Captain von Stockhausen has filed an official testimony that Pike is a Jew."

"Excuse the correction, Standartenführer, but he testifies that he heard Russell call Pike a Jew, which he misheard. But even if he did hear an insult correctly, that does not make Pike a Jew. Surely—"

"Enough! I will not have you calling a captain of the navy a liar. You were the one who recruited Pike as an agent. You were the one who submitted his character assessment. Now tell me, do you have any reason to believe that Frank Pike is a member of the Jewish race?"

"Frank Pike is an Irishman. He is here in Germany

so that he can go back to Ireland, where he will be of use to Germany as an Irishman."

"I asked you a simple question. . . ."

"And the simple answer is no. Pike is not a Jew."

Veesenmayer leapt from his chair and began to pace.

"If Pike is a Jew, then it is almost certain he is a Soviet agent. And if he is a Soviet agent, then it is certain he killed Russell and that the Russians know about our plans vis-à-vis Britain."

I knew he had been suspicious, but he now seemed a full-blown paranoiac.

Veesenmayer loomed over me with a contemptuous smile. "You appear to have taken quite a liking to this man, Herr Sonderführer."

I said nothing.

"A special bond between you two, perhaps?"

I adopted an annoyed tone. He was just fishing, I told myself. He couldn't see the thoughts inside my head.

"I am only doing my job as his case officer. I assure you my allegiance is to Germany."

"Your allegiance is to Hitler! You would do well to remember that, or you'll wake up to the Gestapo knocking at your door."

"Is that all, Herr Standartenführer?" I asked.

He waved me away with his hand.

As I got up to leave, he added in a sickeningly sweet voice, "All that's keeping Pike from Sachsenhausen is Canaris's conviction he can be useful. But as soon as I have a whit of evidence that he's more trouble than he's worth, that support will dry up. And rest assured, De Groot, on that day I will happily send your little Irishman to the *Lager*."

16
Finn McCool in the Bowels of Teutonia

The List

U nlike the poisoning of the treacherous Fenian Seán Russell, the gutting of Dr. Wagner did Finn a power of good. He had finally climbed out of the pit and was growing into his name. Not only had the doctor's murder corrected a past wrong; it had unlocked the mystery of Finn's mission here in Teutonia. It was all thanks to Wagner's briefcase. He had grabbed it after dumping the body.

When he got home that night, he dashed up the stairs to his room. Obelinka was coming out of the bathroom when he reached the top.

"You get new briefcase."

Nothing escaped her attention. "So I did!" said Finn, examining it as if seeing it for the first time.

"Where?" she asked.

"Why, at the luggage shop. Where else?"

"You don't have ration for new briefcase."

"Come now, old girl. Mum's the word, eh? You know I got something for you too."

Finn reached into his coat pocket and produced four handsome *Knackwürste*. Obelinka's face softened as she held the sausage links to the light and appraised them. Unfortunately, they showed signs of their shared occupancy with a murder weapon and a blood-soaked rag.

"There is blood here," she said, frowning.

"Yes, dear. When you deal with butchers, there's bound to be blood."

Once safe inside his room, Finn emptied the briefcase and took inventory. There was: a thin portfolio with the gruesome photographs Crean had shown him, a meerschaum pipe with the carved head of a Tyroler, a pouch of sweet-smelling Cavendish, the morning edition of *Der Angriff*, and, lastly, a brown folder containing documents marked with the official seal of the Reich.

Finn thumbed through the papers and, thanks to his quickening grasp of Teutonian, soon learned that fortune had smiled upon him. He held what appeared to be a medical directory, with names and addresses of more than thirty high-ranking doctors and party members affiliated with an office on Tiergartenstraße.

Wagner, he realized, had been just the beginning. Here was a far better way to fight Hitler than reporting on the fatuous ramblings of a radio broadcast. But there was no need to tell the Anglelanders about it quite yet.

The first name at the top of his directory was Dr. Karl Brandt. Beneath were his titles and fields of specialization:

Brandt, Karl Franz Friedrich

—Surgeon, Head and Spinal Injuries

—Oberführer, Allgemeine SS

—Obersturmbannführer, Waffen SS

—Head, Reich Committee for the Scientific Registering of Serious Hereditary and Congenital Illnesses

—Commissioner, Reich Work Community of Sanitoria and Nursing Homes

—Judge, Hereditary Health Court of Bavaria

Brandt had three addresses listed, one in Munich, the others in Berlin. The first of the local listings turned out to be a Beaux Arts building on the edge of the Tiergarten, with two SS guards and a plaque that said DEPARTMENT OF THE REICH CHANCELLERY. Nothing medical-seeming about it. The second address was at least a doctor's office, located next to Gestapo headquarters on Prinz-Albrecht-Straße.

Finn presented himself there one drizzly morning, claiming to have an appointment. The receptionist *heil-Hitlered* him and demanded to see his card.

"Of course," said Finn, checking his pockets and pretending to search for one.

"I'm sorry, I must have left it at home. My appointment is with Dr. Brandt."

The man narrowed his eyes in suspicion. "I very much doubt that. Dr. Brandt is not here today."

"Oh, I must be confused, then." Finn tried to recall the next doctor on his list, as he and Brandt had offices at the same address. "I believe my appointment today is actually with Dr. Clauberg."

"Dr. Clauberg? You have an appointment with Dr. Clauberg?" asked the receptionist.

"Yes."

"Dr. Carl Clauberg, the eminent gynecologist?" asked the man with an evil smile.

"Yes, well, perhaps it was Dr. Brandt after all. I'll

go home and look for my appointment card," he said, backing away from the desk.

"What is your name?" demanded the receptionist.

"Kein Problem! Tschüss!" said Finn, as he scarpered through the revolving door.

He would need better reconnaissance.

17

JOURNAL

January 7, 1944

By the spring of 1941, Hitler had dropped all plans for the invasion of Britain and devoted himself wholly to his ambitions in the east. The silver lining in this, if one may call it that, was that the Foreign Office pulled its focus from Ireland and directed Veesenmayer's attention eastward too—toward the Balkans. After the Yugoslav campaign began in April, he was rarely in Berlin. And when he was, Pike, to my relief, seemed to have slipped his mind.

With Veesenmayer gone and Pike out of his crosshairs, I anticipated a fine summer together. Our daily ritual could now expand to the city's outdoor cafés, where Berlin returned to life after a long winter. We would amble in the woods and lie out on the lakeshore. We would feel the heat on our bare skin, warming the desire within, melting our inhibitions until the two of us lay glistening with sweat, our limbs radiant and, perhaps, entangled.

But my sunny plans were spoiled when Pike told me he had made the acquaintance of a fellow Irishman, a man named Archibald Crean.

He was a scholar from Belfast who had recently come to Berlin to give lectures on literature. Pike had met him at a *Lokal* in Kreuzberg.

"He's a fascinating sort of fellow, your man," said Pike, referring to Crean, though he was hardly my man. "I wager the two of you'd get on."

"You know you're not supposed to associate with other alien residents," I said, sounding even to myself like a jealous schoolgirl.

I asked if he had at least maintained his cover with this new acquaintance.

"Francis Finn, English tutor and football coach at the Kaiserin Augusta Gymnasium, reporting for duty, sir!"

All the same, I was wary of this new presence in his life. He seemed no longer to be content with just me.

Not long after Pike mentioned this friend of his, he told me he wanted to do some writing in the afternoons and asked for a week's reprieve from our daily regimen. Secretly hurt, I told him that was a splendid idea, writing seemed like a good way to occupy himself, and that it was just as well since I was behind on a number of tasks at the office.

By Thursday, I felt it was my duty, friendship aside, to check on him. After all, I was the man's case officer. But when I dropped by the flat, rather than find Pike scribbling away in a notebook, I found him having tea with a short man in a cream suit.

"Ah—Fluss," he said, remembering in the nick of time to use my alias. "Good of you to drop in."

"I didn't realize you had company," I said with feigned nonchalance. "I thought you were doing some writing."

"And so I was, until the hand cramped up and Crean here ducked in. Won't you join us for a cup?"

"I wouldn't want to intrude."

"Nonsense," said Pike, motioning for me to sit. "This is the man I've been telling you about. Archibald Crean, scholar and littérateur, meet Emil Fluss, cultural liaison with the Spanish Embassy and, may I add, a fellow translator."

Crean gave me his hand. It was one of those overhand grasps, as though he were accepting my invitation to dance rather than shaking my hand properly.

"*Angenehm, Herr Fluss,*" he said. "Whom have you translated?" His German was foreign but crisp.

I couldn't very well list any of the actual works I'd translated, since they bore a different person's name, so I told him my work had consisted mostly of translating German into Spanish.

"*Que suerte. A mi me encanta leer la literatura traducida en Español,*" he said showily. There was something of the cheap stage performer about the man. I could tell he powdered the burst blood vessels on his nose and cheeks.

"Really?" I asked. "You read German works in Spanish translation?"

"Oh yes, though not as often as I'd like. Tell me, what have you done?"

"Well, my work into Spanish has been rather dry and scientific. More Helmholtz than Hauptmann, I'm afraid."

"Say, that's not bad!" said Crean, with an insipid laugh.

"So, Mr. Crean, what brings you to Berlin, and with a war on at that?" If he sensed the suspicion underlying my question, he showed no signs of it.

"Oh, just an opportunity to ply my trade. I'm an itinerant scholar and must go where the winds of employment blow me. I was on the continent already, in

Amsterdam, so I feel that the war came to me rather than I to it. But at the moment it suits me. War feels like a truthful way to live."

I didn't ask him to elaborate on this third-rate, lecture-hall Jüngerism.

He volunteered that he was teaching courses on medieval epic and symbolist poetry, while working on a book about Roger Casement.

"Perhaps you've heard of our German-friendly martyr who suffered gross calumny at the hands of the English," said Crean. "Pilloried as a homosexual."

Pike shot me a mischievous look.

"And what do you think of the new Germany these days?" I asked, ignoring both Pike's peaked eyebrows and Crean's research—which sounded dilettantish.

"A fascinating place," he said. "A little hungrier than ideal at the moment, but fascinating all the same. A German Europe is our only hope of taking the wind out of Britannia's sails."

Pike unscrewed a bottle of whiskey that had come courtesy of Val Kriegsmann and poured us each a dram. "Crean and I have been arguing about Ireland's prospects under a Hitlerian world order."

"And what," I asked, "is the nature of your disagreement?"

"Well, Crean here seems to think whatever's bad for

England is good for Ireland, whereas I'm of the opinion that the vast majority of all possible worlds are bad for Ireland."

"Frank thinks we are a cursed nation," said Crean, followed by a shrill little laugh that I found distasteful.

"I said 'cursèd.' It has a much more poetic ring that way," said Pike.

"Cursed more so than the rest of humanity?" I asked. "More than, say, China, or Greece, or Mexico?"

"Or Poland?" said Crean.

"While it is true that all the nations of man are more or less cursèd, insofar as we must all make our home here in the hostelries of the devil, Ireland is the true Christ of nations. It bears the entire suffering and cursèdness of humanity on its shoulders and, for that reason, it is singular among them."

"I share your sentiments to a degree," said Crean. "As I see it, Ireland is the ark of European civilization. We've preserved its culture once before, during the Dark Ages, and we shall do it again amid the current deluge of Anglo-American materialism. But to be of service, must our fair nation, like Christ, die?"

"In fact, yes," said Pike. "Ireland must die so that we may all live eternally. But it dies only to be reborn."

"In that case," I said, "it seems Ireland is blessed, not cursed."

"Ah, but they mean the same thing, my dear Fluss," said Pike, delighting in the use of my alias. "You see, when five hundred years of colonialism are overcome, and Ireland is a truly whole and independent country, that is just the first step. The second requires the withering of sectarianism, followed by a radical policy of land reform. Then our country must die as a nation and take with it to the grave the entire idea of nationalism. Only when Ireland can be reborn as an island of people not vitiated by national, class, or confessional prejudices will the entire world be freed of their suffering as well. And given there's no good reason to think that will happen anytime in the foreseeable future, with or without the assistance of Hitler, then we may reasonably call Ireland cursèd."

"A marvelous blend of national mysticism, world socialism, and barroom tripe," said Crean, raising his glass and laughing again. I could see that he, too, had been charmed.

"It's as coherent a worldview as you'll find," said Pike.

"In the meantime," said Crean, "I think I'll cast my lot with Hitler. You don't have to like the man; you just have to do business with him."

Crean reached for the bottle and, as he poured us

another round, I wondered why Pike liked this man's company.

I for one had decided I did not much care for Archibald Crean. Though I did eventually find a way to do business with him.

January 8, 1944

Crean was not my sole competition for Pike's company that summer.

Shortly after we were acquainted, a German scholar of Gaelic named Hans Hartmann came to visit. He ran the Irland-Redaktion, a radio service broadcasting Nazi propaganda to Ireland. A polite linguist from Hamburg with perfect English, Hartmann wore his party membership lightly, and the only thing he seemed fanatical about was recruiting Pike to join his broadcast.

Half his broadcasters, he complained, were Welshmen or Americans doing their paltry best to speak in a cartoon brogue. Which is why he was so keen to fill the ranks of his service with real Irishmen.

"Someone who speaks a beautiful fluent Irish such as you would be a magnificent help," said Hartmann, after he and Pike exchanged pleasantries in that language.

"I'm flattered by the offer, Dr. Hartmann. But,

much as I'd relish the opportunity to run my mouth, I don't think I can speak Nazi." He looked in my direction, perhaps recalling the moment when I had come to recruit him. "My tongue would surely trip on phrases like 'the Antichrist of capitalistic Bolshevism.'"

Hartmann waved him off. "Whatever bit of lore you'd like to talk about on air would be welcome service. The simple act of having a native speaker exhort his countrymen to keep the neutrality, both in Irish and in that intriguing Hiberno-American accent of yours, would be of great value. At this juncture, we want the Irish to think of all they have in common with the German cause and not get bogged down by niggling political differences."

Pike laughed. "You'll have to excuse me, Dr. Hartmann, but that's a rather expansive use of the term 'niggling' for a linguist."

"Look, perhaps you could come down to the broadcasting house next week and sit in on our service. See if the shoe fits, as it were."

"Yes, well, I'll have to check my schedule at the school next week, what with football practice and all."

"Of course," said Hartmann, with what I detected was a slight smile.

After Hartmann left, Pike gave me an inquiring look.

"What?" I asked.

"What do you think?"

"If you're asking about broadcasting on the radio," I told him, "I can assure you it's entirely out of the question."

Frau Obolensky came in to refill the teapot. Pike pinched her on the rear and said, "What do you think, old girl? Don't you want us to be on the radio?"

She slapped his head and scolded him in Russian.

"You do realize your whereabouts are still officially a state secret," I said. "It's distressing enough that Hartmann might know your identity. Did you say anything to Crean?"

"Of course not."

"Well, you saw the way Hartmann smiled. Perhaps he recognizes you. If Veesenmayer finds out your identity's been leaked, he'll cut you loose and turn you over to the Gestapo."

"So I'll use a pseudonym. I'm sure Hartmann will agree to it."

"Frankly, I'm surprised you want to do this."

"You've seen my file, Grotius. Propaganda is my métier."

"Then what was all that about not being able to speak Nazi?"

"You heard the man. I just have to burble a bit of

Irish—some chestnut about the horrors of the Williamite Wars or a paean to the murderous glory of Cú Chulainn."

I could tell his idleness was starting to gnaw at him. Out of sympathy, I said I would run the idea by HQ, thinking it would be rejected out of hand.

I should have known that Lauhusen was so besotted, he would agree to anything. "Exactly, De Groot, the radio!" he said, slapping his hand on the desk. "A superb idea. A man must be of service any way he can." He then returned to the barbital dream from which I had woken him.

And so it was decided. Frank Finn was to be on the radio.

18

Finn McCool in
the Bowels of Teutonia

Writer of Deeds

Wagner's death was reported two weeks later
in the *Völkischer Beobachter*. His body had
washed up on the banks of the Havel in Potsdam, but
it was not listed as a murder.

Finn felt ambivalent about this. On the one hand,
he wanted to see his deeds written in print. To see the
Nazi press quake in its jackboots. On the other hand,
if the Reichsärzteführer's death really had been ruled
an accident, then Finn was free to keep lashing away
unsuspected until the bodies piled up.

Perhaps the corpse had decomposed too much
in the water for the authorities to see that he'd been
gutted. Or, as was likelier the case, they didn't want to
stoke the public's already palpable fear about the spike
in murders since the blackout had been imposed. The

S-Bahn Murderer was still on the loose, and there were rumors that another mass killer was prowling the streets of Prenzlauer Berg, though the press was loath to use that term.

"Mass murderers were a symptom of the decadent Weimar regime," said the Torqued Man one day when the topic of crime arose. "It would be a logical contradiction, you see, if the hygienic racial state of the new Germany was afflicted with the same social disease."

They were in the beer cellar in Schöneberg town hall. It had been several weeks since he'd descended the Ratskeller steps.

"Speaking of the new Germany, your friend Archibald Crean seems to be an enthusiast of our regime."

"Oh, I suppose. Though we don't really talk politics."

"He's a curious sort of chap, isn't he?"

"Yes, curious indeed," said Finn.

"But you seem to enjoy his company. . . ."

"Oh, sure. He's good for a laugh, and that head of his is just teeming with epic. He's always going on about red knights in *Parzifal* and green knights in Arthurian romances—why, he knows about knights in every bleedin' color of the rainbow."

"You know, I enjoy talking about literature too. It's been months since we've really discussed books."

"Far too long," he said, sensing the Torqued Man's jealousy.

"And how is your own writing going?"

"Slowly, but it's good to be back in the saddle. Except of course when it's miserable, which is damn near all the time." In truth he hadn't yet written a word.

"I think I've said it before, but I should be happy to read anything, even if it's in a rough state."

"Very kind of you," said Finn.

"If you don't mind my inquiring, and I promise I'll stop hounding you after this, what is your story about?"

"It's about a murderer on the loose in Berlin."

"Ah, a pulp novel," said the Torqued Man, whose cheery reply was unable to conceal the disappointment of a snob. "And who are the victims?"

"Doctors."

The Torqued Man looked surprised, even a bit alarmed. "Why doctors?"

He shrugged.

"Surely your killer must have a motive."

Finn leaned across the table. "Justice."

19

JOURNAL

January 9, 1944

The Haus des Rundfunks, a futuristic fortress near the Grunewald, looked as though it were being overtaken by a fungus from the neighboring woods. Camouflage netting hung down the sides, and false trees and shrubs sprouted from its roof.

Hartmann met me in a lobby lacquered yellow and black and with a reverent Japanese air. He led me to the sanctum of studios at the center and introduced me to the group that had gathered to watch Pike's first broadcast.

"Everyone, this is Mr. Finn's associate, Emil Fluss, attaché to the Spanish Embassy," said Hartmann. He still had that same suppressed smile he had displayed two weeks earlier at tea.

The first to turn and shake my hand was Crean. "Come to spy on your friend, have you, Fluss?"

I had not expected to see him there. I mustered a fake laugh at what was likely an innocuous joke, though part of me wondered if he was speaking code.

"I've never had a chance to see a live radio recording," I replied, "and leapt at the chance when Herr Finn invited me."

In truth, I had invited myself. After all, it was my professional obligation to make sure Pike's new endeavor did not conflict with his duties to us. Also, I was hoping to catch a glimpse of Wodehouse. Pike said he'd run into him at the station during his apprenticeship, and I considered myself a fan. But, while there were plenty of clueless characters about, there was no sign of the punch-stained novelist.

"It's always edifying to see how the sausage is made," said a strabismal man with a red dragon pinned to his lapel. "Usually takes people a few goes before they learn how to speak on the air."

"Don't mind Bevan here," said Crean. "Finn'll be grand. Pretty soon he'll be teaching us a thing or two."

"Us?" I asked.

"Ah, did Finn not tell you? I'm on the Redaktion as well."

I immediately regretted having consented to this radio nonsense. I also felt a tinge of bitterness toward Pike for omitting any mention of Crean. It was clearly strategic, designed to manipulate me, for had I known Crean was involved with the Irland-Redaktion, I never would have let him join.

"I hadn't been on German soil three weeks," said Crean, "before Hartmann sniffed me out and asked me to come aboard. The man can smell Irish blood within a fifty-mile radius."

I asked Crean what he spoke about on air.

"Casement's my man. Roger Casement. Do you know him? Our patriotic saint and Teutophile? Victim of the treacherous English, who forged documents of filth to denigrate his character and perverted all rules of punctuation so they could hang him for treason?"

Of course I knew all about Casement's alleged diaries, detailing his sexual conquests of young men while on philanthropy missions abroad. And the only reason I knew was because Crean never tired of bringing it up. Even more maddening was that each time, he acted like it was the first. "Yes," I said. "You've mentioned you were writing a book on the subject. . . ."

"Well, it's all rubbish, those diaries. Pure concoction," said Crean, ignoring my hint that this was well-trod conversational terrain. Then, leaning in close and nudging me with his elbow, he said, "Though they make for a titillating read if you like them long and thick."

I ignored Crean's innuendo—or was it an insinuation?—and greeted the others. These consisted of a fiery Irish redhead named Rosaleen Lynch, whose searching eyes searched in vain for signs of my being attracted to her, and a gangly ogre of an American Irishman named William Joyce. The latter seized my hand with such violence that he nearly ripped my arm out of joint.

"Spanish Embassy, did you say? What's doing in Spain these days? Franco still putting his house in order?"

Joyce spoke with an absurd Etonian affectation and had a scar that ran from temple to chin, as though his face had been peeled off and a new one stitched in its place.

"As I see it, there's no punishment too severe for those damn reds. Burning churches, raping nuns—it's sickening. Absolutely sickening. He ought to put every single red against the wall and be done with it."

I assured him Franco was carrying out his wishes to the letter.

The politics of the Irland-Redaktion broadcasters seemed as motley and unsavory as their personalities. Rosaleen Lynch was an actress who had come to

Germany in search of fame and stayed for the anti-Semitism. William Joyce seemed, like all the best Nazis, to have been forged in the crucible of failure, impotent rage, and oratory talent. He'd been a fascist under Oswald Mosley in England and had followed the scent to Berlin. He was the man behind the obnoxious persona of Lord Haw-Haw, whose "Germany Calling" was attempting to defeat English morale through mockery. He was also, despite being a fierce Unionist, the voice of another persona on the Irish broadcast, called Patrick Cadogan. Bevan, as far as I could tell, was a Welsh nationalist who shared Hartmann's enthusiasm for arcane languages. Crean liked to think he was unpolitical and saw things with the detached gaze of a scholar. He supported a unified Ireland, of course, though as an unbelieving Protestant. And he seemed to think a new world order under Hitler would be good for *Geist* and *Kultur* and bad for soulless materialism. Then there was Pike. What in God's name was he doing here?

I waved to him in the booth. He looked surprised to see me but returned my smile. He then looked to Hartmann and the sound engineer for his cue, leaned toward the microphone, and began his broadcast.

With the exception of Hartmann, none of us onlookers spoke Irish. Crean, fraud that he was, had only a smattering of phrases. But we were rapt all the same at the sound of Pike's voice. It was warm and melodious, as authoritative as it was playful.

All I was able to decipher in the cascade of foreign words was the announcement of his name. Pike had told me earlier he'd decided to broadcast under the moniker Finn McCool. When I asked him why that name, he was, as usual, shocked by my ignorance of Irish culture.

"Finn McCool, my impoverished friend, is the original broth of a bhoy, the *Urquelle* of all our incorrigible roguery. The legendary hunter at the heart of the Fenian myth cycle, with a chest as ample as two hillocks, a back as broad as a limestone cliff, teeth like boulders, and a hunting horn as shapely as a Saracen's scimitar. He leads the Fianna, a band of wandering woodsmen and misfits. Together, Finn and his Fianna rove the land, seeking revenge for the wronged and working their way out of tough scrapes. He is the antihero's hero. No posture too degrading, no disguise too unmanly for Finn, whose dignity as a scoundrel, liar, and cheat is unassailable. But, cunning and rough-hewn though he may be, utterly unlearned in the refinements of the court, Finn remains a loyal servant to the high king of Erin. What's more, he is infinitely wise. Having eaten of the salmon of wisdom, he needs but suck his thumb to know his destiny."

"And where does that destiny lead him?" I asked.

Finn stuck his thumb in his mouth, then pondered its flavor.

"To death, my dear Fluss—where else? But, first, the radio."

Pike was not the only one seducing souls over the airwaves that summer. At the end of June, Goebbels had announced the war with Russia, presenting it as an act of self-defense against the "conspiracy of the Jewish-Anglo-Saxon warmongers and Jewish power-holders of the Bolshevik Center in Moscow." I could hear in his phrase-mongering the sound of a language being raped and abused, and yet I felt a strange compulsion toward it. I hadn't been back in Germany a year, and yet it was already impossible to imagine a day that did not begin with this town crier screaming his lies through the Bakelite aperture into my kitchen.

Was there really ever life without a *Volksempfänger*? Memories of the many years I spent drinking my morning coffee without an accompanying stream of sonic poison feel fraudulently pastoral. And now, as I hunker in my cellar, surrounded by concrete, that detestable voice with its litany of propaganda is something of a grotesque comfort. It is a daily call to indignation and despair and sustains me in my opposition.

20

Finn McCool in
the Bowels of Teutonia

Baiting the Trap

**And this was the manner by which Finn ensnared
his next fiendish doctor.**

He stepped out of the Hamburger Bahnhof on
a fine summer day alive with war. The city
echoed with the collective, barely stifled groan of
Berliners as they were led deeper into a future with
less food and more dead sons. But it was the sound
of a people who knew how to turn that groan into an
official, bloodthirsty cheer.

He could also hear millions of knots coming
untangled across Europe as the Teutonians invaded
Rusland and the poles of ideology returned to alignment,

the past two years of tail-swallowing sophistry and hypocrisy promptly forgotten. The right was once again saving Europe from Bolshevist barbarism, and the left was back to fighting for humanity against barbaric fascism. But Finn had long since freed himself from the pull of polarity. He didn't need Stalin's approval, or the Anglelanders' for that matter, to kill fascists. As he would show the president of the Red Cross that afternoon, all he needed was the knife in his pocket.

He'd realized the hunting would prove a far cry easier if he knew what his man looked like. So he proceeded down his list to a new target:

Grawitz, Ernst-Robert

—President, German Red Cross

—Physician of the Reich

—Gruppenführer, SS

—Commissioner, Reich Work Community of Sanitoria and Nursing Homes

Sufficiently bigwig from the looks of it, but what really sold Finn on him was that, according to the back pages of the *Völkischer Beobachter*, Dr. Grawitz would be giving a public talk at the Charité hospital on

"The Disease of Homosexuality and How to Cure It."
Not only would he get a proper look at his man's face;
he would get to hear the doctor's thoughts on a subject
he himself had some truck with.

As Finn saw it, perversion was one of the sublime
endowments of humanity, and we should erect
monuments and hold festivals in its honor. The whys
and wherefores of how blood flowed into one's prick
were as natural as the hair growing out of his head. He
was thus all the more curious what catholicon the good
doctor would propose. Surely something sophisticated
and humane, like chopping off a man's testicles and
scooping out a chunk of brain. "Good news, Frau
Schmidt! Your son's a vegetative gelding, but we've
cured him of his sexual perversion!"

The Charité campus was a brick city unto itself. A
veritable *medicopolis*. The southeastern quarter was in
ruins from last year's bombing, with the rubble piled
in orderly, oven-like heaps. It was remarkable, thought
Finn, how structures not forty years old could so
quickly be transformed to look like ancient ziggurats
or burial mounds of a forgotten race.

He arrived just before the lecture began and took
an aisle seat near the front. He wanted to get a good
look at his man. Finn was in his visiting scholar's
guise: clean-shaven and in a tweed suit that was too

warm for Teutonian summer but suitable for stowing arms. The hall was packed, almost exclusively by men, save for a row of sexless nurses and a handful of worried mothers. Likely with sons at home who studied their Plato a bit too intensely and had an unnatural enthusiasm for the flute.

After some introductory gushing by the hospital director, Dr. Grawitz mounted the lectern. He was just as Finn had imagined him: ramrod straight and as hungry for a prick as a Friedrichstraße rent boy. You could see by his pinched face that every sweat drop of his being was directed at suppressing the endless parade of tight-trousered sailors that marched through his mind every minute of the day. Even his mustache looked like a piece of heavy tape to prevent his lip from forming the fellatial O to which it was inclined.

The doctor, dressed in his SS uniform, tugged at his collar—no doubt to let out some of the excess semen backed up in his throat—and in a choked voice began:

"*Meine Damen und Herren,* it is a pleasure to speak to you this afternoon. Before I delve into the topic of today's lecture, I'd like to say just a few words about the age in which we are living. . . .

"As you know, Germany is locked in a war for her survival, and we have now turned our attention to the Bolshevist threat in the east. War, with its vitalizing, purifying effects on the race, brings innovation—in technology as well as knowledge. Thanks to German science and medicine, we are rapidly learning how to perfect the human machine. We already have pills that will keep us fresh and alert for days. Coffee that has been cleansed of its harmful toxins. And delicious snacks that supply us with nourishing vitamins.

"But, ladies and gentlemen, this is just the beginning. Our campaign in the east will at last give us a complete understanding of racial science and the precipitating causes of humanity's most dangerous pathogen: the Jewish-Bolshevistic parasite. I foresee an age in the not-too-distant future of our Thousand-Year Reich of a German people living in a world free of disease. I am honored to say that one of my duties as Reichsarzt is to oversee and coordinate this new empire of experimentation. We will be bold, we will be ruthless, and we will be victorious!"

Here the audience of doctors broke into what they deemed suitably enthusiastic applause.

"It is in that spirit that I am excited to share with you a new cure for a disease that has too long afflicted our nation, especially here in Berlin. . . ."

And so Dr. Grawitz began to remind his audience of the horrors of homosexuality, priming them for the moment he unveiled his wonder cure. The cure, as it turned out, was a simple procedure in which the hormone glands of an ox were surgically inserted into the groin of the patient. Within a matter of weeks, the foreign matter was absorbed into the endocrine system, the testes were reconstituted, and—*voilà!*—the patient was freed from his perverse impulses.

Finn thought he might like to "reconstitute" the doctor's own testes and see where that left him.

A brief question period followed, mostly filled with groveling compliments for the speaker's pioneering treatment. A mother raised eyebrows, though, when she asked whether a hormone implant could really solve the problem of something so metaphysical as a perverted will. The doctors in the audience all laughed.

"Madame," replied Grawitz, "the will is an outdated shorthand for a complex but knowable set of biochemical reactions occurring within the body of the organism. What you call 'will' is simply a concatenation of hormonal secretions dictated by the constraints of heredity and environment. So, in short, the answer to your question is yes. Hormone implants render metaphysics obsolete."

A fellow doctor then stood and raised his hand. "Herr Doktor Grawitz, surely you are familiar with the fraudulent work of the Bolshevik-Jewish-homosexual Hirschfeld, who, before our glorious national revolution, disgraced Berlin with his tawdry Institut für Sexualwissenschaft. It is well known that he performed similar operations using hormonal implants to alter and regulate sexual character. Could you say a few words to explain how your procedure is different, as I'm sure it is, from that of the degenerate Hirschfeld?"

Grawitz then turned a deep shade of aubergine, and the man who had asked the question as an obsequious but misguided attempt to offer up an easy target for the lecturer now found himself the object of scorn.

"Excuse me, sir," said Grawitz with a venomous look, "but I will not suffer the indignity of stooping to answer your insidious question, which is not a question at all but rather a cowardly attempt to tarnish my work by mentioning it in the same sentence as that Jewish swine, whom you clearly know more about than any decent German doctor should."

The man crumpled in his seat, surrounded by the contemptuous faces of his colleagues. It was clear this question had just cost him his career.

While the crowd filed out and Grawitz received the adoration of his subordinates, Finn lurked nearby. He followed him to a nearby *Konditorei*, where he had a coffee and cream cake. Finn watched through the glass from across the street, noticing how after each bite he licked the ersatz cream from his fingers.

After his snack, the doctor returned to his black limousine on Schumannstraße, where his driver was waiting. Just before Grawitz opened the door, Finn touched his elbow. "Herr Doktor?"

He spun around.

"I'm sorry to accost you like this, but I just saw your lecture. I thought it was wonderful."

"Oh. Why, thank you," said the doctor. "It's always a pleasure to share my discoveries with the public."

"I thought, given your research, you might be interested in these," said Finn, handing him the portfolio he'd found in Wagner's briefcase.

Grawitz accepted it with a puzzled look.

"Please," said Finn, "have a peek inside."

The doctor pried a photograph loose. His face dropped. "Why," he said in a low, breathless voice, "would you think I would be interested in this filth?"

"Am I wrong?"

Grawitz scanned the street. "I could have you arrested right now."

"But then you wouldn't get to see any more."

"So you can blackmail me, is that it?"

"Nothing of the sort. I simply know a connoisseur when I see one. You name the place, wherever you feel secure."

A light of recognition went off in the doctor's head. "You're the Irishman, aren't you?"

"At your service, sir," said Finn with a tip of his hat, as a new plan hatched in his brain.

Grawitz told him to meet him the following night at ten o'clock in the public toilet beside the front entrance to the zoo.

And that was how Finn first donned the cloak of Archibald Crean, purveyor of smut.

He knocked on the lavatory door promptly at ten. The hut was dark under the shadow of the massive flak tower, and the only sounds were the nearby roars of imprisoned beasts.

Soon the lock clicked and a sliver of light revealed a wary eye and mustache. "Come in and sit down."

Grawitz's authoritative tone, along with the institutional setting—white tile, metal sink, sanitary napkins—gave Finn the odd feeling that, despite the overwhelming smell of urine, he was here for a doctor's appointment. In a way, he was.

"Now show me what you have," said the doctor, standing over him anxiously.

Finn took out three photographs from a new bundle he had procured from Crean. Grawitz snatched them from his hand.

He had chosen more of the same clinical-erotic humiliation genre. A nurse pouring hot tea down one end of a thick hose, the other held fast by the patient's clenched anus. A prison guard measuring penile girth with razor wire. And a test involving calipers and steel rods that Finn dared not look at too closely.

"Are they satisfactory, Doctor?"

"They're fine," he said, agitated and still greedily eyeing them. "How much do you want?"

"Free of charge."

Grawitz twisted his face into a question mark.

"I'm expanding my clientele," explained Finn. "I ask only that you mention my wares—discreetly, of course—to colleagues who might share your interest."

"Don't be ridiculous," scoffed Grawitz. "I would never discuss such matters with my colleagues."

"Of course not," said Finn. "Yet men of kindred tastes have a way of finding one another."

And this was how Finn lured more white-coated fiends into his trap.

While the Teutonians bore into the Caucasus, Finn penetrated Grawitz's circle of SS doctors. But instead of Panzer tanks and commando units, all he needed to make his advances were bundles of brain-deadening smut. Through Grawitz, and trading on Crean's reputation—which Wagner, before his untimely drowning, must have praised to some of his colleagues—Finn made the acquaintance of Dr. Helmut Poppendick, Grawitz's assistant in the Reich Medical Office, and a psychiatrist, Dr. Paul Lutz.

Both were on Finn's list. Like all the names on his list, they were experts in racial hygiene and were affiliated with both the Reich Work Community of Sanitoria and Nursing Homes and the Reich Committee for the Scientific Registering of Serious Hereditary and Congenital Illnesses, which operated out of that strange building on Tiergartenstraße.

Finn knew he had gotten lucky with Wagner. He couldn't just gut another high-ranking SS doctor in Berlin without spooking the medical community and stirring up the Gestapo. So he decided to bide his time and string along the three doctors on a steady line of medical-grade filth. They all thought they were dealing with Archibald Crean, and so long as Finn didn't sell to any of the real Crean's customers, he saw no reason the ruse would fail. Unless, of course, Finn's three doctors were subsequently introduced to Crean himself. Oh well, thought Finn. He'd have to chance it.

Every week at the Pickled Herring—where
no Nazi doctor would ever set foot—Finn would
purchase a portfolio from the wee Northman.
Ostensibly these were for himself to enjoy in the
idle hours after school. Crean had an endless supply.
And he seemed to enjoy having a fellow Fenian who
shared his predilections.

"You're developing into quite a connoisseur," he
said one day. "I thought you said my art was—what
was the word?—too 'clinical' for you."

"That was my first impression, but then they
lingered in my mind, teasing me, until before long I
found myself hungering for them."

Crean nodded knowingly. "That's often how it is
with rarefied pleasures. I remember feeling the same
way about Stilton cheese when I was a lad."

"I also have a friend who's very keen on them,"
said Finn, imagining that his recent rate of smut
consumption seemed too great for just one man. "He's
a collector of sorts."

"A friend, is it?" asked Crean teasingly.

He didn't believe him. That is, until the Torqued
Man came around to tea one day. "This," whispered
Finn, "is the *friend* I've been telling you about."

"*Ach so!*" said Crean, with an impish smile. He
slipped the man a few friendly winks and nudges, but

the Torqued Man seemed put out by the Northman's presence, as he had since the first time they met.

"Your friend's a bit tightly wound," said Crean, after the Torqued Man had left.

"That's just his way. He's a northerner, a Frisian, which I believe is etymologically linked to frigidity."

Finn advised Crean not to bring up the smut in front of the Torqued Man himself. "He's a very private person. Prefers to go only through me."

"That suits me just fine."

"If you don't mind my asking, how does yourself get this vast supply of delights?" asked Finn.

Crean wagged a finger in mock admonishment. "Now, now, an artist never reveals his secrets, nor a pirate where his treasure's buried. Besides, if I told how I got started, you wouldn't believe me, even though it's true."

"Try me."

"Alright, then. . . . One day late last fall, I was out tramping in the Grunewald, enjoying a crisp afternoon. I had been in Berlin only a month or so, and everything felt new and exciting. Well, there I was, strolling along the banks of the Havel, pondering next week's lectures, when I noticed a large trunk bobbing along the river's edge. What in God's name is that, I wondered. Being the curious sort and having nothing really better to do, I went after the trunk to have a closer look. I heaved the bloody thing onto solid ground, soaking my shoes right through, and damn near split my coat. Once I'd secured it onto dry land, I found a good heavy stone and cracked off the latches. And what would you guess was staring back at me from inside that trunk? That's right, an enormous heap of highly unusual erotica.

"Like you, I was disturbed at first by the dark nature of those photographs. In fact, I ran away from the trunk. Tried to get back to thinking about my lectures, with my heart pumping and my nerves all aflame. I must have walked a mile before I realized I had stumbled on something rare and valuable. Something that shouldn't be rejected out of hand. So now I ran back, afraid someone had already seized it and feeling like a buck eejit for abandoning such a gift. Of course, the trunk was still there when I returned, and I was thrilled. I dragged it to the nearest road and caught a taxi home. My days in Berlin have been blessed ever since."

"You're right," said Finn with a laugh. "I don't believe you." But he pressed him no more on his preposterous story. He knew Crean was being cagey. It wasn't just the volume of resources at his disposal but the sense of artistic ownership he took in the photos, which exceeded that of a mere middleman. He suspected he had his own studio somewhere.

Drawing on Crean's reservoir, Finn parceled out his smut in small doses to his three esteemed clients in covert meetings around the city. While Grawitz preferred the zoo lavatory at night, indicative of his self-loathing, Poppendick liked the thrill of a café table in the Neues Museum, partially hidden behind a marble column. The museum had been emptied of its artifacts since the start of the war, with only a few plaster models to console wandering visitors. Its halls were now used primarily as a public arcade, with a bar and café operating in the main gallery. The psychiatrist Lutz, however, dared not part with his armor of professional authority. He scheduled weekly appointments for Finn at his office under the patient name Eoin O'Duffy, whose fictitious medical file indicated he was being treated for night terrors and neuroses relating to micropenis.

21

JOURNAL

January 11, 1944

Once Pike's radio broadcasts began, the afternoon tea that had once been reserved exclusively for me was now host to a regular parade of the questionable human material that constituted the Berlin Irish.

This enclave of expatriates consisted of educated pariahs who were either genuine admirers of our National Socialist revolution or unprincipled bootlickers. Or, as was often the case, both. If any of them knew that Frank Finn, gymnasium teacher and football coach, was in fact the renowned IRA fighter and forgotten author Proinnsias Pike, none let on. But I sensed an irony in the way they addressed him, as though they were all keeping up the charade either in his honor or at my expense.

Exemplary among these fetid guests was Charles Bewley, the former Irish ambassador to Germany. He'd been sacked for being too keen on Hitler but had chosen to stay on in Berlin. Having forfeited his government pension, he was now writing vitriol against the Jews for a Nazi news agency in Stockholm. Bewley had fluttering eyelids and a forehead so oleaginous it reflected light. The only ideas evident within it concerned the crimes of Jewry foisted upon the free nations of the world, the gross incompetence of Éamon de Valera, and his own close friendship with Goebbels.

"There is an awful lot of hand-wringing in the international press these days about Hitler's treatment of the Jews," he told Pike over tea one Sunday. "But I'll tell you this. Whatever force the Germans have used against the Jews pales in comparison—absolutely pales, I say—with the barbarism shown by the communists in Spain."

Pike listened to this with a bored look on his face. He had known of Bewley back in Dublin, when the man was reputed to be a first-order windbag. After the ex-ambassador finally spent himself, Pike lit a cigarette, leaned back, and said, "Why is it that people who have the strongest opinions about Spain are the ones who haven't set foot there?"

"Well, we can't expect people to run all about the

world before we allow them to have an informed opinion, now, can we?" said Bewley defensively. "That's
what the press is for—at least, that is, an honest press
brave enough to pull back the veil and show the people
what's at play. That's what I consider my mission as a
journalist to be, at any rate."

"You mean your propaganda work with the Swedish
agency?" Pike clarified. "The job Goebbels gave you?"

"He did not 'give' me anything. He merely recommended me because he saw my evident talents."

"For pulling back the veil?" said Pike.

"Yes, precisely."

"Mr. Bewley, you make writing propaganda sound
like working at a curtain shop," said Pike, giving me a
wink.

Bewley cleared his throat, signaling he did not like
being the butt of a joke.

"Tell us, Mr. Bewley," said Pike, now disguising
his mockery as appeasement, "are you still writing
your poems about the old myths? I recall reading a
powerful verse or two of yours about Atlantis back
when I was a lad."

Pike later told me Bewley wrote the most legendary
drivel of a mystical Celtic persuasion. He had agreed to
let the man call on him only in hopes of hearing some
unforgivable doggerel to lighten his mood.

"Certainly," said Bewley. "Though not near as often as I would like. I've been terribly busy with my political writing. For instance, did you know that there are still thousands of unregistered juvenile delinquents—Jews and homosexuals among them—here in Berlin, hiding in the parks and forests, spreading filth?"

I knew about these wild children. While I doubted they were the epidemic Bewley made them out to be, I had seen them on a few occasions scurrying about the Grunewald. I had heard rumors they trafficked in sex, but most of their activity, so far as I could tell, seemed to consist of defacing trees.

"It's true," said Bewley. "They live in underground dens and eat garbage, just like rats. Fitting, that, isn't it? You know they carry plague, consumption, syphilis, the whole lot. Why, it's a public-health crisis of epic proportions."

"You still have the metaphorical powers of a poet, Mr. Bewley," said Pike, before falling into a coughing fit. I noticed he was having them with greater frequency of late.

"That cough sounds serious," said Bewley. "You know, I can recommend a superb doctor. Goebbels referred me to him. In fact, he's even treated the Führer himself. Part of his inner circle in Berchtesgaden, I'm told. Can you imagine? A cozy fireside evening with the Führer? Privy to all his thoughts and musings? I'm told Hitler is quite disarming in person."

"You mean Morell?" I asked.

I had heard of Hitler's physician from Lauhusen, who once dined with him in the company of Canaris. He was a great fat man. Reputed to be the best injections man in the Reich, he treated all the Nazi leadership—Göring, Bormann, Ribbentrop, et al. According to Lauhusen, Morell had the worst table manners of anyone he had ever met. "Ate like he was at a trough," said Lauhusen. "The lip-smacking alone made my brain rattle, but, oh, the smell! It came out of his armpits like there were gas hoses in his jacket. The man's body odor would make you question his character even if he were a factory worker or a ditchdigger. But a physician? What kind of a person would place the care of his body in the hands of such a repugnant fatso?"

"No, not Morell," said Bewley contemptuously. "According to my man"—and here he said a name I can't remember: Braun or Brand, perhaps Brandt— "Morell is a total charlatan. Injecting dandelions and sugar water into desperate starlets willing to pay thousands to smooth out their wrinkles. And now, sadly, he's peddling his sham homeopathy to Hitler. But Dr. Brandt is the genuine article. Why he's the most renowned physician in the SS."

Pike, who had been coughing this whole time, finally hacked up the offending glob into his handkerchief and looked at Bewley with uncharacteristic sincerity. "Dr. Brandt, did you say?"

"Yes, Brandt will have that cough banished in no time. I had a bowel complaint last year, couldn't put down a piece of toast without getting the works all in knots. Brandt put me on a pill-and-enema regimen that had me right as rain within a week. Here, I'll write down his address for you. You can tell him I sent you, but I recommend going soon. He flits all around the Reich these days on important business. And, Finn? When you go, it might behoove you to dress a bit smarter. They're used to dealing with the finest society there."

"Thank you, Mr. Bewley," said Pike, looking at the address with a strange intensity. "I will be certain to consult his expertise."

"Now," said Bewley, "since you insist, I'd be happy to recite a few homespun verses for you."

Thankfully, my brain has not retained memory of the assault on poetry that followed.

22

Finn McCool in the Bowels of Teutonia

An Appointment

Finn continued to transmit to the Anglelanders whatever passed through his ears at the Funkhaus, which—as his Bronx playmates used to say—was bubkes. Meanwhile, real work was afoot.

He returned to the medical office on Prinz-Albrecht-Straße, site of his former humiliation. This time he spun through the revolving doors with confidence, swaggered up to the receptionist, and slapped his appointment card on the desk.

"I believe Dr. Brandt is expecting me."

The receptionist, who seemed to remember Finn, eyed him and his card with suspicion. Disappointed to detect no signs of forgery, he returned it with a hostile flick. "Third floor, second door on your right."

There another receptionist examined Finn's card

and, after looking over his rather shabby appearance, instructed him to wait. The office was empty and painted a sickly green. Pictures of the Führer and Himmler flanked a Teutonian-style woodcut of Hippocrates. Beneath these hung a medical license and a photo of a uniformed man Finn didn't recognize, presumably Brandt. It was a tan, athletic-looking face, with a deeply cleft chin and long features. He would have been handsome if it weren't for eyes that looked like they belonged to a petulant girl, a feminine delicacy that made his jutting, dimpled chin seem all the more obscenely masculine.

A moment later, Finn found himself face-to-face with that unseemly cleft. "You must be Herr Finn," he said, extending a bronzed hand. "I'm Dr. Brandt. Please, come with me."

The smell of disinfectant and the sight of the medical instruments on the counter in Brandt's office made Finn queasy. He tried to ignore the knot in his stomach, cinched with memories from the pit, and donned the cloak of the cheerful patient.

"Thank you for seeing me, Doctor. I imagine you're a very busy man."

"Well, I owed Herr Bewley a favor," he said with a tight smile. "And I always try to see a few patients while I'm here in Berlin."

The Nazi-lickarse Bewley, who usually made Finn want to smother him with Obelinka's throw pillows, had dropped such a fine gift in his lap that Finn had to stop himself from kissing the man. By the grace of God, Finn's catarrh—one of many souvenirs from the Spanish pit—was bothering him that day, and Bewley advised him to see a doctor, using the opportunity to boast that his own physician was none other than Dr. Karl Brandt.

"Is your man good, then?" Finn had asked, as a surge of adrenaline flooded the soft meat of his brain.

"Good? Why, I wager he's the best doctor in Germany. He's even treated Hitler himself. Used to be his personal physician, I'm told. That is, until that fat slob Morell wormed his way into the job."

Finn made a note to remember the name Morell for future reference, but his mind was now stuck on Brandt. "Does he take new patients, this Dr. Brandt?"

"Oh, I doubt it," said Bewley. "He's terribly busy. Splits his time between here and Munich. Nearly impossible to get an appointment unless you know someone." He paused to allow for a crescendo of suspense before making his heroic intervention. "Of course, I might be able to help things along."

"Why, that would be grand, Mr. Bewley," he said. "We'd be indebted to you for the favor."

"We?" asked Bewley.

"That's right," Finn had said, realizing Bewley could not see the well-muscled contours of Finn McCool sharing his own corner of the couch. "Me and my catarrh."

Now Finn was dangling those well-muscled legs [shapely as a teenage bathing queen] off Brandt's examining table, staring into the arsecrack of his chin.

"I understand, Doctor, that you're head of the Reich Committee for the Scientific Registering of Serious Hereditary and Congenital Illnesses?"

Brandt looked surprised. "Yes, that is correct. Why do you ask?"

"Oh, no reason, other than I'm a great admirer of the work you're doing. You see, Ireland is sadly decades behind in the fields of social medicine and eugenics."

Brandt nodded sympathetically.

"In fact, I recently saw *Ich Klage An*," lied Finn, pointing at a signed poster for the film that hung in Brandt's office. "And I thought it remarkable for its candor and its humanity. A top-shelf film altogether."

"I'm pleased to hear that," said the doctor. He looked proudly at the poster, which showed a resolute doctor standing over a confused invalid. "You know, I was chief medical consultant for the film. And truth be told, the story was my idea. Herr Reichsminister Goebbels gave me that poster as a token of his appreciation."

"Is that Fräulein Hatheyer's autograph there?" asked Finn, leaping off the examining table for a closer look.

"Indeed, it is."

Finn sighed with awe. "Tell me, if one were similarly burdened with an ill loved one—that is, someone beyond all hope of a useful social contribution, someone for whom death would be an act of mercy—would your organization be the one to consult?"

"Yes, of course. A number of the organizations I oversee coordinate such things. I'd be happy to have my secretary point you toward the proper resources."

"Thank you, Doctor. That would be lovely."

"Now," said Brandt, "if you don't mind, let's take a look at your throat."

Finn left Brandt's office with a bottle of a high-velocity nasal spray, a fistful of social-medicine brochures, and the keys to the doctor's Mercedes. He had nicked them from the pocket of Brandt's coat while distracting him with his palaver.

Unfortunately, most of the automobiles in the lot were Mercedes-Benzes, and to make matters worse, the lot was directly beneath the windows of Gestapo headquarters. Finn tried the first two rows of cars but with no luck. On the third row, he looked up and caught the gaze of a Gestapo employee drinking coffee in the window. A few minutes later, an officer appeared on the lot and came marching toward him. Finn had just put the key into the door, and while he groped for a suitable lie that would delay what looked like his imminent arrest, it opened.

"Just got the damn thing and forgot which one was mine," he said, waving his keys at the approaching officer and laughing at his own ineptness.

Finn hurried into the car and started the engine. Despite not having driven in the last five years, he managed to put it in reverse, but not before the officer rapped on the window.

"Show me your papers," he demanded.

"Of course," said Finn. The Torqued Man had counseled Finn that while his documents were in order, there were elements in the Security Office that did not look kindly on an Irish socialist living in their midst. Perhaps especially if he was caught stealing a car from a high-ranking Nazi. Finn rummaged in his jacket for his papers, while locating the knife in his breast pocket. He could pull the man's head in the window, slit his throat, and drive off. He tightened his grip on the blade and tensed at the ready.

But just then the officer's attention was diverted by a commotion in front of the Gestapo building. Finn looked in his mirror and saw a Black Maria full of prisoners being unloaded. They appeared to be young boys, no more than fifteen or sixteen, with some as young as ten. But they were dressed as wild Indians and gypsies, clad in colorful rags, women's feathered hats, and leather vests. The boys were shouting in unison something Finn could not make out—a chant, a jeer, a war cry—when suddenly one of the boys, who had his face painted like a cross between a burlesque diva and a Comanche warrior, flung himself at his captor and sank his teeth into his neck.

The officer shouted at Finn to clear out and went off to help his wounded colleague. But Finn was so enthralled with the scrappy delinquents' bravado that he sat idle, having forgotten how narrowly he'd just avoided disaster. He watched the brawl through his mirror, until a mob of police descended on the boys with clubs and knocked the teeth out of the little Indian brave.

The sobering crunch of bone brought Finn back to

his task. He sped out of the lot and re-parked around the corner beside a bombed-out government building.

Inside the glove box he found precisely what he'd been hoping for: Brandt's automobile registration, listing his home address.

He left the keys in the ignition and slipped away.

23

JOURNAL

January 13, 1944

The Berlin of today consists of knots of contradiction. After Hitler has taken such pains to de-Jewify and un-Slavinate it, the city feels more foreign than ever. Everywhere you turn there are workers from the lands of its most recent conquests and beyond: Frenchmen, Greeks, Dutch, Italians, Spaniards, South Slavs, Poles, Estonians, Ukrainians, Lithuanians, Tatars, Turks, Arabs, and, of course, enough Russian prisoners to populate a city on their own. This is a world city bent on destroying the world, the capital of a Thousand-Year Reich that may well not survive the year.

Pike's euphoria at being freed from Franco's prison had faded. And I sensed his fear that Berlin was becoming his new cell.

With good reason. Given the war with Russia, there would be no invasion of Britain. Which meant, unless Churchill invaded first, Ireland was no longer of much value. Meanwhile, life here was becoming bleaker by the day. Rationing grew tighter, Jews were forced to wear humiliating badges in public—as if they hadn't been humiliated enough—and dancing in public was now forbidden. Were they saving Berliners' legs for the next recruitment wave?

Now that fascism and communism were once again at war, Pike must have had occasion to question his decision anew, entertaining fears that he had chosen the wrong side. He masked this with his gallows humor and cheerful pessimism, but I think if he had really been the quipping cynic he purported to be, he wouldn't have deteriorated the way he did.

I was reminded of a story I had read by the banned Prague Jewish writer Kafka—about a caged ape who, faced with no prospect of escape, decides to become human. Humanity not as a lofty ambition or achievement but merely a way out. Red Peter—that is the ape's name, as I recall—frees himself from his cage by becoming an uncaged creature. Like everything Kafka wrote, it was brilliant and absurd, and through the blackest laughter it seemed at once to inspire and deflate all hope of redemption. Pike's position, I came to realize, was not unlike Red Peter's. Faced with no escape, he needed a way out.

That fall of '41, I petitioned Lauhusen to let Pike visit the POWs at Luckenwalde. I thought this would be good for both him and the success of Operation Osprey, which was what we were now calling our plans for a defensive Irish insurgency in the event of a British invasion. The only work that had been done on that plan in months was changing its name from Operation Green to Operation Osprey, again at Lauhusen's behest. The man had a curious fixation with waterfowl. Because Veesenmayer was away in Zagreb, advising the Ustaše on the construction of concentration camps, my request was granted.

The idea was for Pike to interview Irishmen among the prisoners and recruit those deemed patriotic enough to return to Ireland with him and Kriegsmann. I thought this might boost his sense of purpose and renew his faith that he would soon return home. I also hoped it might break the spell of Archibald Crean.

I drove Pike out to the Stalag, about an hour's ride

from the city. The day was gray and blustery. Dead leaves blew across the windscreen. Pike nursed a bottle of black-market *Kräuterlikör* and dozed against the window.

I eyed him while he slept. His face was looking haggard, the lines more deeply etched. And, even though he was developing a paunch and the skin under his chin hung looser, his cheeks were gaunt. I could see how he would look as an old man. Even so, I found him beautiful.

I thought about Maike's face on her deathbed, her features contorted in a grimace. Her image then morphed in my mind's eye into the face of my niece, welcoming and slightly askew, as she watched the nurse inject her. The nurse looked untroubled while she lodged the needle firmly in the vein, then emptied her lethal syringe.

Pike awoke as the car went over a tree branch and saw me looking at him.

"Better tend to the road, Grotius. I think you just ran over a small child."

"What?" I shouted in a panic.

"Jesus, man, it was just a branch. But if you'd watch the road, you'd know I was joking."

"Sorry," I said. "I got distracted."

"By my glittering Apollonian form?" asked Pike.

"Not quite, I'm afraid."

"Oh, go on, Herr Fluss. Don't you love me any-more?"

I didn't know how to respond. Even though Pike was clearly teasing me, the words were a shock. Why would he have said that? Did he think I loved him? Did I love him? I was quite sure he didn't love me. I felt tears well up.

Thankfully, Pike was looking out the window and hadn't noticed. "Seen any good films lately? It's been a while since you gave me the skinny."

I tried to summon a normal speaking voice. "Well, let's see. . . . The last film I recall seeing is . . . *Ich Klage An*," I said, with a faint tremor. I neglected to tell him I'd seen it several times.

"Oh, I think I've seen the posters. *I Accuse?*" asked Pike, translating the title.

"You're improving." Since I had replaced Frau Winter with a suitably dowdy crone, Frau Fichte, Pike's German had dramatically improved. Though his accent was still terrible.

"Go on, tell us about it, then," he said. "Is it any use?"

"Well," I said, feeling the heat rise to my face, "it's about a woman who is diagnosed with multiple sclero-sis, and rather than face a long and agonizing degeneration, she begs her husband, who is a doctor, to assist with her suicide. He consents, gives her a lethal dose of pills, and is then put on trial for murder."

"Oh, stop right there. I won't have you spoil the ending."

"I'll bet you can guess it."

"Let's see. . . . They resurrect the dead wife and she marries the judge?"

"Close," I said. "The doctor defends himself as an angel of mercy who has released his wife from her suffering. He then condemns the court for its crime of forcing people to live with sickness rather than commit the humane and heroic act of killing them."

"Aw Christ, you've gone and ruined it! And, look at that—why, Grotius, you've got tears in your eyes."

I was deeply embarrassed and struggled to regain my composure.

"Was the film really that moving, then?" asked Pike.

I laughed as I wiped another excretion from my eyes. "God, no! It's the vilest propaganda. Not only are they killing Jews, Poles, and what have you. They're murdering children here too. Invalids, the mentally ill—anyone who can't be of use to the regime as a worker or soldier is being murdered by doctors."

Pike looked down at his schnapps as he fiddled with

the cap. "A murderous sort they are, doctors. That's about the height of it."

"They killed my sister's child," I whispered. I hadn't intended to tell him, or anyone, but the words just fell from my mouth.

"What's that?" he asked, turning to me.

"Oh, nothing," I said, clearing my throat. "Just a line from the film."

I recall that was around the same time James von Moltke approached me. I had taken my lunch in the Tiergarten and was enjoying a cigarette on a park bench, soaking in the last light before winter set in, when he strolled past.

We caught each other's eye at the same time and my book was lying facedown on my lap, so there was no pretending we hadn't seen each other.

"Afternoon, Adrian," he said, looking down at me, hands thrust into his fine wool suit.

"James," I said, feeling then somewhat embarrassed to call him by name after so much elapsed time. "What a nice surprise!"

"I thought we'd have seen more of each other by now," he said. Did that mean he wanted to see more of me, or had he been relieved?

"Yes, me too. Nothing like a war to keep one busy,"

I said idiotically. What was next, a discussion of the weather?

But Moltke became grave and sat down beside me and lowered his voice to a whisper. "You have no idea, Adrian."

He then told me he'd just returned from the east, where he'd been sent by Oster to monitor the Wehrmacht's compliance with—or, rather, total disregard for—international law. "It's an abattoir. I don't just mean the violence. I mean the violations. The crimes. I'm writing appeals through all hours of the night. And something tells me they will fall on deaf ears."

I told him I was not surprised. I'd learned enough in Spain to know that war is never waged honorably.

"Even so, it's much worse than you think. I feel the weight of it. Do you understand?"

I told him I did. "It's called despair. It's the chief product of modernity."

"No, it's not that. I don't mean a mood, Adrian. Or a vague sense of decline. I mean a tear in the fabric of mankind. A profanation. A new, truly diabolical chapter in human history, marked by a mass outbreak of radical evil."

It was strange to think we'd once held each other's impossibly young bodies in a twin bed on Broad Street. The recollection felt like something I had read long ago in a novel. But I could still sense the semantic fault lines that had fractured our relationship. The cosmic moral terms veering into the overtly theological. I found it aesthetically off-putting. Not wrong, per se, just not in line with my taste.

In the course of our conversation, I said something to the effect of how repellent Hitler was and how he and his lethal beer-hall vision of Germania were destroying the promise of a Europe tempered by the true humanist depths of our culture.

"You know, a few of us have taken to meeting to discuss precisely such matters," he said. "How the German *Volk* can return to the Christian values that are its essence."

"Oh, yes?"

"You would be welcome to join us the next time we convene at Kreisau. I'm sure Freya shall be delighted to meet you."

"Well, that's very kind of you." I was flattered but a little wary of the way my words had been transformed into "a return to Christian values." Not to mention the added emphasis on his wife.

He could sense my reluctance and probably recalled how his devoutness had once come between us. "We are multidenominational too. Protestant, Catholic, even a few agnostics."

I told him I was honored by the invitation and would let him know, hoping enough time would pass before we saw each other again and the matter would by then have been forgotten. I had little desire to drive hours to the Prussian countryside to hear sanctimonious Junkers pontificate. That was not the kind of saving my soul needed.

24

Finn McCool in the Bowels of Teutonia

Gifts from on High

D r. Brandt lived on a quiet street in the Hansaviertel. Despite a wedding ring on his finger, there was no sign of a wife. Only a sleek greyhound, an animal for which Finn thought the Teutonian word *Windhund* was far more apt. The doctor walked his wind hound every night before bed, usually just a short stroll to the edge of the Englischer Garten and back.

But on this particular night, the one Finn had selected for Brandt's gutting, just as the doctor was about to enter the dark embrace of the park, the air-raid sirens roared to life. It had been the better part of a year since that wail had pierced Berliners' ears, and they had come to believe the attacks were over. Finn paused behind a darkened streetlamp as he saw an air-raid warden accost the doctor and his hound.

"You must seek shelter immediately," said the warden.

"But I live only three blocks from here," replied Brandt.

"Doesn't matter. Take cover now."

"Where?"

"There is a small dugout over there by the Moltke monument."

"That's ridiculous," said Brandt. "It's the opposite direction from my house. Look here, I'm—"

"This is not a matter for debate. Now go!"

The air-raid warden approached Finn and commanded him to follow Brandt to the shelter at the edge of the park.

The dugout shelter was unfinished and still open on one side, putting occupants eye level with the marble boots of the great Prussian general. When Finn descended the steps, Brandt was in the corner soothing his hound, who was agitated by the siren. When she saw Finn, the hound jerked and leapt toward him.

"*Trudchen, nein!*" shouted Brandt, snapping the leash. She whimpered and returned to his side. Brandt looked up at Finn and paused on his face.

Finn himself performed a double take. "Dr. Brandt?" he asked.

"Yes, I'm sorry . . ." said the doctor, unable to place him.

"I consulted you recently about my catarrh. My friend Charles Bewley recommended—"

"Ah, yes, of course. Herr Finn, wasn't it?"

"That's right. Finn McCool."

"Do you live nearby?" asked the doctor.

Just then, two planes flew overhead. In the roving searchlight beams, they looked smaller than the bombers from last year's raids.

"Russians," shouted Brandt over the roar. "They are hoping for revenge."

Seconds later, an antiaircraft gun cracked into the sky, lighting up the night with its enormous flak shells. Finn and the doctor watched as the red and green flares cast a spectral, almost tranquil glow over the city. Even Brandt's distraught hound was awed into silence. But the feeling of peace broke when a flak splinter the size of a cinder block came screaming out of the sky and stabbed into the earth right before their eyes.

"That was lucky," said Brandt.

Finn beheld the twisted chunk of steaming metal. "Lucky, indeed," he said. It was, in fact, a gift from on high.

When the firefight ended—the Russian planes had dropped their payload somewhere on the outskirts of the city before retreating—Finn gestured for Brandt to exit the dugout ahead of him.

Once outside, he bent over and pulled the flak splinter from the ground as if it were a peg from a cribbage board. It sizzled in the grip of his broad, man-killing hands. Finn raised the twisted metal above his head, hefting it like a war club, and, just as Brandt turned to register the blur behind him, brought it down squarely on his skull.

The doctor collapsed on the ground in a convulsion. Blood and brain leaked from his ears. Trudchen barked wildly, as Finn stood over her owner and drove the shrapnel deeper into his head with the heel of his palm. Shortly, the convulsing stopped and Karl Brandt lay still.

Finn admired his handiwork for a spell, then took hold of the wind hound's leash and retreated into the black foliage of the beast garden.

25

JOURNAL

January 14, 1944

Our drives out to Luckenwalde became the new regimen for Pike and me. And the prisoner-recruitment plan had the effect I'd hoped for, at least for a time. Pike's spirits were buoyed in the martial atmosphere among his countrymen. He was a born leader and won their respect through nothing more, it seemed, than friendly insults and backslapping. They were British citizens, either from Northern Ireland or of Irish extraction, and Pike's job was to find the most nationalistic and frustrated among them.

While he got on with the prisoners, sussing out their politics over games of football and cards, I—perched on my stool in the corner, looking like an exam proctor and feeling like a left-out schoolboy—studied his charm. One thing was certain: It was not a question of what he said or did but rather how. Part of this was physical and entirely beyond his control. For instance, his hands were broad and well proportioned. Unlike mine, which were slender and knotted and looked at once dainty and mis-shapen, his had a rough elegance, like a woodsman who could heft a volume of philosophy as easily as an ax. And though his worn body was no sporting ideal, his effort-less manner of inhabiting it communicated strength and intelligence, and this inspired trust. Other traits of his could be acquired—the jesting, the emphatic cursing, the unstudied learnedness, the adoption of nicknames to christen others into his world—though the authenticity behind them could not. Were I to employ any of these techniques for the purpose of commanding authority, they would earn me only derision.

It was during these sessions that I developed a theory about life, which I had long held but never articulated for myself. There are, it seems, two ways of living: *in* the world and *on* it. Those who live in the world find meaning and comfort in their involvement with human affairs. They have a natural enjoyment of con-versing, of helping, of being part of something larger than themselves. They let the life force flow into them, nurture it, and radiate it outward. These are the people who are natural parents and leaders, who form circles, who join clubs and establish institutions, the ones who feel organically connected to a tradition and pass it on in a way that bears witness to their existence as part of an unbroken continuity of life in this world.

Then there are those of us who live *on* the world. Though we are no less entangled in its business or complicit in its crimes than we are sustained by its pleasures, life for us is something we experience as voyeurs rather than participants. It is as if there were a thin film separating our bodies from the rest of the world, such that we are always on the surface of things and forever deprived of communion. Amid the intercourse of humanity, in bonds of family and friendship, we remain encased in ourselves. We live on the world imagining what it must be like to live in the world, wondering what it feels like to truly touch someone, to truly be touched. We may leave legacies, testaments, and other detritus in the wake of our existence, but we will live on in no one. Hitler is a member of this category, but one in revolt. He is taking revenge on the world for having been born merely on it and not in it.

Pike was an enigma, because his authenticity marked him clearly as a being *in* the world and yet, because of his isolation and the contingencies of history, it seemed he could understand the plight of those of us trapped behind the glass. To us he appeared unbounded, a man apart, yet so wholly charged with vitality that his solitude was not, like ours, a state of being cut off from life. Rather, his charisma was the source of life itself. It liberated people from their loneliness. In his company, one had the intoxicating sensation of drinking straight from the hose. Which is why, after such an experience, when you are abruptly deprived of it, your throat becomes parched and the world appears drier and more cracked than ever.

With Pike on my mind today, I decided to visit the Ratskeller. I hadn't been there since he died. It's still doing brisk business—one of the few restaurants in the neighborhood that have been spared destruction. I asked for a seat in the dining room, and as luck would have it, the waiter sat me in the same corner booth Pike and I had once claimed as our own. I was in a reflective mood, and as I choked down the parsnip-and-potato-starch *Frikadellen* in a sauce of nettles and glue, while sipping my liter of beer-flavored water, I thought about the grim fate of those evenings of idle conversation. Pike: his time and talent wasted, felled by illness, then obliterated. Egon

Schulz, my former editor: no doubt shipped east to a living nightmare behind electric fences. Countless others who had occupied the booths beside us had, I'm sure, met similarly dark and senseless endings. But here I was, chewing my patties of privation. Still alive. Surviving. And for what?

"Excuse me, sir," said the waiter, pulling me from my thoughts. "Do you mind if another diner sits across from you?"

"No, of course not," I said, inwardly recoiling. "I'm nearly done anyway. In fact, I'll take the check."

I didn't relish the idea of sharing a meal with a stranger and the crapshoot of conversation it entailed. Small talk with anyone other than intimates, while never appealing, has become a minefield of potentially denounceable utterances. Especially now that defeatist language is at the tip of everyone's tongue.

I stole a glance at my companion as he sat down. No party pin, at least. But I could smell the drink on him. He took off his hat and looked up at me in a similarly furtive manner. I couldn't believe it. It was Rudolf Ditzen. Or as the rest of the world knew him, through his pen name, Hans Fallada.

He didn't recognize me, as he had no occasion to. But we knew each other. Of course, I could hardly introduce myself without breaking my cover—not that I had much to protect these days. But he looked even less keen than I was to have a conversation partner.

I went back and forth with myself like this, until finally it felt too strange to say nothing.

"Excuse me, Herr Ditzen," I said, "I believe we know each other."

His face retracted with anxiety.

"Forgive me, I don't mean to intrude. It's just that I translated one of your books."

"Oh," he said, his features softening slightly. "Which one?"

"The Spanish edition of *Little Man, What Now?* That was me." I decided there was little risk, or rather my ego had already outweighed the risk, in revealing myself. "I'm Adrian de Groot."

"De Groot?" he said, searching his mind.

"We had a brief correspondence several years ago regarding your novel. Your publisher, Herr Rowohlt, put us in touch."

"Ah, I see. Yes, I do recall that. Well . . . thank you," he said.

I had made him uncomfortable. "If things ever return to normal, I would be honored to work on another of your books," I said. "Though I'm afraid the publishing market in Spain has all but dried up in the current climate."

He nodded. "It's a terrible time to write."

"Yes," I said, "and at a time when we need literature the most."

We were speaking in a coded language, feeling each other out for political sympathies. I knew he had been harassed by the regime, labeled "undesirable," yet never to the point of being banned. He was caught in some kind of elaborate dance, which made it hard for me to know where he stood in terms of his own politics. But I knew, because I had read his books, that he had a soul. That he was, at some fundamental level, a contrarian, a misfit, an outsider. Someone who had found a way to turn the blood from his wounds into art. But, as to my orientation, he couldn't be sure until I gave him some clue.

"I hope you won't mind me saying that *Wolf Among Wolves* is a masterpiece."

He gave an embarrassed smile. But this statement of admiration was not enough, since Goebbels himself had been an outspoken fan of that novel.

The waiter came with a beer and schnapps and the grim daily special for Ditzen. I paid my bill and, after he left, added, "I believe it will stand as a testament of conscience in an age that has all but lost it."

With that, the drawbridge lowered and I was allowed to enter. The keep remained impenetrable, but at least I could walk within the castle walls.

Ditzen downed his schnapps, took out his cigarette case and matchbook, and leaned back to smoke. "I hate coming into Berlin. If I had stayed here, I surely would have emigrated. Or killed myself. Or had a bomb dropped on my head. Any of those would be preferable to this," he said, gesturing at his insipid fare. Though I gathered he meant the *Frikadellen* to stand for something larger.

He lived in Carwitz, a small village a hundred kilometers north of the city. The lakes and forests kept him sane, he said. Some days he didn't even think of the war. He and his family grew their own food, had fresh milk and cheese. "Though don't get me wrong," he said, it was hardly an idyll. His wife's family had all moved in with them; the two of them fought a lot; she pestered him about his drinking. "The usual shape of things," he said with a wave of his hand, and beckoned the waiter for another round.

"That in itself would be perfectly bearable with a modest regimen of drink and narcotics, but then I keep getting these goddamn letters."

"What kind of letters?" I asked.

He downed the second schnapps and chased it with a

long swallow of beer. "They're trying to squeeze me," he said, as though that explained it.

After some prodding, I learned that a new publisher, one backed by Goebbels and the Culture Ministry, had picked Ditzen to write a sweeping novel about Jewish financiers, based on a banking scandal of the twenties and a figure named Kutisker.

"They sent me a letter last week saying the only way I'll receive my ration of paper for the year is if I write the Kutisker book. That's why I came into the city to-day—to tell them where to shove their ration of paper."

"Did you really?" I asked, impressed at such boldness and immediately reminded of Pike.

Ditzen averted my eyes and finished off what was now his third round of drinks. "No, not exactly," he said.

He had spilled the matchsticks on the table and was now fiddling with them. "I have my family to think of. I can't just stop working. The cow only gives out so much milk, you know."

I assured him I understood the difficult position he was in. There was no shame in survival, I said. But perhaps along with survival came complicity.

He looked up at me, as though this was the first time my words held any meaning. Then he went back to fingering his matches.

"So, are you going to write it?" I asked.

He chortled. "I could have written the Kutisker book at one point. On my own terms. But not on anyone else's. One thing I'm not is a government shill."

"Of course not," I said, feeling a sudden heat wave of self-loathing.

"They want me for their court jester? Fine. But I'll call the tune of the joke and who's the butt of it. I'll guarantee you this: The joke won't be on me."

And with that he stood up, slapped down a wad of marks on the table, and left.

I peered over his half-eaten meal and noticed he had formed the matchsticks into a pattern. On closer look, they were letters, upside down. I turned my head to read them: HITLER LIES.

No sooner had the words become intelligible than I saw the waiter coming to collect the money. In a panic, I shook the table. The letters came apart, and I left as quick as I could.

26

Finn McCool in
the Bowels of Teutonia

A Grand Plan

**And this was how Finn hatched in his wise brain
plans for a brilliant massacre.**

I n honor of Dr. Brandt's death, disguised as a
casualty of the latest air raid, Finn procured a bottle
of black-market Sekt to share with the Ruslandish
hausfrau.

"Your Finn's been a good little hunter, Obelinka.
Come, put down that knitting and sip on some of
this sparkling," he said from the settee, where he
and his newly adopted hound were reclining. He had
rechristened her Sceolang, the loyal bitch of legend.

Obelinka tried frowning but couldn't suppress a

smile. Her inborn suspicion faded in the face of any object evoking her former aristocratic life. And while she once would not have deigned to drink a Teutonian sparkler in place of real champagne, sleek racing hounds were a prized relic indeed. She nuzzled the wind hound on her way to the kitchen and returned with two goblets.

Finn popped the cork and poured the wine. "*Na zdrowie*, old girl. Here's to better days to come."

Obelinka sneered. "You toast like a Pole, and future is shit. To good days before."

The Ruslandish hausfrau turned out to be right. For, in the months following Brandt's death, the path of Finn's destiny grew bumpier. Grawitz ceased his visits to the public lavatory on account of the renewed air raids that fall. And the only address listed for him in Wagner's directory was that strange, impenetrable chancellery building on Tiergartenstraße. Meanwhile, amid the reshuffling of the Doctors' League, the psychiatrist Lutz was called to Munich. That left only Dr. Poppendick, who, thanks be to God, persisted through the winter with his doses of soul-bludgeoning smut.

To further complicate matters, the Teutonians resumed plans to send Finn back to Erin. They even tasked him with training Fenian prisoners for a mission in which he would defend the island from an Anglelandish invasion. But he dreaded the prospect of leaving without having first crossed more names off his list. He had by this point developed a taste for doctor slaughter and the sense of purpose it had given him. For, while in the eyes of the rest of the world he was rotting in Berlin as either a) Nazi collaborator, b) mindless radio personality, c) lackluster pencil-pushing Anglelandish spy, or d) all of the above, Finn knew the truth—that he was single-handedly driving a stake into the biomedical heart of the Reich.

With a new year under way and the threat of departure hovering, he berated himself for the lost opportunities. He should have thrown Lutz from the sixth-floor window of his office when he had the chance. Or killed Grawitz in that public toilet. Blown his horn, then bit the thing clean off and watched the man bleed out from his mangled stump. It pained Finn to think these might now just be idle fantasies.

Of course, he could still dispatch Poppendick in some hasty manner without much trouble. But Finn was troubled by the thought that these assassinations, this one-man death-dealing insurgency, might be dismissed as the doings of your workaday lunatic. While the isolated killings of Wagner and Brandt had afforded him a measure of security while he was getting his sea legs,

Finn now began to ponder his legacy. To live up to his name, to truly become the immortal hunter of legend, he needed to do something legendary. Something that the bards would sing of for centuries to come.

It was during a late-winter smut exchange at the museum with Poppendick that a colleague recognized the doctor and approached their table behind the marble column. Poppendick had just been admiring a photograph of a bound man having a bedpan emptied into his mouth.

"Sorry to interrupt, Herr Doktor," said the intruder.

"Ah, Herr Doktor Schmidt, what a pleasant surprise," said Poppendick, covering his smut with a copy of *Der Stürmer*. He stood to greet his guest. "Last I heard you were in Lithuania, sorting out the insane asylums."

"Yes, we mopped them right up. Now I'm back visiting family before I return to the General Government."

"Very good."

"And you?" asked Schmidt. "Shame about the euthanasia program."

"Yes, well, frankly, it was losing its footing even before Wagner's death. But we're onto bigger and better things. We certainly have our work cut out for us in the east."

"You can say that again. Well, I won't bother you. I've just come to have a peek at the Nefertiti. Of course, it's not the same as the real one. But the model's not half bad. You know, I've long believed there's not a drop of Negroid or Semitic blood in that face. It doesn't take an expert in racial hygiene to recognize that as the head of a pure Aryan queen."

Poppendick smiled. "I'm inclined to agree, though, it must be remembered, the Semites have clever ways of disguising themselves."

Dr. Schmidt was clearly waiting to be introduced to his colleague's companion, but when it became clear that wouldn't happen, he turned to Finn and introduced himself.

"*Angenehm*, Herr Doktor," said Finn. "Dr. Archibald Crean, though not a medical doctor, I'm afraid."

The man looked at him askance. "Crean, did you say?"

Finn realized then he'd put his foot in it, but it was too late. "Mm-hmm."

Again, the questioning look. Did this man know the real Crean? Finn reached under the table for his hunting blade.

"Well, I'm sorry to interrupt," he said, turning back

to Poppendick. "Just wanted to say hello. I trust I'll see you at the Kaiserhof this fall?"

"The Kaiserhof?" asked Poppendick, puzzled.

"Yes, the Doctors' League Dinner in October? I believe it's the twenty-seventh. Surely you're going?"

"Oh yes, yes, of course. I tell you, things have been so busy lately, I can't think more than a few days ahead."

The two men laughed and took another five minutes to take their leave of each other. Meanwhile, an idea had hatched in Finn's brain.

He would organize a spectacular event to coincide with this Doctors' League Dinner—a massive smut convention. Doctors from the far reaches of the Reich would assemble in Berlin's finest hotel for their annual feast, and Finn would lure them to his illicit showroom somewhere nearby. Of course, his false identity as Crean would likely be blown, but it wouldn't matter. For at that moment, before they could sort out their confusion and while they were all still engorged and gorging on images of tortured human flesh, he would take up his ax and slaughter them to a man.

He couldn't, however, actually kill them all by himself. Not at once. To carry out the kind of massacre he envisioned, he would need help.

27

JOURNAL

January 15, 1944

Apart from our trips to the Stalag at Luckenwalde, Pike spent his days in the company of Crean. Our outings to the Ratskeller diminished to once every month or so, and only at my behest. He would often be drunk by the time I showed up for tea, and Crean would be there with him. I still saw him regularly, as was my duty, and he was still his gregarious, wisecracking self on the surface, but the intimacy of our first year together had faded. And while I had passed those months confused by and pining for that fleeting erotic note, I already looked back on that period with nostalgia.

Much of his and Crean's time together was spent at a dingy hole in Kreuzberg. I knew because I had followed them there once. My intentions had been innocent enough. I had been out securing a flat for an Egyptian agent in Neukölln, when I happened to see the two of them on the U-Bahn platform at Hermannplatz. In point of fact, I first heard Crean's insipid giggle behind me, then saw that Pike was with him. They were walking in the opposite direction. I couldn't help but wonder how they behaved when it was just the two of them.

They emerged on Kottbusser Damm, where they joined the parade of housewives trudging through gray slush with their meagerly provisioned shopping bags. It was only three-thirty but so cloudy it was nearly dark. Pike and Crean walked shoulder to shoulder, or, rather, shoulder to head on account of Crean's diminutive stature. I was too far behind to make out their conversation, but Pike was doing most of the talking, blowing into his clasped hands every few minutes for warmth, while Crean, wearing a pair of ludicrously oversized mittens, clapped and nodded and laughed like a perfect little sycophant. From the looks of it, Pike was enjoying his company—more, I noticed, than he now enjoyed mine. I couldn't understand what I had done to make him dissatisfied with me. It was maddening, because he wasn't cold or unfriendly toward me, not at all. In fact, he was perfectly chummy but without the slightest sign that he genuinely wanted to be my friend or anything more.

I trailed them past the U-Bahn stop to a small alleyway off Oranienstraße, where they ducked into a doorway marked only with the word EINGANG and a crude imitation of the jovial drunk in Frans Hals's painting *Pickled Herring*. I noticed that, as he shepherded Pike through the door, Crean placed his hand on his shoulder and held it there two beats too long. I knew then he was in love with him.

But it was not just jealousy that motivated my suspicions of Crean. It was his whole manner of being. He gave off a fraudulent, subordinate air, like a Gestapo informant. These *Vertrauensmänner* were everywhere, most of them petty criminals or adulterers who had been blackmailed into becoming the whisper collectors of the Reich. It seemed unlikely they would recruit an itinerant Irish scholar, but there was something off about the man, something that irked me. And I became determined to find out what it was.

Having confirmed with the university registrar that Archibald Crean did in fact hold a temporary appointment and lectured every Tuesday and Thursday morning, I planted myself across the street from the university's Faculty of Philology and waited. He arrived in a hurry at five after eleven, looking freshly bathed but nonetheless hungover. I followed him up the stairs to the first-floor lecture hall, where I stood outside for the better part of two hours listening to Crean pontificate on Yeats's "The Second Coming." He spoke fluidly, but what little I could make out was wildly abstruse, with phrases like "the Age of Kali," "antithetical tincture," and "the thirteenth cone." I lurked near the lavatory while the class let out, then trailed Crean, who was accompanied by an overeager student brimming with questions about the geometry of gyres. The student parted ways with him at Gendarmenmarkt, and Crean headed east along the Spree.

I followed him along Köpenicker Straße, past the theaters and neutered cabarets, all the way to Schlesisches Tor. There he entered an alley that appeared to lead to a dye factory. But the lane actually continued past the factory to the base of the Oberbaum Bridge, right at the river's edge. Crean stopped before a ruinous stone structure beneath the bridge that looked like the remains of the old excise wall that had once girded the city. Embedded in it and painted a dull, dappled gray so as to blend into the stone was a door of reinforced steel. On this door he knocked twice, then three times, then, after another pause, once. The door opened. Crean was absorbed into the darkness and the door closed behind him.

I looked for a suitable place to wait where I could see him emerge. This was no easy feat. The structure was hidden from both the bridge and the dye factory. A vessel on the water could make out the ruin, but it was so deeply shadowed by the bridge that I doubted the door would be visible. Only from the small path on which I had followed Crean could one see this strange dwelling. Fortunately, this appeared to be the only way out, so I waited at the window of a café on Köpenicker Straße, ordered a sad approximation of coffee, and kept my eyes glued to the alley.

An hour later, Crean emerged with a portfolio. I let him disappear into the crowd, then went back to the door beneath the bridge. My mind, aided by my cup of pulverized acorn and synthetic caffeine, had been conjuring images of what lay behind that door. Perhaps it was a drug den. Crean did seem the type. Or maybe a brothel. The Kripo had eased prostitution restrictions to raise morale, but this place certainly did not look like it had been sanctioned by the state. If it was either of those two, I would soon find myself considerably out of my element. I could always plead ignorance, say I saw someone knock on the door and decided out of idle curiosity to do the same. But if there was something political afoot, if I had stumbled onto a spy ring or a resistance cell, well, then, that ersatz coffee would be the last I'd ever drink.

So be it, I decided. I had to know what that little imp was up to.

I knocked on the door as Crean had done: twice, then three times, then once. A few seconds that felt like an eternity went by, and just as I was about to leave, the door opened.

"The gentleman is welcome," bade an unseen voice.

I forced myself into the darkness. When the door clanged shut behind me, I couldn't see my own hand in front of my face.

"The gentleman will disrobe," said the voice.

Though this statement made it unlikely I had entered a nest of enemy assassins, I was now alarmed. "Excuse me?"

"The gentleman will remove all clothing, including socks, undergarments, and wristwatch, and place them in the box to his left," said the voice, in the assuring tenor of a trusted sommelier. "Then the gentleman will kindly put on the mask he finds in the box to his right."

Reluctantly, I did as commanded. I could see neither my clothes nor the boxes but felt my way around, making sure my wallet and papers remained in my jacket pocket.

As if it could read my thoughts, the voice said, "Don't worry. The gentleman will find everything as he left it."

I placed the Venetian mask over my face, then stood naked in the blackness, waiting.

"Is the gentleman ready?"

"Yes," I said tentatively.

The darkness receded as a heavy curtain was pulled back.

"The gentleman has entered the dungeon."

To my terror, I now saw that the voice belonged to a man wearing an executioner's mask and a leather harness, which was wrapped tightly between his legs. He gestured with his candelabra for me to leave the vestibule and enter the main room.

I followed his light, my bare feet moving timidly over the cool, uneven stones. Sconced torches along the far wall cast a flickering glow onto a scene that, once I saw it, gave me such a profound sense of déjà vu, I fell to my knees.

It was the *Waldhüter's* Dungeon—the identical tableau I'd first discovered years ago in my father's closet. A staging of wooden racks, crosses, and wheels, and upon them male bodies stretched in extremis, limbs and genitals wrenched and held fast by leather straps, faces contorted in ecstasy. At the center stood the Forest

Ranger, a stout woodsman with an alpine cap and cock as thick as a birch tree. He commanded a rustic arsenal of penetrants and lacerants: deer antlers, boar tusks, goat horns, hawk beaks, the femur of an elk, a rosary of bear claws, the skull of a hare. These the Forest Ranger plunged into the holes of his prisoners, filling the dungeon with their unfathomable cries.

I was transported to the first time I had witnessed these images in my family home. It was not only the graphic violence that had shocked me but its sudden discovery in my father's closet. Once the initial dizziness and nausea wore off, a second wave came over me when I realized that these portraits of blood and pain and prostration and what appeared to be outright torture were perhaps expressions of erotic delight. It was impossible to tell. Surely these subjects must have consented to this kind of treatment, I told myself, for who would let themselves be treated this way if not out of desire? Then again, who could possibly desire such treatment? Though I never looked at my father's collection again, the images lodged in my mind, where they took on a disturbing ambivalence, at once arousing me with tautened male forms and repulsing me with their medieval violence and gore.

But in that horrid dungeon beneath the Oberbaum Bridge, I felt no ambivalence, only sheer horror at somehow having stepped into a dark paternal fantasy. I retreated into the shadow between the torches and tried to bring my breathing under control. Three or four other masked men like me were standing against the wall, observing. Then I noticed that on the far side of the dungeon was a clothed man issuing instructions to someone operating a camera. I realized at last I was in the spectator's gallery of a photography studio.

Just then the Forest Ranger turned from his ministrations and looked our way. He beckoned us with a rake of his antlers, while his cock, swollen and red as a beetroot, twitched in our direction. The others did as they were bid, while I stumbled back against the wall, then ran as fast as my bare feet would carry me. I tripped over my belongings in the vestibule, grabbed them, and sprang for the door.

"The gentleman is not satisfied?" asked the attendant, as I yanked loose the bolts and tumbled still naked into the daylight.

28

Finn McCool in
the Bowels of Teutonia

The Fianna

On a cold March morning, Finn and his hound, Sceolang, were stomping along the mucky banks of the Havel, following the scent of work-shy degenerates. He had learned from the Torqued Man that the wild street urchins he'd seen attack the Gestapo officer lived in these western woods.

The *Wilden*, as they called themselves, were vestiges from the Weimar days, when so-called antisocial behavior was the toast of the town. They had written themselves into the world with pages stolen from the novels of Karl May, with tribal names like the Red Apaches, the Shatterhands, and the Forest Pirates. In their heyday, the Torqued Man explained, hundreds of these boy gangs made their living robbing, whoring, and occasionally murdering.

In the thirties, some of them had grown tired of the
scrounging life and joined the SA for three steady
meals and as much beer as they could drink. In recent
years, most of them had been rounded up—those
deemed redeemable shipped off to youth camps in the
Polish countryside, where they were to be the spear
tip of Aryan colonization—the rest sent to the *Lager*.
But at least one tribe of the *Wilden* still existed on
the fringes of the city. They were run by chiefs, boys
between fourteen and nineteen. Once you turned
the ripe old age of twenty, you had to leave the tribe.
After that, you could be a tramp or a sponger or any
other kind of adult antisocial you cared to be, but you
couldn't be one of the *Wilden*.

The Torqued Man had once mentioned he'd seen
their scrawlings in the Grunewald, marking the
boundaries of their secret encampments. That was
all Finn had to go on as he slogged along the banks
where the Wannsee flowed into the Havel, following
the current north. After hours of soggy wandering,
Finn at last spotted something. A tree with a symbol
carved into it. It appeared to be a hatchet. Upon
closer examination, it was a hatchet inscribed with
a phallus. Given what little he knew of these wild
boys, it seemed an auspicious sign. He circled this

tree and soon noticed another some yards off with the same carving. Before long, he was following a path of identically marked trunks leading from the water into the icy depths of the forest.

At first, he thought a stray acorn or pine cone had fallen on him. But when it happened a third time, and this time hit him in the chest, there could be no doubt. Someone was throwing rocks.

He scanned the glade but saw only dead logs and stones still wearing their winter blankets of snow. He called out in Teutonian, "I come alone and in peace."

In response came a flurry of rocks, this time from all directions. His hound began howling. The rocks were getting bigger and hurt more. One caught him in the jaw, then another on his ear. Sceolang got a sharp stone on the rump and set off yelping into the forest. Before Finn knew it, he was on the frozen ground, curled into a ball.

When the storm ended, he slowly lifted his head, raising his bruised and bloodied hands in contrition.

"Was machst Du, Alter?"

The voice came from a boy perched on a log above Finn. He wore a raccoon-skin coat that bulged under his bandoliers, bloodstained leather trousers, and a stovepipe hat festooned with ostrich plumes and a band of woven lichen. At the intersection of his belts was an enormous buckle painted with the word *Wildfrei.* Wild-free.

"I have a job I'd like to offer you," said Finn.

"We don't work for old fucks. We're our own bosses."

"It involves killing Nazis."

"So what?"

"So, don't you like the idea of killing Nazis?"

The boy shrugged.

"Not too long ago I saw one of your band bite a Gestapo man in the throat."

"Nazis are shit stains, just like reds and liberals and social democrats and monarchists. Fuck them all in the ass."

"Yeah," seconded a younger boy, with brass hoops hung from his ears. "And then make them eat the shit off your *Schwanz!*"

"A winning idea," said Finn.

"He talks funny. Are you an Englishman?"

"We hate the English!" said a freckled boy no older than ten, smoking a pipe.

"Perish the thought. I'm from the next island over, but I assure you that narrow sea makes room for a great deal of difference."

"Hey, Rabbit," said an urchin with a tattooed face

and falconer's cuffs on his wrists, "how 'bout we bugger this old *Arschloch* to death, then cook him up for dinner?"

"Truly, you're lads after my own heart," said Finn. "And I'll gladly offer you to partake of my flesh if you'll just answer me one question: What do you think of doctors?"

A Bronx cheer rang out in the forest.

Having established a bedrock of mutual hatred, the *Wilden* gradually warmed to Finn's proposition. And loath as they were to listen to a grown man, the sheer mayhem and luridness of what he described was irresistible. A mountain of smut? A hall of self-important doctors in their fancy suits? A stabbing orgy and rivers of blood? What more could a group of violent, wayward youth ask for?

"How about payment?" asked the chief they called Rabbit, which, according to Teutonian pronunciation, sounded like *Hrabeet*.

"What sounds fair to you boys?"

"A shitpile of money."

"How about a system of spoils?" proposed Finn. "The time-honored payment plan of warrior tribes the world over?"

"Go on," said Rabbit.

"Well, you can strip the bodies of every man we

kill. Mind you, lads, these are wealthy doctors we're talking about. Clothing, watches, rings, fillings, the money in their wallets—it's all yours. You could even take their scalps, if you like."

"And what about the smut?"

"What about it?"

"We want it."

"Oh, you mean the smut we give to the doctors? But of course—it's yours! I'd be happy to know it's getting put to use. Though it might be a bit bloody after all the slaying's said and done. Hope that's not a problem."

The boys laughed, as though smut without blood were an absurd idea.

"One more thing, *Alter*."

"Name it."

"Your hound comes with us."

Finn looked down at Sceolang, who had returned to Finn's side and was licking her wounded flank.

"Only on the condition that you treat her with decency. No beating, no rock-hurling, no buggering. Do I make myself clear?"

The chief called out to his tribe. "Any *Arschloch* lays a hand on this hound, I'll carve out his eyes. Understood?"

The boys submitted in silence.

"It's a deal, *Alter*," said the chief. He jumped from his log and brandished a knife. He sliced his palm with the blade and held it out to Finn.

Finn did the same, and in the ensuing bloodswap, with Irish humors flowing into the hearts of these feral orphans, a new band of Fenians was born. Finn gave a farewell scratch to Sceolang, who reluctantly took to her new master's side, and the makeshift Fianna dispersed into the woods. A great hunt was in the offing.

29

JOURNAL

January 18, 1944

One afternoon early in '42, while Churchill was threatening to commandeer Ireland's ports and Operation Osprey was still pending, Crean let slip that he and Pike were going to see a film that evening. I was shocked. "I thought you only saw films alone," I said to Pike.

"It's true, it's true. But a special dispensation has been granted on account of patriotic concerns."

The film was *Mein Leben für Irland*, a new Max Kimmich picture about Irish freedom fighters. Crean invited me to join them, but I sulkily declined.

"Oh, come on, Fluss. It'll be a lark. I was gonna ask you too. It's just that Crean here beat me to it. He's got a gob looser than a *sheela na gig* in heat."

Crean giggled, which summoned up for me the cries and shrieks of the *Waldhüter*'s Dungeon. I could no longer look at the man without a chill running down my spine.

Meanwhile, I let Pike's obscure Irish reference lie. I'd noticed he was in the habit of baiting his words with esoterica in hopes I would inquire, but I would not give him the satisfaction today.

"Finn and I are very curious how you Germans depict the Irish cause. But perhaps it will be less interesting for someone who has no pressing concern with our little island."

I sensed Crean was now trying to dissuade me, which of course decided it for me.

"It's true I don't know the first thing about Ireland, but I think I'll go all the same."

We agreed to meet at the Ufa-Palast am Zoo a half hour before the picture. I bought three tickets, then waited in the freezing foyer. I preferred the smaller cinemas to the grandiosity of the Palast. There was something unnervingly government-like about it now, with its imperial gray façade, dripping with swastikas, and the monumental imprint of Hitler's architect Speer. Of course, it had once been a beautiful Beaux Arts building. I had seen the premiere of Lang's *M* there. I'll never forget the convulsed face of Peter Lorre, five stories tall, as he confessed to his unquenchable thirst for murder.

Twenty minutes later, Pike and Crean lolled into view. They were already half-drunk and had brought a bottle of Val Kriegsmann's courtesy whiskey to help them along.

"Grotius, you punctual old sod!" said Pike, clapping me on the back. "Apologies for the delay."

I flashed him a look of alarm, but he didn't notice.

"Grotius?" said Crean. "Since when are you called Grotius?"

"Ah, you've never heard me call him that? When I first met Fluss, at that literary soiree at the embassy a couple of years back, well, you see, he happened to be in the library, thumbing through a volume of that prudent old jurist Grotius. So that's what I first called him."

Crean seemed to accept this impromptu lie, lame though it was, as we filed into the crowded theater.

"Let's sit in the balcony, like last time," said Crean.

So they had been to the cinema together before. What had he and Crean gotten up to in this dark corner? I was of course too embarrassed to say anything, but I noticed Pike didn't countenance the statement. At least he was embarrassed too. But I couldn't understand why he had lied to me. Was I really such a bore that a film couldn't be watched in my presence? Was my infatuation so obvious as to have become repellent?

The lights went down just in time to hide my wounded pride. Pike uncorked the whiskey and we passed it back and forth in tempo with the rousing march of the newsreel. German citizens were donating warm garments to ship to our soldiers who'd been sent east in only their summer wear. A long pan across colossal piles of clothing, a testament to the *Volk*'s heroic sacrifice. Cut to images of train cars filled to capacity with a million Germans' socks and shoes, which, in the denouement, are received by our cheerful troops amid the snowdrifts of central Russia.

The next newsreel brought us closer to the evening's subject: American troops had arrived in Northern Ireland. De Valera had come out denouncing the arrival of foreign troops on Irish soil. Rumors were circulating that an Anglo-American invasion of Ireland could happen any minute. There was Churchill, scowling through his cigar, ready to crush freedom-loving Ireland to slake his imperial lust.

Pike and Crean hissed, though no one else in the audience showed any reaction. We Germans were stockpiling our emotions for an undetermined future.

"Looks like your chance will come soon," I whispered to Pike.

"You'll forgive me if I don't hold my breath," he said.

My Life for Ireland turned out to be an uncanny film. An Irish freedom fighter is sentenced to death for an uprising against his cruel English masters. Sixteen years later, his son has been sent to a British boarding school, which rams colonial ideology down the throats of its wildly handsome pupils. The son befriends a boy who unwittingly betrays him out of jealousy but makes amends by becoming a double agent and heroic martyr for Irish freedom. It is a story of male friendship, patriotic sacrifice, and resistance to cruel and arbitrary authority.

At first, Pike watched the film with sarcastic glee, laughing and wisecracking at the fog-shrouded backlot heath that was supposed to be Dublin and the bowler-hatted, Churchillian landlord who looked more like the fat member of Laurel and Hardy. After British soldiers ransacked the home of a good Irish peasant woman and beat her son, he and Crean were the only ones who cheered as she screwed up her face and shouted, *"Gott strafe England!"* When the English spy explained why he hadn't been able to infiltrate the Irish student circle, claiming, "The Irish stick together like ticks on a dog," Crean translated, and Pike roared and slapped the seat in front of him.

"To the camaraderie of vermin!" he shouted, raising his bottle.

The seat's occupant turned and hissed, "Can't you behave like a civilized person, you swine!"

This only made the two of them laugh more, until the filmgoer threatened to call the police.

But gradually, thanks to me, the story absorbed him. While Pike's German was functional at this point, he still had trouble hearing. So I began whispering translations in his ear a good second faster than Crean could sputter out his. I could tell Crean was trying to beat me, but he was no match for me in terms of speed, to say nothing of his clear inferiority in artfulness. I also had Pike's better, right ear—something I orchestrated when we'd taken our seats. After a few minutes of dueling whispers, Pike, who was receiving a barrage in both ears, shouted, "For the love of Christ, would you two stop? I can't understand a damn thing if you both do it. Crean, let Fluss have it. After all, the man's a professional."

Now, with my voice playing in his head, and my own head swollen with the pride of victory and resting on his shoulder, the story onscreen became an intimate, serious affair.

The Irish prisoners awaiting execution:

"What if it was all for nothing?"

"A sacrifice is never in vain."

The Irish heroine to the spy she is sheltering in her home:

"This is not a real life."

"We are doing this for Ireland."

The new student Patrick, a sensitive, spirited boy, to the charismatic star of the rugby team, Michael:

"Why don't you like me? What have I done to make you not like me?"

I leaned into Pike—the closest I had been in well over a year, my tongue within reach of him—and whispered the story of Patrick and Michael's friendship. United, then torn apart through political forces beyond their control but that ultimately give their lives meaning. Amid rugby matches where the boys sported black-and-white-striped uniforms like concentration-camp inmates, amid shirtless locker room fistfights, amid heartfelt discussions on the nature of friendship in a brazenly homoerotic communal-shower scene. I whispered to Pike as young Patrick fell in love with his schoolmate's mother, as the bespectacled English spy got Patrick to betray the freedom fighter hiding in the mother's house, as Patrick apologized to the rebel and regained his trust by becoming a double agent.

The director Kimmich had fulfilled the Propaganda Ministry's demands to vilify the British, but he had done so in the most subversive way. He had made the British appear German. The audience felt an instinctive hatred for the stiff, authoritarian bureaucrats who ruled their colonies with an iron fist and a smug sense of racial superiority. This would have been amplified for a native English speaker like Pike, to see these supposed British imperialists barking in German. To drive home the comparison of England to contemporary Germany, Kimmich made the school's official graduation ceremony, the moment the young Irish lads are inducted into "behaving like British citizens," consist of burning all their books in a huge bonfire. But instead of obeying the command to destroy, the students abandon the book pyre for the machine-gun turrets they have secretly stationed around the headmaster. The revolt has begun.

As a propaganda effort to turn public sentiment against England, *My Life for Ireland* struck me as a grave misstep. When the lights came on, Pike turned to me. He had been silent for the last hour of the film. "Well, I don't know about you, Grotius, but I have a terrible yen to go mow down some Nazis."

January 19, 1944

Shortly after the Irish film came out, it seemed Operation Osprey might actually happen.

Pike was authorized to choose two men from the prison camp to be trained in preparation for the mission. He tapped a Londonderry schoolteacher named Codd and an Irish mason from Glasgow named McMannis. Codd seemed a thoughtful if taciturn young man, while McMannis was a cheery salt-of-the-earth type whose accent made him all but impossible to understand. We took them from Luckenwalde and brought them back to Nymphenburger Straße, where they were to stay the night. The next morning, I would shepherd them to their demolitions camp in Wiesbaden.

I looked forward to a pleasant evening with Pike and our liberated guests and not a trace of Archibald Crean. Pike had telephoned him to say he was "laid up with the lurgy" and that Crean was not to come around for a few days. Frau Obolensky trebled her cooking and a steady stream of complaint to go with it. Everything seemed on course for an enjoyable dinner party.

But no sooner had Frau Obolensky set the *pelmeni* on the table than a rowdiness erupted among the Irishmen and the night set off toward disaster.

"Meat!" cried McMannis, spearing a half dozen dumplings with his fork.

"And a bit of the *hausgemacht* to wash it down," said Pike, producing a bottle of schnapps.

Here the schoolteacher Codd's eyes swirled in his head as he leapt out of his chair for a drink.

The Stalag, I soon learned, had denied the POWs all but the scantest rations of small beer and only on Sundays. Codd's apparent mild-mannered disposition was really the vegetative state of a dried-out drunk.

The Irishmen plundered the table, devouring the *pelmeni*, slurping up the borscht, and wolfing down the Russian salad while ersatz mayonnaise ran down their chins. All the while Pike laid on bottle after bottle of schnapps, half of which went down the schoolmaster's gullet.

I sensed that the evening could spiral out of control and told Pike to make this bottle the last before bed.

"Aw, Grotius, be a mensch and let the boys have their divilment. There's no harm to come from a sup or two round the table. Isn't that right, old girl?" he said to Frau Obolensky, giving her a playful tug on the ear.

She swatted Pike's hand away. Though she wrinkled her nose at the guests' barbaric table manners and drunkenness, she was clearly touched they had taken a shine to her cooking. Compared to prison gruel, I suppose, it was an improvement.

But the housekeeper's adoring attitude changed when McMannis spied her thick ball of knitting yarn beside the divan.

"Fancy a bit of footy, then, lads?" he shouted, as he kicked the ball over the furniture to Codd, who nearly upended a table trying to receive it with his chest.

Frau Obolensky turned the color of her borscht and went after the ruffians with a table knife. Codd and McMannis made for the door and kicked the yarn ball out into the street.

I followed them, demanding they come back indoors. This was a mistake, as the game immediately became piggy in the middle, with me as the oinking pariah. Painful schoolyard memories surged within me.

"You'll have to be quicker than that, Grotius!" said Pike, who had just joined the fun, as he flicked the ball over my head to the giggling Glaswegian.

"Enough of this!" I shouted, limping after it. Had Pike, in his drunkenness, forgotten about my condition? Or was he purposefully being cruel?

Codd ran into a neighboring yard to field McMannis's pass, but it was intercepted by the block warden, Herr Eich.

Herr Eich was not only responsible for all residents' compliance with blackout regulations; he also reported any suspicious activity. Foreign houseguests, drunken horseplay in the street, the shouting of English—any of these alone would set off sirens in Herr Eich's mind. All three signified a true state of emergency.

"*Das geht gar nicht!*" he shouted, crushing Frau Obolensky's yarn ball underfoot.

"My apologies, Herr Eich," I said. "A childish bit of fun. We didn't mean to disturb you."

"You have disturbed the peace of the entire block. You may not realize it, Herr Fluss, but most of the residents here have important jobs they must rise early for. They do not have the luxury of carousing at ten-thirty on a Tuesday night!"

Nymphenburger Straße was a quiet residential block, mostly private homes inhabited by lawyers, civil servants, pharmaceutical executives, and the like. Our house was registered under the Reich Chamber of Culture as housing for visiting scholars and cultural laborers. But Herr Eich, who had been a vacuum salesman for thirty-two years before his sciatica forced him into retirement, had little esteem for these effete occupations. He regarded me as a deplorable bohemian. And as for the foreign inhabitants, he suspected—more or less correctly—they were all spies.

"Who are these screaming foreigners?"

"Oh, come now, Herr Eich. Don't you recognize me?" asked Pike.

"You, yes," said Eich, "but not these others. Who are they?"

"Just some dinner guests," I said. "They will be gone in the morning."

"Then you won't mind showing me their papers."

Of course, the man had no authority to demand anyone's papers, but if one refused him, then he would have well-founded suspicions, which he would report to the Gestapo. The problem was that the men had no papers with them. They were still at the office. I had planned to retrieve them in the morning, having assumed Codd and McMannis would only eat dinner, then go to sleep. I now realized I had been negligent. If the men were arrested, a bureaucratic ordeal would ensue, exposing us to further scrutiny.

"Is that really necessary, Herr Eich?" I asked.

"Why? Are you hiding something, Herr Fluss?"

"Of course not," I said. "And I resent your line of questioning."

Codd and McMannis were now tussling in the street, laughing as they swiped at each other's legs.

Herr Eich stood scowling. "Even foreigners should know to respect the rules of the country that takes them in."

"Sage advice, Herr Eich," said Pike. "But try telling that to a couple of ignorant gobshites like these ones here. Why, they'd doggie-pile the Führer himself if he were here and give him a Dutch rub to boot. Wouldn't you, you maniacs?" he called out to the Irishmen.

Fortunately, Herr Eich had no grasp of Pike's English. But he had heard the word "Führer" uttered and, coupled with the jesting tone, took it to be seditious. "I have a good mind . . ." he said, but before he could finish his thought, Codd and McMannis suddenly trampled him.

They had tried to tackle Pike but missed, flattening Herr Eich instead. To this day I still wonder whether Pike sensed my predicament and intentionally baited his compatriots into incapacitating the block warden or whether it was just a drunken accident. That was his ambiguous way—only moments before I had thought he was taunting me, and now it seemed he'd come to my rescue.

"My back!" cried the block warden, frozen in a prone position in the yard. The assault had ignited his sciatica. Pike and the others carried him into his house, where they laid him on the sofa with a glass of water nearby and the telephone safely out of reach. At least he would not be able to file a complaint until well after our two guests were gone.

While this solved our immediate problem, it was not without repercussions.

January 20, 1944

I've just learned James von Moltke has been arrested. The Gestapo penetrated another resistance circle—a group run out of the home of the widow Solf. Dozens in custody. Unclear what James's connection is or what his Christian group in Kreisau has to do with it. Terrifying.

Everyone at work is on pins and needles. Himmler's guillotine hangs over us. What will people say under torture? Whose names will fall from those broken mouths?

30
Finn McCool in the Bowels of Teutonia

A Heist

After learning Finn had given up the wind hound, Obelinka stopped speaking to him.

She stopped cooking too, which was meant to be an added punishment, though Finn was quite happy to receive a bit of bread and margarine and a cup of dandelion tea in place of the congealed Russian casseroles that contained God knows what. But he was sorry to have made her sad. They had developed a bond, she and he. As two refugees in a sea of Teutonians, they had grown accustomed to taking refuge in each other. He by making her laugh, she by mothering him. Ever since the Bretonese had left— packed off to Frankenland for a bit of subterfuge, said the Torqued Man—Obelinka and Finn had settled into the domestic tranquility of an aging couple. Tea and books in the morning, lunch and a postprandial nap together, followed by more tea and visitors in the afternoon. He rather enjoyed playing the part.

But during the great Ruslandish silence, the house felt icy. She would not laugh at his jokes or respond to the pinches of her behind. She banged his tea down in front of him and retreated wordlessly to the kitchen. Finn promised Obelinka he would make it up to her.

An opportunity soon arose through his official duties. Pleasant as it was to lark about with the Fenian soldiers on his visits to the prison camp, he'd already formed his Fianna with the *Wilden* of the Grunewald. And he had long made up his mind not to return to Erin before his business here was done. Yet the camp at Luckenwalde, if you squinted your linguistic faculties, sounded like the Teutonian for "Lucky Forest." Surely, there was some good fortune that could be squeezed from this auspicious-sounding place.

That good fortune, he soon discovered, went on four legs and answered to the name Olaf. Olaf was the camp warden's prized Jagdterrier. Though not nearly as sleek or as elegant as Dr. Brandt's wind hound, he was a bright and happy little beast with a great passion for killing rats. He also had a coat like a cozy wool sweater and eyes that made one smile even in a prison camp. Finn knew Obelinka would be smitten.

He selected two Fenian prisoners not for their ability to sabotage or fight off invading Anglelanders but for the simple fact that they were assigned to the camp warden's yard every afternoon to pick up Olaf's evacuations. Finn promised them liberation from the Lucky Forest and a night of mad carousal in exchange for the theft of the hound.

The Fenians carried off the heist in fine style. On the day the Torqued Man was to remove them from camp, they lured Olaf out of his wee house on the lawn with a sedative-laden *Bockwurst* from Obelinka's larder. They then wrapped him in a protective bedsheet and stuffed him in the sack of his own droppings, which they deposited in the refuse bin, as usual, under the watchful eye of the guards. This left only ten minutes, it was wagered, for Finn to come to the bin with a crate of freshly emptied Fanta bottles—which he'd conveniently brought for the lads to enjoy—collect the hound from the bin, and transfer him to the boot of the Torqued Man's car before he expired.

It was a close call. When Finn unwrapped the sheet, little Olaf lay inert. The light had gone out of his eyes. He worried the Luminal tablet he'd given him had been too powerful. But at the smell of a new sausage—this one laced with Pervitin—the hound soon revivified.

Finn stuffed the now boisterous Olaf into his sweater, buttoned his coat, and proceeded to slip link after link down his collar to keep him pacified. On the ride home, he insisted on abdicating the front seat to his fellow Fenians to let them better take in the view of their newfound freedom and passed around chewing gum to everyone to drown out the masticatory sounds coming from within his coat.

Once safely at home in the Nymphenburg, Finn instructed the Fenians to create a distraction to lure the Torqued Man out of the house for a moment so he could present his peace offering to Obelinka. The drunken sleeveens spilled into the street with a makeshift football and sent the Torqued Man running in twisted loops, while Finn unveiled the Jagdterrier.

A tear came to Obelinka's eye as she hugged the handsome little hound to her face.

"He stink," she said.

Finn beamed. They were again on speaking terms.

31

JOURNAL

January 21, 1944

The prospect of an Anglo-American invasion of Ireland faded that spring of '42, and with it any hope of Pike's imminent deployment. Operation Osprey was abandoned, like all the others. I don't know what became of Codd and McMannis after I dropped them off in Wiesbaden; they were likely remanded to another POW camp in Hessen. But Pike showed little interest in any of it. A new restlessness had crept into him. And not just the kind that caused him to go wandering the streets at night and dipping his wick in anything resembling a hole.

I called on him one evening in June, on the first genuinely hot day of the year. Pike was looking mournfully at his tea, with a black bread and margarine so synthetic it glowed. I could hear Frau Obolensky in the kitchen, fawning over her new dog. Presumably the other one had run off in search of a decent meal. I was surprised to see Crean wasn't there.

"He's caught a bad dose of the erysipelas," said Pike.

I suppressed a cry of joy at this news, then, feeling like celebrating, suggested we have dinner at the Ratskeller. We hadn't been there together in ages. "Come on," I said, "it'll be just like the good old days."

Pike humored me, even though I could tell he wasn't in the mood. He claimed to have been working on a novel—a crime thriller of sorts—that was taking its toll. I told him I should like to read it, but he was very secretive about it. He said chefs don't let diners finger the pudding while it's still in the oven, and writing should be no different. I was skeptical how much he was actually writing, since the heavy bags under his jaundiced eyes told me what he had really been up to, no doubt in the company of Crean. He now looked like most Berliners I saw every day on the U-Bahn, a death-mask grimness guarding over immense anxiety and a swollen liver.

I, however, was in an ebullient mood. Not only was Crean absent and nursing a skin infection; word had come from Prague that Heydrich was dead. He'd been shot by the Czech resistance and, in a fitting bit of poetic justice, died only after refusing to be operated on by non-Aryans. A man of principle to the end. How distraught Himmler must have been to lose his hulking protégé.

Tucked into our usual booth, I raised my glass to Pike and, in a whisper, to the wily Czechs who had had the nerve to shoot their Aryan overlord. Pike had already begun drinking and half-heartedly pulled his glass from his lips.

"One Nazi arsehole dead and Lord knows how many hundreds of reprisals there'll be. Not sure that's a calculus worthy of a toast," said Pike.

Pike was of course right, which was why acts of resistance were foolhardy. And while I knew the revenge on the Czechs would be brutal, I still couldn't imagine that only a week later they would obliterate an entire village. "All the same," I said, "I'm glad he's dead."

"Now, now, Grotius, where are your Christian morals?" he asked, mock offended.

"Perhaps Old Testament justice is more fitting for our age," I said.

We drifted into a silence that had become characteristic of our conversations of late. Pike could still wax voluble, but there were now bouts of brooding. Did he do this, I wondered, with Crean? I also wondered if he knew anything of Crean's ghastly hobbies. Surely he would have been horrified by them. But I never did bring it up, perhaps on the remote chance that he not only knew of Crean's interests but shared them.

I scanned the room for potential eavesdroppers and unannounced guests, as had become my habit. I was grateful I hadn't seen Egon again, where I would have had to witness his further humiliation of appearing in public with that repellent badge. Though I feared what had become of him. The deportations of Berlin's Jews had already begun.

"Well, I don't suppose this will come as a shock," I said, breaking the silence, "but I'm afraid there won't be any more visits to Luckenwalde."

"Figures," he said absently.

"But that doesn't mean we've closed up shop just yet," I said. "I have it on good word that Canaris will—"

"Say, remember how young Patrick redeems himself by becoming a double agent, letting the English think he's their man and the Irish all think he's a traitor, but in reality it's his betrayal that allows the uprising to come off?"

It took me a moment to realize he was referring to the film from months ago. "Yes. Vaguely," I replied. "Just how many times have you seen it?"

"Oh, about a dozen now," said Pike. "But isn't that a dazzling thought? The sheer dialectic of it. The initial betrayal opens up a path for greater loyalty."

"You mean insofar as it applies to your case?"

Pike laughed. "My case? You know good and well I'm under strict orders to spend my days wearing out the couch cushions with my arsecheeks. But I've been thinking about what it means to be a real spy. Would you like me to bend your ear on the matter?"

"Please do."

Pike gave himself over to a brief coughing fit, then launched into it. "The thesis is this: espionage as an enchantment of the mundane. The spy takes on a new and dangerous life that is meant to look exactly like the banal one we all live. But behind this banality lies the spy's mission, the reality behind the veil of appearance. This gives occult purpose to the purchasing of eggs, the shining of shoes, the riding of trains—all those *sordid perils of actual existence*. The spy leavens these with the profundity of his choice. That German importer emptying his bowels in a Mexico City toilet? He is in fact making magic. That attentive waiter rolling napkins in Fez—staking his claim on the future. That journalist buying dish soap in Lisbon—taking a stand to say, 'I will that the world go this way and not that way.' They are all re-enchanting the world for themselves, investing the day-to-day drudgeries with meaning."

I gave him a puzzled look.

"What I'm saying, Grotius, is that the spy is an agent in the truest sense of the word. All of his actions, down to the trimming of toenails and riding the trolley, are shot through with the meaning of having chosen. He wills the universal through the particular."

"Well?" he asked after a pause. "What do you think?"

"I think you've seen that silly film about ten too many times," I said. To be honest, all I had remembered of it were the showering youths, but I was quite certain there was no Kierkegaard in it.

"Don't let the metaphysics get in your way. All I'm saying is, a great betrayal is an opportunity. An opportunity to make another, even greater choice. To become an agent on a higher order of magnitude. And that, Grotius, bears consideration." He swallowed the rest of his beer.

"Look, Pike, I'm not sure what you're driving at, but I think it wisest if you concentrate on remaining as comfortable as you can here." I gestured at our surroundings. "For starters, we have the cozy Ratskeller, with its horsemeat *Jägerschnitzel*, sawdust dumplings, and watered-down pilsner. You have your brothels and whatever else in that department I dare not ask." The *Waldhüter*'s rack flashed again before my eyes. "And perhaps I can petition Lauhusen for you to continue visiting the men in Luckenwalde, even without the mission. You never know, things could change again. After all, it's a war."

"Oh, come off it, man. As far as Germany is concerned, Ireland has gone back to being the land of kobolds and fairies. It might as well be on a different planet."

"Well then, why don't you think of this window as an ideal time to write? Concentrate on that story of yours."

He shrugged. "I'm rather busy fulfilling my destiny as an ailing tosspot."

I realized that, despite my encouragements, we had put Pike in an impossible position. He was not a spy. Not so long as he was stuck here in Berlin. And yet he was embroiled in all the pretenses of those who find themselves living in a foreign land with ulterior motives. Unlike a spy, however, his daily actions had no greater meaning. Instead, he was perpetually waiting—the most uncomfortable of existential states. We had sustained him with just enough hope of going home that he couldn't devote himself to anything else, and now that hope was dying.

January 22, 1944

Well, it's official. I'm bombed out. The flat in Schöneberg is a pile of rocks. All my possessions—vanished. Whatever survived the blast is either buried under tons of rubble or taken by looters.

Only the books cause me pain. Grief, really. Who am I without my books? They were my evidence of an inner life, my holds on a better world. Without them, what am I? A cog in this vast machine of death. A lonely creature in a basement.

Pike was also a lifeline for me, similar to my books. Now both are gone. And all I have left is this. These thoughts made flesh.

By the fall, the Irish situation had fully deteriorated. Even if the chance of a British invasion of Ireland were to reappear, IRA attacks on military posts in the north had further deepened the rift between them and De Valera's government, which was precisely the gap we had hoped Pike could plug. My daily duties at HQ were now filled with business from the eastern front—managing a flood of Ukrainian and White Russian anti-communists who were being groomed to raise hell behind enemy lines—as well as a contingent of Boers we hoped to deposit in South Africa with half a ton of gelignite. While most of my work consisted of getting papers in order and securing housing for these new agents, the few I dealt with in person were gruff and given to complaint. Even in Pike's increasingly morose and besotted states, I still preferred his company. I would have taken him on his worst day, with no hope for anything more than his presence.

My dealings with Ireland had dwindled to a monthly briefing. Veesenmayer remained in Zagreb for the year, Kriegsmann was off on missions in North Africa, and Lauhusen remained obscured behind an ever-thickening fog of opiates. The latter had taken to calling me "youngster," which made me suspect he had forgotten my name.

But when I walked into Lauhusen's office for my October meeting, Veesenmayer was occupying his desk.

"There you are," he snarled. "Alright, let's make this quick."

"Where's Lauhusen?" I asked.

"He's dead."

"Dead?"

"As in not living, Grotius. The silly idiot overdosed on his pills," he said, swiveling in the dead man's chair. "Here's another piece of news for you: The Ireland unit is officially closed. That means Pike is finished."

A smile had broken out across his face.

"What do you mean, finished?" I asked.

"Finished is finished. Terminated. He is officially of no use to us, which means he's a liability."

"That's preposterous," I said.

"Irish neutrality is a given. De Valera wants it as much as we do. As hard as you may find it to believe, that neutrality is not contingent upon us paying Pike's room and board here in Berlin. The man is a parasite."

"But—"

"What's more, he's a threat to public safety. Did you honestly think I wouldn't catch wind of his criminal activities?"

"Criminal activities?" I said, genuinely perplexed. Was he referring to Pike's black-market purchases or brothel visits?

"What illness are you suffering from, Sonderführer, that makes you repeat every word I say in the form of a question? Or don't you know that assaulting a gendarme is a punishable offense? I understand poor Herr Eich was mowed down by Pike and his goons right outside his own home."

"Oh, that. It was a block warden, not a gendarme. And it was an accident. Pike didn't even touch the man."

"I'm not inviting you to a conversation on the matter," said Veesenmayer. "You will deal with Pike just as you dealt with the Bretons."

"But . . ." I protested, the alarm showing on my face.

"I want him in Sachsenhausen tomorrow, and I want you to deliver him. Failure to do so will be interpreted as an act of insubordination. Now, thank you, Sonderführer, that is all!"

I saluted with as much contempt as the gesture would accommodate and stormed out of his office.

I had feared this day would come. Operationally speaking, Pike had stopped being useful months ago. But why, I wondered, had Canaris just now relinquished his support? Was it really over that stupid incident with the block warden? I couldn't help but suspect that Veesenmayer, without consulting the admiral, had issued the directive himself.

Not twenty minutes later, I found myself on the top floor in a grand mahogany vestibule, standing before Canaris's secretary. I'd worked in the building for more than two years by then but had never had the occasion, or the nerve, to set foot in the fox's lair. Not since Madrid had I even glimpsed the man himself.

"I know this is highly unorthodox," I said to the athletic-looking young man behind the desk, "but is the admiral in?"

"And who might you be?" he asked.

"Sonderführer Adrian de Groot, Branch II, formerly

of the Kriegsorganisation Madrid. The admiral knows me. Please, I need only a few minutes of his time."

"I'm sorry," said the secretary, "but the admiral does not have any visitors scheduled."

I was about to grovel before the man, when the door to the office swung open and out ran a Dachshund. I heard Canaris bellow, in one of those odd voices that humans reserve for pets and babies, "Mitzi, come back here, you cunning little rascal, you. Keyserling, quick, Mitzi's gone rogue!"

The secretary popped up to scan the corridor for Mitzi, but I had already seen her scuttle down the hallway and, seizing my opportunity, tore after the beast.

I caught her by the stairwell and toted her back as she yelped and writhed in protest. The secretary came down the hallway to intercept her, but I elbowed him aside, Mitzi nipping at his hands, and marched hound-first into Canaris's office.

It was just like the rumors I had heard. Books from floor to ceiling. A Peruvian rug. A Landsknecht arquebus with a beautifully carved stock and intricate silver-work. A woodblock print of an ancient samurai. A huge oil portrait of Franco. A photo of Canaris and Miguel Primo de Rivera in hunting clothes. A Humboldt watercolor map of South America—where, during the last war, Canaris had, legend had it, escaped from an island prison off the coast of Chile, ridden a stolen horse three hundred miles over the Andes, hopped a train across the pampa to Buenos Aires, where he boarded a Dutch steamer under a false Chilean passport bearing the name Reed Rosas, and was, less than three months after being captured, back at his desk in Berlin. In the entire office, there was not a single sign of Nazi officialdom. No swastikas, no Hitler, nothing. Here was a man who was fighting a different war.

"Look, Mutzi! There's our Mitzi Witzi!" said the admiral, holding his other hound like an infant.

He was wearing a louche smoking jacket and leather slippers. I had never seen the man in uniform. He'd aged considerably in the last few years but still possessed a dignified air. Beside him on the desk was Kantorowicz's biography of Frederick II.

Seeing that the face behind Mitzi was not his secretary's, he quickly recovered his normal voice. "Oh! It looks like Mitzi has made a new friend."

"Indeed, Herr Admiral. I just happened to be in the area when she leapt into my arms."

He took Mitzi from me with his hound-free hand and studied my face. I could tell he was straining to place me in his memory.

"Forgive me, Herr Admiral. My name is Adrian de Groot, formerly of the Madrid KO. We've met briefly before."

"De Groot? Of course, of course. The translator with the Dutchman's name. One of Leissner's crack team, right?"

"Exactly, sir."

"Tell me, De Groot. Have you read Lugones yet?"

I was stunned he remembered. It was the Argentine writer he'd asked me about years ago. Thank God I had read him since. "Why, yes, sir. In fact, I have. *Las fuerzas extrañas*."

"And?"

"And you were right, sir. A true master. I particularly admired the one about the gardener who breeds killer plants."

"Good man, De Groot. But now you're here in Berlin, yes?"

He had the habit of addressing everyone informally, with *Du*. I recalled how disarming I had found it upon first meeting him and found it to be equally so now. I immediately felt like the old man's school chum.

"Yes, sir. I've been tending to our sabotage agents awaiting deployment. And, well, sir, one section in particular, the Irish, has just been shut down."

"Ah yes, damn shame, that. Never could get the right angle with the Irish. And poor Lauhusen. He deserved better."

"Yes, sir. My condolences. I . . ." I tried to think of something elegiac to say, but Canaris was already past it.

"Of course, if that damn fool Hitler would have kept out of this infernal Russia business, things might have been different. It's the end of the cycle, De Groot—the Iron Age, as Spengler calls it. The great unraveling."

I knew Canaris was an independent operator but was nonetheless shocked to hear Hitler disparaged in such open terms.

"Well, what's on your mind?" said Canaris, as if just remembering I was still there.

"Sir, it's about how we . . . *decommission* the agents once a cell has been deactivated. After all, they have agreed to work for us. It doesn't seem . . . well, fair that when their contract ends, we then treat them like criminals."

"Yes, I quite agree with you there, De Groot. Modern war's a rotten business. Not like in the days of Stupor Mundi," he said, tapping the book on his desk, "when there was still some honor to it. Himmler, Schellenberg, Kaltenbrunner—all those bloodlusting bureaucrats at the Security Office wouldn't know a code of honor if it slapped them in the face. Well, let me tell you, De Groot. They won't have the final word. They think they pull the strings on this show, but soon they'll see that I still have a sharp pair of scissors."

"Does that mean, sir, you can override the remand order?" I asked, suddenly buoyed with hope.

"No, not a chance of that, I'm afraid. Security Service is calling the shots now on foreign agents in the Reich. If you want decency these days, De Groot, you have to go beyond our borders. Age of Iron, indeed."

I had thought Canaris had magic powers, but it turned out he, too, was just another cog in the machine. For all his maverick eccentricity and hostility toward Hitler, he was, when it came down to it, the same as the rest of us. Clinging to his Kantorowicz in inner exile, all while helping to create the terrible reality he claimed not to condone. I remember thinking as I walked home that you could replace the old knight Canaris with a modern fanatic like Heydrich or Schellenberg and nothing would really change. No sooner had the thought passed through my mind than, like the lightning bolt that knocked Luther from his horse, the revelation struck me: *You could also replace Pike with someone else.*

And that is when, for the first time, the name Archibald Crean entered my mind and made me smile.

I pulled up to Crean's flat in Kreuzberg early the next morning. I had been here once before, the first time I trailed him.

I left the auto idling and rang the buzzer. It was a second-floor flat on a tree-lined street near the Görlitzer Bahnhof. He lived alone and seemed not to have much intercourse with his neighbors.

Crean buzzed me in and was at the door in trousers and a thick robe when I came up the stairs.

"Fluss! What a pleasant surprise," he said unconvincingly.

I adopted the air of someone frantic but trying to remain calm, which was rather natural considering the circumstances. "Crean, I'm terribly sorry to barge in on you like this, and at such an early hour. But I'm afraid it's about Frank."

"What happened?" he said, alarmed. Thankfully his worry had prevented him from asking how I knew where he lived.

"He's still alive, but our friend was struck by a car last night."

"Last night? But I was with him. When? Where?"

Of course he was with him. "It was late, possibly early morning, right outside his door. The motorist struck him and drove on."

"The bastard!"

"I only just heard from the hospital this morning. They say he'll recover, but he took quite a knocking all the same."

"Oh, thank God."

"I thought maybe you'd like to accompany me to the hospital. They moved him to one outside town. But I have my auto out front and am on my way to see him."

"Of course. Just give me a moment to fetch my shoes and coat. Here, won't you come in."

I entered his apartment and stood in the foyer while Crean went to the bedroom to dress. I noticed his overcoat hanging on the rack beside me. I checked his breast pocket and, as luck would have it, found his identity card. Here was the riskiest moment of my plan, and it had fallen right into my lap. Hearing him still padding in the bedroom, I swapped his pass and replaced it with the one I had hastily forged the night before—the skills from my Madrid days were rusty but still functional. Now I could only hope that he didn't check for his papers before we arrived.

Crean came out of the room dressed and reached

across me for his coat and hat. I watched as he fastened his buttons and patted his pockets.

"Have everything?" I asked.

"My cigarettes," he said, annoyed with himself.

"No matter, we can share mine. I ought to cut back anyway."

"Cheers, Fluss."

Off we went, past two hospitals, and out of the city to the north. After we had driven for a good thirty minutes, Crean began to get restless.

"Why in Christ's name did they move him so far?"

"I don't understand it either. Something about needing a kidney specialist."

"Kidney specialist? I thought you said he would be alright."

"Well, that's what they said. I suppose that's because they brought him to the kidney specialist."

"How did he go and get himself run down by a bloody car? There's not a soul on the street that time of night in his neighborhood. It makes no sense."

"I know. But you know how dark it is in the dead of night with the blackout. All it takes is one drunk or negligent motorist. Had the two of you been out late drinking?"

"Not particularly. Just our usual haunt for a few wee pints of the cat piss."

Both Crean and Pike thumbed their noses at our lighter German beers and waxed nostalgic for their beloved stouts, all the while swilling down vast quantities of the derisively labeled "cat piss." When I told them we, too, had dark beer in Germany, in the many varieties of *Dunkles* and *Schwarzbier*, Pike had said, "Oh, you mean black cat piss? Why, your rudest Jerry dark couldn't tie the shoes of the plainest of porters."

This was the first time I had been alone with Crean, at least with him being aware of it. "If you don't mind my asking," I said, "what is it you and Frank get up to on your outings together?"

"Up to? Nothing. A few pints, a few laughs, that's all. Why?"

"Oh, nothing," I said. We were drawing near Oranienburg. I could make out the watchtower and smokestacks in the distance. "It's just that I've never understood why he preferred your company to mine."

"I don't know what you mean, Fluss," he said, with evident discomfort.

"At first I thought it was because he was embarrassed by my affection for him. But it's clear you're in love with him too."

"In love with him? Look, Fluss, I'm afraid you've jumped the rails. I don't know what in the world—"

"I really don't mind. He's an extraordinary man.

But I want you to understand that I'm not doing this out of jealousy. I'm doing this for him."

"Doing what?" said Crean as we approached the gates of Sachsenhausen, emblazoned with a sinister wisdom about the liberating powers of work.

"*Arbeit macht frei?*" said Crean, reading the iron letters. "Say, what kind of hospital is this?"

Two armed sentries approached the car.

I rolled down the window as the guard *heil-Hitlered* me. I gave him my credentials and Pike's internment papers.

"Is this the prisoner, Herr Sonderführer?" he asked, pointing uncertainly at Crean in the front seat.

"Of course it is," I said, like he was an idiot for even asking.

"Prisoner? What in the bloody hell is going on?" asked Crean.

The guard saluted and waved me through. I drove past the watchtower into the vast triangular camp-grounds, with Crean now in a panic.

Two more guards brought me to a stop at the Appellplatz. Three gaunt, bald prisoners were on the roll-call line, frozen in a squat with their arms stretched painfully in front of them. When I got out of the car, I noticed them looking at me and muttering. Then they began to yell unintelligible curses.

Looking again, I realized these living ghosts were the very same Bretons, Pike's former housemates, that I had delivered here over a year ago. Seeing the wrecks they had become—a wreckage I played a hand in, and an evil no amount of cynicism could conceal—I felt something within me break. I had done this to them.

But in that moment it was only an inchoate feeling, and there wasn't time to dwell on my guilt. Crean was screaming about the mistake that had been made as the guards dragged him from the car. He kept demanding they look at his identity pass. The guard snatched the pass from him, examined it, and smiled.

"Alles in Ordnung, Herr Finn."

Crean looked my way, and a flicker of understanding passed across his face.

32

Finn McCool in the Bowels of Teutonia

Hibernation

And this was how Finn was unmanned and slept through his long-dreamed-of doctors' appointment.

The leaves of Berlin died on the trees and the Doctors' League Dinner loomed. Finn had arranged for a great inventory of smut to be supplied by Crean shortly beforehand. Per their routine, they would make their broadcasts, then repair to the Pickled Herring to drink their pints and deal in *Dreck*.

But when Finn arrived at the Funkhaus, instead of seeing Crean in the booth, he saw Patrick Cadogan, the irritating Irish persona of the even more irritating Billy Joyce, sharing the microphone with Rosaleen Lynch as they sang a risible duet of "Londonderry Air."

When the broadcast ended, Joyce emerged from the booth in his usual obnoxious manner, slapping the backs of all misfortunate enough to be in the station. Despite claiming an Anglo-Irish pedigree, he was at heart a phony American. His voice was an adenoidal whine, and his attempt at a brogue was something like an English foxhunter imitating a Bowery Boy.

"Your man Crean was a no-show, Finny," said Joyce, as he socked Finn on the shoulder [thickly sinewed as a medicine ball].

Rosaleen Lynch came out of the booth in tears. "Oh, Finn, it's terrible. I think Archie's been arrested." She buried her head in his chest, and Finn got a noseful of harsh chemicals swirling up from her red coif.

"Arrested? How do you know?"

"We were supposed to walk together to the station today, but when I turned onto his street, I saw him being ushered into a black motor car."

"Ushered by whom?"

"It was that clubfoot friend of yours, the one who came here to the station. Archie said he thought he was a spy."

Finn said he would look into the matter, that he was sure there was nothing nefarious about it, and for Rosaleen not to worry.

"I'm a mess, an utter mess, I tell you. I don't want to go home alone tonight, Finn. Will you come with me?"

He needed to find Crean and, more important, Crean's smut. But, gallant by nature, he agreed to escort her.

Rosaleen lived in an elegant flat in Mitte and invited him in. She put on the kettle while he listened to the radio and admired the sumptuous living space.

"Quite the hovel you have here," said Finn, following the arabesques of the cornice molding as they erupted in a spray of floral ejaculations.

"It belonged to some smarmy Jew," she shouted from the kitchen. "You should have seen all the dusty books and filth he had on the walls. I had to have the place fumigated with Lysol before I could move in."

"And here I thought that was just the toxic scent of your character," said Finn under his breath.

He had been debating how he felt about having a twirl with old Rosie. Obvious cons: her raving bigotry. Obvious pros: a warm, welcoming hole, presumably below a fire-red pubis. Did the former make the latter less compelling? Certainly. But did it render it *uncompelling*? On that he was undecided.

Rosaleen set the tea tray down on the side table. "Why don't you play mum?" she said, kicking off her shoes and laying her head on Finn's thigh.

Finn poured the tea, then stirred in the powdered milk and synthetic honey.

"What could Archie have possibly done to get himself detained?" asked Rosaleen, looking up at her expropriated ceiling.

"It's a mystery," said Finn. "I've always known him to be upright and law-abiding."

"Do you think that clubfoot of yours really works for the consulate?"

"You mean Fluss? I think so. Though who really knows the truth of anyone else?"

"Well, as for me," said Rosie, turning over so that her chin lay firmly in Finn's lap, "I've made a point my whole life of being honest about my feelings and direct in expressing them."

"I can see that," said Finn.

She looked up at him, smiling, as she grazed her fingers upon Finn's inseam. She had worked her way into his pants and had just laid hands on his glans when he noticed out of the corner of his eye a photo on the armoire. He could make out Rosie standing beside a familiar jug-eared face.

"Who is that you're with in the photo over there?" he asked, squinting.

"Where? Oh, why that's General O'Duffy. I had the pleasure of meeting him right before I came over to Germany."

"Eoin O'Duffy is a fascist cunt," said Finn involuntarily, as he felt his horn go soft.

Rosie sat up, stunned. "What did you just say?"

"Eoin O'Duffy bore the fascist brunt . . ." he said. "The brunt of the Irish Catholic duty toward Spain, that is."

"Oh, Jesus, Mary, and Joseph, I must be losing my mind," said Rosie, pulling her hand out of Finn's trousers. "This whole business with Archie has my nerves so frayed, it's affecting my hearing."

She stood up and smoothed out her skirt.

"Well, I should be going, anyway," said Finn, buttoning his pants.

"I'm sorry to tease, Finn, but I just won't be myself until I get my vitamin injection."

"Yes, well, perhaps another time."

"I should like that," said Rosie. She touched his

cheek at the door. "And, Finn? Do please find out what happened to Archie."

The Torqued Man was waiting for him at the house. He appeared even more twisted than usual, but in a different way. As though he had undergone a reconfiguration of his parts.

"Where have you been?" he asked.

"Just out gallivanting," replied Finn.

"Well, there'll be no more of it," said the Torqued Man, thrusting Finn's valise at him. "Come, we must go."

"What's going on?" asked Finn.

"The Teutonians have ordered you be sent to Sachsenhausen."

"Is that where you're taking me?"

"Of course not. Officially you're already there. Now get in the boot."

Finn then understood what the Torqued Man had done. He had saved him, and in doing so, he'd gone and cocked everything up.

He blew a kiss to Obelinka in the upstairs window and lowered himself into the Torqued Man's hold.

The next time he saw the sky, he was on the shores of a great body of water. "The Wannsee," said the

Torqued Man. "This cottage," he said, gesturing at the shaded wooden house near the lake, "was my sister's home. Now it is yours."

He brought Finn inside and handed him a thermos. "Drink this broth and rest. There are potatoes and nutrient bars in the kitchen. I'll check in on you every couple of days."

Finn drank of the thermos and looked out across the moonlit lake, rippling apart like all his finely wrought plans. Crean was gone, and with him his supply of smut. He had built his plan for the Doctors' League Dinner around smut. It was smut that would lure the doctors to the basement of the Hotel Kaiserhof. It was smut that would distract them while his wild boys climbed out of their hiding place in the laundry wagons and blocked all the escape routes before the ensuing massacre. And it was smut that had made these ne'er-do-wells willing to cooperate in the first place. Without their promised cut, Finn knew, the *Wilden* would turn on him like a pack of jackals.

He could make out the dark wooded edge of the Grunewald on the opposite shore of the lake. As destiny had woven it, his new hiding place was only a short paddle from where the young ruffians made their camp. Better to propose another form of payment ahead of time, thought Finn, than risk inciting their ire on the night of the big event. He found a rusty but seaworthy dinghy beside his new home and paddled across the lake to the *Wilden*'s lair.

He had come a long way since his first pelting. He was now adept at reading the runes of the tree carvings that crisscrossed the forest in a vast network of secret trails. And he knew the bird calls and wolf howls to use to announce his presence without setting off the alarms. This seemingly remote patch of wilderness was really an invisible *Gleisdreieck* of antisocial society.

When he arrived in the torchlit glade, the tribe was in the middle of one of their brutal initiation rituals. The outer ring of watchmen acknowledged his presence and absorbed Finn into their chain. Inside the circle, a naked boy of about thirteen was being beaten with birch branches. When the beating finally stopped, his tormentors formed a tight circle around his flayed body and doused him with hot streams of piss. It steamed into his eyes and ears and into his fresh wounds. Even the wind hound Sceolang, who seemed to have adjusted well to life in the forest, left her mark on the initiate.

A bottle of rotgut that had been making the rounds arrived in Finn's hands. He took a long pull. It burned his throat something delightful and suffused his whole body with warmth. He passed the bottle on.

Chief Rabbit tucked his long and handsome horn back into his pants and called for his adjutants. These came bearing an old Prussian helmet and a long bayonet. The chief donned the spiked helmet, took up the bayonet, and bid the initiate kneel. The boy wobbled to his knees, shaking with piss and blood, and looked up at Rabbit. Despite his degraded state, there was a glimmer in his eyes. The chief raised the bayonet, intoning in gibberish Apache, and dubbed the boy a fully fledged brother of the *Wilden*.

Upon witnessing this spectacle of homoerotic juvenile bonding, inspiration flooded the wise brain of Finn McCool. Who needed smut to lure the Nazi doctors to the basement of the Kaiserhof, when he could offer them a live show instead?

Only the thorny matter of a surrogate payment remained. But surely he and his young associates could work out something to their liking.

"*Was ist los, Alter?*" Rabbit called to him. The wild boys turned to see what news brought Finn McCool to their forest. "What did you think of our ceremony?"

"Savage, to be sure. Even a touch nauseating. But moving all the same."

"You geezers are such sentimental fucks."

The chief took up courtly repose on the *Wilden*'s

hallowed *Stoßsofa*—the fucking couch—and snorted a line of Pervitin.

"So, everything ready for this weekend?"

"Just about," said Finn. "Though your ritual has given me a new idea."

Finn laid out his vision of the live performance.

"What about the smut?"

"Well, we've hit a bit of a snag with that. A trifle, I assure you."

The wild boys booed.

Rabbit was displeased. "That smut's part of our agreement, *Alter.* No smut, no gut."

So much for the fellowship of the Fianna, thought Finn. "Surely some other form of payment would be acceptable to you boys. Food? Booze? Women?" At this last suggestion, the *Wilden*, who were all hardened misogynists and homosexuals, laughed. "Sorry," said Finn, "I misspoke."

Another bottle of their potent scaltheen came around. Finn took a swig. This one burned even more. The warmth rose through his chest all the way to his head.

"Now, tell me what you'd like."

Those were the last words Finn remembered uttering before he was overcome with dizziness and dropped like a stone.

When next he woke, he was in a strange bed inside a strange house. His head and chest were still on fire. He tried to make out his surroundings through the blear. On the nightstand, a cross, and on the dresser, a family portrait, the man in SA uniform, the woman holding a small child with a lolling head. He heard a distant kettle boiling, then footsteps. The Torqued Man appeared in the doorway.

"Welcome back," he said, handing Finn a cup of tea. "Drink this."

"Where am I?" asked Finn.

"The cottage. I brought you here three days ago. You've been asleep for most of it."

The Torqued Man explained how he had returned to the cottage the next day with more food and found Finn passed out in the dinghy, just drifting on the lake, and had swum out into the frigid waters to rescue him. "You've fallen ill. You're running a fever."

He told Finn to rest, that he would take care of him, that nothing needed doing. And with that, Finn fell back against the Torqued Man's pillow and into sleep.

The Doctors' League Dinner came and went— without an orgy of smut, without a bloodbath at the hands of Finn or the *Wilden*. Instead, Finn remained bedridden. Fall turned to winter, and a long, cold darkness unfolded upon the land. The Teutonian army stalled on the banks of the Volga while the icy stocks of their rifles ripped the skin from their gloveless hands. The Jews of Berlin, in the next logical step of their systematic un-personing, were rounded up and shipped east, where those lucky enough to live would be suffocated, poisoned, and drowned by those same doctors who had recently smoked cigars and swapped lewd jokes in the banquet room of the Hotel Kaiserhof. All the while, Finn slept.

He drifted in and out of consciousness, never fully awake when he woke nor fully asleep while he slept. He passed weeks in bed, punctuated only by somnambulant walks to the living room sofa, where fever and exhaustion reclaimed him. In his addled dreams, he returned to the Spanish pit. To the garroting post. To the white room. To Arturo, the cellmate to whom he had begun teaching Irish and English. The first phrase he taught him in both languages: *Eoin O'Duffy is a fascist cunt.* The phrase echoed in Finn's slumbering mind like it was bouncing off the walls of a cave. It would carry on the wind while he dreamed he was creeping through the boglands, clad in a bronze hauberk and gripping a man-killing ax the size of a submarine. It would circle the walls of his cell while he tore against his medical restraints before the looming figures of his tormentors.

Usually they were pumping him full of some new drug—testing the biopsychic triggers of the red psychosis—when their images would dissolve into the Torqued Man. There he was, spooning broth into his mouth, wiping his forehead with a damp cloth, and crumbling Vitamult bars into repulsive nuggets of nourishment. He rubbed Finn's limbs to keep his muscles from atrophying. He turned him to avoid bedsores. He read from books or talked to him in a soothing whisper—a medley of German, Spanish, and English—counseling him to rest. Finn was thankful he had fallen into the care of this man, a man whose care was no longer entangled in professional duty, and who had put himself at considerable risk to help him. Perhaps he had misjudged him. For the first time since the Torqued Man had spirited him away from the Spanish pit, Finn felt a flicker of gratitude.

But always in the background of his dim consciousness was the nagging anxiety of an unkept appointment, the feeling that he was expected elsewhere.

33

JOURNAL

January 25, 1944

I need to remind myself to be grateful. I am alive.
Not only that—I enjoy the luxury of two places to call
home in this city, while hundreds of thousands are
bombed out. They rove the streets like sleepwalkers,
barrowing their sad belongings over the debris. It's
safe to say at this point that Frau Obolensky must be
dead. And no one at HQ has said one word about new
agents to handle. I am going in to work just a couple
of times a week, and only in order to stay apprised of
the storm that is still gathering. Nothing more since
Moltke's arrest. But fearful thoughts are aswirl. Will
Himmler have enough leverage to get his hooks in us?
Will Hitler give Canaris the sack? It is yet one more

hovering uncertainty as death continues to rain down from the sky.

January 26, 1944

This just in: General Oster has been put under house arrest. For what, I don't yet know. Someone said he was helping Jews escape. But isn't that always the first thing that's thought of? That's not all—I've been hearing rumors that Lauhusen may have actually been involved in one of these resistance circles and killed himself to avoid betraying his fellow conspirators. Can you believe it? He could barely stay awake for a ten-minute meeting, and now I'm to understand he was plotting an uprising? Was it all a façade?

January 27, 1944

My conscience was only mildly perturbed about Crean. Like the vague anxiety I used to get after a night of too much drinking, afraid I'd said or done something stupid. Part of this owed to the fact that I found him repugnant. I told myself someone of Crean's dark predilections would probably find a prison camp highly stimulating and thought little more of him.

But soon after, the skeletal faces of the Bretons began

haunting my sleep. I'd managed to keep them out of my dreams for more than a year, yet seeing the effects of the hell I'd delivered them into had battered down those walls, and for them—whom I'd stamped with the same fate as Crean and for no higher purpose—I began to suffer.

It is only now, recalling my deed, that Crean joins the Bretons—along with Gretchen and Pike and Maike and James von Moltke and the publisher Egon Schulz and the people of Spain and, God, so many others—in the ledger that weighs on my soul. Even if I would damn Crean to save Pike again and a hundred times over (I would), I can no longer think of this as the heroic act of resistance I once deluded myself into believing it was.

My sister's house, where I took Pike, was more or less as I had left it after Gretchen's death. Two years had passed, and I still hadn't gone through her or Maike's things. The only items I had managed to purge were Klaus's SA uniform and my father's trunk. I had also come a handful of times to beat back the weeds, trim the hedges, and keep the outside of the house looking like it was still lived in. I'd heard reports of squatters occupying vacant summer homes and didn't want to be faced with the embarrassment of having to call the authorities on a family in hiding.

Pike stretched his cramped limbs in the living room and looked around. "What a bourgeois double life you lead, Grotius. Why, this could pass for the home of a spinster."

"This was my sister's house," I said.

"Aw, that's a pity. And here I thought you were going to teach me how to needlepoint."

The walls and tables were covered with all manner of hackneyed handicraft. Marzipan fruits, wooden soldiers, paper ornaments, crocheted psalms, ceramic animals, personified nutcrackers, brightly colored postcards—all these Maike had hoarded as a child and cluttered her house with as an adult.

Pike picked up a trophy of a nude athlete swinging a swastika-emblazoned discus and raised his eyebrows at me.

"Her husband's," I said. "Also dead."

Pike spotted the wheelchair in the corner. "That was your niece's?"

"Yes. How did you know?"

"You once mentioned her. What was her name?"

"Gretchen."

"Gretchen," he repeated. "I've always loved that name. *Ewig-Weibliche* and all that business."

I showed him to the bedroom. The last time I had been in there was to change the sheets after Maike died.

I could still smell death in it. It unnerved me to think of Pike sleeping there, but I hoped it would help break the morbid spell that hung about the room.

Once he was settled in, I explained to him again the precariousness of our situation. "According to the Abwehr, the Foreign Office, and the Security Office, you are now interned in Sachsenhausen."

"And how is it I'm not?" he asked.

Of course, I would never tell him about Crean. I told him I had pulled a sleight of hand with the paperwork and he needn't worry about the rest.

His look let me know this was a thoroughly inadequate answer, but he didn't inquire any further.

"That means you should take care to be seen by as few people as possible, especially since it's out of the question for you to pass as German."

"*Was meinst Du?*" said Pike in his terrible accent. "*Mein Deutsch ist ganz flüssig.*"

"Be that as it may," I said, "I will soon get you forged papers making you a foreign worker. They won't be great, but they'll be better than nothing. The real trouble, however, will be with food. There's no feasible way for you to receive your own ration cards. I can share mine, of course, but that will only go so far."

"Not to worry," said Pike. "I'm acquiring a knack for foraging."

I told him I would return in a couple of days, and as I was leaving he stopped me at the door.

"Grotius," he said, fixing me with rheumy eyes. "Say goodbye to Crean for me."

Did he know?

With Pike reliant solely on me in this remote suburb, I had envisioned a rekindling of our former intimacy. We would listen to the wind howl on the lake while we sipped our mugs by the stove. We would go for walks in the neighboring woods. When the weather turned warm, we would take Klaus's dinghy and go fishing and swimming. My fantasies, a mingling of old Berlin memories and my early days with Pike, roared back to life.

But it was all wishful thinking. If Pike felt the least bit of gratitude at being rescued, he showed no signs of it. Instead, he slunk off into the woods alone. And the next time I returned to the cottage, I found him passed out in the dinghy, dead drunk in the middle of the lake.

I had already begun to fear for his health. His hearing, bad when we first met, had steeply declined in the past year, such that I nearly had to shout to be heard. And he carried that cough like a cowbell, rattling his presence to anyone who happened to be nearby. Now that he was at Wannsee, I worried he would drown in the lake, or collapse in the woods and freeze to death, or not hear the air-raid siren and be blown to bits. He needed rest. He needed someone to give him the care he was too stubborn to accept on his own.

I had found some old Luminal tablets in the cottage that Maike had used to quell Gretchen's seizures. The principal side effect, according to the apothecary's label, was drowsiness and fatigue. I reasoned that if my tiny niece could take them, then they couldn't do much harm to Pike or his battle-seasoned liver. So I began grinding a tablet or two into his food, which consisted mainly of the Vitamult bars that, due to some requisitioning error, lined the halls of Abwehr HQ. They were apparently brimming with nourishment and tasted so awful the bitterness of the Luminal went undetected.

At first his reactions were alarming. Fevers, dizziness, rashes, slurred speech, as well as the desired drowsiness. I soon adjusted the dosage, though, and the fevers abated. But he was still too weak to leave his bed for more than a few minutes at a time. This state of affairs, needless to say, was not how I had envisioned our companionship. I did not want to see Pike ailing. I certainly did not want to hurt him. But it was my duty to protect him from Veesenmayer and this criminal state that wanted to dispose of him, just as they had my niece and so many others. I would not let them do it again. And if that meant Pike had to be kept in bed, then so be it.

34

Finn McCool in
the Bowels of Teutonia

Convalescence

With the first bloodening of spring, Finn stirred from his hibernation. The fog lifted from his brain, and though it did not entirely recede, it let in enough light for him to feel more man than vegetable.

The Torqued Man was there at his side. "You must build up your strength slowly," he said, lifting the bowl of broth to his lips.

But Finn was in no mood for taking it slowly. He was impatient with his convalescence. One day, waking to find himself alone, he leapt from his sickbed and threw himself into the icy waters of the Wannsee. The cold felt like an old friend. It tautened the fibers of his atrophied muscles and electrified his benumbed brain. Soon his hunger returned. But he would drink no more broth or insipid porridge. Nor would he permit another fetid Vitamult bar to pass beyond his lips. His spirit demanded the fruits of the forest instead—earth roots and bramble berries and river fish.

He spent his days following the kestrel's cry through the reedworks, crawling behind fox tracks on the forest floor. He was not the only one. Since he had been asleep, Teutonians had been finding it harder to fill their bellies. Their ration cards earned them increasingly meager cuts from the butcher and more mulch baked into their bread. The Grunewald and the marshland of the Havel had become dotted with scroungers of nature's bounty like himself. But Finn was always the first to unearth its treasures, having learned the secrets of woodcraft from his days with the *Wilden*. Though, regarding the *Wilden* themselves, he kept his distance. He harbored suspicions that the little shitehawks had poisoned him for reneging on the smut, and he did not care to meet his demise at the hands of thirty pubescent psychopaths.

Finn stuffed himself with wild beets and fennel and nettles and dandelion and ground ivy and goutweed and wood ears and bear's garlic and waldmeister and scurvywort and watermint and butcher's-broom and bird-in-the-bush and candlesnuff and coltsfoot

and penny bun and blackthorn and wolfberry
and spleenwort and dog violet and purslane and
buckthorn and hound's-tongue and chicory and
alehoof and goatsbeard and mallow and pfifferlinge
and pike and eel and loach and bitterling and asp
and tench and vole and toad and duck and goose and
hare and shrew.

When he had eaten his fill, Finn picked his teeth
with an elder limb and let out a belch that sent
Berliners running for their air-raid cellars. Within
moments, his vigor returned. The life-sap lit his eyes
and swelled his loins. And in that clear-eyed state
that only a mountain of fresh game and roughage can
induce, he recalled a story the Torqued Man once told
him while sitting at his sickbed.

The quilt that covered his ailing body had once
belonged to the Torqued Man's niece. She was a
sweet girl named Gretchen, who had been cursed
with a sickness. A sickness from which there was
no recovering, one that was the very fabric of her
life. But, contrary to the doctors' rulings, it had not
become the entirety of her life. For all their expertise,
they could not see beyond her twisted frame, beyond
the seizures that convulsed her with such sudden
violence she looked like caught prey whipped in the
jaws of a wolf. They could not see that captive in her

body was a mind with memories and affections, with an awareness of its own quickened state, with stories of having lived and hopes of life to come.

"They could not see," the Torqued Man had told him, "that Gretchen, like everyone, had something we call a soul. To Dr. Heinze of the Brandenburg State Welfare Institute, my niece, Gretchen, with her palsied and unproductive limbs, appeared as nothing more than a cyst on the racial body. I was told he and his nurses would care for her, but they simply *excised* her."

The Torqued Man spoke these words candidly, as though to himself. For Finn's eyes were closed, and though he appeared to be in a feverish slumber, the story lodged in his brain. He'd been so angry, said the Torqued Man, that he wanted to kill the doctor and his nurse. Of course, he would never do such a thing. Wasn't that the great frustration of life, said the Torqued Man. So much wanting. Such a yawning gulf between desire and action. "There are things I have wanted, Finn. Things I've yearned for." And with that he bent down and kissed the sleeping Finn on his lips [delicately parted and soft as fontanelle].

This memory of the Torqued Man's tale at his sickbed penetrated Finn's brain and woke him to his former purpose. He had been so attached to the

Doctors' League Dinner, then so distraught by the unraveling of his grand plan, that he had forgotten how much dignity there was in humble work. There was a doctor nearby that needed killing. It was as simple as that.

Whatever the cause of his illness, he now considered it a blessing. The Doctors' League Dinner massacre had been an idea born of pure ego and met with poor planning, a desperate swipe at immortality in fear of dwindling time. Organizing an illicit sex-show-cum-mass-assassination in the basement of a five-star hotel was complicated enough. Doing it with a group of savage adolescents would have been like herding cats.

But the hammer had not dropped. The Anglelanders never invaded Erin and now, even if they did, Finn was free. Thanks to the Torqued Man, the Teutonians believed he was in prison. Though it was a shame about the wee Northman Crean, he realized he had been spared a catastrophe. Destiny was now offering him the chance to return to fundamentals.

That's why this time, on a late April afternoon in 1943, when Finn took the train to Brandenburg, he brought only his hat, coat, and hunting knife. As the brochure in the Torqued Man's cottage promised, the Brandenburg State Welfare Institute was located in the charming gothic town center of Brandenburg an der Havel, within easy reach of the train station.

Dr. Hans Heinze, child psychiatrist and director of the erstwhile euthanasia project, had given specialized medical care to many hundreds of young lives unworthy of life. The treatment varied: lethal overdose, poisoning by gas, or simple starvation. But they always achieved the same perfect outcome. A total eradication of the sick body. Their little patients went home in even littler urns, like the one that the Torqued Man kept on the mantel in the cottage.

And yet, despite such impressive results, last year the higher-ups had pulled the plug on the program. Granted, Dr. Heinze had gotten an earful from parents and churchmen screaming bloody murder. One lunatic had even threatened to slit his throat after a relative of his had received care. But he, Dr. Heinze, was of the mind that the public had to be educated to understand health. Inevitably, there would be some friction. But if you wanted to make progress and shape the outlook of future generations, you couldn't simply kowtow to public opinion. After all, just look at the public. Some people could barely keep themselves alive! That's why there were experts in the first place. Would you trust a man off the street to sew your pants? Of course not! That's what tailors were for. So why should you trust

something as precious and complex as the health of
the race to your average citizen? Since dismantling the
domestic euthanasia program, the Doctors' League had
focused all its energy on the east. Admittedly, there
was more room to maneuver out there. And far more
of a dire threat to be confronted, racially speaking. But
where did that leave people like Heinze and his team
of nurses? Back to the humdrum days of prescribing
Pervitin to lethargic children and sedatives to the
hyperactive and deviant. Meanwhile, the nation was
squandering good money and labor just to enrich a few
barons at Bayer and let the racial stock stagnate.

Such must have been Dr. Heinze's thoughts as he
made his rounds to the catatonics on the east wing.
Meanwhile, Finn had been loitering outside the
hospital doors, waiting for the receptionist to empty
her bladder. Luckily, her afternoon snack of coffee
and amphetamines ensured he didn't have long to
wait. He entered the vacant lobby, walked down the
east-wing hallway, and asked the first white-coated
man he saw if he might be Dr. Heinze. Yes, said the
man, he was in fact Dr. Heinze; how might he be of
assistance? Finn asked if he could have a quick word,
ushered him into the nearest room, and stabbed the
man in the throat. An honest job well done is all one
should ask for in this life.

Unfortunately, a nurse tending to a catatonic boy behind the partition heard the doctor's deathgroan and pulled the curtain back to inquire. Before the nurse could scream, Finn had cut her throat too. She collapsed on top of the doctor in a bloody heap. The young patient remained frozen in his thousand-yard stare. Finn dragged the bodies behind the partition, patted the young lad's hand, and wished him a speedy recovery before exiting through the window.

He felt a bit queer about killing the nurse, a touch more like a cold-blooded murderer than the insurgent assassin or heroic hunter he fancied himself. Not that women couldn't be evil or that the nurse had been any less guilty than the head doctor. She, or another nurse just like her, had very likely been the executioner of the Torqued Man's niece, while Dr. Heinze simply barked orders. But there was something about killing lower down on the chain of command that offended his working-class sensibilities. And, call him old-fashioned, but slaying the opposite sex didn't sit well with him either. After all, didn't women have enough men hunting them?

Despite these misgivings, the nurse's death proved a boon. For though the killings made the papers, no one suspected a political angle. Instead, there was cautious speculation that they were the doings of a

"troublemaker" terrorizing nurses in and around
Berlin. In the last six months, this apparition had slit
the throats of four *Krankenschwestern*—sick sisters,
another Teutonian word Finn loved—in Spandau,
Potsdam, Tegel, and now Brandenburg. Dr. Heinze
was being written off as collateral damage. He had
likely happened upon the killer in the act and tried
to intercede. The police suspected this interference
accounted for why the perpetrator had not left his
customary puddle of semen on the corpse. The child
patient who had witnessed the whole gruesome event
remained trapped in his catatonia. Doctors were
uncertain when or if he would ever speak.

Though he never told the Torqued Man about
the slaying of his niece's murderers, the act marked
a new twist in the braided spirals of their destinies.
The Torqued Man had always liked having someone
to care for and was now doing so in defiance of
the Reich. His caregiving had become an act of
subversion. This made Fluss a double agent of sorts,
which must have been a balm to his conscience. And
though Finn, once he was well, grew too restless to
play the surrogate niece for more than a couple of
hours here and there and spent most of his time in the
lakelands, he now enjoyed the Torqued Man's visits
more than ever. For one, the man was no longer his

handler, whose friendship, no matter how sincere, had originally been the directive of his Teutonian masters. And Finn, having shed the anxiety of occupation that once hummed in his brain, now felt the Torqued Man's longing to be less of a trap. Now they were just two men.

Two men fueled by pain and desire and the pleasure of touch. Caresses were exchanged, and perhaps a horn or two was blown again, though the cottage did not exactly shake with an orgy of rutting. Instead, the Torqued Man and he were now content to sit on beer crates in the evenings and take in the moonlight and the lake-lapped silence. On the occasions they did speak, it was of elemental things: childhood loves, the shape of the sky, the shadows cast by trees.

35

JOURNAL

February 1, 1944

Not long after my swap of the Irishmen, I ran into Professor Hartmann of the radio service. I was at Nymphenburger Straße, settling in some new South African saboteurs, when he came by in search of Pike.

He was surprised to see me. "I didn't realize you resided here, Herr Fluss."

I told him that I used to, and that I came by every now and then to check on the charwoman, whom I felt kindly toward.

He asked if I had seen Mr. Finn or Mr. Crean. The two of them had up and vanished, he said, and he feared they'd been arrested. I said I'd heard nothing of any arrests and knew nothing of Crean but that Finn had mentioned something about going to Copenhagen to visit friends.

I heard Frau Obolensky yelling at the South Africans upstairs and used it as a pretense to get rid of him.

But this was not the end of it, as a few days later two Kripo officers called at the door of my flat.

I was in the middle of my morning calisthenics when the bell rang. I rushed for my robe and answered the door perspiring and out of breath.

"Interrupting something, are we?" asked the smirking officer, who looked like he had stepped out of a propaganda poster. He nudged his stouter, less racially-ideal-looking partner to attune him to the innuendo.

"Just my exercises, if you must know," I said peevishly.

"Oh, is that what they call them?" said the stout one.

"Gentlemen, is there something I can do for you?"

"Are you Emil Fluss?" asked the Aryan.

"I am."

"We'd like to ask you some questions. May we come in?"

I offered them the two chairs by the window, while I leaned against the bookcase. Strange to think it no longer exists.

"When was the last time you saw Archibald Crean?"

"Crean? Well, I'm not sure. Some weeks ago. Why, is he alright?"

"When is the last time you saw him?"

"Well, let's see. I think it was about three weeks ago. We went to the Schöneberg Ratskeller for a drink."

"Just the two of you?"

"No, in the company of another Irishman: Frank Finn."

"And do you know the current whereabouts of this Frank Finn?"

"Herr Finn told me he was going to stay with friends in Copenhagen. I haven't heard from him since."

"Do you know the name of these friends in Copenhagen?"

"I'm afraid I don't."

"How do you know Herr Finn?"

"He came to a function a couple of years ago at the Spanish Embassy."

"That's where you work?"

"Yes, I'm a cultural liaison there." I didn't want to invoke my Abwehr credentials except as a last resort, fearing it would only draw attention to Pike.

The stout officer examined my antique poster of the 1898 Feria de Sevilla, while the Aryan asked me if I had ever given Crean a ride in my automobile.

I told him I didn't own an automobile, which was technically true.

"Do you ever borrow one for work?" he asked.

"Of course."

"And did you ever invite Archibald Crean into it?"

"Absolutely not. I use the car strictly for carrying out professional duties, none of which have the slightest to do with Herr Crean."

Eventually they got tired of my high-handedness and left.

I nursed Pike through the winter on bouillon cubes, tea, and the ubiquitous Vitamult. Only much later, to my chagrin, did I realize the expiration date on them was a year past. I immediately replaced them with buckwheat porridge and potatoes, but from then on I wondered whether it was perhaps those nutrition bars, and not the Luminal, that had done him in.

Fortunately, he began to improve. On days when he was lucid, some semblance of our meandering conversations from the Ratskeller returned. When talking was too much for him, I read him Kleist, who had shot his beloved and himself on these very same shores and whose stories suited the sickbed.

By spring, I had tapered Pike off the Luminal. I

didn't want him to develop a dependency, and I had only one bottle anyway. He was soon up and about, back to wandering the forest.

And then something miraculous happened. Though he was out foraging most of the day, in the evenings we would sit together and watch the lake. Something in him opened up on those moonlit nights, and I sensed a tenderness in Pike I had never known. A compassion that finally acknowledged everything I felt for him, and even if he did not fully reciprocate it, he accepted it. No manipulation. Just acceptance.

"We've had quite a ride together, you and me," he said one night out of the blue. "Haven't we, Grotius?"

Now that he was recovered and we were alone, he had returned to calling me by my original alias. I then realized I had never told him my real name.

"My name is Adrian. Adrian de Groot."

He laughed until his eyes welled with tears. "And to think you've been saddled all these years with names that sound like faulty plumbing. Adrian. What a fine name. Well, it's grand to meet you, Adrian."

He put out his hand. "I'm Proinnsias."

I had all but forgotten his original name. He was always just Frank, and in my mind Pike. But that, too, had been a cover.

I took his hand. We kept them entwined for several beats longer than a handshake, then he pulled me toward him. It was the first time he ever kissed me.

We lay together, bare and laid bare. Proinnsias and Adrian. Adrian and Proinnsias. Two stripped souls at the end of the world.

But as abruptly as this portal opened, it shut. Those miraculous days evaporated like a dream, and Pike began his precipitous decline. The essential Pikeness of him started to drift away. He was not cold or hostile, but his personality retracted; his affect became diminished. I feared he had suffered a series of small strokes, likely caused by drinking and despair, but perhaps as a consequence of my ministrations, be it the Luminal or the Vitamult.

Whatever it was, something of Pike—Proinnsias, Frank, even Finn—was lost.

As though to mark the transformation, I soon presented him with the new identity pass I had forged. Francisco Gallego: a Spaniard from Vigo. There were a number of Spanish workers in Berlin, and though he spoke with an entirely unconvincing accent, his Spanish was at least fluent. Pike seemed to enjoy this reconnection with Spain and laughed when I presented him with this new, and his final, alias.

Strangely, he began to adopt this persona even when

we were alone. He would answer me in Spanish, until I began responding in kind.

"You should rest," I would say to him. "You're destroying yourself out there in the woods."

"*Pero me hice amigo de los árboles.*"

But why did he need to make friends with the trees when he had me? "*Soy tu amigo también,*" I said, realizing my jealousy now extended to plant life.

"*Sí, sí,*" he replied absently. "*Somos amigos. . . .*"

By the end of last summer, we had stopped conversing in English entirely. More alarming, he also took to peppering his conversation with fictional memories of his alias, working on his father's fishing boat in Galicia or fighting in El Rif as a soldier in the Foreign Legion.

I didn't know how to react to this perplexing behavior. I couldn't tell whether Pike was just amusing himself with fantasies or if he was genuinely succumbing to delusion. But there was no use fighting it. I simply went along with the pretense, hoping the veil might part again and one day he would return.

Since Stalingrad, all of Germany had been doing just that—going along with the pretense. But by the spring of 1943, we could no longer pretend the situation was anything other than dire. Goebbels trotted out his new slogan of "total war is the shortest war"; and to seal the people's commitment, he closed all bars, clubs, cabarets, and any restaurant or shop deemed too luxurious. From then on, our only distractions from war and survival would be theaters and the cinema, where all the words that came out of people's mouths had been vetted by the censors.

While I would never agree with any policy that came out of Goebbels's mouth, it was a relief to know Pike could no longer scamper off to his dive in Kreuzberg or any number of places that would have otherwise lured him out of hiding. Aside from the cinema, which he seemed to have lost interest in, the only place he had to turn was the forest.

The air raids had returned that spring. They were nothing compared to what we are experiencing now, but they jarred us into a new dismal reality. And come summer the writing was on the wall. First there was the "tactical disengagement" at Kursk, which meant the Russians were now on the offensive. A few weeks later, the Allies invaded Italy and Mussolini's regime collapsed like a marionette with its strings cut.

It was around then that writing of a more literal sort began to appear on walls around the city. At first, they were isolated incidents. The words KRIMINELLER HITLER glowing in phosphorus paint on the façade of a bombed-out apartment block. NAZIS RAUS carved into the fence of a garden colony under the S-Bahn. A public lavatory in Hindenburg Park with GOD SEES ALL scrawled over GOD PUNISH ENGLAND—a relic from bygone days. I had read about the execution of the Scholl siblings earlier that year for writing similarly defeatist slogans around Munich. I found their idealism staggering. Foolish, admirable, reckless, courageous— yes, all of those. To give one's life for the scrawling of a word or two? It seemed so pointless and, at the same time, utterly filled with purpose. Yet, bit by bit this last year, these acts of literary subversion have begun crop- ping up throughout the city. Just yesterday I saw one that made me laugh. That is, before I shivered. The LSR of the Luftschutzraum, formerly signaling the direction of the nearest air-raid shelter, now offers a chilling piece of advice: LERNT SCHNELL RUSSISCH.

Who are these high-minded vandals? I often think of Ditzen and his matchsticks. What does it mean for a man to write a propaganda novel to support his family while engaging in minuscule acts of resistance in the shadow of his dinner plate? And what would have hap- pened had I not shaken the table?

36
Finn McCool in
the Bowels of Teutonia

The Poisonous Mushroom

And this was how Finn began to hunt for the Poisonous Mushroom Dr. Morell.

Enlivened by the hospital murders, he began stalking the streets near the Zoologischer Garten at night, hoping to catch a fresh scent of his old quarry Dr. Grawitz. The sporadic bombings of spring had faded, and with the heat of summer boiling his blood, the Red Cross president surely would return to his furtive trysts in the public toilet.

The darkened streets off the boulevard were stocked with boys offering themselves to the night. Many of these young hustlers came from Finn's former allies the *Wilden,* who crept from their forest lairs to rob and pleasure the citizenry. Though he steered clear of the little lunatics when they were en masse and in their wooded lair—whatever they dosed him with had banjaxed his works for months—he kept on cordial terms with a few of the night crawlers.

He was outside a Kinoplex, consulting with one of them, a pugnacious urchin named Buckskin, who was no stranger to toilet liaisons. Finn had just recruited him to help trap Grawitz in exchange for a liter of Waldmeister schnapps and three comic books, when he heard his name in the form of a question.

He turned around. It was Rosaleen Lynch.

"Finn!" she said, surprised. "I thought that was you!"

Finn said hello and quickly ushered her away from his business associate.

"My word, Finn, where have you been? How are you? You look ill. Is everything alright? Who is that you were talking to?"

"No one. Just some kid asking for a fag."

"When you disappeared, we assumed you had been arrested too, just like Archie. Everyone at the station is worried they'll be next. But, really, Finn, what happened to you?"

Finn steered her by the shoulder to a dark corner beside the Kaiser Wilhelm Church.

"Rosaleen, you can't tell anyone you've seen me. I assure you, both Crean and I are safe. But I can't get into the details. All I can say is that we're working with German intelligence on a top-secret mission."

"What? Are you serious?"

"See," he said, pulling out his *Kennkarte.* "As far as anyone is concerned, I'm a Spanish national."

"Francisco," she said, gaping at his forged identity card. "I knew there was something more to that clubfoot than he let on!"

"To do our work, Crean and I needed to go underground. That's why it is imperative you tell no one you've seen me. Do you understand?"

"Yes, of course. I promise I won't say a word. But if you've gone to ground, then why are you out here on the K-damm?"

"A man's entitled to a little entertainment every now and then," Finn said with a shrug, failing to register that the cinema behind him had been boarded up for weeks.

"Oh, Finn, darling," she said, hugging him. "I'm so happy to know you're alright. But I'm afraid I have to run. I'm late for my magical injection."

"Your magical injection?" he said, confused.

"Yes, I'm sure I told you about my vitamin injections before. I can't stop raving about them."

Finn seemed to recall her saying something about an injection once.

"My homeopath, Dr. Morell, is simply a miracle worker."

"Dr. Morell, did you say?" asked Finn, suddenly alert. The name had gone through him like an electric current.

"Yes, one little prick and you feel like you've been reborn."

"I'll have to remember that line for future use."

"I'm serious, you naughty boy!" she said. "Everyone who's anyone uses him. My friend Heidemarie Hatheyer—yes, the film star!—she's the one who fixed me up with Morell. She kept saying she swore by these all-natural injections, that her voice got smoother, her wrinkles disappeared, that she lost three kilos in her stomach and gained two in her bust. I couldn't believe it, so I had to try it for myself. And you know what? She's right! They're a miracle! I'm told Hitler himself gets injections from Morell. No wonder—the man's a proper genius. He even sells his own patented recipe of vitamin bars. Though you wouldn't think it to look at him. In fact, he doesn't look healthy at all. For starters, he's enormously rotund, and he smells like an old train car. Why, when I first saw him and his greasy face, I thought he was a Jew. But I'm told it's the Swiss Italian in his genes. They can be quite swarthy, you know."

Finn was no longer listening. All he needed to hear was that Emerald Rosie knew the doctor who treated Hitler.

"And when is your appointment?" he casually inquired.

"Why, in ten minutes," she said, looking at her watch. "If I don't go now, I'll be late."

Finn said he'd be happy to accompany her.

The chrome waiting room of the Kurfürstendamm clinic felt like the inside of a giant martini shaker. The only reading materials were a menu of hormone treatments—the Rise and Shine (*Raus aus den Federn*), the Sharp as a Tack (*Blitzgescheit*), and the Rejuvenator (*Die Auffrischung*)—along with a stack of brochures touting the myriad health benefits of Vitamult bars. Finn felt his gorge rise at the mention of those foul bricks the Torqued Man had fed him throughout his illness, which had no doubt made him worse. While the brochures claimed their secret recipe of mountain herbs and essential vitamins was fueling the elite fighting forces of the SS, Finn was certain Vitamult's real ingredients were yeast, beet sugar, and cat vomit.

When the secretary received an urgent phone call for the doctor and paged him to the front, Finn at last caught a glimpse of Morell. He read the contours of his portly face, with its loose-hanging lips and wire-rim spectacles that pinched the skin around his temples. At once Finn realized that this man was the reason he'd been hibernating for the better part of a year, the reason his plans for the great massacre at last year's Doctors' League Dinner had gone astray. This was the doctor he'd been waiting for.

Rosaleen Lynch emerged, freshly stuck, with flushed cheeks and an insufferable energy. Finn got rid of her with a promise to call on her soon, then returned to the clinic to wait for Morell.

Unfortunately, the doctor came out an hour later and got straight into a black motor car waiting at the curb. It was an official vehicle, with little swastikas mounted on the hood, and though the chassis groaned under the weight of its precious cargo, it sped away before Finn could think of a way to delay it.

When he returned to the clinic the next day, the doctor was not in. Nor was he accepting appointments in the foreseeable future. The third day, the receptionist grew suspicious. When he returned the following week, the clinic was closed.

He decided to call on Rosaleen Lynch, as promised, to find out what had become of her magical-injections man and maybe, if the portrait of the fascist cunt Eoin O'Duffy could be put facedown, offer her an injection of his own.

"Finn!" she said, opening the door. He could tell she was drunk.

He put his finger to his mouth to quiet her. Her block warden was likely listening.

"I was just in the neighborhood and thought to drop by."

He heard the radio coming from her flat, plus a man's voice humming along to the music. "But I see you have company. I don't mean to bother you."

"Oh, it's no bother at all. Please come in."

"No, no, I don't think that would be a good idea."

"Who is it?" asked the man inside.

"It's just my friend Fra—Francisco. Please, come in."

Finn wished he could retract his knock.

Rosie's guest came to the hallway. He was young and brimming with racial superiority. His pomaded blond hair glistened under the chandelier.

"Francisco? Isn't that a Spanish name?" asked the young man. "You don't look Spanish."

"Ah well, what can I say? Spanish father, Irish mother. Just like De Valera."

The Aryan looked at him blankly.

"Karl-Heinz is a detective with the Kripo," said Rosaleen.

"Ah, you don't say?"

"The youngest on the squad, isn't that right, Karl-Heinz?"

He shrugged with self-assurance. "Only by three years."

"And he just got promoted to Homicide! Kommissar Lipke—catcher of killers!"

"Well, congratulations and grand to meet you, Kommissar. In any event, I was just in the vicinity and thought to say how-do, but I really should be going. . . ."

"Oh, stay and have a drink, Francisco," said Rosaleen, rolling the R and elongating the vowels, as though they were all three having a laugh at his ridiculous joke of a name. "Karl-Heinz, talk with Fran while I go fix us another round. *Aber auf Englisch!*

"He's been practicing," she said to Finn, before disappearing into the kitchen.

"So," said Finn, "the Criminal Police, you say? That must be an intriguing line of work."

Karl-Heinz shrugged again. "So far it's been a lot of dull paperwork and asking questions that don't have answers."

"Is that so?" said Finn.

"But that was in Missing Persons. Homicide should give me something to sink my teeth into."

"Yes, I quite imagine," replied Finn. "Plenty of murderers walking the streets of Berlin these days."

"Actually, regarding statistics, the new Germany has very few murders."

Karl-Heinz's English had not yet grasped the nuances of double entendre. Finn groped for another question before the young detective started thinking of his own. "So, then, how did Rosaleen and yourself meet?"

The Kripo detective told him in slow but exacting English that he had been out shopping for trousers one Sunday at Wertheim's—or, rather, the Aryanized department store that went by some conglomeration of letters but that everyone still referred to as Wertheim's—when he overheard a woman talking in English. He didn't recognize her, yet there was something powerfully familiar about her voice. It gripped him, this eerie feeling of intimacy, and yet he was certain he had never seen this woman before. Then he heard her say the word "Jew" and the revelation nearly knocked him over. She was Emerald Rosie the Jew Hater! He listened to her broadcast twice a week to practice his English. For, once the war was finished, Karl-Heinz explained, there would be vast English-speaking domains incorporated into the Reich, and unlike his colleagues, who barely knew their native German, he was a vanguard thinker (though Finn supposed the real reason Karl-Heinz was studying English was because he liked to watch American movies). But the great relief he felt upon recognizing Rosie's voice now gave way to nervousness. Did he dare approach her? Would that be proper? Was she tired of being hounded by her adoring public? Or would she appreciate it? He was so overcome with indecision, by the time he worked up the nerve to introduce himself, she was gone.

"He's my biggest fan," said Rosaleen, who had returned with a tray of vodka highballs.

Finn was confused. "But if she was gone, then how did you ever meet?" But he would soon regret his curiosity.

"That's the thing!" said Rosie. "It wasn't until he came round the broadcasting house to investigate Archie's disappearance."

Finn winced at the sound of Crean's name.

"How do you two know each other?" asked the detective, looking at Rosaleen.

"We work at the station together," she said, glancing uncertainly at Finn. "Or, I mean, we used to."

Karl-Heinz shot him an inquiring look. "Then I'm surprised I never questioned you about the disappearance of Herr Crean."

The whole evening was going pear-shaped. He'd swung by to have a peek at Rosie's ginger bits, and now his life and mission dangled by a single fiery strand.

Finn rushed to explain that he used to help with the cables and the like but that he'd left well over a year ago. "Grunt technical work, nothing glamorous like Rosie here. And, yes, terrible mystery about your man Crean," said Finn. He needed to get out of there.

"You know, another man disappeared right at the same time as Herr Crean."

"Oh?" said Finn, feigning surprise.

"Another Irishman—a man named Finn."

"I don't believe I knew the gentleman. . . ."

"So your voice has never been on the radio?" asked Karl-Heinz.

"Not to my knowledge," said Finn. "Why? Do I remind you of someone?"

The detective paused to think. "Not really. Though maybe Patrick Cadogan."

"You flatter me," said Finn.

"Where do you work now?"

This was fast becoming an interrogation. "At the munitions factory in Moabit."

"Bad luck," said Karl-Heinz. "Sounds like a demotion."

Finn drank down his vodka soda and adopted a sullen look, hoping this would deter the detective from inquiring more into his work. He had to leave before this ambitious peeler and radio fanatic recognized his voice and began to unravel the lies.

But he still wanted information on the fat doctor. He casually brought up that the last time he saw Rosaleen he had accompanied her to that clinic on the K-damm where she got her vitamin injections. "Was wondering if you might refer your man to me. Morell, was it?"

"It's rotten news," said Rosaleen, "but Dr. Morell's closed his clinic until further notice. I'm all out of sorts because of it. You know, Heidemarie told me she just about flung herself out the window, she was so distraught without her weekly pick-me-up."

"What happened to him?" asked Finn.

"Well, his receptionist won't say, but . . ." she

said, lowering her voice, even though an officer of the police was sitting right beside her. "Heidemarie, who's close to Goebbels, said that Hitler's become Dr. Morell's sole patient and that he now keeps him at his side around the clock, administering injections. They say the Führer simply can't function without them. And it's no wonder—I mean, what with the stress of managing this war."

"Careful, now," said the detective. "I wouldn't want to have to tell my colleagues in the Gestapo you're suggesting our beloved Führer is a drug addict."

"You're the one who said it, you little rat. Not me!" Rosaleen threw herself on Karl-Heinz's lap and they collapsed in a fit of laughter and kisses.

Finn swallowed the rest of his drink and made for the door, leaving the two lovers to their mock denunciations.

37

JOURNAL

February 10, 1944

Vermehren, one of our agents in Istanbul, has just defected to England along with his wife. Apparently, he, too, was connected with that resistance group, the Solf Circle, and was warned of his impending arrest. Now he's sharing whatever he knows with the Allies. It's quite possible he gave them our codes. The atmosphere feels combustible.

Not surprising, considering half the city has already burned. There are so many homeless now, they look like a defeated army camped out on the streets, haunting the cavernous depths of collapsed buildings. When the *Gulasch* cannons wheel into the neighborhood, throngs line up with whatever bowl they can improvise. I recently saw a man slurping soup from his hat. Those with more pride roast rats over fires made from the debris of their homes. Yet the radio still blasts its daily schmaltz, with ballads about singing nightingales and tavern romance, and not two blocks from the mobile soup kitchen is a queue, just as long, of people waiting for tickets to *Faust*.

February 13, 1944

Kriegsmann came to Berlin in the fall of '43. Naturally, he wanted to see Pike. I knew he would be furious to hear he'd been interned and might well demand to see him in Sachsenhausen, thereby exposing my sleight of hand. So I told him the truth—that Pike was alive and well and hidden safely in the vicinity. Except neither was true by then. His health had taken another turn for the worse, but he refused to stay indoors. His chest rattled with every labored breath, and a tremor ran down his left side. I pleaded with him to let me take him to a doctor, but he wouldn't hear of it.

"You know what doctors do," he said to me in Spanish. "You told me yourself."

"But they don't kill everyone," I said.

"I'd prefer not to test their selection criteria."

I put Kriegsmann off the first time, more out of

shame than lack of trust. I felt responsible for Pike, and his wretched state reflected poorly on me, like the negligent parent of an injured child. But when he told me Val was taking the train down for the weekend and insisted on seeing her old friend, I had no choice but to agree.

The Kriegsmanns had loomed enigmatically in my mind ever since meeting Pike. Helmut of course I knew—a forthright gentle giant who seemed always to hit his mark but never to question where he was aiming. But it was Val that was the mysterious part of the equation. Pike had always referred to the Kriegsmanns as a unit, though I sensed that Val was the anchor of his affection. She was, with the erstwhile exception of Crean, the only Irish friend he had left. And while I had once chafed at hearing glowing reports about how wonderful the Kriegsmanns were, I thought their presence—especially that of the elusive Val—might help bring Pike back to himself, and maybe to me.

I gathered them from their hotel in Mitte and drove them out to Wannsee as evening fell. They were, I admit, a radiant couple. Against even the gray backdrop of our beleaguered city, they looked like film stars. Helmut, lantern-jawed, in a tan suit. Val, incognito in a silk kerchief and sunglasses, which she soon removed to dramatic effect. Her eyes were piercing green and her hair a lustrous pile of strawberry blond. But, as I was to learn, she had a kind of overbearing, self-centered energy that I despised.

Just as we came up the drive, the air-raid siren sounded. The Kriegsmanns had picked an odd time for a weekend visit. The bombing campaign that now seems as though it will never end was then just beginning. The South Africans, who had recently embarked for Portugal, had been lucky to get out when they did (and to have been spared the fate of the Bretons). The authorities had ordered the evacuation of unemployed women and children to the countryside. But they had no plan. Everything was in chaos. The details of the evacuation order changed by the day, until eventually, because there was no viable means of escape and no coherent direction from the government, many remained stuck. Even Goebbels was getting tangled in his lies over the radio, and the machine-gun fire of euphemisms and neologisms that over the years had brutalized our poor language now began to jam in his mouth.

We hurried into the house to take refuge. It lacked a cellar, but under the crossbeams was better than nothing. Pike was nowhere to be found. I went to the kitchen to look out back in the yard where he liked to sit. Through the window I made out his silhouette offset against the shimmer of the lake. He seemed to be lolling beneath a tree, whittling a stick as though nothing were amiss. I called to him, my voice inaudible above the siren. The Kriegsmanns and I ran out to him. He turned and saw his old friends, and for a brief moment, the brightness came back into his eyes.

"Can't you hear the siren, Frank?" shouted Val.

Pike smiled. "Sounds like Finn McCool blowing his hunting horn."

The air raid failed to materialize that evening, and Pike even resumed speaking in English for a few hours, which I found both heartening and bewildering. The four of us dined on pork loin à la Val and cognac. There were even raspberries and fresh cream for dessert. The Kriegsmanns appeared to be thriving during this war.

Val, who seemed to live in a bubble of charmed cluelessness, told of the most amazing seashells they had collected on their last outing to Skagen. And of what a glory the tomato-growing season in Copenhagen had been. "Great big lumps of them, darling," she said to Pike. "So shiny, you could practically see yourself!"

"I hear the Danes have lost the right to self-government," I said, attempting to interject a sour note into the proceedings.

"They had a good thing going before," said Kriegsmann. "They should have cooperated and made things easier on everyone."

"I always tell Helmut, just because the world has gone mad, that doesn't mean we have to start raving too."

"Val's always managed to keep her chin up," said Pike. "A girl who knows the value of a proper laugh."

"Oh, speaking of, Frank darling, I've brought you the latest clippings from 'Cruiskeen Lawn,'" she said, referring to a Dublin column she'd introduced him to. "Dad's been sending me the *Times* in bundles every week. They're beyond brilliant. And so unbelievably funny I just about peed myself."

The two of them descended into a private exchange of laughter concerning the rollicking wit of the author, bouncing between English and Irish, while Kriegsmann and I drank deeply from his cognac.

By the end of dinner, everyone was well lubricated. Pike and the Kriegsmanns recalled their college pranks in Dublin, occasionally remembering to address me out of politeness, as though the stories were for my benefit. Eventually, I did us all a favor and went to wash the dishes.

"Oh, you poor man," said Val, noticing my limp. "How'd you hurt your foot there?"

I caught Pike's eyes for a moment, before looking away, embarrassed.

"I . . . have a congenital limp. A clubfoot actually."

"Oh, you don't say?" said Val, full of sympathy, yet unable to resist the train of thought that came chugging through her mind. "Just like Goebbels."

I went to the kitchen, seething. I scrubbed the dirty plates in a rage while Pike and the Kriegsmanns continued to reminisce.

When I returned, Val was teasing Pike for having left Dublin. "We were all having a whale of a time, but then this one here," she said, ruffling his hair, "up and fecks off to Spain to 'fight for the soul of Europe.'"

"We shall all be repaid," I said, "for what we have done to the soul of Europe."

That put the brakes on their trip down memory lane.

Eventually, Kriegsmann managed a reply. "Well, Hamburg was a good start. The Allies will have their revenge, and it won't be just against our armies."

"Yes, I suppose before long we might have to move back to Dublin. Pity. Ooh, or maybe Argentina."

After a spell of silence, Pike tottered to his feet. "*Damas y caballeros,*" he said, raising the bottle of brandy. "Here's to a life spent waiting for death. *Viva la muerte.*"

He drained the bottle, bid us good night in Spanish, and staggered down the hallway to bed.

Little did I know it was the last drink I would ever share with him. It still rankles that the Kriegsmanns stole it from me.

Not long after, Pike collapsed in the Grunewald. Apparently, a forager found him unconscious on the ground and had him taken to the nearby hospital in Schmargendorf. When he woke, he wrote a letter to Val Kriegsmann, by then back in Copenhagen:

Got lost in woods. Now in care of nun, await soul ascent. Say goodbye to all in Éire.
Con amor, Francisco

A confused Val then telephoned her husband to ask why a Spaniard in a Berlin convent was saying good-bye.

Kriegsmann searched the Catholic hospitals and found him only a few hours after he had died. A nun was cleaning his face with a warm white towel, said Kriegsmann, and Pike looked serene. That night, just as the RAF fliers had promised us, the western part of the city was "Hamburg-ized." And, along with it, the mortal remains of Proinnsias Pike.

I told myself it was out of concern for my safety that Pike entrusted his final words to Val Kriegsmann rather than me. And while this explanation sounded eminently reasonable—for it was quite possible Veesenmayer had shared his suspicions of me with the Gestapo—I was, I admit, hurt by this final act of neglect.

And yet, when I picked up the pen here in my private bunker shortly after receiving news of Pike's death, hoping to sort out my thoughts on this man who exerted such a pull on me these last years—a man who at once drew me in with his charm and a fleeting caress while shutting me out with evasiveness and numbing irony—I found I bore him no grudge. Just a bottomless yearning that clung to those few days by the lake, beyond time, where I saw him and he saw me.

Perhaps it was pity that kept me from resenting him. For he was, above all, a tragic figure. A man destroyed by history.

But pity can only go so far before it turns to contempt. And for Pike I felt no contempt. Only love.

38

Finn McCool in
the Bowels of Teutonia

The Hausfrau

There was no sign of the fat doctor that whole
summer. And the clinic remained closed into the
fall. Hitler would no doubt be requiring ever higher
doses of his doctor's concoctions, as Germany's "war for
survival" was becoming more truthful than Goebbels
ever intended the phrase to be. If things went on like
this, Morell would never leave the Führer's side. This
realization depressed Finn. For, even after his return
to elementary man-hunting, he'd never been able to
give up his dream of a crowning slaughter. Try as he
might to cultivate the virtues of humility and the simple
nobility of workaday achievements, his heart burned
with ambition. Morell had rekindled these flames.
Finn's original vision of a massacre in the basement

of the Kaiserhof had given way to a new dream—the assassination of Hitler's doctor. How romantic and world-historical it all sounded. The words alone made his spine tingle. But would Morell ever return?

What was essential, lest he fall into another deadening winter slumber, was to keep busy. The radio broadcasts were of course off-limits, and as far as Finn was concerned, good riddance. He had long given up hope of any meaningful direction from Angleland, which meant he had only his own desires commanding him. But dreaming big and doing nothing, that was just the loafer's mask he donned for the Teutonians. He mustn't let it become his true face. He mustn't let the perfect become the enemy of the good. No—let the world take him for a lazy idle schemer while secretly he tended to his garden.

So Finn pressed on with the ensnarement of Dr. Grawitz. It was a knotty plan, and there had been some delays of late. The young gigolo Buckskin, whom he had initially recruited for the task, had been rounded up and shipped off to Sachsenhausen, where he and the other work-shy inmates were being worked to death. A grim *contrapasso*.

Thankfully, another brave boy-whore, Hatchet Willi, stepped forward to take his place. But Willi didn't give

a fig for comic books or schnapps and wanted only a
pile of cigarettes. Two cartons to be exact, which was an
exorbitant fee. But Finn, not wanting to disappoint—and
to be honest, since the last debacle, he feared the little
savages—agreed to the terms. To stockpile enough wild
game and home brew to trade for four hundred Slovakian
cigarettes took considerable time and unaccustomed
bouts of sobriety. But it was important to Finn that the
esteemed Dr. Grawitz meet his fitting end, in the jacks.

Finally, with the leaves already blushing with death
and Hatchet Willi with enough tobacco to fill his young
lungs with tar, the hunting of Grawitz resumed. The
gigolo held up his end of the bargain and, not long after
patrolling the black corners of the zoo, succeeded in
catching the eye of a particularly agitated mustachioed
man near the lavatory.

Finn gave him the signal from his blind in the bushes,
and the two of them slipped into the toilet. As instructed,
Hatchet Willi undid the latch while administering a
vigorous, hands-free fellatio. This allowed Finn to creep
in behind Grawitz, whose heavy grunting drowned out
the squeak of the hinge. Finn waited for the doctor to
climax, then buried his knife deep between his shoulder
blades.

Grawitz tried to scream, but his mouth had already
filled with blood.

Hatchet Willi licked his lips, while his late trick clunked headfirst into the sink.

All around, it was a merry evening.

The killing put a little spring in Finn's step for a few days, but then the thrill faded, revealing the despair that hung overhead and threatened to descend.

He wondered if the police were beginning to put things together at this point. Yet, perhaps to avoid the scandal of what had clearly been the result of a lavatory sex act gone wrong—Finn had so hoped to read the headline: RED CROSS PRESIDENT FOUND STABBED IN ZOO TOILET WITH PANTS AT ANKLES AND TOBACCO-STAINED SALIVA ON GENITALS—Grawitz's death was reported as an accident resulting from a faulty hand grenade. And, indeed, when Finn walked past the zoo, the toilet had been blown to smithereens.

After Grawitz, the trail of doctors went cold. Poppendick no longer frequented the Neues Museum; Lutz was presumably still in Munich and nowhere to be seen. And Morell? He had appeared only long enough to infect Finn with the idea of him, to haunt then elude him for the rest of his days. The obese physician had become his white whale.

But in the meantime, Finn needed more doctors, police investigation be damned. Which meant he needed the list he had obtained from Wagner. It was at his former lodgings in the Nymphenburg, along with the transmitter he'd used to talk with the Anglelanders—all left behind when he was spirited away into hiding.

The Torqued Man had warned him not to venture into town, but he was especially adamant that he stay away from the Nymphenburg. Obelinka and the current Boerish residents might say something to the wrong person. No one could be trusted. On top of that, block warden Eich was still on the prowl and would be certain to report the loathed Fenian's return.

So Finn returned under cover of darkness. The block warden lived two houses down on the second floor. His light was out, but Finn could detect his shadow at the window, where the blackout curtain was pulled back and moonlight glinted off his binoculars.

Unable to risk the front steps, Finn circled to the far side of the house. There he hoisted himself up the storm pipe and stretched his legs across the brick to the yellowed sill of the living room window. The latch had long ago corroded from the highly acidic, cider-rich streams of the Bretonese, and Finn was able to heave his top half onto the ledge and kick himself in the rest of the way. He made a loud thud when he landed on the living room rug, but the house gave no sign of stirring. He took the stairs slowly and, with a gentle turn of his key, entered his former bedroom.

Thankfully, there was not, as he had feared, an Afrikaaner sleeping in his bed. Instead, the room appeared as he had left it—with the green ashtray and brass lamp on the desk and the map of Berlin tacked to the wall. He knelt down beside the small bookcase, where he had left his cache. He moved the case noiselessly and was trying to get a fingernail under the floorboard, when he heard a low growl behind him.

Fin turned to see Olaf, the scruffy hunting *Hund* he'd abducted from Luckenwalde, baring his teeth. Beside him in the doorway were the thick, varicose legs of the Ruslandish hausfrau.

"Looking for these, Gospodin Finn?" said Obelinka in a flawless English she had never before displayed. She held the list and the transmitter in each hand.

"You startled me, old girl," said Finn. "I see you've found my buried treasure."

"We need to talk."

"It seems you've been practicing your English, Obelinka."

"And you've been a very bad boy, Finn," she said.

"If this is about arranging a spanking session, old girl, I can assure you—"

"You stupid man. We're on the same side, and you've gone and mucked it all up."

No suitable innuendo came to Finn's mind.

"I recognize this transmitter because I have the same one," she said.

"You're with the Anglelanders?" asked Finn, stunned.

"As apparently you are. As was Crean. That is, until you got him thrown in a concentration camp."

Obelinka proceeded to tell him that Crean was an SIS agent operating a pornography ring, with clients among high-ranking Nazis. He was gathering valuable information on organizations such as the Propaganda Ministry, the Reich Chancellery, and the Doctors' League. He had even blackmailed some of his clients into informing, lest he expose them as sexual degenerates. But then one of his top informants—Wagner—got killed under mysterious circumstances.

"Before Crean disappeared, a doctor named Schmidt told him he'd met a man impersonating him. An Irishman with an appalling accent and an alcoholic's face. That was you, I take it?"

"Couldn't have been. You know my German's as unblemished as my liver."

"And I assume this," she said, shaking the list of doctors, "came from the briefcase. The briefcase that just so happens to be monogrammed with the initials G.W., the same initials of the former head of the Ärztekammer, who just so happened to turn up dead." Obelinka gave him a stern look. "You've been killing them, haven't you?"

Finn grinned sheepishly, like a child caught with his hand in the sweets jar.

"First Wagner," she said, "then nothing for nearly two years, until a Dr. Heinze and his nurse get their throats cut in Brandenburg. And then, just a few weeks ago, a Dr. Grawitz blows himself to bits in a public toilet. All names on this list. All killed since you arrived."

"The truth is, Grawitz was stabbed. And Brandt was my doing too. Nevertheless, you're remarkably well informed for a housekeeper."

Obelinka laughed. "That's what all men think, which makes this the easiest cover in the world. They see a fat old woman and pay me absolutely no mind. They don't realize I have ears that can hear and are attached to a brain that can think. You all assume I do housework all day, when really I spend a few minutes cooking and cleaning and the rest of my time paying attention."

So that was why her cooking was so awful, thought Finn. "I, for one, have always appreciated your charms, Obelinka."

"Oh, you're a randy old goat. But this isn't about me. This is about you and how you've single-handedly ruined a top espionage operation. What's more, you've likely gotten Crean killed. Do you know what it's like to work in the brickworks of Sachsenhausen?"

"I had nothing to do with Crean."

"Bollocks!" spat Obelinka. "Fluss took him instead of you, because he's in love with you. It's a shame how you've led on that poor clubfooted queer all this time. You're an incorrigible flirt."

Finn, not accustomed to the sensation, blushed.

"But why did the Anglelanders tell me to infiltrate the Irish broadcast, if they already had Crean there?" he asked.

"Because you were supposed to be in Ireland. SIS got suspicious when you came back. They assigned Crean to keep tabs on you there, because they didn't trust you. And it seems they were wise not to."

Finn protested that all he had been doing was slaying Nazi doctors and single-handedly driving a stake into the biomedical heart of the Reich.

"Biomedical heart of the Reich? Now you've gone completely soft in the head. What in the world do you think blotting out a handful of doctors will do to win the war?"

Finn shrugged.

"No assassination short of killing Hitler himself is going to put an end to this madness," said Obelinka.

"There is one doctor whose death would do just that."

"What are you talking about?"

"Theodor Morell. He's Hitler's personal physician."

"How do you know?"

"I know one of his former patients. I even saw Morell in the flesh, just before he left Berlin," Finn said wistfully. "He was pumping half the elites of Berlin full of his concoctions. But that's all over. He's supposedly with Hitler in his secret fortress out east."

"But what's the point anyway?" asked Obelinka. "How would killing him kill Hitler?"

Finn repeated the rumor Rosaleen Lynch had told him, that the Führer was hopelessly addicted to Morell's injections. Simply couldn't function without them. That's why Morell was now ordered to be at his side at all times.

"So if the patient can't live without his doctor," explained Finn, "and you kill the doctor . . ."

"Then you find someone else to be his doctor?" said Obelinka.

"No!" said Finn. "If you kill the doctor, you kill the patient! Only Morell knows his way round those concoctions and dosages—they're his own bleedin' recipe. Trouble is, he's in an unknown location, hundreds of miles away."

The familiar buzz of the oven timer came from the kitchen.

"Well," said Obelinka, "you've clearly lost your mind, and my *bubliki* are done. You should know that I have to tell SIS what you've been up to."

She left the room with her *Hund* and started down the steps. Halfway down, the creaking stopped, and then Finn heard her rush back up. She appeared in the doorway, breathless.

"Where does Morell get the material for his injections?"

"How should I know? Why?"

"If you want to poison someone's soup, you don't have to do it at the customer's table. You can do it in the kitchen, then let the waiter bring it out."

"Is this a Ruslandish proverb I'm unfamiliar with?"

"Instead of killing Morell, which stands a rather ridiculously remote chance of actually killing Hitler and makes me truly question your sanity, if you could poison whatever he injects Hitler with—vitamins, did you say?—then, well, just maybe you could use the unwitting doctor to administer the lethal dose."

"Why, of course!" exclaimed Finn. "The vitamins! Listen, old girl, do you have any of those un-stomachable Vitamults lyin' around?"

"More than I can stand. Fluss saddled the South

Africans with a dozen apiece, but they wouldn't touch them. I tried to sneak them into their suitcases before they left, but the smell gave me away. Not even the rats want anything to do with them."

He bid her go fetch one. Obelinka's words had just reminded him of the Vitamult brochures beside the menu of hormone treatments at Morell's clinic. In his interminable wait for a glimpse of the doctor, he had read the copy a dozen times. He recalled that both the pamphlets for the hormone treatments and the vitamin bars bore a blue logo that looked vaguely familiar and a name that made him think of a Turkish bath.

Obelinka returned with her arms full of bars. "Take them all."

"One will do, thank you," said Finn, grabbing one. He examined the wrapper. Sure enough, it bore the same cerulean stamp: HAMMA INDUSTRIES.

"Hamma Industries, doesn't that name sound familiar to you?"

"Hamma? Not that I know of. Here, take these awful things too." She threw a bundle of large envelopes at him.

"What's this?" asked Finn.

"Crean's pornography. The poor fool. He left the negatives and a handful of prints with me for safekeeping. They're of no use to him now, and I can't bear having the vile things in the house. They haunt my dreams. But if they really are Nazi bait, then I suppose you might . . . Wait—" said Obelinka, interrupting herself. "Hamma. Don't they have an advert near the Oberbaumbrücke? You can see it from Köpenicker Straße, above the Spree."

The image came to him at once. HAMMA. Painted in blue letters over the ghostly palimpsest of the Rubenstein cooking-oil factory in Friedrichshain. The headquarters of Hamma Industries. Here must be where they made not only Vitamult bars but the special formula that coursed through the bloodveins of the Führer himself.

"By God," shouted Finn, "you're a regular Ruslandish genius!"

He stuffed the envelopes of smut into his coat and kissed Obelinka on her forehead. "Now, be a dear and tell the Anglelanders I'm off to kill Hitler."

He stopped by the kitchen and grabbed a piping-hot *bublik* from the oven. In his giddy state, it actually tasted grand—well, almost. Then to the pantry, where he pocketed the industrial-sized jar of rat poison. He had taken neither the list nor the transmitter. There was no need for those now.

39

JOURNAL

February 22, 1944

Since this mess is the closest thing I have to a journal
and now likely a final testimony, I will record the chaos
that has been unleashed: The Abwehr is dissolved. Canaris has been placed under house arrest somewhere
in Bavaria. The wave has finally come crashing down,
and just like that, we are shipwrecked.

As feared, the members of the Solf Circle broke
under torture and named several of our agents involved
in alleged anti-Nazi plots. I fear how this redounds
upon James, already in custody a month. No word
on Lauhusen's role, presumably because he's already
dead—praying that saves me from suspicion by proxy.

Everyone is scrambling for lifeboats. You've never

seen such panicked groveling. "Who has connections? Who can give me a recommendation? Who can secure my transfer abroad?" It's like a bad farce of what we've put the Jews through these past ten years.

Meanwhile, there's nothing at all funny about my situation. I have sent word to a handful of old contacts in Madrid in case there's anything for me there in the Foreign Office. But am doubtful as they, like everyone attached to Canaris, have seen their currency plummet.

March 8, 1944

Nothing for me in Madrid. Leissner has been removed. Himmler and his Security Office now control all foreign intelligence. All blood vendettas, no matter how petty, are being repaid. I fear the Reichsführer even remembers I once guffawed at his belief regarding the whereabouts of the Holy Grail.

Meanwhile, the bombings have resumed, and with a terrible new twist: They have started attacking in broad daylight. The terror of darkness now reigns throughout the day.

Perhaps I will not need a new job. Perhaps none of us will.

40

Finn McCool in the Bowels of Teutonia

Final Victory

Such were the memories that flitted through Finn's brain while he lay cramped in the ductwork of the Hamma factory. He had passed the afternoon silently regaling himself. And even though he had lived it, the story of his transformation here in the bowels of Teutonia—from a laboratory specimen fit for the garroting post into the legendary hunter Finn McCool—sounded like a far-fetched fiction. Perhaps next time he would tell it to himself a different way.

It was now dark. The clerk had finally packed up his papers and mustard jar and left. Finn wiggled forward and pressed his head against the metal grate until the screws popped loose. It clanged onto the desk below, followed by the crash of his stiffened body.

The fall knocked the sensation back into his limbs. He staggered over to the filing cabinet and, after a few minutes of searching, found what he was looking for: the home address of the sole proprietor of Hamma Industries, Dr. Theodor Morell.

Finn laughed when he saw it. *Inselstraße 24–26, Schwanenwerder Island, Wannsee.* He and Morell were practically neighbors. The man he'd been hunting for months lived just off the path of his daily foraging route.

And, oh, what a timely discovery it was. For, as of this morning, there had been a new development in what Finn was calling Operation Poisonous Mushroom. A new development of the most opportune sort.

As reported on the front page of the *Völkischer Beobachter*, Hitler had returned to Berlin to celebrate the martyr Horst Wessel's birthday. Likely at the prodding of Goebbels, who knew the people of the capital could use a little cheering up these days. After the "strategic retreat" of Stalingrad, it would be an immense help to see that their Führer was still hale and optimistic as ever about final victory.

If Hitler was back, that meant Morell was back

too. Surely he would take the opportunity to come home and call on his poor, neglected wife. Though, considering the man's hygiene and waistline, she probably appreciated her beloved best from afar. But, even if only to pick up fresh underwear for the bunker, Morell would certainly come home. And Finn could not miss his chance to pay a house call.

Slinking down the stairs to the factory floor, Finn spied a row of industrial stew vats belching and roiling beneath their lids. He had enough poison to kill a whole scrum of Hitlers, yet he mustn't dump it in the wrong concoction and, instead of killing his man, wipe out an innocent squad of sportsmen munching their nutrient bars.

Finn climbed the ladder to the largest of the vats. He lifted the lid and peered in. The smell almost floored him. Its putrescent cat-vomit odor and hue were unmistakably Vitamult. He checked the other cauldrons but was unsure how he should recognize Hitler's special brew among them. Then he noticed the pots were labeled. *The Rise and Shine, the Sharp as a Tack,* and *the Rejuvenator.* Only the smallest vat was without a marking. This he ascended and was met with a fragrance so evil he knew immediately it was the Führer's.

Finn poured in the full dose. Swirling colorlessly into the vat of bubbling barnyard secretions, his Hibernian seasoning looked right at home. He shut the lid and leapt from the ladder before the fumes could unman him.

Now he had an insurance policy. If Morell somehow slipped through his fingers, his deadly sting would still reach Hitler through the doctor's envenomed syringe. Obelinka would be proud of this prudent, comprehensive approach. No matter what happened, in a matter of days or weeks—either from withdrawal or strychnine poisoning—Hitler would be dead.

The Reich would crumble. The war would end. The plague of fascism would be eradicated. And the film negatives of that brain-deadening, soul-chilling smut—the smut that had excited the lust and fueled the murderous bureaucrats of the biomedical state— would grow brittle in their hiding place beneath the floorboards of the Torqued Man's cottage and eventually disintegrate.

The *Wilden* would come out of their forest hideouts and find loving homes to hug away their antisocial natures and wholesome sport clubs to corral their anarchic energy.

The concentration camps would be liberated,

all injuries and expropriations would be duly compensated, and a just coalition of Jews, Gypsies, Slavs, socialists, and homosexuals would rule over Teutonia for a thousand years.

The Anglelanders would hail Finn as the secret agent who single-handedly won the war, and along with a medal of honor, they would send a formal letter apologizing to him for having underestimated his talents and would relinquish their vitiating hold on the northern lands of their neighboring island.

His Taoiseach, Éamon the Valorous, ruler of a united land, would inscribe Finn's high deeds into the annals of the Fenian heroes, and the fine folk of Erin would continue to sing of him for centuries to come. They would sing of a man from the far-flung crumb of the continent, who, during the blackest moment of the blackest century, came from the pit of Spain to the bowels of Teutonia—not as a collaborator, or as a prisoner, but as a hunter.

Quitting the factory in Friedrichshain and following the gentle current of the Spree, Finn lit out for the western lakelands.

41

JOURNAL

March 23, 1944

It's finally happening. The rivets are coming loose. Amid general catastrophe, the particular shape of my own undoing has suddenly appeared.

There I was this morning, sipping ersatz coffee in Frau Obolensky's abandoned living room and listening to unconvincingly gleeful reports of the Luftwaffe's bombing of Modena, when the doorbell rang.

It was the handsome Kripo detective. The same one who'd questioned me over a year ago about Crean's disappearance. Only this time he had come here, to Nymphenburger Straße. As if that weren't bad enough, he was with two other plainclothes officers: bird-faced men who looked like brothers, possibly twins hatched from the same bad egg. Something about them screamed Gestapo. I fear they are the uncanny heralds of my doom.

"*Heil Hitler,*" they said in unison.

I muttered the required response.

"Are you Adrian de Groot?" asked one of the twins.

"Yes," I said, feeling my stomach drop into my shoes at the sound of my real name.

I noticed the Kripo detective smile, evidently satisfied to know I had lied to him earlier about my identity.

"What's this about?" I asked irritably, as though I didn't have time to deal with such a trifling matter as the police. They had an instinctive sense of hierarchy and made sure always to kiss up and kick down. But, of course, I no longer had any official protections. I was clinging to the desperate hope the old conditioning would keep them at bay.

They wanted to know whether I was residing at my sister's residence in Wannsee.

"On occasion," I said. "Why?"

"And you are also residing in this house?"

I was still technically listed as an occupant and, though it had been vacant of any foreign agents for months, I had been availing myself of its cellar as my bombproof writing den. I looked around me. "It appears that way."

"This house is now the property of the Reich Security Office."

Frankly, I was surprised the Security Service had not already expelled me or, for that matter, repossessed my car. The upside of bureaucratic chaos, I suppose.

"You think I don't know that?" I said sharply. "That's why I'm here, making sure no squatters or loafers tamper with the official housing of the Reich. You've no doubt seen my name on the housing registry."

"What official position do you currently hold?"

"You surely already know the answer to this question if you know who I am and where to find me. With the Abwehr folded, my official attachment is now to the Foreign Office." I had no idea if this was true. For the past three weeks, I had been busy simply staying alive.

Luckily, my answer seemed to suffice.

"When was the last time you were at your residence in Wannsee?"

"I don't know. A couple of weeks ago, I think." This was a lie. I hadn't been since Pike's death, but I didn't want to give them the impression I was an absentee owner, lest the People's Welfare League pluck it from me and assign it to a bombed-out family deemed more deserving.

The officers exchanged glances.

"Is anyone else residing in your home in Wannsee?"

"No, of course not."

"A neighbor reported seeing two men there on multiple occasions. Did you have guests?"

"When?"

"Ever."

"Is it now a crime to have houseguests?"

"It is if they are illegal houseguests. Now answer the question."

"I have had a guest there on occasion."

"Who?"

"Oberleutnant Helmut Kriegsmann of the Brandenburger Elite Commandos, if you must know. Now, shall I tell him you've been meddling in his affairs and obstructing the business of state?"

"Several reports have been filed against you recently," said one of the twins.

"What reports?" I said, still managing to maintain my indignant tone amid the genuine panic that was now creeping over me.

"One of your blackout curtains has been raised for the last week. Your neighbors have reported it on at least two separate occasions."

I would have been relieved, but two things unnerved me. First, how had my blackout curtain been raised a week ago when I hadn't been there in months? And second, why had the Kripo and perhaps the Gestapo become involved in a basic ordinance infraction that should have been a matter for the Ordnungspolizei? They must have suspected me of hiding someone.

"Forgive me, Officers. I must have raised it to clean the windows last time I was there, which, come to think of it, was probably closer to a week than two weeks ago. I'm duly embarrassed that I could have been so careless but will gladly pay the fine to compensate the *Volk* for my unintended thoughtlessness."

"Three infractions carry a mandatory ten-day period in custody," said one of them, as though challenging me to have a witty repartee to that. Then, after the threat had hung in the air long enough: "You're quite lucky that only two reports were filed."

"Yes, Officer. Very lucky indeed. I promise I'll see to the curtain immediately and remit payment to the Wannsee constabulary precinct posthaste."

Just when I thought my bluff had worked and they were losing interest, the young Kripo detective, who had been quiet and smiling all the while, piped up.

"Do you remember me, Herr De Groot? You were going by 'Herr Fluss' at the time. I don't suppose you have anything more to tell me about the disappearance of Archibald Crean now, do you?"

I flexed my toes as hard as I could to channel the

blood away from my head and keep my expression mild. "Detective, I'm sure you can understand that I was obligated, for reasons of state security, to present to you under my required alias, but I assure you I spoke the truth. I had nothing to do with Mr. Crean or whatever happened to him."

"And what about Frank Finn?"

"Like I told you, the man took a trip to Copenhagen, and I haven't heard from him since. Let's just say, gentlemen," I said, chancing another bluff, "Mr. Finn traveled there on confidential matters of intelligence, and, unless you wish to undermine the war effort, I urge you to desist from inquiring further."

The young detective looked down at his notes, which I took as a sign of victory.

"Your niece died at the Brandenburg State Welfare Institute in December 1940, yes?"

His question knocked all the feigned bluster right out of me. They saw the confusion blossom across my face.

"She was in the care of Dr. Hans Heinze," he said. "The same doctor who was murdered almost a year ago, along with his nurse." Did I happen to know anything about that, he asked in a pleasant tone.

I told them I vaguely recalled reading of the nurse killings and that a doctor had also been killed as collateral damage, though I hadn't realized it was the same doctor as Gretchen's. But wasn't I angry about my niece's death, he suggested.

"I was upset, if that's what you mean. The way people are upset when a loved one dies."

They all smiled at one another—a gesture more chilling and sinister than any form of interrogation.

"Of course," said the young detective, his eyes twinkling into mine.

"Are we all done here, Lipke?" asked one of the twins.

The detective nodded. "For the moment."

The other birdman told me to stay nearby in case they had more questions for me in the coming days. Then, as a parting shot: "In the meantime, lower that blackout curtain."

Something is wrong. Deeply wrong. They will soon uncover the truth of my connection to Pike and figure out what happened to Crean. But can they really believe I had something to do with the death of the doctor who murdered Gretchen?

Oh, but that's not all! My God, how could I forget? This is the madness of narrative. What an illusory sense of order! As though we experience life as a meaningful unfolding, when in fact it is a never-ending series of trapdoors.

I drove out to Wannsee to shut the stupid blackout curtain and erase any lingering signs of Pike's occupancy, in case they decided to search the house. I was glad I had gotten rid of my father's collection when I did. Many of the roads had been blocked for weeks on account of the rubble, but thankfully the Potsdamer Chaussee had been repaired enough for use.

When I arrived at the cottage, it was untouched, save for the raised curtain. I was usually meticulous about such things and couldn't understand how I could have neglected to lower it. As far as I could tell, there was no trace of Pike's inhabitance. I had been anxious that he might have left behind his false identity papers, but there was nothing there. Nothing in the closet or under the bed. The only things in the pantry were a pile of Vitamult bars, which seemed to have bred and multiplied on the shelf.

I surveyed my sister's home, host to so many deaths in recent years, and my eye caught at the urn on the mantel. I don't know what compelled me, since I had no reason to suspect that it contained anything other than the dregs of my niece's short and unlucky life. Perhaps its position on the mantel was slightly different from how I last remembered it.

In any event, something drew me to it, and I lifted the urn. It was surprisingly heavy. Too heavy. I opened

the lid and peered inside. In it was a rolled manuscript, wrapped in wax paper like fresh meat from the
butcher, lying on a bed of Gretchen's ashes. I undid the
wrapping and read the title page: *Finn McCool in the
Bowels of Teutonia: Concerning His Murderous Exploits in Berlin.*

What in God's name has Frank Pike left me?

42
Finn McCool in
the Bowels of Teutonia

Eine Spritze

Allthough was quiet at Villa Morell. Presumably, the good
doctor and his wife were abed. After all, it was
almost midnight, and Finn could well imagine how
tending to the Führer's corporeal upkeep tuckered a
man out.

He surveyed the property. The animal-secretions
business had been good to Morell. It was an Italianate
monstrosity, no doubt built by a nineteenth-century
sewing-machine mogul or mattress king who fancied
himself a doge. With pedimented windows, a rooftop
balustrade, and a belvedere for taking in the private
lakefront view from on high, the only thing that
broke the spell of Venetian splendor was the swastika
flapping limply above the front lawn.

But security at his palazzo was remarkably lax.

No halberd-hefting sentries, no ferocious mastiffs prowling the grounds. Not even a light, save for a dim glow on the second floor. A hallway night-light perhaps.

Finn, giddy with thoughts of plunging his dagger into the fattest belly of the Reich, went to the French doors facing the lake and set to work with his pick.

It took a few fumbling tries to revive the muscle memory, but as all things learned in childhood can never be forgotten, he soon heard the click of the latch.

Just then the floodlight switched on.

Finn jumped back into the dark.

A minute later, the door opened. "You're early!" snapped a woman's voice at him in Teutonian.

Finn remained frozen, unsure whether he should acknowledge his existence.

"Alright, let me have a look at you," said the voice.

Whoever she was expecting, thought Finn, it certainly wasn't him.

"Well, hurry up, then. I haven't got all night." As she spoke, her face came into the light. She was a comely woman, the doctor's wife. As comely as they come, in fact—silk wrap falling off her shoulders, hair up in a seductive heap, and the haughty, well-preserved face of a wealthy actress, with dark eyes, fine lips, and a nose he wanted to suck.

Finn stepped into the light, bracing himself for the inevitable confusion and screams he would have to stifle.

But instead of a scream, the woman only let out a long, exasperated sigh.

"Alright," she said. "I suppose you'll do. Though you hardly look like a 'Mediterranean Brigand.'"

And with that, she harried him inside, leading him through darkened rooms and up a grand staircase.

"I'm taking twenty percent off the price, and you can tell the service if they don't like it, then they should stop the phony advertising. What's your name, anyhow?"

"Francisco," mumbled Finn, still trying to find his bearings in this strange game, though he was beginning to catch the scent.

"Well, at least the name's believable. But if you're a Sicilian pirate, then I'm Hermann Göring."

Finn assured her she wasn't, though he could speak to her in Iberian tongues if she wished.

"Please do. Your German gives me a headache."

He followed her into a sumptuous bedroom, where two large candles were burning beside the canopy bed.

"Now, take off your clothes and put these on." She handed Finn a silk tunic and a red satin neckerchief and disappeared behind a Japanese screen.

Events were not unfolding as Finn had envisioned. His mind was set on justice. He had a foe to vanquish, a war to win.

Mrs. Morell tossed her wrap over the edge of the screen.

But wasn't this a plausible step in that direction? After all, he could use her to get close to Morell.

"What about your husband?" he asked, unbuttoning his shirt.

"Away at war," came the reply from behind the screen.

Finn frowned. Had his intelligence been wrong? But surely as reputable an organ as the *Völkischer Beobachter* printed only the truth. If Hitler was back in Berlin, Morell must have come with him. Perhaps he hadn't informed the missus?

"Come on, let's see what you're working with," said the doctor's wife, who now stood before him in all her glory, save for a pair of black boots that laced so far past the knee, they grazed the curls of her crotch. She was a ferocious beauty, such that it defied Finn's powers of cognition to picture her mounted by that fat slob husband of hers. No wonder she sought the comforts of a gigolo.

Never one to disobey a woman in such circumstances, Finn did as instructed. He sloughed off his trousers and let her admire his horn, which began to crack and sway with vital sap.

"Not half bad," she said, biting her fingers. "A bit gnarly, but not bad at all."

She helped Finn tie the neckerchief round his head, and then brought out a length of nautical rope.

"And what's that for?" he asked.

"To tie you up," said the doctor's wife, like it was a stupid question.

Finn eyed the rope warily. Images of vile smut along with memories from the Spanish pit flooded his vision.

"Oh, don't tell me this is your first time," she scoffed. "Now, give me those hands."

Finn held out his hands tentatively. "Just so long as we're clear, I don't go in for laceration, suffocation, or— and I'm sure I need not mention it here—defecation."

"Well, you'll just have to hope I honor your wishes, won't you?" she said, securing Finn's hands and tying them expertly to the tall canopy bedpost he stood beside. "Because now you're my pirate prisoner. And you are currently held fast belowdecks while my husband, the captain, is asleep. You're being transported back to the imperial court to stand trial for the hundreds of men you killed and the many thousands of women you raped. But not before I've had a chance to have my way with you. Understood?"

"*Todo entendido,*" said Finn, jumping into the role. He was a quick study in these arts, and, before long, he and Mrs. Morell were sniffing and licking each other in all the choice spots.

Finn cut a swath through her fur with his tongue while she stood on the bed. Then she got down on the floor and blew a fair tune on his horn. But, ever the actress, it was the sound of her own voice and sight of her own reflection that brought her the most pleasure. She told him how angry the captain would be if he found out what a terrible slut his wife was. How fallen she was for enjoying his reprobate cock, his terrible cock, which had punctured countless maidenheads and ripped through the guts of so many innocent girls. How she would sooner kill herself than bear a miscreant sired from his infernal seed, a swarthy degenerate for whom the gallows were too good. And she did this all while staring at an image of herself in the full-length mirror. Finn humored her by muttering amorous threats about splitting her in twain and filling her so full of pox she'd rot from the inside out. These played well enough, and she took no undue advantage of his vulnerability, save for a few bum slaps and scrotal tugs. All was shaping up to be a most agreeable, albeit kitschy, bout of coitus.

He was hilt deep in the doctor's wife, bringing

matters to a climax, when a man appeared in the doorway.

Mrs. Morell let out a shriek and uncorked herself. "Who the hell are you?" she cried.

"I am Stefanos? From the service?" said a bronze, curly-headed Greek with a confused smile. "Sorry, I knock at the back door like you said, but no one answer and the door is no lock, so I just follow the sound here."

"What on earth are you talking about? I only ordered one of you."

"Yes, that was me," said Stefanos. "Lotte says to me you are in mood for Sicilian bandit."

His gaze, followed by Mrs. Morell's, fell on Finn. "Then who the hell are you?" she asked, facing her erstwhile pirate ravager and his drooping horn.

"Sorry, is this still part of the role play?" asked Finn. But Mrs. Morell failed to find the humor in it. He was trying to assure her this was all a silly little misunderstanding, one he could clear up if only she'd untie him and let him fetch his wallet, when the doctor's wife cut him off and screamed at the top of her lungs: *"Theo!! Komm raus! Schnell!!"*

Just then, the door behind the full-length mirror flew open and out stomped the blubberous, exposed form of Dr. Theodor Morell.

It was really him. Face-to-face. The Poisonous Mushroom.

"Theo, this asshole's an impostor! A pretty good one, but an impostor all the same!"

Morell narrowed his eyes at Finn.

"I'm calling the police!" said Mrs. Morell, who now felt genuinely violated.

"No, no, dear. Let's not be rash. We don't need to bother the police with this. Besides, that would create difficulties for the service, and we don't want to make trouble for Stefanos here. Isn't that right, young man?"

Stefanos nodded uncertainly. His mind was no doubt clouded by the numerous rolls of flesh that poured out from Morell's open robe—identical to his wife's and yet a study in contrast. Beneath it was a pair of sweat-soaked women's knickers, all but hidden in the overhang of his gut.

"*Liebchen,* why don't you take Stefanos downstairs and pay him for his trouble. Meanwhile, I'll have a word with our impostor here."

Mrs. Morell gathered her robe and left with the Greek gigolo.

"Oh," he called after her. "And bring up some of that *Baumkuchen* when you come back. With cream!"

Morell shut the door and approached Finn, who had been fingering the knots of his bindings to no avail.

"So," said Morell, with evident satisfaction. "I saw you fucking my wife."

The man smelled rancid. A film of sweat shone on his face and chest, no doubt from all the furious wanking he'd been doing behind the mirror.

"That seems to have been by mutual design, sir. Though, technically speaking, I did not ejaculate, so I'm not sure it counts as a proper cornute."

"But you didn't come here to fuck my wife, did you?"

"Truth be told, I did not," said Finn. "Though I was more than happy to oblige. In fact, I won't even charge you for the service, like that strapping Hellene surely would have."

"If you did not come here to fuck my wife," asked the doctor, tilting his head at Finn like a curious *Hund*, "then why did you come?"

"I'm collecting donations for the orphan fund."

Morell chuckled, as he went to pour himself a drink from the boudoir's sideboard. "After midnight?"

Finn strained against his bindings, but there was no loosening them. The doctor's wife had lashed him tight to the mast. "Charity never sleeps, Herr Doktor."

Morell, who was chipping at a block of ice, paused. "So, you know who I am?"

"But of course," said Finn, looking him squarely

in the eyes. "You are the Master of Injections. *Der Spritzenmeister*. The most important physician in all of Teutonia."

Morell gave a slight bow. "And whom do I have the honor of receiving into my home and into the warmest recesses of my wife? And, please," he said, twirling the ice pick between his fingers, "let's dispense with the raillery."

"The name's Crean, sir, Archibald Crean. A native son of Éire, as you might have sussed from my distinctive grasp of Teutonian. I apologize for the violation and subterfuge. I assure you they were unintended. I simply found myself swept up into your good wife's theatrics and didn't want to disappoint. In truth, I came here in the dead of night because I had heard rumor of your return and wanted to seize the opportunity to put to you a business proposition. You see, I've had a number of dealings with your colleagues in the medical profession, men of discerning taste, who spoke of you in only the highest terms."

Morell squinted at Finn, looking for the deceit. But his curiosity had been piqued. "Go on."

"I'll get right to it, Herr Doktor. I deal in erotic photographs. And I had it on good authority that you are an aficionado of such pleasures. And, well, understanding that you are usually busy attending to

your—if I may speak frankly—illustrious patient, in
what I can only imagine are highly secure environs
with few material comforts or sensual delights, I
thought perhaps you would be interested in taking
some of my wares with you. I now realize I went
about things far too rashly, and again I apologize, but
my judgment was clouded by a sense of urgency and
a fanatical enthusiasm to be of service to you and the
Reich."

Morell took in this torrent of speech, mulling
it over as he scratched his chins with the ice pick.
Then, surveying his captive, who still sported the silk
neckerchief and tunic and stood naked from the waist
down, said, "So, you are the Irishman I have been
hearing about."

"Precisely, sir. At your service."

"And these wares, as you call them, I suppose you
have them here?"

"Of course. They're in the breast pocket of my coat,
just over there on the far side of the bed."

"In due time, in due time," said Morell. He downed
the drink he'd neglected, then approached Finn
from behind, pinning him against the bedpost with
his enormous mass. "But it seems foolish to concern
oneself with simulated eros when presented with the
pleasures of the *Ding-an-sich*. Don't you think?"

He lifted Finn's tunic from behind and drew the pick slowly down the length of his back, bringing it to a rest at his coccyx. He gradually applied pressure. Finn began to spasm as the pain shot out in all directions—up his spine, down his legs, out his genitals.

"I recommend keeping still," said the doctor, lowering the pick between his cheeks. "You could perforate a rectum quite easily, and I'm afraid colorectal matters are not my specialty."

Finn felt the scrape of cold steel upon his anus.

"More like an avocational interest," said Morell. He then licked his fingers and moistened the tip of his member. "As you know, my area of expertise is injections. And it looks as if you could do with a little *Spritze*."

Just as Morell prepared to heave himself on Finn, his wife returned with a plate of *Baumkuchen*. "*Du Schlingel!* I should have known you'd be having fun without me."

"Where's the cream?" asked Morell, poutily eyeing his cake.

In the doctor's distraction, his ice pick had drifted from the vulnerable region of Finn's crack and now hung harmlessly against his cheek. Seizing his moment and summoning the rage coiled within his legs [ham-shaped rockets], Finn sprang free of the doctor's grasp and leapt up the bedpost, onto the bed. Then, bouncing on the mattress, he shot through the canopy and jerked his bound hands with such force that the long post snapped between them like a twig.

He tumbled off the bed and crashed against the wall. The splintered bedpost, still stuck within his bindings, clattered down beside him. The corpulent doctor came at him with his ice pick, and Finn—seeing the Poisonous Mushroom loom before him like an execrable growth upon the earth and knowing that the fullness of his destiny had come—began to torque.

The veins of his temples burst as his eyes rolled in his head and spun like the reels of a slot machine. His tongue shot from his mouth, cracking his teeth, and turned like the propeller engine of an attacking airplane. His horn, still slick with adulterous quim, rose like a serpent piped from its nap and spit a lash of salty semen in all directions. Finn's hands [ample as oven mitts] caught the doctor's thrust and slowly, bone by crunching bone, began to work the Spritzenmeister's own needle backward into his big slapper of a gut.

The doctor grunted and shook, the sweat rolling off him in great sheets. He fought with all his might. He kicked at Finn's testes, which hung like grapefruits between his knees. He snapped at Finn's spinning tongue with jaws grown powerful from gluttony. He blew his miasmic breath into the saucer-sized nostrils of Finn, clouding his brain and making him unsteady.

But Finn would not relent. And the doctor's ice pick began to do its work. It punctured the surface of the great tympanous belly 'til the Poisonous Mushroom began to bleed. His guts hissed and roiled in anticipation, and the doctor let out a howl that woke the wolves. Little by little, Finn drove the injection into the man's stomach. Any other man would have long been gutted, but Morell's layers of fat were thick and bottomless. Finn was just about to drive the needle home and had stepped back to gather himself for a final thrust when his foot landed atop the broken bedpost.

Wobbly wood scrap underfoot, he rolled backward and fell against the window, whereupon he smashed through the glass, tumbled arsewise over the sill, and crashed like a twisted flak splinter onto the ground below.

43

JOURNAL

March 24, 1944

Sick with confusion. I can hardly write. Can any of it be true? Couldn't even bring myself to finish it. It's thrown me into intestinal havoc. I don't believe I've ever read something whose immediate effect was to incite violent diarrhea. "Bowels of Teutonia" indeed! If this keeps up, I'll soon run out of sawdust and my overflowing bucket will force me out of hiding.

I will try to sort out my thoughts here. Writing has at least restored my breathing to normal. Perhaps the bowels will follow suit.

Very well. Clearly it's a work of fiction, autobiographical to be sure but a fantasy nonetheless. Did Pike not tell me he was working on a novel? Well, this must be it. Though I'm not sure "novel" is the right term for this ungainly thing, which is by turns mock epic and puerile espionage potboiler, whose ludicrous plot nearly collapses under the weight of its overblown diction.

So, if it is a fiction, why am I so worked up? Does part of me still think it's real? Or is it just wounded pride? Am I supposed to see my own reflection in the Torqued Man? An internally racked and well-intentioned coward—is that really how he thought of me? Someone to be placated and humored? And yet I must remind myself that a "well-meaning coward" was only what the character Finn McCool, not the real Pike, called me before murdering Seán Russell. And all of that is surely fiction!

Alright, I suppose some of what he reports is plausible. Many of his facts are out of order, of course, but regarding the general sequence of events, let us review:

Was it possible Pike was recruited in Spain by the lawyer Baroucin, who himself was a double agent? Yes, but then this would mean England knew nearly every move the Abwehr was making, which is . . . well, this would mean they infiltrated us almost from the start and . . . yes, fine, I grant it is possible. And murdering Russell on the U-boat? Well, yes, of course he could have. But to return to Berlin when he could have gone home? And then this insane murder spree of Nazi doctors? What of the idea that Archibald Crean found my father's trunk of smut, as it is called, and turned it into an industry by which Pike, I mean Finn, lured Nazi doctors so as to murder them? But how could Pike have made up that first part? It's the uncanny kernel of truth embedded within this thing that makes me ill. He did say the doctors in Spain had conducted various experiments on him, but he seemed to laugh about it. And it's true Gerhard Wagner wound up dead of mysterious circumstances. Of the doctor Karl Brandt, I don't recall. But there was that report in the paper about the Red Cross president accidentally blowing himself up in the toilet. All the same, he's just taking real events and then weaving them into his fantasy, presumably because he lacked the powers of imagination to invent ex nihilo.

But how then did he know about the Brandenburg doctor and nurse who murdered Gretchen? Did I tell Pike about them? Perhaps I did. I confessed many things while he was sleeping in his sickbed. Was he, in fact, awake? But the idea that he killed them as an unsolicited favor to me, as some kind of courtesy, to carry out what I could never bring myself to do—well, it's pure madness. And I suppose, in some perverse way, touching.

Only now the police are sniffing around, and whatever semblance of truth is hidden in that ridiculous fantasy is now rippling off the page and into my life. I can only assume the young detective mentioned in Finn's story—the one he encounters at the flat of Rosaleen Lynch, at which point I couldn't read another page—is one and the same as the handsome Kripo Kommissar who has taken such an interest in me. I distinctly recall one of the hideous twins calling him Lipke. It was this uncanny coincidence that made me cramp so violently and throw the evil thing aside. The thought that Pike said or did something to implicate . . . no, no, no more—the bucket calls!

March 26, 1944

How foolish I feel. It's all a fiction. And I worked myself up to a near apoplexy over it.

I couldn't resist reading on in Pike's tale—and tale, as in tall tale, is how I now think of it. Though I still haven't finished it, as I got no further than the moment he mentioned storing Crean's pornography under the floorboards of my sister's cottage. Once I read that, I did not turn another page. Nor did I have time to ponder at length the staggering coincidence of Pike restoring the offspring of my father's horrible legacy to the very womb from which I'd ripped it years ago. Or the supposed revelations—preposterous!—that both Crean and Frau Obolensky are British agents. No, my only thought was that, on the off chance that a shred of Pike's manuscript was true, I had to get to the cottage immediately.

Of course, the car wouldn't start. It was out of petrol, and there was none readily available.

As expected, the S-Bahn line between Schöneberg and Zehlendorf was cut, so I had to ride the ring to Westkreuz. But in my fraught state I got on a train going the wrong direction and didn't notice until I was already in Treptower Park and at my wit's end. I was consumed by those criminal photographs pulsing against the floorboards in my mind, which evidently had no qualms about plagiarizing Poe. I kept picturing the Gestapo searching the cottage and then grinning when they noticed that stepping on a certain spot on the rug produced a distinct squeak.

Three heart-pounding hours later, I arrived in Wannsee. It was a moonless night. Smoke from the bombings still hung thick in the sky. I had forgotten my pocket torch, so the walk to the cottage was in total blackness. I could barely see the door well enough to fit the key in the lock.

But once inside, everything looked normal. No signs

of a police raid. I went to the corner of the living room, peeled back the rug, and lifted the loose floorboards, just as I had done twice before—once as leverage over Klaus and once to unburden myself of my father's legacy. I looked down below and promptly found . . . nothing.

There was nothing there. The cache of film negatives and photographs from that ghastly dungeon did not exist. At least, not in my possession. Not in my reality.

I collapsed in a puddle of relief. I had been driven half-mad by a fiction.

All that has happened is I forgot to close a blackout curtain, and Pike wrote a fantasy sprung from his own predicament, albeit with a few startling coincidences. That is all.

44

Finn McCool in
the Bowels of Teutonia

Lump of Sugar

When Finn came to, he was looking up at the sweetest rosebloom of a girlish face, framed in white. She was wiping his loins with a wet sponge. I must be in Tír na nÓg, he thought—the Land of the Young. His horn thumped against the starched bedsheet in exultation, and he raised his head to kiss the lips hovering over him. But at the slightest movement, his body seized in protest.

"*Immer sachte,*" said the nymph, gently pushing his forehead back against the pillow. "*Sie müssen sich erholen.*"

Queer, thought Finn, that the nymphs of Tír na nÓg in the far western sea beyond Aran should speak such fluent Teutonian. "Where am I?" he tried to ask, but his voice came out sounding like a rusty crank.

The nymph gave him a glass of water. Finn drank mightily from it, then tried again. This time, his voice returned. *"Wo . . . bin . . . ich?"*

"Im Krankenhaus," said the nymph. She smiled at him, caressed his cheek with the back of her soap-scented, perfectly pink hand, and left.

The sick house. Finn racked his brain for other locales in Celtic eschatology, but sick house was not one of them.

A few moments later, he heard a familiar voice. "So, you're alive."

"Obelinka?"

Gradually, she came into his field of vision.

"How in God's name did they let an old girl like you into the Land of the Young?"

"More like Land of the Dead and Dying," said Obelinka, once again in her newfound perfect grasp of English. "I hadn't set much hope by you, to be honest. But the nuns here are used to hoping in the absence of any."

"Nuns?" said Finn. "You mean that lusty nymph in the kerchief . . . ?"

"It's a wimple, you simpleton. But at least your libido's intact. It might be the only thing that is, after the spill you took."

"Where am I?" asked Finn for the third time, now thoroughly confused.

"The hospital."

With that dour word, all traces of Tír na nÓg vanished from his brain. He was in the land of doctors, but that heavenly nurse of his seemed as far from a white coat as . . . Suddenly, Finn remembered everything. "Is he dead?" he asked.

"Who?"

"Morell! The Poisonous Mushroom! The Spritzenmeister!"

"Lower your voice," said Obelinka, leaning in closer. She looked around at the other hospital beds, filled with those wounded in the latest air raids. They were burned and mangled, with disfigured faces and scorched limbs, but she worried some of their ears might still work.

"And, no, he's not dead. Not unless he had a heart attack on the flight back east."

"But I half gutted him!"

"Well, be that as it may, when he was chasing us across his lawn, I saw nothing more than a scratch. The man moves surprisingly fast for such a lard-arse."

"You were there?" asked Finn.

As it turned out, Obelinka had been on his tail all

along. Not only had she tracked Finn to and from the Hamma factory on the night of the attempted gutting of Morell, but apparently she'd scooped him from the front lawn in the nick of time—either tossing him over her shoulder like a sack of turnips or trundling him in a handcart she kept tucked under her skirts for such occasions—then tramped through pitch-black woodland on thick Ruslandish ankles all the way to the hospital in Schmargendorf.

"So you came to save me," said Finn.

"I came to gather credible intelligence, since I knew you wouldn't be doing so. And, since we've already lost Crean to this mess, I won't stand for another casualty of your addled brain."

Finn recalled treading the canopy pole underfoot. "If it weren't for that fucking bedpost!"

"What in God's name were you doing there, Finn?"

"I told you, I was winning the war. Kill the doctor, and you kill the patient."

"And like I told you, you're out of your bloody mind! Do you seriously think Hitler couldn't find another doctor? As you well know, the Reich is teeming with them."

Finn shrugged as much as his broken shoulders would allow. "Hitler or no, it would have been a fine thing to slay him. Ah! But I took out an insurance policy, old girl. Your idea, in fact."

"What do you mean?"

"I spiked the punch."

"Meaning?"

"Meaning Morell lives, but Hitler is dead! Or he soon will be!"

Obelinka noticed the eyes of the noseless patient in the neighboring bed turn toward them. "You must be quiet," she said to Finn. "Now tell me precisely what you did."

"I broke into the Hamma factory and dumped the whole larder's worth of strychnine into the vat—the very vat of hormones Morell pumps into dear ol' Adolf's bloodveins."

"What do you mean, 'the whole larder's worth'?"

"The rat poison you keep in the pantry. I used all of it. It'll be eating through the Führer's organs in no time!"

"What rat poison?" said Obelinka bemusedly. "I never kept any rat poison in the pantry."

"Of course you did. That giant jar on the uppermost shelf on the left."

"That's ersatz sugar, you fool. Some loathsome blend of saccharin, sawdust, and whore's perfume."

"But there was a skull and crossbones drawn on the jar's label."

"That was one of the cheeky Bretons' doing. They brought it home to me before you showed up. I used it once in a cake and never again, though I hadn't thought about killing rats with it. . . ."

"But . . ." said Finn, agog. His mind was unspooling in all directions, and he felt a lump the size of a billiard ball form in his throat. "That's what I used to assassinate Seán Russell."

Obelinka laughed. "Oh, Finn, you poor confused man. I'll grant you might have given him a tummy ache and left him with an appalling taste in his mouth. But assassinate? I think not."

The revelation was too much for him to bear. Morell was alive. Hitler was alive. Even the treacherous Fenian Seán Russell, though dead, was so by no hand of his own. Had it really been just an ulcer? But what about Wagner and Grawitz? And Brandt? And the executioners of the Torqued Man's niece? Were those not the work of his stag knife?

Finn felt the coiled springs in his brain come loose. Something misfired, and the carefully stitched seams of his self rent and unraveled. He had come undone.

45

JOURNAL

April 20, 1944

The world is not yet ending. Or, rather, it is, but it's a long process, and the final explosion lies somewhere just beyond the horizon.

Meanwhile, nature refuses to capitulate. Blind and stupid in the face of our desecration, another spring dawns. The phosphorescent yellow shroud that has hung over this ruined city since November has finally receded. The sun still shines in the sky. The birds still chirp in the trees. And these battered Berliners still go about the grim business of living, rooting through the rubble for cigarette butts to stuff in their pipes. We suck life from the ruins until there's nothing more to suck.

I'm here in Wannsee, writing aboveground and out

of doors for the first time. Given the dizzying events of the past month, today, with the first hopeful moment in well over a year, I find myself moved to take up the pen in daylight. It feels like my first visit to a nudist territory: initially terrifying, then exhilarating, and before long perfectly normal.

Not that I will make a habit of this. But today is a special day. Our dear, deranged leader and absentee warlord turns another year older, and I will honor the occasion with a gift. Of course, I'll have to feed these sheets into the stove as soon as I've written them.

If I recall correctly—for my journal is safely hidden at the moment—the last entry I made was right after checking the floorboards at the cottage, somehow convinced that Pike's story posed no real threat to me. Is there anyone stupider than one's former self? Anyone more clueless, more worried about the wrong things, more blind to the motives that drive us and the reality staring us in the face?

No sooner had I written that entry and gone upstairs to make a cup of tea to sip while I read the end of Pike's story, having convinced myself that I at last knew how to read it, than the knock came. And with it, the start of the single most harrowing and defining chapter of my life.

I opened the door to the two bird brothers, each of them flanking Kommissar Lipke, all of them smiling at me. They wanted to ask me some more questions, they said, but this time it was necessary to take me into protective custody.

I don't remember the conversation after that. Those terrible words cut some vital cord within me, because I knew perfectly well what "protective custody" meant. It meant they could do with me what they wanted. No need for an arrest, a formal charge—I was their plaything for as long as they liked. I could have shouted, "What's this about?" And perhaps I did. But it would have been pointless. It didn't have to be about anything.

As I feared, the car turned at Potsdamer Platz in the direction of Prinz-Albrecht-Straße. Toward Gestapo headquarters.

But when Lipke noticed this, he became indignant. "What are you doing?" he shouted from the back seat to the bird brothers in front. "This is my case, my jurisdiction—go to Alexanderplatz."

The bird brothers looked at each other. "We have oversight, Lipke, in any case we choose. We advise you not to be so uppity."

But uppity was exactly what Kommissar Lipke was.

"Gentlemen, I hardly need remind you my uncle is Reichskriminaldirektor Nebe. If he hears that the Gestapo is poaching on Criminal Police work, preventing the Kripo from working homicide investigations, and has to take time out of his busy day to meet with Herr Himmler, who I'm sure is even busier, to inform him that the clearly articulated divisions within the Reich's security apparatus are not being adhered to—"

"Alright, alright, you've made your point. But we're coming with you."

The car turned back onto Leipziger Straße and headed across the river. Though I did not appreciate it then, the outcome of this dispute is likely the sole reason I am able to write these words today.

They put me in a small room with two opposing chairs and a table. I was seated in one and the young Kripo detective took the other. The birdmen loomed in silent menace behind me.

"Herr De Groot, can you confirm your whereabouts on the afternoon of April twenty-fifth, 1943?" asked the detective.

The accumulated tension and the absurdity of the question made me burst into laughter.

"You find that question humorous?"

"No, it's just that I can't possibly answer that—not without my logbook," I replied, "which was destroyed when I was bombed out of my flat in January."

"So you have no alibi for the afternoon in question."

Alibi? For what? That date meant nothing to me as far as I could recall.

"I didn't say that, Herr Kommissar. I only said I can't immediately recall my precise whereabouts on an afternoon one year ago. But I believe that would have been right around the time I was tending to a group of visitors from South Africa concerning matters of state. Honestly, I don't know, given the recent tumult of jurisdictions, whether I am at liberty to divulge further details of those operations."

"Let me jog your memory, Herr De Groot: Do you recall visiting the children's wing of the Brandenburg State Welfare Institute that afternoon?"

So it was that again. Not about Crean or Pike or my Abwehr associates or my stupid blackout curtains. It was about the doctor.

"No, I'm quite sure I didn't. I hadn't been there since my niece's death, at the end of 1940. Of that I am certain."

"You said a few days ago that you had been upset by your niece's death. Were you upset with anyone in particular?"

"What do you mean?" I asked.

"Did you blame the doctor for your niece's death?"

"No, of course not," I said unconvincingly.

But hadn't I once threatened Dr. Heinze with violence, he asked, when I learned of her death?

I had no recollection of doing any such thing, I said,

as I felt the blood in my cheeks betray me. I thought back to that moment, in the days following Gretchen's death, when I found myself shaking outside the hospital in Brandenburg, the word "murderers" on my lips. But it was true. I had no recollection of making any specific threat.

I was upset, I said, that was all. It's possible I spoke to the doctor severely. In any event, I said, that would have been well over two years before the doctor and nurse were murdered. "That's a bit too long for a crime of passion, don't you think?"

"Yes, it is. But for a premeditated murder, I'd say it's a most judicious window."

"That's preposterous!" I said. "I've never murdered anyone."

The young Kommissar exchanged private glances with the silent Gestapo agents behind me.

"How, then, do you explain the recent testimony of a patient who claims to have witnessed the murders first-hand? A young Werner Essenfeld, eleven years old, was a catatonic patient in Room 113A, where Dr. Heinze and his nurse, Frau Mittler, were killed. Two days ago, for the first time in four years, he spoke."

"A medical miracle," said the Gestapo agent behind my left shoulder.

Yes, a miracle that the boy himself hadn't already been murdered by the hospital staff.

The detective looked at me for a reaction to this news.

"According to his testimony, the killer, a man of medium height and pale complexion, came into the room with Dr. Heinze and, just before stabbing him, said the following words: 'This is for Gretchen.'"

"What do you say to that, Herr De Groot?"

So it was true. My God, it was true. Pike's story was true.

"Okay, Lipke," said one of the birdmen behind me, after I'd sat there a minute in shock. "Let him marinate."

Whereupon I was stripped down to my underwear, marched to a black windowless cell, and left to decompose. For how long I cannot say. It could have been two days. It could have been ten. I wager it was somewhere in between.

Time vanished into the darkness. Even the normal animal rhythms went silent. I was too nauseated to eat and had little need to move my bowels—a blessing considering my sole outlet was a chamber pot discernible only by touch. The only punctuation came in the form of a stale roll and a pitcher of water deposited through my slot. I could not see my hand in front of my face. All I had to tie me to a reality beyond my own thoughts was the feel of cold concrete, the sounds of clicking boots and distant screams.

I was terrorized by the thought that the police would find the two manuscripts—my journal and Pike's story—when they searched the Nymphenburger house. Thank God some part of me had the foresight to hide both of them before coming up the stairs that morning, as was my habit. But had I hidden them well enough? Would they think to poke a broom handle into a defunct pipe in the cellar ceiling?

There were waves of anger down in that hole too. I had been hurt by Pike's words. They felt like a betrayal. Why had he done this to me? What had I done to deserve this? Why should I be punished for his actions? Pike had deceived me. But why? Why did he only pretend to be my friend?

And yet there were those few precious and ineradicable days just before he drifted away for good. Days without pretense or deception. Just us together. And how could I claim he did not care for me, when, after all, he had killed for me? Unasked, unbidden, he had done me this mad kindness. I spiraled through these thoughts until exhaustion put an end to all thinking.

I was woken with a bucket of cold water. Then

dressed in someone else's clothes and given another roll and a lukewarm cup of tea. The guard told me I would be interrogated within the hour and returned me to my dark cell. Now fully conscious, I was taut with anticipation, even though I knew there was nothing I could do to prove my innocence. I had thought of turning over Pike's story to them, but to find it they would also find my journal.

A whole day must have elapsed before they finally brought me to the interrogation room. Kommissar Lipke sat at a table behind a large lamp. The Gestapo agents were gone. Perhaps he had successfully elbowed them out of his investigation, or they were busy digging for new evidence to bury me.

The detective switched on the floodlight. I cannot describe the pain one feels when, after days of total darkness, thousands of watts of light explode into your retinas. But I now know that light has a sound, like screeching train metal, as it screams into your brain.

He laid a file on the table. "Please have a look."

It's the journal, I thought, with a heavy, sinking feeling. I had signed my own death sentence.

"Open it."

I squinted at it again, fumbling at it with my shaking hands. I then realized the file was far too slim to be my journal, or Pike's manuscript for that matter. It was something else.

I opened it but could barely make out the words. Gradually, my eyes focused enough to read the heading: DIRECTORY OF THE REICH COMMITTEE FOR THE SCIENTIFIC REGISTERING OF SERIOUS HEREDITARY AND CONGENITAL ILLNESSES.

"This was found in the house you were occupying at the time of your arrest. Would you like to explain how it came into your possession?"

I told him I didn't know.

"Would you like to explain why the names of these doctors have all been crossed out?"

I told him I didn't know.

"Don't you find it an intriguing coincidence, Herr De Groot, that all these doctors are dead?"

I said nothing.

"Where did you get this directory?"

I told him it wasn't mine, that the house had been host to several occupants over the years.

"Then you are saying one of the foreign agents under your oversight was in possession of this directory?"

I said I didn't know.

"Who can vouch for your whereabouts on the afternoon of April twenty-fifth, 1943, between two and six p.m.?"

In the hole, I had reconstructed that day from memory as best I could. I had gone to Tirpitzufer in the morning to sort out the fake documents our Boers would need once they were smuggled back to Africa, then driven out to the cottage in the afternoon to deliver Pike another meager share of rations. He was of course gone. I stayed a few hours, on the off chance he'd return before dark, then, giving up, drove back to my flat and had dinner alone. In short, a perfect lack of alibi.

"No one," I replied.

"Where did you get this directory?"

Lipke fired barrage after barrage of these same questions at me under the lights, raising his voice until he was shouting in my face. And then, quite abruptly, I was returned to the hole. No one laid a hand on me. With darkness, light, and time, they had all the tools they needed to crush a man's will.

But, you see, it was precisely in this crushing of my earlier will, the will toward self-preservation, that I finally discovered a new one. A will that had been latent in me for years, that I'd fought for so long to ignore, and that there in the blackness flowered. Just like that, my thoughts changed and I found a way out. I recalled the caged ape of Kafka's story and hugged myself with excitement. There was no escape. That much I knew. But there was a way out.

46

Finn McCool in
the Bowels of Teutonia

Krankenhaus

The nun wiped Finn's privates with such regularity
you could have taken tea atop them. He had to
hand it to the Teutonians on matters of hygiene. Sure,
they ran amok with the concept when applied socially,
but confined to the literal scrubbing and scouring of
surfaces, they were nonpareil. Though there were
signs that the lusty nun's sponge baths were motivated
by more than just cleanliness. Not only were they
administered daily and each time longer than the last;
she also used her hands more than the sponge, even an
occasional pinky on the perineum, and lathered him
so thoroughly that at the end of each session his horn
positively sparkled.

Alas, it was the only part of him that did. His limbs
were still in bandages, and a deep gloom pervaded

his brain from crown to stem. At his lowest moment, believing he was at death's doorstep, he sent final word to his old Fenian girl-chum in Daneland, bidding her pass on a farewell to his clan back in Erin. He would have liked to write the Torqued Man too, for he at least owed him a goodbye, but he didn't want to compromise him. He asked the nun to post his letter and waited for his body to cough up his soul.

Sensing the deep funk her charge had fallen into, the Christbride redoubled her efforts to buoy his spirits, honoring her vow to show charity wherever it was needed. And while those chaste, life-affirming sponge baths were surely appreciated and must have helped circulate the vital sap through his veins, they were not enough to fix him.

That monumental task fell to his fellow invalid. Each day more beds were filled by new casualties from the Anglelandish air raids. The faceless man who once occupied the bed next to Finn had died and been replaced by a legless child. One afternoon, the boost from his midday bath long since dissipated, Finn lay gazing at the ceiling, waiting for either death or the next day's horn-laving to come, when he felt the eyes of the little lad upon him.

He turned his head, still a slow and painful ordeal, and returned the boy's look. They spent some minutes this way, eyes locked. When Finn finally caught on and realized he'd been informally challenged to a staring contest, he threw the match with a climax of dramatic bulges and a flurry of blinks. His opponent enjoyed this, and the game soon changed into a contest of facial contortions.

Much as this sport made Finn's head throb, the laughter it elicited was a salve upon his wounds. He spent the afternoon this way, exchanging queer faces with the little legless boy called Emil.

"Emil?" said Finn, after the boy had told him his name. "And your family name wouldn't happen to be Fluss, would it?"

The boy found this funny. "No, my name's Hauser. Emil Hauser." And then he got very sad and began to cry.

"What is it, Emil? Are your injuries paining you?"

No, it wasn't that, said the boy. It was just that his father's name was also Emil Hauser. And his father was dead.

"And what about your mother, Emil?"

Not the right question, it turned out, as the poor lad had twice the tears for his mother. She, too, was of course dead. The same roof that had crushed the boy's legs had fallen on her head. Finn gave the boy his condolences.

"Life's a real kick in the teeth, son. I'm sorry you've had to learn it so soon."

"Why do you talk funny?" asked Emil, distracted by the peculiarity of Finn's Teutonian.

"Because I'm from a strange and distant land," said Finn.

"Which land is that?" asked Emil.

"The land of Erin, they call it," said Finn.

"And where's that?" asked Emil, a curious lad with a great thirst for knowledge.

"Across the North Sea, on the windward side of a dour but mighty place called Angleland."

"That land I know," said Emil. "They're the ones who've taken my legs and killed my mum."

A terrible, cowardly way to wage war, thought Finn. Surely the world was a better place when warriors gutted one another on the field of battle. But where was the honor in man-slaying like this? Did this six-year-old's pair of obliterated legs or his mother's smashed skull really put a dent in Hitler's war machine? No, by God, the approach was all wrong. The steaming injustice of it all boiled in Finn's brain—a clear sign that there was yet life in him.

With his horn kept immaculate and his young hospital mate pumping him for stories of his homeland, Finn slowly healed. He regaled the

boy with tales of the great hunter Finn McCool
and his merry woodsmen of the Fianna, his loyal
hounds Sceolang and Bran, and the adventures of
shapeshifting and trickery and great boastful lies with
which they filled their days in the green forests of
Erin.

Finn told him of the deer he once came upon in a
clearing and how, just as he was poised to fell her, she
transformed into a beautiful woman, and how Finn
took this deer woman for his wife, and she bore him
a son, Oisín, but not before changing once more into
a deer and escaping back into the forest. As a result,
Finn did not know his son until years later, when the
lad was about six or seven, and he came upon him in a
smoke-filled grove, where Oisín was roasting a boar.
Seeing that Finn had just bagged a tusker himself,
the boy challenged him to a cook-off. And observing
the identical way each handled his hunting blade and
manned the fire, Oisín and Finn recognized the other
for father and son. After which Oisín joined the merry
band of Fenians and the two of them were as entwined
as the double spiral of Epona.

The little orphan Emil delighted in this story of
recovered paternity and bade Finn recount it daily.
Each time, Finn embellished and altered the tale,
until the setting of Erin gradually morphed into the

Grunewald, only a stone's throw from their hospital
beds, and young Oisín became a boy who, though
missing his legs, could swing through the forest on
branches and vines like an orang-utan.

In this way, Finn and Emil became fast friends.
And though Finn had never in his forty years felt the
paternal pull, he sensed within his wrecked self the
budding of a new capacity—if not fatherly, then at
least avuncular.

Then Obelinka returned.

"We're going back to Angleland, Finn."

"What? Why?"

"We've been recalled. In case you can't already tell,
the RAF plans to bomb Berlin to bits. It's no longer
safe here."

There was some semblance of protest on his lips,
though nothing he could articulate. He had no clear
purpose. No plan. No mission.

Anyway, Obelinka had already arranged
everything. They were to escape up the Havel by
canoe, join the canal that flowed into the Oder, and
then float downriver until they reached the Baltic
coast. A fishing troller sent by SIS would pick them up
outside Stettin and carry them to neutral Swedeland.

She had just explained to him the extraction

plan when Finn saw the familiar figure of Helmut Kriegsmann walk past the doorway and down the corridor.

He alerted Obelinka to this development.

"What?" she said, alarmed. "How does he know you're here?"

Finn explained he might have written a letter to his wife and she may have put the pieces together and told her husband.

"You fool!" cursed Obelinka. "Quick, you have to hide."

"But why? Kriegsmann's no harm."

"The man's an elite commando, and I don't want him mucking about."

"So we'll escape later."

"It has to be tonight. Everything has been set in motion. Any delay means we'll miss the boat and then we're stuck."

"Just hop on the transmitter and tell them we need some more time."

"That's not how this works, Finn! Besides, I've smashed our transmitters—they're too dangerous to carry on us while we travel. Now quick, hide!"

But Finn was not going anywhere quickly. His foot was still in a cast, and he hadn't stood up in ages.

The nun, who was across the room spooning gruel

into a patient's mouth, noticed Finn's distress and stood to come over.

"You go," he said to Obelinka. "I have an idea."

She gave him a skeptical look, as if to imply ideas were not his strong suit, then slipped out.

When the nun approached, Finn, hoping he'd read her kindness correctly, grasped her hand and uttered his plea. "Merciful sister, please, my life is in your hands. A man just walked in, a very bad man, who wants me dead. He scorns the love of Christ and wants to finish the job he started when he threw me from the third-floor window. Please, dear sister, can you save me?"

"Who is this man?" she asked, instantly at the ready, as though she'd been waiting for ages to expand her repertoire of care.

"A dashing fellow in a field officer's uniform. He'll come in here any second looking for me. I know it's against your vow to lie, but could you lie to save a life, even if it's the miserable life of a contrite sinner such as myself?"

"Yes, of course," she said, exasperated, "but what do you want me to say?"

"Wrap my head in bandages and tell him I'm not here."

She ran to the doorway, peered into the hall, then

ran back. "There's no time for that. The man is coming now!"

She jerked Finn's bedsheet from its tuckings and draped it over his face. "Hold your breath!"

Finn opened up the great bellows of his lungs [each the size of a zeppelin] and sucked in so much air he made the rest of the hospital light-headed. A few seconds later, he heard the well-mannered voice of his Teutonian warrior friend—one whom history had simply placed on the wrong side—inquire whether a foreigner resembling the man in this photo had been admitted as a patient.

"Yes, sir," said the nun. "He was indeed here. But I'm afraid he's dead."

By God, his Christbride was a consummate liar.

"Oh. Dead, you say?"

"I'm sorry, sir."

"When did he die?"

"Just a few hours ago."

"Really? What of?"

"Fever, *mein Herr.*"

"Is that him?" said Kriegsmann.

Finn gathered she had pointed at his draped corpse.

"Can I see him?"

"It's best if you stay there at some distance, sir.

There's been a typhus outbreak, and since he died of fever, we oughtn't take a chance."

Finn was running out of air. His lungs were sending urgent, unheeded messages to his brain as he heard the sister's footsteps approach. "Don't move a muscle," she whispered as she bent down and pulled back the sheet to reveal his face.

"Yes, that's him," said Kriegsmann solemnly. "Thank you."

She replaced the sheet over him. He was about to explode.

"Would you like to claim the body, sir?" he heard the nun ask.

What the hell was she up to?

"No, not yet. I'll ring later to make those arrangements."

"Very well, sir. Again, my condolences."

Flashes of light sparkled in his mind's eye and he felt a tingling throughout his body. Finally, the sheet peeled back again, and there, while he gasped for dear life, was his cunning little liar of a redeemer, smiling down on him.

47

JOURNAL

April 21, 1944

Backed into a corner with darkness in all directions, I could finally be honest with myself. Why had I been so drawn to Pike in the first place? He had charisma, a certain roguish charm, and a playful learnedness— yes. But at the root of all those qualities was a sense of self-possession. He was a sovereign self. He would not be cowed or corralled into anything. But it was precisely his association with us that called this essential aspect of his character into question. I couldn't reconcile the two. It had perturbed me. And, in my attraction to him, I was moved by some vague desire to help him, to preserve his integrity. But, as I had just learned, Pike never compromised. He had resisted to the end.

It was perhaps a kind of quixotic madness, a sickness that drove him to kill, but he had done the very thing I had always wanted but been too cowardly to do: revolt. To throw off this disgusting cloak of rationalizations, complicity, and guilt, in which for nearly a decade I had wrapped myself.

I had wanted to pretend the Abwehr was something apart. I had wanted to pretend my aversions and private opinions kept me above the swamp, floating on a cloud of inner exile. I had wanted to pretend saving Pike by sacrificing Crean was an act of heroic defiance, when it was simply an expression of my desire. But it was also my desire—to go along and keep myself out of harm's way—that made me deliver the Bretons to their horrible fate.

Kant had it wrong. There is no distinction between duty and desire. Rather, duty is just a name we give to desire when we desire something difficult. We are faced then with a choice between conflicting desires. Do we choose one and violate our desire for moral dignity, or do we choose the other, that of revolt, and violate our desire for safety and comfort? To put it another way, the question is simply: In which way do we want to suffer?

There in my hole, I finally understood what Pike meant about the damnedness of choice. He had worn the mask of cynicism, having me believe he'd chosen to escape his Spanish pit, as he called it, simply out of the will to live. I had seen through the mask, though I hadn't seen through to the truth. But now I understood. And with it, I understood the truth of myself. Apart from hiding Pike, I had consistently followed my desire for safety and comfort. His appearance in my life, I now realized, had disturbed me because I sensed in him a fantasy of my own repressed wishes. Beneath my worry, my anger, my hurt feelings, there—still intact—was a more authentic feeling: longing. Not just a longing for Pike, but a longing to be like him. I wanted to be damned in the way he had chosen to be.

And now the parameters of my choice had been radically simplified. I could endure their interrogations, their tortures, all the while maintaining my innocence, only to have them pin on me whatever charge they wished. Before long, the Gestapo would get their hooks in and unravel the truth about Crean and Pike. Some kind of a perfunctory show trial in the People's Court surely awaited me. If not a death sentence, then its equivalent in the *Lager*. So much, then, for the desire for self-preservation. That meant the choice now before me was either to refuse responsibility or to accept it. I could stubbornly cling to the truth of my innocence on the futile hope I would be exonerated, or I could heed that other long-nursed, long-neglected desire. As Cervantes's Knight of the Sorrowful Face once said, and will say for eternity, *I know who I am and who I may be, if I choose.*

The next time I was pulled from the darkness and sat in the chair before Kommissar Lipke, I looked at him calmly and said, "There's no need for further questions."

"Oh, really," he said, laughing at my commanding tone. "And why's that?"

"Because I confess. I killed the doctors. And the nurse. I killed them all."

48

Finn McCool in
the Bowels of Teutonia

Downriver

O belinka returned after dark and pulled Finn
from his bed. His muscles were atrophied, and
he walked with a limp on account of the bulky plaster
shoe round his right foot. But he could move. This
he had discovered earlier that afternoon, at the same
time he learned that his holy redeemer and lady of the
sponge was not so chaste as he'd supposed. Finn had
thanked the sister for granting him succor, a show of
gratitude that somehow found him sucking her nipples
in the mop closet. She had given him life in death and
now, verily, Lazarus had risen.

"Let's go," said Obelinka testily.

But Finn would not go without first saying goodbye
to his young friend Emil. He'd been sleeping all day on
a morphine jag to ease the agony of his phantom limbs.

Finn hobbled over and put a hand to the lad's forehead. He hadn't meant to wake him, but the boy's eyes popped open.

"I thought you were dead," said Emil.

"Me? No, you were just dreaming, my boy. I'm right as rain. But I'm afraid I do have to go."

"Where?"

"Back to my homeland."

"To Erin?" asked Emil, excited. "Will you take me with you?"

"Oh, wouldn't that be marvelous? But it's a long way, as you know, and it's a twisted, dangerous journey. You'll be happier here with the good sisters. And just wait 'til you hit puberty. Then you'll really enjoy yourself."

"But I want to be part of your Fianna and swing through the trees like Oisín."

"Finn!" said Obelinka. "It's time."

"I'll tell you what," Finn said to the boy. "You rest up here and get your strength back, and as soon as you're feeling fit, I'll send for you. And then you can join me in the forest with all the other merry Fenians, and we'll fill our days with feasts and hunting. Now, how's that sound?"

Emil nodded. *"Gut."*

"Alright, then, it's a deal." Finn spit into his hand

and extended it. Emil did the same, though the poor lad's mouth was dead dry on account of the opiates, and the two shook on it.

The Ruslandish hausfrau heaved the canoe into the current, with Finn lodged in front, then nimbly leapt in.

"Two on the right, two on the left," she called out like a seasoned cockswain, her paddle cutting through the water with remarkable force. She was an extraordinarily able woman, it turned out, culinary matters notwithstanding.

They had taken the S-Bahn to Pichelsberg, just past the Olympic Stadium. Obelinka had stowed a canoe there in the foliage along the banks of the Havel where it splayed into a dozen little channels and inlets. She had already laden the boat with two gallons of tea and a chewed suitcase of stale *bubliki,* beside which sat her prized replacement *Hund,* the little Jagdterrier Olaf, wagging his stump of a tail on the hull.

The *Hund* now sat, front paws on the bow, watching the rippled reflections of moonlight, while Finn struggled to keep up with Obelinka's furious stroke.

"Once we reach Spandau, it's thirty miles upriver

to Liebenwalde, where the Havel meets the Oder Kanal."

"Jesus," said Finn, gasping for breath. "And how much oar-slapping after that?"

"I have a canal boat arranged there to take us the rest of the way. Now, mind your cadence!"

Finn complied as much as his weakened muscles would allow while he withdrew his faculties of sensual perception and contemplated the question of ultimate ends. He was confident his ox-strong paddlemaster Obelinka would, barring squall or torpedoing, carry them safely to Swedeland. But then what? She would likely turn him over to SIS, who, as Finn understood it, were rather annoyed with his off-book activities. They might be keen to make life difficult for him. Desk detail in a frigid office in Stockholm perhaps. A Swedish winter had killed a surly eccentric like Descartes—what's to say it wouldn't take him too? Or, even worse, what if they brought him to drizzly London, where he would surely die of a combination of pneumonia and despair? And to die abed when there was a war on? Be it of weather-related causes or weltschmerz, it was unconscionable.

To think, just two weeks ago he was lying in hospital waiting for death to take him. Thankfully, little Emil and his concupiscent nun had helped him over that hump. Not only that—the latter had rendered him officially dead, at least as far as his friends were concerned. Which meant he could now live in the bowels of Teutonia unfettered. Why, the Christbride had done him an even better turn than she knew. He was now free to become fully wild. Free to become a true creature of the forest. Free to continue his work as a foreign agent wreaking intestinal havoc on Hitler's empire.

Kriegsmann and the Torqued Man would mourn him, to be sure, but then they would be fine. In fact, the Torqued Man would be relieved of his burden, absolved of all responsibility.

Ah, but that was rather disingenuous, wasn't it, to think his death would be a favor to the Torqued Man? Like the self-serving bit of bollocks he'd foisted upon poor Emil, telling him he'd be better off an orphan in this crumbling metropolis and that he'd send for him eventually. The truth was, much as he was fond of the boy, he couldn't be saddled with the responsibility of looking after him. Besides, even were he to stay on in Berlin, how could he continue his one-man insurgency with a paraplegic child underfoot?

It was then that an idea flashed into Finn's wise brain. Young Emil needed someone to look after him.

The Torqued Man needed someone to look after. It was a perfect fit—a merger of the two Emils! In a stroke, Finn could resolve the gnawing sense of dereliction he felt toward both of them. The Torqued Man would at last have a fair surrogate for his invalid niece, the little legless lad would have a proper guardian, and Finn would be free.

Of course, there was the question of how to do it without alerting the Torqued Man to the fact that he was still alive. Perhaps he could just leave the boy in a large basket on the doorstep? But which doorstep? And how to keep the boy from crawling off? And even if those logistics were solved, how to prevent Emil from divulging Finn's existence to his new foster father? Yes, there were still many knots to untangle. But these were mere details in an otherwise sound plan.

As he dipped his oar left and right against the current, two things were now clear to Finn. First, if he followed his Ruslandish hausfrau across the Baltic, he would be of no use to anyone. And second, for all his colossal failures and delusions of efficacy, if anyone was going to drive a stake into the biomedical heart of the Reich, it was he. How exactly, he did not yet know. But he had decided.

He gave a final stroke to help Obelinka on her voyage, then flung himself over the side.

"Finn!" he heard her shout.

Olaf let out a bark, but Finn was soon drifting downstream, beyond reach of the *Hund*'s scent and the scant moonlight.

"What are you doing, you madman?" cried Obelinka. "Come back!"

"Godspeed, old girl!" he called, then disappeared beneath the current.

He floated downriver, resting atop his oar and kicking with his good leg. The water was frigid, but a regained purpose burned within him. After drifting past their put-in at Pichelsberg, he soon spied Schildhorn, that familiar phallus of a peninsula, discernible even in the dark.

Thrust into the plump thigh of the Havel, Schildhorn was for the *Wilden* hallowed ground. In warm months they enjoyed terrorizing visitors to the beach, groping bathers and raiding their picnic baskets. And in the off-season they congregated around the monument, smoking fag ends and etching tributes to the life priapic. The towering cross had been built by mythopoetic Teutonians of the previous century to hail the march of that wide-warring Saxon Albert the Bear against the pagan, impertinent Slavs.

In recent years, under the *Wilden*'s stewardship, it had acquired a rich patina of puerile effacements.

Finn climbed ashore near the monument—at the moment deserted—and shook the wet from himself like a *Hund*. The forest smelled of smoke. Perhaps the *Wilden*'s campfire was nearby.

As he limped beneath the forest canopy, he could just make out a faint wail—either a cat's cry or an air-raid siren. It was possible his hearing was not what it used to be, or perhaps some river water was still lodged in his ear.

The smoke became thicker, all but obscuring an orange glow in the surrounding forest. Suddenly, a gust of wind parted the veil of smoke. He felt a blast of heat, then for a brief moment saw: The trees were on fire. And the flames were coming toward him.

He escaped to the eastern edge of the woods and emerged by the train tracks. The intersection looked uncannily familiar. Yet nothing was the same. He saw the green logo of the S-Bahn station Obelinka and he had walked to earlier that night, just two blocks from the hospital, but the area around it had been transformed into a hell pit. The whole street was ablaze.

He gimped his way back to the Krankenhaus,

where only hours earlier he'd patted young Emil's head and communed with a sister of Christ in a cleaning closet. He now found it a heap of scorched stone.

Finn searched the burning rubble for Emil and his nun, or, for that matter, any living creature. But it had been a direct hit. There was nothing left. Only the charred, shrunken corpses of the holy and the sick.

49

JOURNAL

April 22, 1944

What did it matter that my confession was a lie? But was it even a lie? Pike was under my care, after all, so in some sense I was right to claim responsibility for his actions.

Besides, with the evidence against me and my suspect status as an agent of the recently liquidated Abwehr, I was going to pay, anyway. So why not pay for something that was worth the price?

It seemed everyone around me had already become part of the resistance—Lauhusen, Oster, Moltke, and God knows who else. Likely even Canaris himself. I thought back to the admiral fingering his biography of Frederick II, powerless to help while vowing he would still have the final say. Was it more than impotent bluster? Had he in fact been biding his time? And now that he'd been freed from house arrest and reinstated to the laughable position of Minister of Commercial and Agricultural Warfare? Perhaps the old fox was mobilizing more than beetroots. Then of course there was Pike. And, if his story was to be believed, even the loathsome Crean and our cranky Russian housemaid were not what they seemed. Everyone, that is, except me. But now Pike and I were a team, with a clear division of labor between *Tat und Schuld*: He did the deed and I now bore the guilt.

After I confessed, Kommissar Lipke returned with a typewriter and took my statement. I recounted everything the way Pike had written it. From the first murder three years ago of Wagner, whom I stabbed and dumped in the Spree; followed after a hiatus by the killing of Dr. Heinze and his nurse at the Brandenburg hospital; and finally, early last fall, the murder of Grawitz in the public toilet by the zoo. I gave the details Pike had given, all save the killing of Brandt, whose death Lipke never mentioned and must have still been thought an accident. I also left out the smut, which was a complicated subplot I didn't care to broach. And, since I had not yet finished reading the manuscript—Finn was still frozen in time outside the Hamma factory on his way to Morell's house—and had seen nothing in the papers indicating otherwise, I could only assume Pike's bogeyman Morell still lived. Along with his chief patient, who was still very much alive.

The rest I made up. For instance, where was the murder weapon? I told them I threw it in the Havel. How did I happen to find Ernst Grawitz in a lavatory? I had seen him on the K-damm earlier that evening and followed him. Why had I stopped the killings for well over a year and then resumed? I was busy at work, I said. Somewhere, over the course of my confession, it struck me that I had resumed my old vocation. I was, with the help of Kommissar Lipke, translating Pike's purple Hiberno-English into bureaucratic police German.

After collecting the details, Lipke looked up at me. "Why did you want to kill these doctors, De Groot? Was it simply revenge for your niece? And if so, why did you wait over two years before killing Heinze?"

"No," I said. "On this point I want to be clear. Originally, I wanted nothing more than to avenge the state-sanctioned murder of an innocent child. But I soon realized the problem was much larger than merely one bad doctor. To kill only Dr. Heinze and his nurse would have been to ignore the murderous nature of the entire medical apparatus of this regime. Therefore, my motive from the start—and you can write this down verbatim and share it with your colleagues in the Gestapo—has been to single-handedly drive a stake into the biomedical heart of the Reich."

I was sent to Plötzensee Prison to await trial. Compared to my time in police custody, the nine days I spent there were almost pleasant. In fact, my cell was roughly the same size as my Nymphenburger cellar nook, and the last several months of life in Berlin had been so bleak and constrained, I had little trouble adjusting.

A strange calm had come over me. We spend our lives avoiding death, hoping every door we open to the future won't bring in that unwelcome guest, though we all know he's sure to pay us a visit. Now that I had finally opened the door to death, and opened it knowingly and on my terms, I felt at peace. The lessons those long-suffering Greeks had tried to teach themselves—about imperturbability, equanimity, and the like—had always been intellectually attractive to me, though I had never experienced anything like ataraxia. Now I think I actually felt it. A freedom from disturbance. My daily meals of stale bread, sour margarine, and cold acorn coffee, which came in a dented metal jug delivered through the door slot, once would have demoralized me. Now they were a source of detached amusement. That I had nothing to read was, instead of a crushing blow of boredom, a mere triviality. For what does the man with only a month to live care that he can't read another novel?

The only thing I wished for and deeply missed was the ability to write, which is why this moment right here, with the lake breeze on my neck and my pen racing to keep up with my thoughts, feels magnificent. I did, in the absence of writing materials, take to dictating in my head. I narrated several times what I have in the last day recorded here, but I also found myself crafting a précis of my life, an auto-eulogy of sorts. Of course, no one would ever hear it or read it—I would likely never write it—but there is something to the idea that a life, even for the one living it, is only intelligible as story. And I took comfort knowing my story was going to end this way. Even if I hadn't exactly lived as an enemy of this regime, at least I would die as one. Pike, it turned out, had given me a gift.

Every afternoon from one to three, we were let into the yard. It was a damp gray square with only a few weeds for greenery and the dull yellow sky overhead. But I remember it fondly. For here, in spite of the prohibition on talking, was where we escaped our isolation. The custom was for prisoners to walk the square clockwise, and while silence prevailed in the vicinity of the guards, one could hear dozens of jaw-clenched conversations proceeding out of official earshot.

On my second day in the yard, a familiar voice called my name. I looked over my shoulder and saw James von Moltke give me a furtive wave. His hair had thinned considerably in the months since I'd last seen him. He didn't exactly smile at me, but there was a light of recognition in his eyes, as though to say, "So you've ended up here too."

With my teeth clamped tight, I told him everything that had happened since his arrest, how the Abwehr had been dissolved and how the chaos raining down on the city streets had swept through the halls on Tirpitzufer. Oster was still under house arrest, I told him, and it seemed Canaris himself had been neutralized.

"Yes, I've heard. It's open season now. And with defeat inevitable, soon anyone with half a conscience will be here. Only by then it will be too late."

"What are you being charged with?" I asked.

"They haven't decided. But they know we were talking about a world without Hitler. One way or another, I'm sure the People's Court will invent a suitable reason to separate my head from my body.

"And what are the charges against you?"

"I killed several high-ranking SS doctors."

He laughed. I hadn't intended to say it in a glib or deadpan manner, but Moltke thought I was joking. "That's a good one, De Groot. But really . . ." he said, waiting for me to tell him the truth.

I explained to him I was serious and told him I had confessed to four politically motivated murders.

"You?" he said, shocked. I told him of my assassination campaign in greater detail, and he seemed both mortified and impressed—though, over the course of our conversations the next week, I gathered more the former. Moltke had not given up his Sermon on the Mount morals and seemed to think the role of the anti-Nazi resistance was to be the voice crying out in the wilderness.

"Murder is murder. God cannot sanction the snuffing of a human life, no matter how evil the wrongdoer. I still do believe that," he later said to me, though I could sense a hanging "but" in his tone.

"But what about Hitler?" I said, after moving out of range of a guard.

He had spent long hours pondering this very question. "I was against it, and I still do believe it is a sin. . . . But I also believe that it is we, not God, who must live in the world of men, and we must rely on His mercy to forgive us our sins."

"You sound like a man," I said, "who is at once a Christian and a lawyer."

Moltke smiled, but I could tell the matter weighed heavily on him. "And you, Adrian—you are what? A littérateur and an assassin?"

I detected a note of incredulity in his voice.

"Beauty and justice," I said. "Didn't Plato say they were virtually the same?"

"I suppose," replied Moltke. "But he also said poets are liars."

It was a strange rekindling of our student days—Balliol College green had given way to the gray prison yard, but the same dynamic persisted. Philosophical conversations tempered by teasing and with just a hint of mutual aversion—I to his Christian earnestness, he to my shallow aestheticism. But our lipless conversations were a bright spot in the otherwise cinder-blocked days that I assumed would be my fate until, as Moltke said, they decided to unjoin my head from my body.

Why did it have to come to prison, I wondered, with death looming overhead, for James and me to rediscover each other? The world bends to the arc of a cruel irony.

One afternoon, I confessed to him.

"I've killed no one, James. No doctors. No nurses.

I'm as innocent as an Easter lamb. And that is also the true mark of my guilt."

"I know, Adrian," he said, gently squeezing my hand out of view of the guards. "But it's not too late for forgiveness."

Then, after breakfast on the tenth day of my captivity, the turnkey opened the door to my cell and ushered me to the warden's office.

The warden angrily stamped a set of papers and handed one to the guard. "Get him out of my sight."

"What's happening?" I asked. Had the moment come already? But surely they couldn't execute me without first some kind of a trial.

"The charges against you have been dropped," explained the warden. "Though if I had my way, I'd keep you locked up for being sick in the head! Now get out of my prison!"

The guard shoved a bundle of my clothes at me, escorted me to the gate, and just like that I was free.

50

Finn McCool in the Bowels of Teutonia

Forest Father

After the brutal business of the destroyed hospital, Finn retreated to the woods, to the still-vast stretch of lakeland spared the flames that wicked night.

He grieved for his young friend and the amorous nun, but he also planned—for from that pile of burning bodies, Finn had plucked an idea. A way forward, a breakthrough, or, as the Teutonians said, *ein Durchbruch*, which had the virtue of sounding like the crunch of brick and bone such an insight had cost him. He had been so narrowly focused on man-slaying that he'd overlooked the obvious virtues of sabotage. The idea had dropped from the sky and burst like a bomb inside his brain.

He didn't have to kill the doctor or poison the stew.

All he had to do was cut off the supply. Set fire to the factory and send all those precious hormones up in smoke. Why, it couldn't be simpler. And in no time at all, Hitler would be prostrate and pining for his vitamins.

Finn tried to pull himself into fighting shape. He fed on the last yield of forest plants, already shriveled in the frost, and strengthened his limbs on sodden footpaths, until the only souvenir from his evening at Villa Morell was a slight limp. With each passing day, though, he found it harder to fight off hunger and cold. Realizing he could not get through the winter— let alone carry out his plan—on his own, he decided to overcome his fears and once more seek out the *Wilden.*

He found their camp this time in the wallows surrounding the Barssee. As he trudged around the icy lake, following hastily carved signs, he wondered why they had chosen to make their nest in this Bog of Allen place of desolation. It was soggy, inhospitable terrain, with hardly any sun and mud that sucked your shoes clean off.

He gave the kestrel's cry to signal his arrival. But no reply came. Something was amiss. There was no hail of stones, no posted sentries. Only the sharp smell of human shit.

A dozen boys were huddled beneath a miserable lean-to, not at all up to the gang's usual standards. There was no birch-bark covering to keep out the wet, no hanging moss or dried leaves to insulate the floor. Why, even the hallowed fucking couch was waterlogged and in tatters.

The boys were sniveling and filthy, snot frozen on their upper lips and angry rashes across their cheeks.

"Lads," said Finn, "what's become of you?"

The boys looked up at Finn from eyes sunk deep within their sockets. *"Hrabeet ist tot."* Their chief was dead.

"Well, who's next in line?" asked Finn. "Surely you have a succession protocol in place?"

"Of course we do, you geezer, but none of us wants to stomp in a cat's skull, drink a boot filled with piss, or any of the other rituals Rabbit put in place."

"Can't say I blame you, lads. But have you considered having a vote on it instead?"

"We tried that, but none of us was able to secure a simple majority," said one of the older boys, about thirteen. "No one trusts the other to lead us."

"It's a problem we adults face too, I assure you. Speaking of," said Finn, noticing there was not a boy over fourteen among them, "where are the older members of your crew, the lads with downy mustaches and fully formed libidos, like Hatchet Willi?"

"Dead," said a few. "Gone," said the others. They recited a litany of arrests and knife fights and gangrenous infections that had liquidated the senior members of their group. Those remaining were a particularly green crop, with several new recruits who, like young Emil, had been recently orphaned.

"And what's become of that fine wind hound?" asked Finn. "Why is Sceolang not here wagging her tail?"

"She's dead too." At this, one of the boys burst into tears. And Finn, seeing their crinkled faces and thinking of all the dead innocent things he had known, felt the salt water leak out of his own eyes.

"We miss our parents!" cried one of the youngest boys, about nine.

"Quiet, *Penner!*" scolded his brother. "How many times do I have to tell you the old sods are kaput?"

But the boy's lament seemed to have opened up the floodgate of grievances.

"I'm hungry!"

"I'm sick of being wet and cold!"

"Why can't people just be nice to us?"

"Yeah, I'm tired of eating cum and shit!"

"Now, hold on there," said Finn. "Who here's been making you eat his evacuations?"

All the boys averted their eyes. Eventually one of them muttered a name.

"Wolfi."

The orphans told Finn how an older boy named Wolfi routinely preyed on them, destroying their camp, stealing their food, and forcing the most vulnerable into humiliating acts. He was also, Finn learned, the same vicious cunt who had killed his *Hund*.

"He said he'd fuck us all to death if we don't do whatever he says."

"But it's not fair! He's not our leader. We didn't elect him. Hell, we don't hardly know him."

"Rabbit would have never let this happen to us," said one.

"Rabbit was a twisted fucker too, you know," countered another.

"Yeah, but at least he kept us safe."

Finn was observing how this Hobbesian discourse would play out, when one of the boys the oldest and most sophisticated of the group jutted a chin in his direction. "What about him?"

All eyes in the lean-to now fell on Finn.

"You mean this funny-talkin' geezer?" asked another, nonplussed.

"Finn's not like other adults," the veteran went on. "Sure, he's old as hell, but he has a wild spirit. He's a degenerate, but he's decent. He's like a fun, irresponsible uncle who gives you booze and cigarettes, but you never have to worry about him raping you."

"I appreciate the eulogy," said Finn, "but—"

"That's why I say we make him our new leader."

Several of the boys cheered.

"But what about the rules?" protested one. "Remember, no one over nineteen?"

"Finn's probably over a hundred!" gassed one of the little fuckers.

Only a hair over forty, he wanted to say, but he resisted the urge to correct.

"Fuck the rules, boys!" said a spirited ten-year-old. "We make the rules now! And I vote for the geezer!"

"Me too!"

"So do I."

The vote went round the huddle, and before long there were ten votes for Finn and two holdouts.

"It doesn't matter," said the oldest. "We have ten of twelve. That's a majority by any count. The geezer's our new leader."

Finn ruminated on this offer. Here were boys, like his late friend Emil, in need of care. They were an unruly, miserable lot, to be sure, but perhaps he could actually help them. Not tame them, no, he wouldn't want to do that, but maybe curb some of their most repellent antisocial impulses and show them a bit of decency. In exchange, he could have a true Fianna— not that tenuous agreement between him and Chief Rabbit, which was a transactional relationship at best, based on smut and possibly terminated with an act of poisoning. No, instead, he'd have himself a loyal band of pint-sized *guerilleros.*

At last he spoke. "Lads, I'm honored. Truly I am. And I genuinely sympathize with your plight here in the lawless bogs, derelict of leadership and prey to vicious scoundrels as you are. But I couldn't possibly accept—that is, unless you agree to a few conditions."

"You want to piss in our wounds too?"

"No, son, nothing like that. Now, look, I'll lay out my terms, but I'll only accept if the vote's unanimous. That means you'll have to argue it out until there's a consensus, you hear? All twelve must be in agreement. And if not, I walk away. We'll have no tyranny of the majority or stifling of minority voices here. Is that understood?"

The boys assented.

"Good. Then the conditions are as follows:

"First, if I'm to be your leader, then you must give up indiscriminate assaults on the citizenry."

"What's that mean?" asked one.

"It means we only steal from the more-or-less wealthy, and we only attack those in uniform or sporting party pins or otherwise revealing themselves to be in need of a stick of hickory to the face."

One boy raised his hand. "Do train uniforms count as uniforms?"

"Interesting query," said Finn. "I don't see why not. It's really more about the spirit than the letter of the law, anyway."

"What are the other conditions?"

"The second is that you forswear that soul-deadening smut that's been known to circulate amongst you. Now, I know I once trafficked in the stuff myself—in order to serve a just cause, mind you—but I should never have even considered letting minds as young as yours anywhere near it. As I see it, that plan's failure was a gift. But don't misunderstand me, boys. I'm no puritan. I support the love of the masculine as much as I do the feminine. And you're all free to indulge your inclinations—or lack thereof—as you see fit, but let's focus them on warm, willing bodies or, when those are absent, on good, honest depictions of sex acts and engorged genitals with a bit less misery involved."

This created a bit of grumble, but no one seemed outright opposed.

"The third and final condition," said Finn, "is you help me set fire to the Hamma factory."

"What's that?"

"An evil factory in Friedrichshain, the foundational link in a supply chain supporting the precarious health of Adolf Hitler."

The boys failed to be galvanized by this information.

"If we burn down this factory, we'll kill Hitler."

Thus worded, the prospect dazzled them. But some of the boys still had trouble following the logic.

"Is Hitler going to be in the building when we burn it?"

"Well, no."

A sigh of disappointment ran through them.

"So we won't actually kill him?"

"It's probably just what those schoolmasterly fucks call a metaphor," said another.

"It's not quite so direct, boys," explained Finn. "But I assure you it's more than mere metaphor. See, there's a clear causal chain, starting first with the factory and then . . ." He could see he'd lost them again. So he tried a different tack.

"This factory is where they make Vitamult bars."

"You mean those shit bricks of mashed carrot and ground donkey dick?"

"Precisely," said Finn.

"And we get to torch it?"

"That's right, lads. Burn it to the ground."

The twelve of them conferred for about four seconds. It was unanimous. Finn McCool had become a father.

51

JOURNAL

April 23, 1944

There was a car waiting for me when I exited the prison gates. The back door swung open and a man in military uniform poked his head out.

"Get in."

I got in.

"I don't believe we've had the pleasure, De Groot. I'm Leutnant Fabian von Schlabrendorff, adjutant to Generalmajor von Tresckow of the Reserve Army Command."

Neither of these names was familiar. I was still in shock that my life had suddenly, inexplicably, been returned to me. And after I had already made peace with surrendering it.

"You're a lucky man, De Groot. Reichskriminaldirektor Nebe himself ordered your release."

"Why?" I asked.

"Apparently you made a false confession."

I was mystified. How could they know? I had reported the murders just as Pike had written them. Did that mean . . . ? My mind hit a wall of questions. Had Pike made it up after all? Had he committed the murders but narrated them differently? Had someone else been arrested? Had Lipke altered my statement? Come to think of it, I didn't recall reading my confession after he prepared it. And why had this reserve officer just ordered me into his car, where he seemed to be regarding me with an air of amusement?

"How did they know?" I asked tentatively.

"No idea," said Schlabrendorff with a shrug. "Anyway, whomever you killed or didn't kill or lied about killing isn't my concern. You're here because it has come to my attention that you're in a unique position to help Germany in a crucial moment of its history."

Seeing that I found his sentence unintelligible, he elaborated: "Moltke has vouched for you. He said you were ideally equipped to help us out of a tight spot."

I still had trouble understanding. How had James communicated beyond the confines of the prison?

"And because, unlike Moltke, you were lucky enough to have your case handled by the Kripo rather than the Gestapo, one of us was likely in a position to influence the investigation."

"Us?" I asked.

"A number of patriots in the officer corps, many of them your former colleagues in the Abwehr as well as some in the Criminal Police, have decided enough is enough."

"What is enough?" I asked.

"This war. This catastrophe."

I was finally starting to catch on. And it seemed I had grossly underestimated Moltke's little faith circle. "Do you mean . . . ?"

"That's right—Hitler must be eliminated."

Those words of sheer fantasy, now uttered so bluntly.

"And you want me to help?"

"Yes."

"Do I have a choice?"

"Of course."

A new way to be damned. It was another gift. "Good. Then I agree of my own volition."

"Good."

"But how?" I asked. "And please don't tell me you want me to kill Hitler's doctor."

"What?" he said, perplexed. "Morell? No, of course

not. Look, just listen and don't interrupt, because we haven't a moment to spare. . . ."

Schlabrendorff then proceeded to tell me of the most extraordinary circumstances. Just before our former deputy head of espionage, Hans Oster, was placed under house arrest, he delivered a set of British-made bombs to Army High Command; they were being stored in a secret location in the Bendlerblock, where they awaited deployment in an operation to assassinate the Führer. This was a stroke of good luck, for following the dissolution of the Abwehr, the Security Service had searched HQ from top to bottom but not the neighboring Bendlerblock—until yesterday, that is, when a zealous officer, likely snooping around at their behest, found the bombs hidden in a depot on Tresckow's wing. He noticed their foreign make and demanded to know their provenance.

"What is urgently needed," Schlabrendorff explained, "are forged documents showing that the bombs came from Spain, using British materials stolen from a shipping convoy, and in preparation for a sabotage mission to coincide with Operation Felix, the aborted Spanish–German attack on Gibraltar. All this paperwork needs to be backdated, appearing to have come from Franco's people and been processed through the Abwehr KO in Madrid in the summer of 1940, before being passed on to Tresckow, who was with Army Group A in Paris at the time. It requires someone with flawless Spanish, someone who knows the KO Madrid documentation protocol, and, finally, someone who can forge all this, including Leissner's signature.

"I've been told that you, De Groot, are the one man in Berlin who can accomplish this. And with it, you can help spare Germany the worst of this catastrophe."

I asked him how long I had.

"Yesterday I assured the man we had the paperwork filed somewhere and would supply it to him immediately. I can put him off today, but that gives you, at the very latest, until first thing tomorrow morning."

I told him we would need rubber stamps and tools to carve the seals and that if he could supply those along with paper, typewriter, and a pot of coffee with actual caffeine, I could do it.

I worked all through the night on the documents. I was weak from prison, but I used every ounce of strength I had to make sure they were perfect. At dawn, I passed the forged papers to Schlabrendorff on a bench in Hindenburg Park where I had once sat with Pike. He told me he would contact me in two weeks' time, but that I should be ready to go to ground at a moment's notice.

And so here I am, seventy-two hours later. I am free, my lungs filled with fresh air, and I have now completed the most important translation job of my life: the one that will kill Adolf Hitler.

52

Finn McCool in
the Bowels of Teutonia

Flying Column

Finn spent the winter forging a new society in the
woods. He learned that, if properly harnessed,
the productive energy of a dozen well-nourished,
puberty-straddling boys is simply staggering. The
first thing they did under his lead was pillage the
Havel and the Wannsee, and the Krumme Lanke
and the Teufelssee, and the Pechsee, Barssee, and
Schlachtensee, and every other freshwater refuge
of perch, loach, tench, and eel. They set upon the
creatures with gaff and net and smoked them by the
hundreds. Amply fortified, they then embarked on
turning their ruinous camp into a place to call home.
Finn moved them to dryer, higher ground, with
natural redoubts on the ridge of a glacial moraine.
There they dug a trenchwork of pit fires that burned

hot and showed very little smoke. He had them collect stones from the riverbank, which they laid as sunken foundations for their subterranean shelters, topped with tightly matted birch bark, sealed with pine resin, and virtually invisible to passersby. The quickest and ablest of them he took on outings to burglarize the palatial homes along the Wannsee, stealing staples like potatoes, cigarettes, and bread—along with whatever else they could get their little hands on. Together, their manpower provided warmth, sustenance, and protection. At Christmas, they celebrated in their cozy encampment around the crackling Yule log, exchanging gifts of stolen goods, homemade schnapps, and hand-carved catapults.

Come the new year, with everyone hale and in high spirits, Finn began schooling them for combat. Being feral children, they were already scrappy by disposition and well versed in tussling and throwing rocks, but Finn had greater aspirations for them. He was not going to make a hames of it, as he had the Doctors' League Dinner. This go-round, he would take his time. He would train his men. He would transform them into a swift flying column and a Fianna worthy of the name. Meanwhile, the Hamma factory continued belching its glandular fumes into the Berlin sky.

So Finn was patient and thorough, like a good

father should be, and the little ruffians loved him
for it. He drilled them in tactics of ambush and
encirclement. He taught them how to outflank
the enemy and how to beat a Parthian retreat. He
instructed them in rudimentary demolitions, arson,
and knife-fighting. They roved the forest playing war
games, staging maneuvers in the snow. When the air
raids gave them cover of darkness and sound, they
set off small, muffled explosions near the river, using
bombs made from the peat-rich bog turf, which they
dug out of the wallows and dried in the winter sun.
On quiet nights by the fire, Finn would tell them
redacted war stories. He stripped them of the senseless
suffering and bureaucratic horror that was at the heart
of modern conflict and fortified his own exploits with
feats he recalled reading in *Seven Pillars of Wisdom*.
He even felt the ancient spark of those guerrilla days
in Erin, when he was scarcely older than these young
misfits now in his charge. That life, the one he'd
chased to Spain but largely missed out on, he was
finally living here, of all places, in the parklands of the
Teutonians' demon metropolis. And for the first time
since arriving in this evil city, he'd managed to adopt
both the original cover the Torqued Man had given
him and the role the Teutonians had recruited him to
play: He was a school coach and a leader of men.

By the first thaw of March, his collection of wild orphans had become a proper platoon. That's when the sadist Wolfi, in the company of two other boys, had the bad luck of stumbling into their camp. It was the first they'd seen of him since Finn had been elected. He'd assumed the boy had, like most predators when deprived of easy prey, simply lost interest. But Wolfi, as they gleaned from his overheard conversation, had been away these last months at Hitler Youth training camp in Belgium. They had selected him, along with other HJ members over fifteen and with similarly outstanding records, to form a new Panzer division of the SS. And now he was home to see his family one last time before being sent to France.

Wolfi's two companions were clearly jealous of his imminent deployment and now trying to impress him with sadistic boasts.

"Didn't you say those little vermin lived around here?" asked one. "Looks like I brought my knife for nothing."

"Yeah, Wolfi. I thought you said we'd get to have some fun."

"Hold your horses, young 'uns," said Wolfi, bayoneting an icy puddle with his stick. "They're around here somewhere."

"You know, Hans-Peter and I found a den of gypsies up in Wedding while you were away. We put the fear of God in them."

"Yeah, and then we reported them."

Finn and his *Wilden* listened to all this from behind camouflaged blinds. He had heard enough to determine these boys were acceptable targets for their first combat mission. He motioned to his Fianna to encircle the enemy. Silently, the lads surrounded the frustrated sadists. Then, on Finn's kestrel cry, his warriors let loose their catapults. The rocks caught Wolfi and his friends in the face and sent them running, blood streaming from their eyes, right into a barrage of sharp rocks from the other direction. Now the enemy was paralyzed, injured, and terrified—all while the *Wilden* remained hidden.

On Finn's next signal—the woodpecker's knock— came a hail of flaming turf sods soaked in margarine. Expertly lobbed, they landed at the sadists' feet and ignited their clothing. Wolfi and his friends, alight and screaming, ran aimlessly through the woods, crashing into trees and tripping over rocks. Meanwhile, the synthetic butter seeped through their trousers and scorched their flesh. Finn and his Fianna trailed them, making sure the woods did not catch fire, and watched as their enemies eventually fell through the ice of the frozen bog and extinguished themselves. Though wonderfully maimed, the little bastards were still alive and would likely continue to live, assuming they could find their way home before freezing to death.

Finn gave the owl's hoot to fall back, and his Fianna retreated wordlessly into the woods, back to their hidden camp, to the safety and muffled walls of their underground lair, where they celebrated their victory in rowdy style.

They were ready.

53

JOURNAL

April 24, 1944

I am more confused than ever.

This morning before first light, I returned to the Nymphenburger house to retrieve my journal and Pike's story. The police had thoroughly ransacked the house, yet the manuscripts lay undisturbed in the cellar pipe.

And now I have just finished reading *Finn McCool in the Bowels of Teutonia*.

Can it be true—he's alive? But he must be. He narrated the hospital, the nun, even . . . Which means he had to have written this after I learned he was dead, which means he was alive this whole time. Is he here now? Alive?

May 1, 1944

I've searched the Grunewald every day for the past week. Two of the mangy boys I encountered there offered me sex for hire. The other one stole my cigarette lighter. None of them would countenance my questions about a middle-aged Irishman in their midst. Several times, though, I felt I was being watched. I could picture Pike smirking over my shoulder, but whenever I turned, there was only a bird perched on a branch or an old woman foraging woodruff.

Whether or not he is still alive, I feel him here. He lives in the city's woods, in their fugitive, untamed spirit.

I don't know if the truth of Pike's story nearly cost me my life or if the fiction of it spared me, and I suppose I never will know. But I know this: Pike's story saved me.

He may not have loved me quite the way I loved him, but he cared. He cared enough to say goodbye. And that is enough.

May 8, 1944

Schlabrendorff assures me that, thanks to my actions, the plan now proceeds as intended. The bombs remain in the depot, unmolested. By summer, I am told, Hitler will be dead. It will not save us from the catastrophe that already engulfs us, but our revolt of conscience will be known. Not just in words but deed.

And should it fail, at least I will have done my part. A small, unseen, and unglamorous part to be sure, a few dissembling flicks of the pen. But that, alas, is the role of the translator.

As for these pages, I cannot bring myself to burn them. Foolish as it may be, I want them to stand as a testament. Perhaps out of vanity but perhaps, I tell myself, out of lingering hope.

54

Finn McCool in the Bowels of Teutonia

Final Testament

They crawled from the forest at night to a gloomy city choked with rubble. Following the phosphorescent curb paint, they fanned out in discreet pairs to cover the twenty klicks to Friedrichshain, where the Hamma factory was brewing its final batch. The boys were sharp and strong, their bodies hard from fishmeat and their minds free of the beclouding influence of smut.

Only Finn walked alone and enwrapped in the obscene images he'd used to bait the Nazi doctors. On his person he now carried, like every member of the Fianna, a hunting blade, a sewn pocket full of turf bombs, and a dozen nicked cigarette lighters. But lining his coat and trousers were also the film negatives and prints from Crean's studio, the ones

Obelinka had given him and that he'd hidden beneath the floorboards of the Torqued Man's cottage.

He had recently gone back there. The cottage was empty and smelled as though it had lain vacant all winter. He thought back on the last time he'd sat with the Torqued Man, looking out over the lake and sharing a drink to ease their loneliness. He wondered how his friend now fared. He hoped he'd survived the bombings. He wagered he had, for the Torqued Man struck him as a survivor. Someone who could bend his form to fit the cracks and fissures of disaster. He was a translator, after all. A man who contorted himself to express others' thoughts in his own tongue. It was a kind of wizardry, that.

Finn pulled back the living room rug, pried open the floorboards, and retrieved the cache of smut from where it had resided since before his failed attack on Morell. He was glad he'd resisted destroying it, though he had felt the occasional doubt whenever he imagined the Gestapo raiding the cottage and the Torqued Man being stuck with the bill. But some part of him knew eventually the smut would come in handy. And now he'd found the perfect use for it.

He put the prints and negatives in his rucksack, swapping them out for a tightly rolled sheaf. It was his testament. He'd spent the past winter writing it, stealing the quiet morning hours in the forest while his *Wilden* slept. Ever since his resurrection in the Schmargendorf hospital, he'd understood that if he was to leave a discernible legacy beyond the grave, he'd have to put it down in words. For a man writes his story in deeds only if there is someone there to sing it—to render the work of blade and blood into pen and permanent ink.

So Finn had written his story. He began as one does in epic, in medias res, crammed in the duct of the Hamma factory and in the middle of an undulating journey of triumphs and defeats. And he had followed it through backward and forward, from the moment he was sprung from the Spanish pit, to this very moment here in the cottage, all the way to the great burst of light at the end.

He knew he could count on at least one man to read it. And a story only needs one reader. In fact, a story is really only ever written for one reader. Who knows—perhaps his would even translate it.

Finn put the manuscript into the urn. It seemed a fitting place for it—in the ashes of the innocent, the handiwork of doctors and fascists, the very wreckage from which Finn's murderous exploits took flight.

He left the urn askew at the mantel and raised the blackout curtain at the window. It was his way of saying farewell. For, wild Fenian that he was, he didn't want to leave without saying goodbye.

The Fianna reunited at the factory. They caught their breath against the southern wall, with the poisoned Spree twinkling below and the air-raid sirens wailing. Four of the lads had narrowly averted being corralled into a shelter, and one of them had been bitten by a dog. But everyone had made it. Their four-hour march across the city, however, was a mere prelude to the night's main event.

Finn ripped the lining from his coat and trousers and distributed the smut sewn within.

The boys looked up at him, confused. "But you said . . ."

"Now, look here, boys," he whispered. "This filth is to be our kindling. We'll hide it in all corners of the factory. As for these strips of film, well, now, they're extra special. It's made of what they call nitrocellulose, stuff that's just asking to be set alight. And it'll turn our humble fag-lighters and turf-bombs here into flamethrowers and blockbusters."

He could see their eyes glow with excitement even in the dark.

Armed with their incendiaries, Finn and his Fianna set about impregnating the fortress. They had become adept at scurrying up drainpipes and shimmying through windows left ajar. In a matter of minutes, they were inside.

But the stench of the place nearly undid them. Accustomed to pure forest air, their nostrils burned and their eyes watered and they felt a powerful urge to retch.

"That, lads, is the smell of Hitler's insides," said Finn. "Now, have a hurl and let's get to work."

They fought through their nausea and papered the place with smut. Soon the factory was covered in a rich tableau of the *Waldhüter*'s Dungeon. Finn went up to the belching cauldrons, the ones he'd visited before when he unwittingly added a sugar substitute to the Führer's regimen. Now he placed his turf bomb wrapped in pornographic negatives under the hissing stew and got his fire to the ready. He signaled for the *Wilden* to do the same.

On his call, he gave the cry of the dove—for it was Operation Dove that had been his first aborted mission and the seed of all future ones here in Teutonia. The boys struck their lights. With thirteen puddles of fire roaring and feeding on the flatulent fumes, Finn and his Fianna made a mad but well-rehearsed dash for the exit.

He was bringing up the rear when he noticed one

of the younger boys still inside and frozen in a trance. His gaze was caught on a piece of smut that had failed to ignite. Finn saw the image that snagged the boy's mind and immediately understood his paralysis, for it showed a gentleman of hearty endowment undergoing a trans-urethral probe with a stag horn.

"Found one that put the heart crossways in you, son?" said Finn. "Come on, then." And throwing the stricken lad over his shoulder, flames licking at his heels, he made for the door.

He set him down outside, and the boy ran to join the others by the water's edge, where they were to regroup before following the river back home.

But an air attack was now under way. The sky right above them had become a cacophony of buzzing planes and flak artillery. Finn signaled for the boys to retreat and find shelter, indicating he'd meet them back at camp.

"Finn, come with us!" they shouted.

But Finn wanted to watch the factory burn. He wanted to see it crumble with his own eyes, until he was certain Morell's empire of viscera—and with it, the Führer's own vital sap—had been vaporized into a foul-smelling memory. He was not leaving until it was destroyed.

When it became clear their leader would not escape

with them, and flak splinters began whistling by, the Fianna reluctantly obeyed and dispersed.

They were good boys, thought Finn. Savage, thieving, enamored of violence, but good boys all the same.

That was the last recorded thought to enter Finn's brain before a plane swung overhead and dropped its payload directly onto the Hamma factory. In less time than it took for him to turn his head, the world became a great burst of light.

No words could penetrate beyond that all-consuming brilliance to see into the mystery of Finn McCool's life or death, to learn of his future exploits or what all his high deeds amounted to. For he had already told his tale.

And so Finn and his Fianna disappeared into the forest for good, to those distant hunting grounds in the realm beyond story.

S-E-C-R-E-T

Date: 08 September 1945
CPTN CHARLES CARSON

OFFICE OF STRATEGIC SERVICES, BERLIN
APO 401   US ARMY

TO:
CPTN FLOYD WEEKS
BERLIN DISTRICT INTERROGATION CENTER
APO 755 US ARMY

Floyd:

The Brits should consider
themselves lucky. Never have I
read so many pages of filth. The
MSS you recovered consist of
a deviant's diary spliced with
an obscene pulp comic. The one
true thing I can conclude from
DE GROOT's diary is that he is a
homosexual and that he will say or

do anything to save his own skin.
I advise you and SIS to beware the
man's eagerness to cooperate and
set little store by his claims
to have been a participant in
the JULY 20 PLOT to assassinate
HITLER. Truly, every miserable
German I come across these days
would have me believe they were
part of the resistance. On the
other hand, I highly doubt he
merits judicial attention. For
what it's worth, my recommendation
would be to leave DE GROOT right
where he is: clearing rubble at
the Coca-Cola plant.

As for FRANK PIKE, possible
alias FRANK FINN, I don't think
the present MSS will help anyone
get a straight story. According
to one of the accounts, this
FINN single-handedly murdered
several high-ranking Nazi doctors,
including Dr. KARL BRANDT,

who is currently in American custody, awaiting trial. Among the slew of actions that beggar belief in this narrative, this FINN claims he was working with British intelligence operative OBOLENSKY, who, as SIS never tires of reminding us, has emerged from this war as hands-down the most valuable Allied agent in Berlin. It was her communiques that allowed for the strategic bombing of key industrial sites such as the Siemens campus and the Hamma factory. I would recommend interviewing her on the off chance she could confirm any elements of the FINN account. Though last I heard, after she helped crush the commies in Greece, the Brits sent her to Malaya to ferret out reds and recalcitrant Japs.

Just one question: Didn't you tell me a while back that

SIS is looking for an agent who
disappeared in 1942—one by the
name of CREAN?

I'll hold off burning these
until I hear word from you.

Yours sincerely,
Charles

Historical Note and Acknowledgments

I'd like to acknowledge the flesh-and-blood lives on which *The Torqued Man* is loosely based. Frank Ryan was an Irish republican and socialist who went to fight the fascists in Spain, where he was captured and sentenced to life in Franco's prison. He avoided this fate when, in 1940, German military intelligence recruited him to help coordinate Irish operations for Hitler's planned invasion of England. But Operation Sea Lion, as the invasion was called, never panned out and Ryan, after an abortive U-boat trip back to Ireland, was left cooling his heels in the Reich until he died of poor health in 1944. The question of how an anti-fascist and restless soul like Frank Ryan not only passed the time but wrestled with his conscience in Hitler's Berlin was one that struck me as more amenable to the task of the novelist than the historian. This led me to the UK's National Archives, where I read British military files and interrogation reports on Dr. Kurt Haller, an Abwehr agent who was Ryan's spy handler in Berlin. Immediately, I became interested in the story—both the very limited one narrated in the documents as well as everything left unsaid and open to the imagination—of the relationship between the German spy handler and his Irish charge. The rest, as they say, is history, or rather fiction.

———

I'm also grateful to the many excellent people who helped make this book a real thing in the world.

Enormous thanks to: My agent, Susan Golomb, and my editor, Noah Eaker, for putting all their wisdom and energy behind me. Susan, I feel lucky to have you in my corner, knowing exactly what's needed and how to make it happen. Noah, I couldn't have asked for a better interlocutor and editor. Working with you to realize this vision has been a delight from start to finish. And you even got your brother to read it (thanks, Adam!). The whole team at Harper: Mary Gaule for keeping the train running smoothly; Kathy Lord, copyeditor extraordinaire; my publicist, Tracy Locke;

Becca Putman for putting the word out; Leah Carlson-Stanisic for the interior design; and Milan Božić for the cover design, for generously inviting me to submit an illustration of my own and bringing it brilliantly to life.

To the friends who lent a helping hand: My man in Berlin, Ian Morgan, for the Teutonian lessons and for saving me from the Hans Gruber Effect. Colin "DDR" MacNaughton and Josh "Jingles" Sommovilla for reading early work and cheering me on; Trey Houston for manning the camera; Mia Harlock for helping a guy out; Ben Greenberg for going out on a limb when I could have been another Fante Bukowski. And to beloved friends, in SF, around the Bay and beyond, for all the bonhomie and laughter.

Thanks, of course, to my family: parents Ben and Elaine for fostering my bookish tendencies and supporting me in everything, including my oblique approach to a career path; my sister, Melissa, for our decades of inspired silliness together; my niece, Addie, for confirming the joys of the creative life; Uncle John for the trusty green desk and the encouragement; and my father-in-law, Karl, for showing me that long, hard runs are the best.

And to the most important person in my life: Sami—thank you for everything. You know in art as well as life what to cut, what to keep, and how to make it good.

About the Author

PETER MANN has a PhD in modern European history and is a past recipient of the Whiting Fellowship. He teaches history and literature at Stanford and the University of San Francisco. He is also a graphic artist and cartoonist. This is his first novel.